American

HEROES
AGAINST ALL ODDS

Black Mesa

Aimée
THURLO

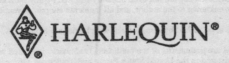

S0-AGF-648

HARLEQUIN®

TORONTO • NEW YORK • LONDON
AMSTERDAM • PARIS • SYDNEY • HAMBURG
STOCKHOLM • ATHENS • TOKYO • MILAN • MADRID
PRAGUE • WARSAW • BUDAPEST • AUCKLAND

This book is dedicated with love
to the three people who made it possible:
My husband David Thurlo, whose seventeen years on the
Navajo Indian Reservation gave me the basis for *Black Mesa*.
Professor Alfonso Ortiz, for the insight
into his Tewa culture and for the humor
that made dealing with him such a pleasure.
And Sue Stone, because she's always there
and her support makes a world of difference.

HARLEQUIN BOOKS
225 Duncan Mill Road, Don Mills,
Ontario, Canada M3B 3K9

ISBN 0-373-82229-4

BLACK MESA

Copyright © 1990 by Aimée Thurlo

New Mexico
State Facts

Nickname:	Land of Enchantment
Date Entered Union:	January 6, 1912 (the 47th state)
Motto:	*Crescit eundo* (It grows as it goes.)
New Mexico Men:	William "Billy the Kid" Bonney, *outlaw* Christopher (Kit) Carson, *army scout, trapper* Tony Hillerman, *author* Dennis Hopper, *actor* Jim Morrison, *singer, songwriter*
Flower:	Yucca
Bird:	Roadrunner
Fun Fact:	New Mexico is one of the four corner states, bordering at the same point with Colorado, Utah and Arizona.

He leaned back on the ground and guided her to lie against him. He brought her lips to his.

His kiss was soft at first, neither urging nor coaxing. Her heart leaped to life and a slow tendril of heat began to wind its way through her. She parted her lips slightly and slid her tongue forward to tease his.

With a groan, he pulled her even closer. His mouth smothered hers, a raw urgency tugging at his restraint. She moaned softly.

"Tell me you need me, schoolteacher, as much as I need you," he said in a husky voice. "Say it."

She had just started to answer when a loud thump shattered the moment.

"What the—" Justin moved to one side and saw a fireball arc across the sky toward them....

About the Author

Aimée Thurlo is a nationally known bestselling author. She's written forty-one novels and is published in at least twenty countries worldwide. She has been nominated for the Reviewer's Choice Award and the Career Achievement Award by *Romantic Times Magazine*.

She also co-writes the Ella Clah mainstream mystery series, which debuted with a starred review in *Publishers Weekly*.

Aimée was born in Havana, Cuba, and lives with her husband of thirty years in Corrales, New Mexico. Her husband, David, was raised on the Navajo Indian Reservation.

Books by Aimée Thurlo

Harlequin Intrigue
Expiration Date #109
Black Mesa #131
Suitable for Framing #141
Strangers Who Linger #162
Night Wind #175
Breach of Faith #200
Shadow of the Wolf #217
Spirit Warrior #246
Timewalker #275
Bearing Gifts #304
Cisco's Woman #377
Her Destiny #427
Her Hero #441
Her Shadow #457
**Redhawk's Heart* #506
**Redhawk's Return* #510
Christmas Witness #544
Black Raven's Pride #572

*Four Winds
**The Brothers of Rock Ridge

Dear Reader,

Black Mesa was a work of love for me. Like the hero, my husband, David, was raised on the Navajo Indian Reservation. Our home, however, is a stone's throw from one of the Rio Grande Pueblos. *Black Mesa* combines those elements of our lives into a powerful story about choices.

My husband and I come from two different worlds, but the love we share has kept us together throughout the years. Like it was for us, the hero and heroine must strive to see past the differences that stand between them, and find the courage to follow their hearts.

Black Mesa is a glimpse into worlds most people never see. I hope it'll touch your hearts.

Walk in beauty,

Aimée

Please address questions and book requests to:
Harlequin Reader Service
U.S.: 3010 Walden Ave., P.O. Box 1325, Buffalo, NY 14269
Canadian: P.O. Box 609, Fort Erie, Ont. L2A 5X3

Prologue

The boy stood in line with five others, all trembling with fear. His blanket had been discarded and lay on the ground in preparation for what was to come.

As the pungent fragrance of burning piñon filled his nostrils, John Romero watched in pensive silence. Time had wrought many changes over all of them since he'd sponsored the boy at the Rite of Water Giving. Billy Tsosie had been an infant then, but before he left the kiva tonight, he'd be a man. It was time for the finishing. Here, deep within the womb of the earth mother, Tsosie would become a part of all the life that surrounded him, and one with his tribe.

To John Romero the years had passed much too quickly. He looked back on his own accomplishments with a heavy heart. His goal had always been to make the pueblo a better place to live while maintaining the traditions that had held them together. Respect and adherence to their own ways had helped them survive for centuries before the coming of the Spanish and after. Yet, somehow, he'd lacked vision. He'd fought to open the doors to progress, closing his eyes to the subtle dangers. Although he'd found ways to increase the tribe's holdings, benefiting all, the price they would have to pay now threatened their very existence. The increased wealth had acted as a magnet for the evil that had wound its way into their midst, an evil only he and the one he had summoned could fight. Would there be anything for Billy Tsosie and the other boys to inherit?

There was a deafening thump on the roof of the *sipofene*, a small private room attached to the kiva. The sound brought John Romero out of his musings. The sacred matter at hand would require all his concentration. Yet his thoughts continued to strain in a different direction, separating him from the very things he held dear. A sense of futility and failure chilled him to the marrow. As Billy turned and glanced at him, John reached deep within himself, seeking the calm he needed to honor his duty to the gods.

Billy's eyes were wide with alarm as the pounding noise came closer. John gave him a nod, silently reassuring that all would be well.

Suddenly the masked god of the Summer People stood before them. His head was blue, with eyes and mouth outlined in black. A single horn, striped in black and white, grew out of his head and extended up about an arm's length. A corn husk adorned his ear as a pendant.

Without preamble, the hunt chief stepped forward and asked the first boy if he wished to be finished.

The youth nodded once, not trusting his voice.

Consent given, the hunt chief gestured to one of the *Kossa*. The sacred clown of the gods came forward to assist the god of the Summer People.

The god continued down the small line, initiating each of the boys. When the task was concluded, he stepped back and faced them. The god stood motionless for a moment, then suddenly reached up and removed his mask.

The shock that initially appeared on the boys' faces was quickly replaced with a proud glow. They were now sharing in the secret. The familiar face behind the sacred mask would never be revealed to anyone uninitiated.

John Romero smiled as the boys were encouraged to try on the mask themselves. By the end of tonight, another cycle would be complete. He felt a strong bond to these boys. They were part of the endless chain of events that tied their past as a people to the present and ensured their future. As long as they held fast to the knowledge gained from the old ways, they'd have the strength to persevere. John studied the faces around him and invoked the aid of his *Po wa ha*, the guardian spirit who aided him through his earthly trials. Yet deep within himself, he doubted the tribe or he would survive what was to come.

John watched the proceedings in silence. His part here was over for now. His presence would not be required again for a few more hours. With a respectful nod to the hunt chief, he wordlessly slipped out of the kiva.

John Romero gazed overhead at the thick blanket of stars the Anglos called the Milky Way. Some tribes called the same stars The Path of Souls After Death. This seemed particularly appropriate now. Nothing, except a life-or-death matter, could have taken him away from the kiva this evening. But his friend had telephoned before the start of the ceremonies with an urgent message. He too had discovered what was happening. Now he feared for his life.

With great concern John Romero considered their chances for survival. The information they possessed was not sufficient to defeat their enemies. It was, however, dangerous. Their one hope lay in combining forces. Together, perhaps, they would be able to find the answers they needed to stop what was to come.

John walked through the village, his old, comfortable paratrooper boots padding softly against the sandy earth. He'd left his truck in the graveled area next to the pueblo's bank on the other side of the plaza. As he traversed the nearly deserted grounds, the massive adobe walls of the pueblo homes loomed out of the darkness.

Surveying the empty parking lot in one glance, he strode to his truck and slipped inside. Ten minutes later, he reached the main gate which led to and from the pueblo. Whenever the tribe was engaged in closed rituals, it was kept padlocked. The area was patrolled frequently by tribal peace officers as an added measure against intruders.

No one was around now. The moon had slipped behind a cloud, surrounding him in a veil of darkness. His only companions, the stunted trees illuminated by his headlights, seemed like spirits in the night. Using his key, he opened the gate and drove the truck through. He had returned to lock it once again when he heard a branch snap behind him. Before he could even turn his head, he felt the thin cord at his neck.

Powerful arms began to squeeze the garrote. His eyes bulged and the bright lights of consciousness started to dim in his brain. Desperately he slammed his elbow into the chest of his adversary, but his massive attacker only grunted and tightened the cord. Remembering his knife in the growing haze of half awareness, he groped for his belt and found the deer antler handle.

His fingers were growing numb as his lungs screamed for air. With all his remaining reserves of strength, he yanked the razor-sharp, six-inch blade from the sheath. Then, in one mighty surge, he slammed the knife into his attacker's abdomen, ripping upward against the rib cage.

With an almost inhuman gasp, his assailant stiffened. He arched away from him, clutching his torso in a futile attempt to stem the flow of blood. The man staggered backward a few steps, then collapsed. By the time he hit the ground, he was dead.

Gasping for air, John Romero stared at him, recognition dawning slowly. He'd only seen this man once before, but it was someone his friend had trusted. Had he eavesdropped on their conversation earlier that day? If so, how much did their enemies know about them already?

Danger was closing in on them. He hoped that it wasn't already too late for his friend. He'd have to hurry and pray that they had come after him first. What he'd feared most had begun.

A few minutes later the body of his attacker was beneath a tarp in the back of his truck. Quickly he grabbed a juniper branch and erased the evidence of their struggle. As he worked the remaining blood into the sand, a shiny figure brushed to the surface caught his eye. He reached down for it. His stomach tightened as he realized his prized hunting fetish had been broken in the fight. It was a bad omen. Yet there was no turning back now.

Chapter One

Kelly Ferguson stared at the slate countertop that ran along the back wall of her classroom. Getting labs set up for her Santa Fe Middle School students was time-consuming, but she loved teaching earth science.

She glanced at the rock samples placed inside numbered plastic beakers. The stock container in which she'd kept some of her most important igneous rocks had been misplaced. She'd need to find several more samples before tomorrow. She looked up at the clock above the chalkboard. It was almost five o'clock. If she hurried, she could make it to Black Mesa and gather samples before dusk. While there, she could also stop to take some instant photos of the rock formations. She picked up an old Polaroid camera and a film packet from the supply room, along with a stack of papers to grade, then locked the door.

As Kelly strode down the hall toward the main entrance, Adrian Lowell stepped out of the art room where he'd been substitute teaching that day. Her pace slowed almost imperceptibly, dreading the encounter. She realized he must have been waiting for her to leave; substitutes almost never stayed late.

Adrian leaned against a section of lockers and grinned. "Hi, Kelly, it looks as if we're about the only ones here. Since I'll be taking Mr. Sanchez's class tomorrow again, I thought I'd get some things ready. How about you?"

"Nothing special. Just the usual," she said trying to cut it short. She knew he was getting ready to ask her out and was hoping to duck the issue. He seemed nice enough on the surface and cute, too. He stood five foot ten, had light brown hair and a very trim, athletic build.

Yet she'd noticed a strangeness in his brown eyes that made her feel uneasy. "Well, I'd better be going," she said, trying to walk past him.

"Do you have any plans for tonight?" Adrian asked hopefully, loosening his tie with his free hand. "I know a great little restaurant just east of the plaza."

There it was. He had been working up to this all day. She could tell from the way he'd focused his conversation on her at lunch in the teachers' lounge. Not wanting to hurt his feelings, she tried to decline gracefully.

"Thanks for the offer, Adrian, but I've made other plans. Maybe some other time," she said, glancing at her watch. "I've got to get going now. I'm late."

She turned to walk away, when he reached out and grabbed her shoulder. "It's that Indian lawyer, isn't it..." He stopped in midsentence when Bart, the night custodian, came around the corner. "Never mind, see you tomorrow, Kelly," Adrian said, releasing her.

She could still feel the pressure of his fingers where they'd dug into her shoulder. "I'll be seeing you," Kelly said, hurrying away. How did Adrian know about John, and what made him think they were dating seriously?

Adrian must have heard her talking about John in the teachers' lounge at some point or another. That's the only thing that made sense. Adding a good-night to Bart as she passed by, she walked quickly to her small red truck in the staff parking lot.

The matter settled in her mind, she turned her attention back to the present. She had to take the fastest route out of the city if she was going to be able to collect those samples before dark.

Heading west along Upper Canyon Road, Kelly made her way toward the plaza. She turned right on Delgado Street, and drove over the narrow concrete bridge that crossed the tiny Santa Fe river. The traffic was surprisingly light. Most of the evening rush was already home or out of the area. There was a white station wagon behind her and a few other cars further back, but that was all.

She made a right onto Palace Avenue, and headed in the direction of the La Fonda Hotel, the tallest building in the city. Walls of adobe and coyote fences outlined the residences and art galleries, sometimes indistinguishable from one another. A few tourists occupied the narrow sidewalks, doing the last of their sight-seeing before dinner.

As she entered heavier traffic, she noted that the white station wagon was still there, several car lengths behind her.

She drove further west and then turned north. Still the station wagon remained in the same position. Was someone following her? But who and why?

The situation was beginning to alarm her until the car turned east toward the mountains on a side street and disappeared from sight. She breathed a sigh of relief. Whoever it was would never know how he'd frightened her. Maybe she'd just been working too hard lately. She was starting to sense danger where none existed. Well, she wouldn't let her imagination ruin the rest of her day. She drove toward U.S. Highway 84, ready to resume her former plans.

As she left the city behind, vast, empty stretches of the upper Rio Grande Valley greeted her. Sage and piñon dotted the landscape in random patterns that added a touch of green to the rocky expanses. She searched for the particular outcropping of black rocks her Pueblo friend, John Romero, had shown her during a hike. For centuries the men of his tribe had gathered obsidian there for tools and knives. The women had come for the basaltic rocks that could be shaped into metates and used for grinding corn.

As her thoughts turned to John, she found her earlier good mood returning. The pueblo had been closed for the past week, but the religious observances would be finished tomorrow. And John had asked her to join him for the festivities that would follow. She looked forward to seeing her friend and sharing the part of his culture he'd opened to her.

There was also the arrival of Justin Nakai to look forward to. John had spoken highly of his Navajo friend, attesting to his gentle spirit and strength of will. Justin apparently worked for some government agency in Kansas City, and had succeeded in the white man's world, John claimed, without ever losing sight of himself as an Indian.

John's sister had also alluded to a different sort of excitement created by Justin's impending arrival. Kelly still remembered Maria telling her in confidence that Justin Nakai had buns worth dying for.

What would the man be like?

After a twenty-minute drive she turned off the main highway onto a network of dirt roads. The surrounding land belonged to the state, though it was leased by the pueblo to graze sheep and cattle. Counting the turnoffs, she headed into the sunset. Kelly wound a path to the hillside she was searching for, north of the solitary bluff the Pueblo people called Black Mesa.

Making efficient use of her time, Kelly gathered her samples in a paper sack and finished taking the photographs. Then as she walked back along the rocky trail toward her pickup a sudden discovery stopped her dead in her tracks. Directly before her was a prayer stick imbedded in the ground. Feathers were tied around the painted and shaped cottonwood marker.

She stared at the Pueblo artifact, then glanced around uneasily, wondering if anyone had seen her. She'd obviously trespassed on pueblo land. Since it was a time of closed rituals, she could be in a great deal of trouble. John had warned her to be careful and not to go down the wrong road. But they all looked alike out here.

Kelly quickened her pace, breaking into a jog. The sun was setting rapidly and this was no place to be lost, particularly after dark.

Jumping behind the wheel of the truck, she placed the camera and photographs on top of the homework papers she'd brought. The truck started instantly, and moments later she was speeding down the dirt road. Shadows were lengthening with each passing minute, and a shiver ran down her spine. Anxiously she tried to follow her tracks to make sure she didn't get lost again. Unfortunately the landmarks were fading as quickly as the light. She switched on her headlights and slowed down. The last thing she needed now was to blow a tire on the rocky ground.

She stopped at a crossroads, trying to reorient herself, but neither path looked familiar. Making a quick choice, Kelly headed down the road to her left. She hadn't traveled more than fifty feet when she realized she'd made a mistake. This path was only taking her down into a large arroyo, where she knew the ground was dangerously soft. Fearing she could get stuck, Kelly shifted into low gear.

Suddenly her headlights fell upon a group of Indian men wearing ceremonial masks. They were gathered around a bright gasoline lantern about fifty yards farther up the wash. The glow bathed their circle in a champagne-colored light that gently skewed the eyes' perception. In the eerie haze, she saw one man lying on some kind of ground cloth. Another, wearing a feathered mask resembling the sun, was on his knees, as if praying. She stopped the truck, reluctant to go any farther into the wash.

Mesmerized, she watched those closest to her. Their faces were covered by large cylindrical masks, with mule deer antlers on the top and muzzle noses that protruded outward from each. Teeth were painted on the sides. All the ceremonial costumes were limited to the masks, however. Jeans and sports shirts served as a reminder that even here the old and new mingled and coexisted in a truce forced by the changing times.

She could hear someone speaking, but the words were muffled by the low roar of the pressurized gasoline lantern.

As one of the others moved around the kneeling man, he raised his head and saw her. He cried out in a loud voice that echoed clearly down the arroyo and through her opened window.

The others turned around, spotting her immediately. For a moment no one moved. Abruptly two of the men in the deer masks broke into a run, coming directly toward her.

Terrified she'd interrupted one of the tribe's secret rituals, Kelly instantly placed the vehicle in reverse. The engine died. In a panic, she reached down and turned the key in the ignition, holding the gas pedal all the way down. The truck lurched back and died again. Cursing aloud, she took the truck out of gear and tried once more, afraid to look up. With a roar the engine thankfully started. Quickly she backed out of the arroyo and wheeled around on the dirt road. In a shower of gravel and sand, she sped away. The men in deer masks stopped chasing her at the top of the arroyo.

She had no idea where to go next in order to find the highway, but she had to get away from there. Some religious societies considered death the only acceptable atonement for sacrilege. Of course, nowadays most of the tribal members wouldn't go along with that. Yet she had no intention of putting it to a test. No matter what they had in mind, it was not bound to be a pleasant experience.

Kelly rammed the accelerator to the floorboard. Ignoring the way the truck bucked and fishtailed in the loose earth, she hurtled down the dirt road as fast as she dared.

Several minutes later, the arroyo far behind, she slowed the truck down to a safer speed. She had no idea where she was. As she took a deep breath, a light reflecting off her rearview mirror caught her attention. Headlights were closing in behind her, the powerful beams bouncing up and down as the vehicle approached at high speed. She gunned the gas pedal again and slid around the curve, praying they wouldn't catch up with her. Without thinking, she selected roads randomly at each intersection. To her surprise, her choices were correct. The main highway loomed ahead on a small rise.

She glanced back, a strangled cry escaping her lips. The vehicle behind her was catching up. Its headlights glared into her eyes, and she could hear the roar of the engine. Forcing herself to focus on the road ahead, Kelly maneuvered toward the Interstate ramp just a short distance away. Surely they'd stop following her once she was off tribal lands.

As she reached the highway her hopes were dashed. The large blue pickup following her squealed its tires as it careened around the curve. It went up the asphalt ramp just seconds behind her. Using the temporary advantage of reaching the good road first, she pushed her truck for all it could muster and drove as if death itself was chasing her. The speedometer rose up past eighty and the little red pickup shook beneath her.

Beyond the reach of her headlights, she saw a well-lit gas station ahead. A refuge! Body trembling, she reduced her speed and took the off ramp. Kelly slowed her truck and drove onto the gravel beside the building. In her rearview mirror she could see that the vehicle following her was pulling off to the side of the road about a quarter of a mile behind.

Almost running, she hurried inside. The burly half-Indian proprietor glanced up curiously from the show he was watching on a small portable TV. "Can I help you?"

Her heart was pounding so hard she was afraid he'd hear it. Forcing a smile, Kelly picked up a bag of potato chips from a rack on the counter. The men who were pursuing her would probably not come after her inside the gas station. She'd just have to remain where she was and wait them out. To ask for help here would only compound the problem, especially since she would have to explain *why* they were after her.

"Hey, I think I've seen that movie before." She was trying to act casual and make small talk. Only her voice sounded unnaturally high to her, and she was almost out of breath. She paused for a second more. "It's one of the classics, isn't it?"

"It's Humphrey Bogart's best," the man replied, "and just getting to the good part, too. They're trapped by a hurricane, and Bogey's caught in a mess of trouble with some gangsters."

Her hands were still shaky. As she started to hand some change to the proprietor, one of the quarters slipped through her fingers. It rolled across the dusty tile floor toward the service-bay doorway, then fell flat. "This isn't my day," she muttered and went to retrieve it.

She stopped suddenly as an Indian man stepped into the room and blocked her way. She stared at him, her throat so tight she couldn't make a sound. He was tall, his eyes were a piercing black, and his skin, smooth mahogany. His raven hair was trimmed short, almost military in style.

"Let me get that for you," he said. His voice was soft, yet it had a strength that commanded attention.

Was he one of the men who'd come after her? A glance revealed a car in the garage where a mechanic was working. The man tried to hand the coin back to her. "Here you go."

He didn't seem Pueblo somehow, only she couldn't quite identify his tribe. He was wearing a light blue sports jacket over an open-collared shirt and had on jeans and brown boots. His age she could only guess at—more than thirty and less than forty.

Realizing that he was trying to return her money, she extended her hand. "Thank you," she stammered, thinking that he'd probably concluded that she was a bit on the dim-witted side.

With a glint of amusement in his eyes, the man pulled a soft-drink can from the refrigerated unit by the wall and paid the proprietor.

"How's Wally doing with that nail puncture in your tire?" the owner asked casually.

"He'll be done before too long." The man shook his head slowly. "Those spares they put in new cars sure aren't worth much. I'd have never made it back to Santa Fe on that little bicycle tire. I was lucky you were still open. When Wally's finished, I'm going back to Santa Fe for a new tire." He shifted his attention to Kelly.

She tried to think of something to say, but the intensity of his gaze made her brain switch into neutral. He seemed to be looking right into her soul. Then, a moment later, he turned away and walked back to the garage area.

She took a deep breath, then let it out slowly. His clothing was like that of many Southwestern men, yet his catlike grace and searching eyes suggested a hunter. Her skin tingled with a disturbing warmth and her pulse was still racing. What an incredible presence!

"Ma'am?" the proprietor broke into her thoughts.

Her face reddening, Kelly turned and paid for the chips. She leaned against the counter and pretended to be engrossed in the movie. "Do you mind if I watch just a little more of that? *Key Largo* is one of my favorites," she asked.

"Not at all. Pull up a chair if you like." He waved his hand in the direction of an old chrome and yellow vinyl chair that must have originated in someone's kitchen.

Kelly scooted the chair near the open door where she could watch the vehicle that had followed hers. Its outline gleamed faintly in the moonlight.

After twenty minutes, she saw the headlights turn back on. Her body stiffened and she held her breath praying they weren't coming after her. Then she saw the truck do a three-point turn and start back down the highway in the opposite direction.

She sighed with relief. They were returning to tribal land. Perhaps the impasse had given their tempers a chance to cool. As common sense prevailed, they'd decided to return to their rituals.

Thanking the proprietor, Kelly walked out to her truck. Her body was drenched with perspiration even though the temperature was in the mid-sixties. She shivered slightly as the cool desert breeze touched her skin. All she wanted to do now was go home, take a long bath and go to bed. She'd had enough excitement to last a lifetime.

Kelly had traveled about a mile down the deserted freeway when she spotted a set of headlights approaching her from behind. As her heart began to drum in her ears she saw a large truck closing in behind her. It looked like the same one that had followed her before, but she couldn't be sure. Her hands began to perspire making it difficult to grip the steering wheel. Then it started. The blue three-quarter-ton pickup smashed its massive bumper into the rear of her own smaller vehicle.

She bit her lip to keep from screaming and tried to accelerate to get away. She pushed the gas pedal all the way to the floor and her pickup lurched forward. But her little engine was no match for the other vehicle on open roads. The larger truck overtook her immediately and pulled alongside.

She looked pleadingly across at the other truck, but the windows were tinted, and all she could discern were outlines. Not being able to see those who were trying to harm her made it even worse. Her terror grew, and she tried to slow down and inch away toward the shoulder of the road.

With a deafening crunch, the larger vehicle smashed into her front end. Her tires squealed in protest. The steering wheel spun hard to the right and slipped through her fingers. Her truck skidded off the road into the soft dirt shoulder then lurched and jammed into the ground. An eerie sensation gripped her as the truck angled sideways, toppled over and then began rolling into the dark emptiness below.

She was tossed forward and back, the seat belt cutting into her torso. Then, mercifully, everything was still. She opened her eyes, dizzy and disoriented. Her head throbbed. She glanced out her shattered windshield trying to make some sense out of the crazy landscape. It seemed wrong somehow, like a scene of an alien world in a science fiction movie. Through sheer willpower she tried to force away the cottony dullness that surrounded her mind.

With effort Kelly focused on an area beyond the hood, trying to seek out familiar patterns. As her thoughts began to clear, she realized she was upside down. The roof of her truck had been crushed so it almost touched her head, despite the seat belt harness that held her.

Her arms were wrapped oddly around the steering wheel but everything in her aching body seemed to work. Freeing her hands, she gripped the wheel tightly with one and tried to release the belt with the other. If she was careful, she'd be able to ease herself down without smashing her head against the roof of the truck.

It was difficult from her angle to find the seat belt connector, but slowly she began to trace her hand along the harness. She'd have to get away from the car and hide out until she was sure they wouldn't be coming to finish her off. Finding the release mechanism at last, she pressed it but nothing happened. It was jammed.

Kelly had started to try again when she heard the sound of footsteps approaching through the brush.

Chapter Two

She cried out in frustration as the belt refused to yield.

"Just stay calm," a man's voice said, the sound distorted by the buzzing in her ears. "Don't try to move yet." A light shone from somewhere onto her face.

She knew he must have been looking in at her from the driver's window. Only she couldn't see him because of the way she'd twisted around trying to get free. He moved to the front of the vehicle, the beam of the high-powered flashlight leading his way. In the glow, Kelly caught a glimpse of his dark boots.

"Talk to me if you can," the man urged. "I need to know about your condition before I can figure out how to help you."

Into an early grave? Kelly hesitated, uncertain of his intent. What if he was only making sure she couldn't fight back before he finished her off? She heard him walk around the vehicle, inspecting it. At least her hearing was beginning to clear up.

"I'm going to have to get you out of there soon," he said. "Your fuel tank has been punctured and there's gas all over the ground. If you can understand what I'm saying but you can't speak, make any kind of sound, and I'll understand. We're both in a great deal of danger as long as we remain near this truck." His voice was now coming from behind her.

Dully she identified the smell stinging her nostrils and knew he was telling the truth. The scent was growing stronger with each passing second. Praying she wasn't making a fatal mistake, she answered him. "I'm okay, but the seat belt is stuck. I'm trying to work it loose."

"Wait. Let me see if I can get inside to help you. Your door is too damaged, but maybe I can force the passenger's side. Hang on, and if you can, trust me. I *will* get you out."

His tone, more than his words, had an oddly reassuring effect. Intuitively, she felt certain fate had placed her in capable hands.

The pickup rocked slightly as he struggled to open the door. "I'm going to have to run back uphill to my car. There's a lug wrench in the trunk that will serve as a crowbar. With that, I'll be able to open this." He bent down and peered through the cracked window on the passenger's side. The bright beam of his flashlight filled the cab.

She turned her head slightly, glad that it didn't hurt too much and, for the first time, caught a glimpse of his face. It was the man she'd met in the gasoline station.

"Remember me?"

"Yes," she said, managing a smile. He wasn't the type of man she was likely to forget easily.

"I'll be back to get you."

She held on to his words, using them to bolster her courage.

He returned a few minutes later. "Okay, now grab on to something if you can for support."

She heard him grunt, then with a shrill squeak the door gave way. Placing the flashlight beside him so it illuminated her, he added, "I'm going to cut the seat belt, but don't worry. I'll catch you. Let me do all the work, and we'll have you out of here in a second."

He held her head in the crook of his arm and cut through the strap with a pocket knife. As her body slipped down, his arms cradled her against him. "There we go. How do you feel?"

His chest was warm and comforting. "I'll live." She managed a smile.

"That's the idea," he replied, inching backward on his knees out of the cab. "Can you grab the flashlight? I've angled my car so that the headlights shine down the hillside, but we're still going to need it to see."

"I've got it," she replied. His body was strong and hard, yet he was surprisingly gentle as he held her.

Clearly wanting to distance himself from the vehicle as soon as possible, he carried her away from the overturned truck first, stepping around the dozens of school papers scattered along the slope. Then, out of immediate danger, he started the climb back to the road.

She could feel his muscles strain as he made his way up the brush-covered incline. When they reached the top of the hillside, he stopped by the side of the car. Gently he lowered her onto the ground.

"I don't know quite how you managed to do that," she said, feeling terribly self-conscious, "but I appreciate the lift."

He laughed, the sound full and masculine. "You're not very big, you know." She tried to sit up, but he stopped her. "Don't do anything abruptly. Test everything out a little at a time. Is there any spot that hurts more than the rest?"

"No," Kelly answered hesitantly. With his arm around her for support, she slowly worked up to a sitting position. "I'm okay. Just bruised."

"You're a very lucky lady. Your truck is a mess." With an almost imperceptible trace of reluctance, he released her.

Kelly glanced down the hillside, all the details of her accident replaying themselves vividly in her mind. She shuddered. "Thank you—" she met his eyes "—what you've done..."

He nodded once, gravely. "What's your name, schoolteacher?"

"Kelly Ferguson." She extended her hand. From all the papers scattered about, he didn't have to be a detective to deduce her profession.

"I'm Justin Nakai." He shook her hand, then cupped it between both of his. "You're freezing. Let me fix that." Before she could protest, he took off his coat and slipped it over her shoulders.

The gesture touched her. "John was right about you," she said and smiled.

He considered her statement. "You're a friend of John Romero's."

"Yes, I've known him for some time. He told me you'd be arriving tonight. You and I were to have met tomorrow evening at the celebration following the close of the religious observances."

Instead of commenting, Justin leaped into a thoughtful silence.

She forced herself not to interrupt his thoughts. John always said Anglos were too impatient, and she didn't want to live up to his claim. As a teacher she was used to dividing her day into seconds, minutes and hours. Yet, as one of her Tewa friends had explained, time wasn't meant to be a framework used to wall up lives, but something to move through. No tick of the clock set the right moment. Intuitive awareness was a much better guide.

Justin Nakai stood and walked to his car. Kelly watched him, curious as to what he was planning to do. She saw him reach into the trunk and take out what appeared to be two paper-wrapped candles.

When she realized they were flares, she bolted awkwardly to her feet, her muscles sore and stiff from the accident. "No, don't do that!" she said, as he ignited them both.

Justin regarded her speculatively. "We'll need help and emergency vehicles," he explained, placing the flares on the shoulder of the road.

She tried to keep her body from shaking but couldn't quite manage it. "It would be better if you could just give me a lift into town."

His eyes narrowed slightly, his expression alive with curiosity. "I'm sorry, but we can't leave the scene of an accident. The police need to be brought in. Besides, that gas spill constitutes a fire hazard. We're really close to pueblo land and I'd hate to see a range fire get started out here. It would be very hard to contain, particularly since this has been a dry year."

Kelly nodded and didn't argue further.

"Let me take you to my car. You can rest in the passenger's seat. I'll lower the back down." Justin wrapped his arm around her shoulders.

Nervously Kelly looked up and down the highway, but no headlights were in sight. She didn't relish staying out on this solitary stretch of road any longer than was necessary. Yet, there was nothing else she could do. If she told Justin what had really happened, she'd be risking his life as well. As a Navajo, he too would be viewed as an outsider in possession of secret knowledge. According to the Pueblos' beliefs, power shared was power lost. Any breath of secrecy surrounding Pueblo rituals threatened their very existence, and self-preservation was a strong motive for action.

There was only one thing she could do. She'd have to omit a few facts, but somehow manage to get the urgency of the situation across to him. "Justin, we shouldn't linger around here any longer. I had that accident because some nut came by really fast and forced me off the road. If he decides to return, we may be in a great deal of trouble."

He walked around to the driver's side. "Don't worry. I don't think anyone will bother you now that I'm here."

Their eyes met, and for an instant she had the impression he'd pieced together far more than he was letting her know.

"Someone will be by soon to help," he assured. "This road isn't as deserted as you might think. Commercial trucks use it quite often. Well, 'often' for these parts, that is," he smiled.

Kelly stretched out her legs and leaned back against the seat, trying to find a comfortable position. She was completely exhausted. The terror she had experienced had drained her. The high-tension charge of acute fear needed energy reserves to be sustained. The only thing her mind could register now was fatigue and a chronic, low-level anxiety.

Uncomfortable with the silence between them, she tried to make conversation. "John told me that you two met in law school at the University of New Mexico in Albuquerque. Only you went to work for the government, while he decided to pursue a law practice."

"John's life is here. Being with his own people is important to him."

"But not to you?"

Justin smiled. "The Navajo were a nomadic tribe once, and I guess I inherited a little of that. I wanted to see what else was out there."

"Well, I'm glad for my sake that you accepted John's invitation to visit," she acknowledged gratefully.

Justin saw headlights off in the distance. "Wait here. I'll be right back."

She grabbed his arm without even thinking. "No, don't. You have no idea who that might..."

He disengaged himself gently. "I can take care of myself." He glanced up and studied the approaching pickup. "Besides this isn't the same vehicle you tangled with."

Surprised, she sat up abruptly. "How do you know that?"

"I looked your truck over when I was down there getting you out." He opened his door and stepped out. "Whoever tried to kill you was in a blue vehicle. Their paint is scraped all over the driver's side of your truck."

Without further explanation, Justin left the car. A bright yellow truck, with its custom camper shell, had stopped on the shoulder before one of the flares.

Justin went up to the driver. "There's been an accident here. I'm going to need your help."

"I've got a C.B.," the elderly man replied, peering down curiously at the overturned pickup. "We're not linked to police frequencies, but I'm sure we can raise a trucker who'll stop and telephone them for you."

"Thanks. It would also be a good idea to have some paramedics come to check out the driver."

A few minutes later, the man glanced up at Justin. "I reached a trucker on the outskirts of Santa Fe. He's going to call the emergency people. What else can we do for you?"

"We'll be fine now. Thanks for stopping and for all your help."

Justin watched the man drive away, then started back to his car. Methodically he tried to organize the evening's events into a logical pattern. What on earth had the schoolteacher been doing out alone on this road at such a late hour?

He'd seen the camera in her overturned pickup, along with some of the school papers. It was an instant camera, so she'd probably had some photographs in her purse or the glove compartment. Had she secretly been taking photos of some of the Pueblo ceremonies? Maybe someone had seen her and notified tribal officials. The problem was, he had difficulty believing they would have run her off the road. The Pueblos were adamant about their right to privacy, yet harming anyone went against the basic tenets of their culture.

He remembered a rare discussion on the subject he'd once had with John. Like the Navajos, the Pueblo tribe had a deep reverence for all living things. It was the foundation of their religious beliefs. To take a life, particularly during ceremonials was to create inharmony. The consequences of such an act could, according to their teachings, profoundly and adversely affect the whole community.

Then again, there had been a few unpleasant incidents reported in the past, attributed to the tribe's more radical factions. On occasion they'd proved to be extremely dangerous to curious outsiders. Had that been the case tonight?

Justin slipped behind the driver's seat and shifted so he could look at her squarely. "The state police will be notified, but I'm sure it'll be the tribal police who'll respond," he said. "This road runs through Pueblo land so it's considered primarily their jurisdiction."

"Then it'll probably be Sergeant Suazo who'll come out," she said with a resigned sigh.

"You've met the man?" he observed. Maybe she'd been accused of spying on the Pueblos before.

"Yes, but whenever I'm at the pueblo, I do my best to avoid him. To be fair, he seems to prefer it that way," she admitted candidly.

Justin said nothing. He'd only met Suazo a couple of times before, but the man was as friendly as a cornered rattler. "Does John know you were on Pueblo land tonight?" He took a shot in the dark, just to see her reaction.

She stared up at him quickly, alarm etched in her features. Then slowly, as if she'd guessed his gambit, her expression relaxed. "John showed me a place *adjacent* to Pueblo land where I can gather rock samples for my earth science class. That's where I was before all this happened."

There was more to her story. The facts all pointed to that. Later tonight, when he saw John, he'd ask about her. He was curious to find out what kind of relationship his friend had with her. She was unmarried. He'd noticed the absence of any wedding ring, or sign of one, on her hand earlier. He'd also bet his last dollar it wasn't due to lack of offers. She was quite beautiful even now, despite everything she'd been through. She was independent, too, a quality he admired in a woman. Even though she was badly frightened, she was still relying on her own strength to see her through. "I'll be meeting John this evening. Shall I tell him what happened?" Justin asked, again watching her reaction. Her face remained unreadable, a lady of mystery to the end, it seemed.

Instead of answering, she sat up and called his attention to the road. "Look, there's someone approaching now. Police, I imagine, from the lights."

He waited a moment. "Suazo," he said at last. "I'll go meet him. You stay here and try not to move too much."

"You know, normally I argue when someone tries to give me an order, but right now I'm just too tired." She sighed and settled back into the seat.

He chuckled. "I'll remember that." Leaving the car, he walked up to the tribal policeman's vehicle, a green and white four-wheel-drive Bronco with blue and red emergency lights flashing.

Suazo stepped out, hand resting lightly on the butt of his revolver, and strode toward him. "Nakai," he acknowledged. "I heard you were due to show up sometime today. I thought you'd have been at the Romero house by now."

"I was delayed getting out of Kansas City," Justin answered. "Are they still in the kiva?"

Suazo glanced at him in silence for about five seconds, then shrugged. "Probably on and off until tomorrow. Who knows?"

Justin felt Suazo's reluctance to even allude to the pueblo's religious activities. He was well aware that the Dinéh, as most Navajos referred to themselves, weren't generally held in high regard by the Pueblo tribes.

"I'm going to have to see your driver's license, Nakai, for my report."

"I understand," Justin replied, reaching for his wallet.

Suazo stared at Justin's government issue identification and shield for a moment in the beam of his flashlight, then uttered a low curse.

"FBI special agent? Just my luck. All this time I thought you were some kind of legal paper pusher with the BIA." Suazo paused for a moment, thinking, then continued. "This *is* just some accident you came along, right? Not some case you're working on?"

"I just happened to be the first person on the scene, that's all. I'm here to visit friends at the pueblo. Now let me brief you on what I found here when I arrived." He told Suazo the facts as he had determined them, then waited.

"She has camera equipment in her truck?" Suazo's eyes narrowed. "I'm confiscating that." He strode over to Justin's car. "I better get started questioning her. By the way—'' he stopped in midstride but did not turn to look at him ''—remember this is my jurisdiction.''

"I'm on vacation. Handle it any way you want." Nonetheless, Justin intended to stay close. He wasn't sure if his interest was due to the woman herself or the puzzle she posed. He only knew he was reluctant to abandon this completely.

Suazo opened the door to the passenger's side, and stood just outside as he began to question the woman. While Justin watched, the Pueblo man listened to her story about being run off the road. When she was finished, he gave her a cynical look. "Come on, lady, give me a break. Someone deliberately forced you off the road out here, and you want me to believe you don't know why? This area isn't exactly brimming over with crazy men. It's not likely you were a random target. Try again."

She was about to answer when the rescue team arrived. Suazo remained close by as the paramedics unloaded their equipment.

"I'm not through with you, Ms. Ferguson," he warned. "There's something you're not telling me. I'm also taking your camera and any film I find in with me. If there are any photos of the tribe's rituals there, you'll be prosecuted. You can count on that."

She glared at him. "Taking the camera won't do you much good, Sergeant. It's an instant camera. The pictures I took, though, should be somewhere in the cab of my truck. Study them as long as you want. All you'll see is a variety of rock formations. You can also search the rest of my things, if it'll set your mind at ease."

So now it was out. Justin must have seen her camera and told Suazo. They both suspected her of spying on the Pueblo. The thought filled her with anger, then anxiety. If they discussed their suspicions with any of the tribal members, it was going to make things even worse for her!

"I'll go through your truck carefully, you can count on it. Instant photographs come out on thick, heavy paper so they're not likely to go far," Suazo affirmed, starting down the incline.

Justin gave her a quick look. "I'll go with him and bring back your purse. I'm sure you'll want it back tonight."

By the time the paramedics finished giving her a checkup, Justin returned. "What's the verdict?" he asked, placing her purse beside her on the ground.

"I'm fine, just as I told you," she answered. "I'll be sore for a few days. That's all."

"We still recommend that you go in to the hospital with us for a more thorough checkup, ma'am," the eldest of the two paramedics advised. "We didn't find any problems, but it always pays to be on the safe side."

"Thanks, but that's not going to be necessary." She started to walk away, then realized that without Justin's help, she had no other way home. She glanced at Justin. "I hate to impose, you've done so much already, but I'd really like to go home. Could you give me a lift?" She gestured toward the wrecker which had just arrived at the scene. "My truck's not going anywhere on its own power, I'm afraid."

Justin could feel Suazo looking at him, speculating whether he'd try to interfere with his investigation. He should have said no and let Suazo arrange for her transportation. Yet he couldn't quite find it in him to turn her down. "On one condition. We make a stop by the hospital first."

"You're tough to bargain with," Kelly replied with a sigh.

He didn't say anything, but rather waited patiently for her answer. She nodded. "All right, I agree."

He started to walk her back to his car, when Suazo stopped him. "Nakai, a word with you."

Justin left Kelly's side, and joined Suazo out of her hearing range.

"Remember, you have no jurisdiction here," Suazo growled immediately. "This is my case. I don't want you involved."

"I'm not involved in your investigation," Justin answered flatly.

"Your interest in the woman is...personal?" Suazo asked.

Justin resented the question, and he found himself resenting the man who'd asked it. "Yes," he replied at length.

As Justin walked back to his car he saw his passenger was already inside. His gaze lingered over her. He was attracted to her and might as well stop sidestepping the issue. He tried to remember how long it had been since he'd had a woman in his life. Realizing he was having a tough time calculating the answer, he chuckled softly. Of course, he'd never been one to date casually. When he sought out the companionship of a woman it was because there was something special about her. He'd always found it difficult to understand colleagues who saw dating simply as an antidote to being alone. From childhood he'd been taught to be comfortable within himself and had spent many nights with the stars as his only companions. "You ready to go?"

She nodded. "I've placed you in a bad position, haven't I?" she observed wryly. "You're late meeting John, and now it appears Suazo's angry with you, too, because you're giving me a ride home."

"If Suazo's annoyed," he replied, driving off, "that's his problem. We're not doing anything wrong. As far as John's concerned—" he gave her a crooked half smile "—I'll give him a call from the hospital.

He won't worry, though. He knows I've never been good with schedules.''

Kelly nodded in silent acknowledgment. It was hard not to be affected by the man beside her. Justin exuded a raw vitality that sparked the air between them like lightning streaks across the sky. The strength and wildness of his heritage remained a part of him despite his modern-day clothes and short-cropped hair.

"When I talk to John shall I give him any message from you?" he asked, hoping to learn more about her connection to his friend.

"If you want to tell him what happened, it's okay. Only make sure he understands I'm not hurt, and that I plan to be there tomorrow."

The more she avoided direct answers, the more curious he became. "Why didn't you tell Suazo all of the truth?" he asked bluntly.

"Justin, I'm exactly what I've said I am," she answered wearily. "I'm a schoolteacher who came out here to collect rocks for her earth science class. I'm no threat to anyone. If you're asking me to logically explain why someone would try to kill me—" she shrugged helplessly "—I can't do it. As far as I'm concerned murder isn't a rational act."

Skillfully worded, yet still evasive, Justin observed as they arrived at the hospital. He escorted her inside. At least the panic that had gripped her earlier was all but gone. Was she responding to him personally, or was it simply having company that had made the difference? He found himself hoping for the former, then forced the thought from his mind. It was time to restore balance to his thinking. "I'll wait for you out here."

"I'll try to make it quick," she answered.

"Don't rush. I'm a very patient man." He held her eyes for a second longer than was necessary. Had John also felt the impact of this woman's sensuousness? He remembered the way she'd fit into his arms. It had made him want to keep her there where she'd be safe. "Very patient," he reiterated.

She nodded once, then disappeared stiffly through the emergency room doors.

KELLY FOLLOWED THE NURSE to the examining room. There she answered the doctor's questions automatically, but her mind remained on Justin. His words had teased her imagination. The temptation to entertain herself by speculating as vividly and as creatively as possible was strong. Fantasies seriously hampered clear thinking, however, and at the moment that's what she needed the most.

Kelly stepped out into the lobby area twenty minutes later and glanced around. Even in a crowded room it wasn't hard to spot Justin. His bearing seemed unconsciously to dominate the space around him.

He strode toward her. "Ready to go?"

She nodded. "I'm fine except for bumps and bruises. They said that if the muscle soreness gets too uncomfortable, an aspirin or two should take care of it. Thanks for letting me borrow this." She started to slip out of his jacket.

"Keep it for a while," he answered. "I don't need it." He walked with her to the entrance, then stopped. "Wait here in the lobby and I'll pull the car up to the doors."

This time she didn't protest. Lost in thought, she watched him go outside. Justin was highly intelligent and not easily put off. Her answers hadn't satisfied him, nor Sergeant Suazo for that matter. Yet, there was nothing else she could do. Circumstances had forced her into a very tight corner.

Justin drove up, and a moment later they were on their way to her cottage. Kelly pretended to be absorbed in the passing scenery, but in reality she was acutely aware of everything about him. The cologne that clung to his jacket was musky and earthy, and the masculine scent surrounded her senses. She glanced at him out of the corner of her eye. His shirt was opened wide at the collar, hinting at the strong, smooth expanse beneath. She remembered the gentleness of their touch and a pleasant warmth enveloped her.

"Do you like teaching in New Mexico?" Justin asked, interrupting her musings. "There're so many cultures that intermingle out here, I imagine it must create some unique problems."

The question took her by surprise. She'd expected more inquiries about the accident, or the events leading up to it. This topic was a welcome relief. "I like working with the kids here. I can't think of many places you could go where there wouldn't be cultural difference to contend with. Out in the Southwest, though, people seem more relaxed about things so they're more tolerant. The kids are especially that way."

He glanced over at her, then back at the road. "Do you work after hours often, like today when you were gathering rock samples?"

She nodded. "Teaching is a round-the-clock job. The time you spend in the classroom is only half of it. There're lesson plans, papers to grade, parent conferences and a million other details involved. Still, I love my work."

"By the way, all the rocks you collected for your students have been scattered by now. Why don't I pick you up tomorrow morning and we can go gather some more? You still need them, don't you?"

She smiled. There it was. Back to the same subject, though the route had been circuitous. "As a matter of fact, I do. I'd really appreciate a ride, too. Only we'll have to get up real early if I'm going to make it to school by eight-fifteen."

"I'm an earlier riser, no problem." He paused, then casually added, "You said John showed you that place?"

"Yes, he did. Ask him about it, if you'd like," she countered defensively. "Justin, I realize seeing my camera has created a lot of questions in your mind, but believe me, I wasn't spying on the Pueblo. The photos should have proven that to you."

"The contents of your purse and glove compartment were all dumped out on the roof of the cab. Suazo and I sorted through it, but we found only two photos. One was a close-up of a rock formation and the other showed Black Mesa. Suazo said he couldn't tell for sure where it had been taken from, but it could have been somewhere on Pueblo land. We also discovered an empty film packet. That means there were more photographs. What happened to them?"

Her mouth dropped open slightly and she fought the sinking feeling that spread over her. "You mean the rest are *gone*?"

Chapter Three

Justin let the moments of silence drag on. "I suppose it's possible the other photos were scattered along with your class papers when the truck rolled," he added a bit skeptically.

"That's got to be it," she affirmed. "They'll be found tomorrow, then you'll both believe me."

"If nothing else turns up, you're in for an unpleasant time with Suazo," he warned. "He's bound to think you've found a way to hide them and that's why we only found two."

Following her directions, he drove up a narrow gravel lane. Nestled at one end was a small cottage hidden under a cluster of cottonwood trees. "I can help, if you can bring yourself to trust me."

"There's nothing more I can say," she replied. She took a deep breath then let it out again. "Why don't you come inside and have a cup of coffee or a drink. I'm sure John won't mind if you're a few more minutes late at this point. You can use my telephone to call him and let him know."

Justin smiled. "Sounds good. It was busy when I tried to call earlier."

She wasn't really sure if he'd accepted her invitation because he wanted to find out more about the accident, or because he wanted her company. Either way, she was glad they didn't have to part just yet.

He followed her inside to a small living room. A pile of grade sheets covered the desk at one corner of the room. Beside it, textbooks and three-ring notebooks filled a large bookcase. Everything there, however, had been stacked horizontally as often as vertically, giving the shelves an uneven look. The first impression was one of order, but a closer study revealed she was a person obviously not bothered by small details.

That trait was not one he could understand easily since it went against his nature. Details were the cornerstone of his work and blended well with his fondness for organization.

"Come on. There's a telephone in the kitchen you can use. In the meantime, I'll put some water on and make some tea, or coffee, whichever you prefer."

"Tea's fine." Justin picked up the receiver from the wall unit and dialed. "It's still busy." He saw her putting the teakettle on. "What can I do to help?"

Kelly gave him a hesitant look. "I'd love to be able to get out of these dusty clothes. How about pouring the water into the teapot after it boils? Everything else is ready."

"No problem. I think I can handle that," he answered with a ghost of a smile.

"In that case, you're in charge."

"That's just the way I like it," he replied as she started to leave.

"Glad you're happy," she quipped. "After all you've done for me, I can at least play by some of your rules."

"And if I ask too many questions?"

She grew serious. "I'll answer those I can." Not bothering to explain her words further, she hurried to the bedroom.

Closing her door, Kelly undressed quickly. One aspect of what had happened to her tonight still worried her greatly. Once John heard what had happened to her, he'd probably guess the rest of the story. As her friend, he'd be placed in the middle of what had proven to be a very nasty situation.

If the tribe ever figured out that she'd been the one who'd accidentally intruded on their ceremony, they would not forgive easily. The parents might have their kids pulled out of her classes. Worst of all, the rapport she'd worked so hard to establish with them would disappear forever.

She thought about the scene she'd witnessed. Something about the voice of the man who'd called out still bothered her, only she couldn't quite pinpoint why. The mask had muffled it.

Slipping on a pair of jeans and a lavender knit top, she hurried to meet her guest. "Did I take too long?"

"Not at all."

"Have a seat. I'll pour the tea for us," she offered.

He sat across from Kelly at the kitchen table. "By the way, I saw a photo of John and you in your living room. It looks like it was taken at a celebration of some kind."

"It was. It dates back to the first time John and I combined forces professionally. I was called to testify on behalf of a Pueblo student who was being kept at home for weeks at a time. John, as the tribal attorney, was in charge of presenting the boy's case. The boy was needed to work the fields because his father had been ill. John and I came up with a solution. Through a work-study program that extended his school year, we figured out a way for the boy to do both. After the matter was settled, John and I went out for a victory dinner.''

Minutes later they finished their tea. Justin's gaze softened as he looked at her. "You're a good hostess, but you must be exhausted. I'll be going now so that you can get some rest."

She smiled wearily as she walked him to the door. "I got a second wind there for a bit, but I think that's all used up."

"Thanks for tea and for the company."

He stood before her, his body almost, but not quite touching hers. She was very aware of his nearness. "You helped me out a great deal today, Justin, I'll never forget that. If there's ever anything I can do for you..."

"Get some rest," he answered with a nod. "I'll see you again in the morning, say at six-thirty? Will that give you time enough to gather a few samples?"

"Sure and thanks for offering to take me."

As he walked to his car, she watched him through the small window in her front door. He had great shoulders. Her gaze drifted lower. And Maria had been right about everything else.

Standing by the open door of his car, he turned back to look at the house. In the glow of the car's interior light, Kelly could see a trace of a smile on Justin's lips. Somehow, he'd known she'd be watching.

JUSTIN FELT THE COOL night air as it streamed through his open window. Now it was time to go to the pueblo and ask his host to forgive his delayed arrival. He'd tried to call several times but John's line had been continually busy.

He thought of John and the friendship they'd shared for so many years. He was looking forward to visiting with them. After they'd caught up on news about each other, however, he intended to ask his friend about Kelly. That relationship puzzled him. John wouldn't have risked an emotional involvement with an outsider. He'd have searched within his tribe for a companion and friend who'd better understand his life-style and religious beliefs. Yet, with matters of the heart, plans often went awry.

Justin stopped at the gas station near the pueblo and called the

Romero home again. Someone would have to meet him at the main gate and let him in.

This time he got through. Ten minutes later Justin approached the sturdy wooden gate that led onto pueblo land. Just on the other side he saw an old, battered Ford pickup.

A man got out of his vehicle, then walked forward to the gate. "You're my brother-in-law's friend?"

"Yes, I'm Justin Nakai," he identified himself and stepped out onto the road so he could be seen in the glare of both sets of headlights.

"Are you John's brother-in-law?" He'd lived in the white man's world all these years, but the second he returned, the old customs came back naturally. As a Navajo, he was reluctant to refer to anyone by their name in their presence, seeing it as a sign of bad manners. Though admittedly the Pueblo custom was not the same, he still felt bound by the traditions of the Dinéh. It pleased him that his friend's relative was greeting him the Navajo way.

"I'm Raymond Johnson, Maria's husband. By any chance, have you talked with John since you arrived in town?"

"No, I haven't spoken to him," Justin replied, puzzled.

"I had hoped..." The sentence trailed off cryptically. "Maybe you should hear it from Clarita. I'll lead you to the house."

They arrived a few minutes later. John's sister and mother were standing just behind the screen door, their silhouettes outlined by the light within. As they greeted Justin, they looked at him anxiously. He didn't know what to say, it was obvious something was wrong. "I'm sorry about my late arrival," he apologized to his friend's mother. "I stopped at the site of an accident to help."

No one spoke, but the alarm in their faces made his blood freeze. "It was an Anglo woman out on the highway. No one was hurt, and I drove her home." Justin decided not to mention the schoolteacher until he had a chance to talk to John first. He followed the others inside. "Excuse me, but is something wrong with John?"

Maria glanced up at Justin as she led her mother to a chair. "He's gone."

Justin's body tensed. "I understood he would be busy attending to his kiva duties most of today and tonight."

Maria tossed her head, brushing her long, black hair away from her face. "That's true. Only they said he left but never came back." She stood near the window, her eyes focused on the well-lit path that led to the door.

"'They' said?" There it was again, the Pueblo tendency never to reveal too much. "Who do you mean?" He felt a surge of adrenaline warming him. His senses sharpened to wary alertness.

"The ones who were there tonight," she replied obliquely. "After they came by, I called my aunts and uncles but no one had seen him in the pueblo anywhere. We'd hoped he'd gone to meet you because his blue pickup isn't here."

As she turned, he could see the faint light of hope still shining in her eyes. With a heavy heart, he shook his head. "I haven't seen or talked to him at all today."

"Then something has happened to my son." Clarita glanced at them through tear-filled, fearful eyes. "He would have never neglected his kiva duties." Wrapping a colorful cotton shawl over her shoulders, she walked slowly out of the room.

KELLY SAT UP SUDDENLY, her bruised muscles protesting the urgency of her movements. She tossed the covers aside. Her body was drenched in perspiration. Quickly she switched on the lamp on the nightstand. As light illuminated her bedroom, she looked around. She was alone.

She forced herself to breathe deeply, then dropped back against the pillow, shivering. It had only been a bad dream. Yet, it had felt so real! She could have sworn she'd seen a man standing by the foot of her bed, watching her.

Taking a deep breath, she reached to turn off the light once again. Suddenly she heard a familiar creaking outside. Without hesitation, she shot out of bed. Her nightmare, she was certain, had been triggered by this.

Kelly crept through the darkened house and went to the phone in the den. She started to dial the police, then put the receiver back down. After what had happened earlier today, she might have too much explaining to do. She thought about calling John—and Justin—but then realized she'd face the same complications.

Gathering her courage, she went to the kitchen. She'd recognized the noise as the creak of her backyard gate. Unlatched, it always made that strange high-pitched squeal as it groaned in the wind. Turning on the outside light, she peered cautiously out the study window. She had to know if it had somehow come unlatched on its own. Her heart almost stopped as she saw the back gate closing. Someone was just leaving! For a moment she couldn't move. Somehow, she'd been followed to her own home!

Chapter Four

Justin had been out all night with John's brother-in-law, driving up and down the highway searching for his missing friend. Despite their efforts, they'd found no trace of John or his blue pickup truck. Justin would have to wait until the ceremonies were over before moving his search onto Pueblo land.

He knew John could be in trouble close by, yet he was helpless to act because of tribal restrictions and customs. He was forbidden even to approach those who had last seen John. It was frustrating to have his hands tied in this way, when his training demanded he take immediate action.

Clarita Romero had finally been persuaded to go to her bedroom at about five in the morning, after they'd returned tired and dusty and unsuccessful. Despite the constant assurances John's sister Maria had voiced, a terrible sense of foreboding filled the household.

Knowing he would be unable to sleep, Justin had asked John's brother-in-law to escort him off tribal land once more. He had left before sunrise to check out Kelly Ferguson's crash site, on the off chance that it could have something to do with John's disappearance. Aided by a flashlight in the predawn half-light, he walked up and down the highway looking for the photographs she claimed should have been there. Scores of school assignments were scattered along the route, but he found no trace of the missing photographs, or of John.

Unwilling to remain away from the Romeros' for long, he headed back to meet Raymond at the gate, as they had arranged.

Raymond's first words told him that there was still no news of John. Justin stood out in the porch of the Romero home, as the first rays of sunlight bathed the pueblo in its unearthly red glow. The strong easterly breeze was beginning to subside as the ground began to warm once again. Justin cleared his mind as he watched the sunrise. His decision was made.

When Clarita came out to fix an early breakfast for everyone, he approached her. "I'd like your permission to talk to people about John's disappearance. My training as a special agent may be useful. I have no official jurisdiction here at the moment, but I am your son's friend and I would like to help." He paused, trying to find the right words. "John and I have been very close since we met. Even though we haven't seen each other very often, he's still like a brother to me. Once the pueblo is reopened at noon today, I'd like to be free to do what I can to bring him back safely to his family." Would she understand his need to help and trust him to conduct his investigation in a manner that would not dishonor them or pry into Tewa ritual? It was hard to put into words what he felt in his heart.

Clarita paused to think before answering. "You are not one of us, but John told me once that your roots trace back to ours. You belong to the Navajo Naashashí clan. They are the Bear Enemies, a Tewa clan. Your ancestors and ours share the same blood."

"Yes, that's true."

"My son will need help. I know he's in danger. I'll speak for you with the rest of the family."

Justin stepped out into the backyard, his weary gaze resting pensively on the Rio Grande to the west. The feel of the good New Mexico earth beneath his feet reminded him of his roots and all the things he loved most.

It had been almost three years since he'd worked in the field. He'd been successful there, conducting investigations into criminal activity, sometimes going undercover and always in contact with the public. Yet, doing his job well had meant being forced to accept unwanted promotions to show the "right attitude" or "for the good of the Bureau." Eventually he'd found himself "advanced" into a desk job, supervising and training others instead of doing the work that best suited him.

It was strange how things worked for those outside the Dinéh. The Navajo way taught a man to look for harmony. In order to walk in beauty, it was important to find one's place within the Circle of Life. Once a man discovered what it was he did best, there was no need for promotions. Working with those who valued advancement and social position above all else was at times very difficult.

Now, on behalf of his friend, he'd go back to doing what he was meant to do. He'd employ every ounce of training and knowledge the department had given him. Even more, he'd draw from the qualities he'd learned as a Navajo boy, for in those he found his greatest strength. Insight, patience and the ability to read people had made him into the modern day hunter he'd become.

Clarita came outside and met Justin. The uncertainty was beginning to take its toll on her. Deep lines etched her face and her hands trembled slightly. "Do what you have to do to find my son." She handed him two long, smooth pieces of white quartz. One was grooved allowing the other to fit over it. "These are the *xayeh* which were used during John's naming ritual. Through them our family, in all its generations, will give you the wisdom you need and guide your search."

He recognized what she was giving him. They were also known as lightning stones because when rubbed together in the dark they'd glow and give off sparks. To those who believed, they were proof that their ancestors still lived in spirit form. He accepted them somberly, knowing the deep religious ties they held for her. "Thank you for trusting me and for giving me these. I'll guard them well."

An hour later Justin pulled up to Kelly's cottage.

She heard him arrive and waved from the den window. He'd changed into jeans and a green flannel shirt, but his clothes were dusty and he looked tired. Had he and John gone out early, perhaps on a hike or across the cornfields?

"Hello," Justin greeted her as she opened the door. "Are you ready to leave?"

"Just let me get a windbreaker and my school stuff, they're in the den."

Within minutes they were on their way out of Santa Fe. Following her directions, Justin drove to the collection area. Kelly concentrated hard on the landscape, paying special attention to all the small landmarks. She was determined to stay well north of Pueblo land this time.

With Justin's help, it didn't take long to gather the igneous rock samples she needed, and soon they were heading back to Santa Fe.

Justin watched her out of the corner of his eye. Silently he considered telling Kelly about John's mysterious disappearance. Under the circumstances, however, that didn't seem to be a good idea. First, he wanted to talk to the Romeros and find out more about her. He wanted to trust her, but she'd been in some kind of trouble last night, and it could have had something to do with the people of San Esteban.

He was almost tempted to ask if she might have involved John in the problem she was having. Her only references to him had not been particularly revealing. She either knew nothing at all, or was a consummate liar.

Minutes later she was getting out of his car at the school. "I'll pick you up this afternoon. We'll take a look at your truck, then go out to the accident site and look for your things," he said.

"Fine. I'm really anxious to find some of those photos to show you and Suazo. My reputation is at stake here."

"If they're still there, we'll find them," Justin said, not really sure if that was reassuring or not.

With a quick thank you, she walked toward the building, limping slightly from last night's bruises. Justin watched her for a moment, then drove away, anxious to speak with Sergeant Suazo about John.

KELLY STOOD on the sidewalk where the buses had loaded up minutes before, waiting for Justin. The day had been hectic, and she had spent her lunch break in her classroom munching on a school "mystery burger" and grading papers.

She jumped when someone tapped her on the shoulder.

"Hello again." Adrian beamed. "I haven't had a chance to talk to you all day. You must have had lunch in your room. Have a lot of catching up to do?"

She tried to be civil. "Actually I was grading papers all day because of a big geology test."

"You must be exhausted, particularly after being up all night at the pueblo. I saw that Romero guy bringing you to school this morning. You got here just in time." Adrian's voice was becoming a little strained.

"Adrian, if it's any of your business, which is isn't, the pueblo wasn't open to outsiders last night, so I couldn't have been there. And the man you saw was Justin Nakai, a Navajo friend of John Romero's," she snapped, not caring for his suggestive comments.

"I didn't mean to make you angry. I was just going to ask you if you need a lift. But I guess your Indian friends are taking good care of you. Here comes one now," Adrian spat out, noting Justin was entering the parking lot. "I guess I don't meet your racial requirements."

She glared at him and practically bit her tongue to keep from reacting. She would not dignify a comment like that with a response. Stepping off the sidewalk she greeted Justin, who had just pulled his car to a stop.

A short time later they arrived at the wrecking yard where her truck had been towed. She'd already called her insurance company and arranged to have a loaner car delivered the next day. Now there was the more immediate problem of what to do about her truck.

One look at it quickly confirmed her worst suspicions. The little red pickup was beyond repair. Her heart plummeted. She'd been lucky to survive. She and Justin searched the vehicle for the missing photographs, but found no trace of them. Disappointed, she stood with Justin before the wrecked vehicle.

"Judging from those scrapes and dents," she heard a familiar voice behind her, "there's no doubt someone deliberately pushed you off the road. Exactly what were you up to at the pueblo last night?"

Kelly spun around and came face-to-face with Sergeant Suazo. "I wasn't at the pueblo," she said uncertainly. "What are you doing here?"

"I'm just doing my job. What about you, Nakai? Has the FBI suddenly taken an interest in traffic accidents? Or are you looking for reasons behind John Romero's disappearance, too?"

Kelly froze, taking Suazo's words in. "What do you mean, John's disappearance? And who's the FBI agent?" She looked at Justin, whose expression had gone from noncommittal to disgust. "Are you with the FBI?"

Before he could answer, Suazo cut in. "You mean she doesn't know you're a special agent?" He gave Justin a surprise look. "Let me guess. You're undercover," he added cynically.

"I think you've said enough, Sergeant. I don't think Ms. Ferguson even knew that John is missing, much less had anything to do with it. So far she's a victim, not a suspect." Justin's voice was getting close to sounding angry.

Kelly went from bewildered to angry in a heartbeat. Impulsively she turned to Justin. "What's happened to John? Tell me!"

Suazo stood there waiting for Justin to answer, a pleased look on his face.

"We really don't know. He failed to return home after leaving a tribal ritual last night. We've been looking for him since then, but haven't found any trace of him."

"I know he was involved in religious ceremonies. Are you sure he's not somewhere on Pueblo land?" Her heart was beating at a rapid pace.

"Where do you think I've been looking all this time?" Suazo answered irritably. "Now that we've established that, I'll be leaving. By the way Ms. Ferguson, I've left instructions that this truck not be moved or altered until my investigation into your 'accident' is settled. And don't sell it to the wrecking yard until then, either."

"If your department is impounding it, then you're going to have to pay the storage bills," she countered angrily.

"Let the lawyers figure that one out," Suazo smiled, then turned and walked away.

As soon as Suazo was out of sight, Kelly turned on Justin. "What the hell kind of game have you been playing with me?"

Chapter Five

He stood there for a while, waiting for her to settle down. The gesture just made her angrier. But this time her anger turned cold and impersonal. "You knew about this situation with John all along, but you didn't tell me," Kelly challenged. "John's my friend. Didn't it occur to you that I'd want to know?"

"There was nothing you could have done about it. It seemed to me you had enough problems of your own."

"Maybe so, but I would have still cared," she answered. "When did you *really* first find out?"

"Last night when I arrived at the Romero home. You were probably sound asleep by then."

Recalling her intruder, Kelly felt a shiver run up her spine. What on earth was going on? Were the two events related? She dismissed the possibility. Had it been John, surely he would have identified himself.

She caught Justin observing her carefully. "Is something wrong?" he asked.

"No, nothing you don't already know about," she stammered. Then a thought occurred to her. Dear heaven, how much had she revealed to him unwittingly since the hit and run? She'd had no idea he was in the FBI!

She struggled to remember everything she'd said, but her mind became a total blank. Desperation gave her courage, however, and she gathered herself quickly.

Perhaps it was time to mend a few bridges. Justin was obviously trying to help the Romeros find John, in spite of Sergeant Suazo. "Sorry. I shouldn't have lost my temper. You've done so much to help me."

"You needed a hand. I was glad to be there for you," he answered with a gentle smile.

"That's something one friend does for another," she replied thoughtfully. "Are you my friend?"

"I'd say we're getting there," he answered cautiously. He walked with her back to the car. "Make yourself comfortable. I'll be right back. I have to go inside and make a quick telephone call."

Justin strode into the building. Using the pay phone on the wall, he dialed the Romero home. It was time to stop trying to handle the search on their own.

"Yes?" a young woman answered.

He recognized Maria's voice. "Hello, this is Justin. Any news about your brother?" A heaviness settled over his spirit as he received a negative reply. "I think we should call the Santa Fe and state police in on this. If he could have, he'd have come back by now."

"Justin—" Maria's voice was low and sounded strained "—you don't think...he's dead...do you?"

"There's no evidence of that at all," he assured her calmly. Seeing the man behind the counter watching him, he turned away and lowered his voice. "We just have to keep looking until we find him. Maybe there's a logical reason behind all this, and he'll turn up this evening." Privately he knew from his own experiences in law enforcement that many missing people turned up dead or were never found. But Maria and her mother did not need to know that. Not yet, at least. Maybe never, if fate was on their side.

Justin hung up the telephone and walked slowly back to the car. A heaviness settled over him as he thought about John. Later, in private, he'd ask Maria about the relationship between John and Kelly. It was not the kind of matter one discussed over the telephone, though it was very important that he get a straight answer as soon as possible. He didn't believe in coincidences. On the same night John had disappeared, someone had tried to murder the schoolteacher now sitting in his car. There had to be a connection, though at the moment he had no idea what it could be.

Justin slipped behind the driver's seat and shut the door. She smelled of wildflowers. The soft, clean fragrance suited her well. There was a wholesome yet earthy quality about her that pleased him.

"By the way, I went by the site of your crash. I only had a few minutes to look around, but I didn't find any photographs."

She bit her lower lip nervously. "They're there somewhere. Thanks for at least trying to find them, though. Has Suazo looked for them?"

"He said he had looked, but if he found anything, I haven't been told."

"Are we going by there now?" she asked. She was hurt that he hadn't told her about John or his job. It was a sure indication that no matter how nice he seemed he didn't really trust her.

"That was my plan," he agreed. "It'll be easier with both of us looking."

Soon Justin began to slow down, and she began to watch for the place where she'd almost been killed. A cold chill ran up her spine as she remembered the events.

"There ahead," she said. "But what's the smoke from?"

Justin said nothing, but pulled to the side of the road quickly. "Be careful where you walk. Don't disturb any footprints or marks on the ground. I want a chance to study them. It seems someone else has been out here since this morning."

Justin stepped out on the driver's side, and walked up and down the road, looking at the ground. Kelly walked slowly. Her legs still had a tendency to cramp, particularly after she'd been sitting awhile. As her gaze drifted over the area, a shiver ran up her spine. This lonely stretch of desert had almost become her grave. The realization gave their task a sobering urgency.

Kelly went with Justin to a small culvert that ran underneath the highway. A dying fire was giving off small plumes of smoke and the faint scent of gasoline. Upon examination they discovered that most of the smoldering embers were actually pieces of her class assignments.

"Someone came out here, gathered up a lot of my papers, then burned them. Why, Justin? Are they opposed to homework, or what?"

He stood there thinking for a few moments, then bent down and stirred through the ashes with a small stick. "At least there were no photographs in this fire. That type of paper would leave traces behind."

"But why burn my class papers?" It just didn't make any sense.

He considered it for a moment. "How about to get rid of something on them?"

"Who could be threatened by essays on the rock cycle?"

"Not the papers themselves," he countered patiently. "But rather the fingerprints of whoever picked them all up. I think they must have been looking for something else, too, perhaps the photographs. I'll tell you one thing, they're sure being careful. Some of the tracks by the highway have been rubbed out, probably with a piece of brush. They didn't even want us to see footprints."

"Then the photos may still be around here, unless whoever it was took them when they left. I think we'd better keep looking."

They walked down both sides of the road, picking up the few papers they found in case a photo was trapped beneath, but they had no luck. After about fifteen minutes, they climbed the incline back up to the road.

Turning to look down the road, he tilted his head slightly to one side. "I have an idea," Justin said. "If the photos were on the seat with the papers, and the truck turned upside down, they might have fallen to the floor and lodged behind the dashboard. But when the wrecker turned the truck back over..."

"They'd have blown out of the cab of the truck as it was being carried back to Santa Fe. That means they could be somewhere farther down the road. We'll have to drive back slowly and check."

They returned to his car and began the trip back. Every time a car came upon them, Justin waved them around so he wouldn't have to speed up. After about three miles, Kelly told Justin to pull over. When he came to a stop, she sprang from the car. Kelly ran to a bush not ten feet from the gravel shoulder. Hung up in the sagebrush, the glossy photograph caught the sunlight, sending tiny pinpoints of light dancing skyward. "Look, it's one of mine! You see? I was collecting rocks!" She handed him the photograph and stood back, waiting. "This proves it."

Holding it up close, Justin studied it carefully. "This is one of those you took yesterday, right?"

"Right," she admitted, wondering why he was being so guarded. "See Black Mesa off in the distance?"

"I recognize it, but the angle is all wrong. We weren't at the same spot you took this picture from this morning. And there's something else here, too." He pointed to something she'd failed to notice earlier. A prayer stick was clearly visible in the left foreground of the photograph.

They'd just found proof that she'd been on Pueblo land yesterday, the one thing she'd been trying to hide!

THE RIDE TO THE PUEBLO was awkward for both of them. She knew Justin was waiting for her explanation.

"I guess I did stray onto Pueblo land yesterday," she admitted finally, "but please believe me. It was purely accidental. The fence lines in that area come and go so it's hard to orient yourself. When I saw that prayer stick I realized I was in the wrong place. I hurried out of there as fast as I could and headed in the opposite direction."

"And then what?" he insisted.

"I got lost on the roads for a while when it got dark, but finally I was able to find my way back to the main highway. Then I saw you at that gas station."

"And that's it?" he asked skeptically.

"Then I had my accident. What else can I tell you?" she said, hoping he wouldn't press the issue.

After several minutes, he spoke again. "Now that school's almost over, what are your plans for the summer?"

She noted with relief that he'd changed the subject. "I'm meeting with Elsie Whitecloud later this afternoon to discuss a federally funded summer program for the Pueblo children. We'll be teaching special classes to build reading and comprehension skills in science. I applied for a grant and got it, so now we have to work out the details."

"So much for your summer vacation," he observed.

"I didn't really want or need one," she answered honestly. "Earning extra money is something a teacher always has to do, especially in New Mexico. Thirty-nine states pay their teachers more."

"Some things never change. My schoolteachers back in Shiprock usually had second jobs, too." Justin glanced at her thoughtfully.

"I'll make my visit with Elsie a short one, then walk over to the Romeros'. I want to see Clarita and the family as soon as possible."

Twenty minutes later they arrived at the pueblo. Justin followed her direction to Elsie Whitecloud's home. As he finished parking, the green and white tribal police Bronco pulled up next to them.

Seeing Sergeant Suazo in his dark glasses and khaki uniform, a big black-handled revolver on his hip worried her. He hadn't seemed so aggressive earlier. Had he spoken to the religious societies and discovered her activities of the night before?

Her hands became clammy and her mouth went totally dry as Suazo came toward her. Gathering her courage, she stepped out of the car to meet him. To appear hesitant would only make things worse.

"I've been waiting for your visit with the Whitecloud woman, Ms. Ferguson. I have to ask you a few more questions," Suazo said brusquely.

Her chest constricted, but she forced herself to remain still. "How can I help you, Sergeant?"

"When was the last time you spoke to John Romero?"

Her eyebrows furrowed. "About a week ago, I think. He'd called to invite me to the festivities tonight."

"Those are now going to be held in private homes. Plans have changed since the man is missing, out of respect for his family."

"You haven't uncovered any leads yet?"

"No, but we're still working on it." Suazo watched her carefully. "Why were you so nervous when I first came up? Anything else you want to tell me?"

"I...I don't know what you mean, Sergeant," she stammered, but composed herself quickly. "If you're still looking for John, however, you might try his law office in Santa Fe. I'm sorry I didn't think to suggest it before. It's possible he went there after he finished his religious duties. He spends the night on his couch many times when he's working on a case."

"I've already checked that out," Suazo answered sharply. "I know how to do my job, Ms. Ferguson."

"Sergeant, if my friend's missing, I want to do everything I can to help," she stated firmly. "I'll call his associates in town and find out if they've seen him."

Suazo shook his head. "Your interference is the last thing I want. The people of San Esteban have been handling their own affairs for centuries, Ms. Ferguson. We don't need any outsiders' help. The less of your kind we have around here, the better."

As Elsie Whitecloud came out of her house, all eyes shifted in her direction. She was a striking woman with jet black hair, copper skin and dark features. At forty, she had a mature, confident manner about her that commanded attention.

She stood beside Kelly, allying herself with her friend. "I couldn't help overhearing, Sergeant." She challenged him with a bold gaze. "Despite your views on the subject, isolation is neither a reasonable nor a practical way to live. We coexist with others in this area and we need to equip our young for the challenges they'll meet. Ms. Ferguson is here to help us accomplish that. As I told you earlier today, she's most welcome at my home, and in this pueblo."

"Just stick to your duties as a teacher then, Ms. Ferguson. You'll be making it a great deal easier on yourself if you do." He turned and walked away.

"Thank you, Elsie," Kelly said softly.

Elsie nodded, then with a smile turned her attention to Justin. "I heard about your arrival last night. Tell John's family to let me know if there's anything at all I can do for them."

"I'll do that," Justin replied, looking back and forth between the two women. If Kelly had friends like Elsie Whitecloud and the Romeros, perhaps his skepticism about her was unwarranted. He'd wait until he learned more about her from Clarita before he made up his mind.

"I'll probably be at the Romeros' when you come by later. If I have to leave before you get there, I'll make sure someone can give you a ride home." Justin turned back to his car.

"Justin," she called out, "let me know as soon as there's any more news about John."

He nodded. Wordlessly he got into his vehicle and drove off.

JUSTIN SAT in the Romeros' living room. The tension in the air was oppressive, like the still heat just before a desert storm. Emotions threatened to boil to the surface during the long stretches of silence. Nothing new had turned up, even though several law enforcement agencies had joined the search. Suazo had interviewed the moiety chief and the boys who'd seen John before he disappeared, but had failed to uncover any leads at all.

Suazo glared at Justin. "Am I going to keep tripping over you everywhere I go?" he growled.

Before Justin could answer, Clarita spoke. "It's my wish he be here. My son could be hurt and in need of help. This is no time for personal feelings or ambition."

Suazo took a deep breath, and crossed his arms against his barrel chest. "Nakai has no jurisdiction here. This is a tribal police matter."

"I've said all I'm going to on the subject." Clarita crossed her arms, and looked away as if the conversation was concluded.

Suazo glared at Justin, persisting in his argument. "You have no right to interfere with our business. This is a Pueblo matter, it doesn't concern the Navajos."

"My friend's mother has asked for help, and this Navajo intends to give it."

Suazo was about to reply when they heard a knock at the front door. Clarita rose wearily, and went to the door. "Come in," she invited, opening the screen door.

A tall, brown-haired man in a gray suit came into the room. "Clarita, I came by to see if there's anything I can do to help. I know you must be very worried about John."

Suazo muttered a dark oath. "Great, another Anglo comes to solve our problems."

Clarita shot Suazo a stern look. "If you can think of anything that might help us find him, Murray, I would be grateful."

"I've tried, but I haven't been able to," he answered dejectedly. "I'll keep trying, though."

Clarita nodded. "Let me introduce you to the others. You no doubt know Sergeant Suazo," she said.

"We've met," Sullivan clipped out.

"This is Justin Nakai, a friend of my son's."

"I heard about you," Murray said. "John mentioned his Navajo friend from Shiprock often. Perhaps there's something you can tell the police that might be of help in locating John. Is there someplace he might go in a crisis that only the two of you know about?"

Justin shook his head. "No, there's nothing like that, but I plan to look into the matter. Maybe I can learn a thing or two that may help out."

Murray smiled. "I'm sure we all want to help find John, but shouldn't we leave the investigating to the experts?" he suggested kindly.

Suazo snorted, but said nothing.

Clarita broke her silence. "Our Navajo friend *is* an expert. According to John, Justin is one of the finest field investigators the FBI has. He's been given commendations on three separate occasions."

Murray did a quick double take, then turned to look at Justin intently. "You're an FBI agent? John never said anything about that! With you and Sergeant Suazo on the job, we'll have news about John in no time at all, I expect."

Clarita looked at the men gathered around her living room. "Our house is open to all of you as long as you wish to stay," she said softly. "I'll bring some coffee for you." She stood and began to walk toward the kitchen.

"Just water for me, Clarita, please. I'm still taking medication for stomach problems." Murray pulled out a little medicine vial and extracted a white tablet. "So the FBI is looking into this case now?" Sullivan continued, ignoring Suazo completely.

"No," Suazo interrupted before Justin could answer. "This is still a tribal matter." He looked at Sullivan with obvious distaste, then back at Justin. "Mr. Sullivan is another sign of all the progress the Pueblo is making," Suazo said sarcastically. "He's the director of the bank here. They hire some of our people in exchange for doing business on our land. John was the one who recommended they be allowed to place one of their branches here. They call it the United Tribal Bank. Some of us opposed it, but speeches rich with promises are hard to fight."

Sullivan said nothing, then turned to look at Justin. "Actually

John's done a great deal for this pueblo. As the tribal attorney, he represents all the pueblo's financial interests. We do a great deal of work together on those matters, and so far it's been a very profitable arrangement for everyone."

"Do you perhaps have any suggestions of where we could look for him?" Justin asked.

"The sergeant asked me that earlier this morning, but I just don't have a clue. I wish I did. The bank has to make several financial decisions on real estate ventures we've got pending. Without John's vote, though, everything has to remain at a standstill." He paused, then in a less formal tone added, "Besides, John's a buddy of mine and I'm concerned. I want to do whatever I can to find him."

"More help," Suazo muttered under his breath. "Just what we needed."

Justin kept his attention focused on Sullivan. "I'd appreciate you letting us know if he contacts you."

"Your duty ends after you report it to the tribal police," Suazo countered.

Justin didn't reply. He was distracted by the sight of Kelly walking up the hard-packed dirt path to the front door.

She knocked, then without waiting, opened the door and entered. Justin realized from that one action that John's family held her in very high regard. Even though no doors in the pueblo were ever locked, only good friends or relatives of the family would have been at liberty to do as she'd just done. He contrasted the custom to the traditional Navajo way. In Dinéh settlements it was considered polite for a guest to wait outside the dwelling until the host came out to greet him. He preferred the way of the Dinéh. It prevented potentially awkward situations.

"Hello." Kelly glanced around the room. "I can see from your faces that there's been no further news."

Suazo jammed his hands into his uniform pockets. "Another one who wants to get involved. We could use less help, and more answers. Like what happened to the other photos you took, for instance."

Kelly stared down at the floor, trying to decide what to do. The last thing she needed now was for Suazo to learn about the one photograph they'd found.

Chapter Six

Justin spoke immediately, settling the question of whether to admit anything to Suazo. "This afternoon we found a photograph a few miles from the site of the hit-and-run, off Pueblo land. It was of rock formations just as she said. I've returned it to her because legally, neither one of us can keep it."

"Only one? How convenient!" Suazo looked directly at her, then wordlessly strode across the room. Putting on a pair of gold-framed sunglasses, he stalked out the door.

"He's not very personable, is he?" Murray commented, gazing down at his glossy black shoes in embarrassment.

Kelly exhaled slowly. "That's a kind way of putting it." She realized Justin had protected her by not telling Suazo all he could have. Relief flooded through her as she realized that he must have believed her trespass had been unintentional.

"Where's the sergeant?" Clarita inquired, coming back into the room with the drinks.

"Gone," Murray spoke, taking his glass of water as Clarita held the tray before him.

"I thought I heard your voice out here, Kelly." She placed the tray down on the coffee table within easy reach of everyone. Her face and eyes mirrored the strain she was under. "You've heard what happened?"

Kelly nodded. "Clarita, I'm so sorry. What can I do?"

"Talk to *him*." She made a quick traditional gesture, pointing her pursed lips in Justin's direction. "Maybe he can learn something from you that will help in locating my son."

Excusing himself, Murray Sullivan left the house and started back toward the bank.

"Justin and I met yesterday," Kelly explained, "and I'm going to do all I can to help find John, believe me." Seeing Clarita's puzzled expression, she added, "He pulled me from my pickup after someone ran me off the road."

"You were in an accident, and now John's missing? What is this world coming to?" Clarita slumped visibly, and Justin rose to help her. She waved him off with her hand and stood erect on her own. "If you both will excuse me, I think I'll lie down for a while."

"Let me help you to your room," Kelly insisted, taking her arm. Clarita nodded.

Justin watched Kelly in silence as she walked with the elderly woman down the hallway. Kelly had courage, but with it also was a special womanly gentleness. She wasn't afraid to open her heart and show she cared. Yet there was too much mystery surrounding her. Until he knew more, the attraction he felt was nothing more than a dangerous distraction.

Kelly returned alone a few moments later. "I wish John's father were still alive. Clarita needs someone to lean on."

"She has her family. They'll be there for her." Justin didn't like to hear anyone speak of the dead in that way. To call them by name, or to wish for their return, went against everything he'd ever learned. Breaking those taboos still made him uneasy. He decided to change the subject. "Are you ready to return to Santa Fe?"

She nodded.

"Good, it'll give us a chance to talk," Justin answered. He really didn't think Kelly was directly involved in John's disappearance. Yet, she did know something she wasn't telling, and his hunter's instinct told him it was important. Worried about his friend, he grew determined to find out what it was.

Kelly sat in Justin's car and stared out the window at the passing scenery. "I really wish I could figure out where John might be," she said as they reached the highway. "I keep thinking that it must have something to do with the tribe's religious rituals. Perhaps John went into retreat. Some of their societies do that from time to time."

"That's true. But if that were the case, someone would have come forward by now to inform the family."

"You're right." There had to be some way she could be of help. He'd shown some trust in her. Now she wanted to show him she was worthy of it. An idea formed in her mind. "I've spent the last year working on specialized projects that involved kids from the pueblo," she said after a long pause. "I've met many people and made friends here. I'm going to make some discreet inquiries. Maybe I can turn up something."

"That's not a very good idea," Justin warned. "You might be putting yourself in even more danger. From what I can see, you've got enough enemies of your own." He watched her out of the corner of his eye.

"What happened last night frightened me. But there's nothing I can do about that situation. On the other hand, I can at least try to help John. I owe him a great deal." She shifted so she could face him. "When I first started programs for the Pueblo kids, I met with a lot of resistance. The tribe is very independent, and individual members are hard to get to know. It was John's support that helped me gain their trust." She tucked one leg beneath her. "Now, when it looks like he might need my help, I have to be there."

He nodded slowly. "You also need a friend who can help you. I could be that for you, if you'd confide in me."

"You've already done a great deal for me. First at the accident site, and then later when Suazo brought up the matter of the photograph. I want to thank you for that." She stared absently out the window. "Getting you into a heap of trouble now is no way to repay you." The words slipped out before she realized what she'd said. Quickly she tried to cover. "I mean, Suazo probably thinks you lied about where we found the photo. He could make trouble for you."

Her words took him by surprise. Was she trying to protect him? But from what? She was a tiny little thing and stubborn, but her motives continued to puzzle him. "You're afraid of something, but it's got nothing to do with either Suazo or those photos. Whatever it is, you don't need to stand alone."

"I know." Her voice was steady, unnaturally so. She was certain her problems had nothing to do with John. If only she hadn't trespassed on that ceremony! Still, she couldn't change that now. Confiding in Justin and thus endangering his life too, since he was as much an outsider here as she was, would accomplish nothing.

As he turned the car and pulled into her drive, Justin saw the apprehension etched in her face. She looked anxiously around her property as if searching for signs of danger.

"I've got a plan that might work to both our advantages," Justin proposed.

"Why don't you come in? You can tell me about it," she invited quickly.

"All right."

Justin followed her inside, silently questioning the wisdom of accepting her invitation. An elusive but powerful sensuality surrounded her, though she didn't seem to be aware of it. Quickly he brought his thoughts back into line.

Twenty minutes later they sat on her couch, iced-tea glasses in their hands. "So, we agree. We'll concentrate on John?" she asked.

He nodded. "Yes, but my offer to help still stands. If you ever need me..."

Her eyes strayed to the patio and she remembered the intruder. A sudden chill passed through her. Afraid he'd noticed, she stood. "Let me bring you more tea."

"Sounds good. Let me help." He walked with her into the kitchen and placed his glass on the table beside hers.

Her hand was still trembling as she grabbed the pitcher and began to pour. Tea spilled onto the table. Cursing softly, she reached for the paper towel dispenser on the far wall.

Justin leaned back against the counter and gently forced her to face him. "Tell me how I can help you."

"You can't," she answered, dejectedly.

Kelly wasn't sure who started it, but a moment later she felt his arms wrapping tightly around her. She buried herself in his embrace, enjoying the warmth of his body against hers. She did trust him, even though he didn't really trust her.

A moment later he eased his hold and stepped to one side. That's when she realized she must have made the first move. His back had been to the counter. Feeling awkward, she avoided looking directly at him. Instead she feigned great concentration on the task of cleaning the table. Justin was clearly a man who lived by logic and intellect. Allowing her emotions to lead her, as she usually did, had only resulted in embarrassing him.

"Let me tell you about my plan," Justin said, walking with her back to the living room. "It has some merits and some drawbacks." He sat facing her. "As a Navajo I'm bound to encounter some resistance when I try to ask questions about John. Traditionally the Pueblo Indians were the victims of Navajo raiding parties, and to this day, some of them have yet to forgive us," he said with a wry smile.

"So you do want my help!" she interrupted enthusiastically. Seeing the annoyance on his face, she realized that once again she'd acted too impulsively. Justin's sense of timing was part of who and what he was. Interfering with it wasn't likely to foster good will between them. "Sorry. You were about to say?"

He managed a patient smile. "I don't want you to actively investigate. That might prove dangerous. Yet, between the adults and the kids you know, you're in an ideal position to gather information without pursuing it."

"You want me to spy, but not really get involved," she observed, lips pursed. "I'm not sure I can do that. I'm not much good at halfway propositions."

"I had a feeling that's what you'd say," he commented. "But consider the advantages. If we're working together, it'll be easier for me to keep tabs on you and offer you some protection."

Keep tabs on her. The phrase stayed in her mind. If only he wasn't so determined to find out the circumstances surrounding her accident. This was probably his way of staking out her activities without being obvious.

"Think about it carefully. You need an ally and, in my own way, I do, too."

If his reasons had been difficult, she would never have hesitated. It would have been wonderful to be able to spark some old-fashioned male gallantry and protectiveness in such an attractive man.

"I'll help you all I can, but you're going to have to trust my discretion and let me approach people my own way. I'm not good at hiding what I'm thinking."

His expression never changed. "I know."

His answer caused her face to burn. "The people I know at the pueblo trust me because I've always been honest with them," she went on matter-of-factly. "They're aware that John and I are friends and would probably think it very odd if I *didn't* start asking questions. There's no way they'd believe I'd just let it slide."

He walked around the room, hands deep inside his jacket pockets. "Okay. Handle it whatever way works best for you. Only remember to tread carefully when you're dealing with religious matters. You don't want to make things harder on yourself, or bring trouble to anyone else."

Kelly nodded somberly and walked to the patio door. The danger out there stalking her had left her no place to run. "I'll be very careful, don't you worry."

"Does your family live in Santa Fe?"

His question surprised her. "Why do you ask?" she countered.

"It might be a good idea for you to stay with relatives for a while."

"This is my home. I don't have anywhere else I can go," she answered honestly.

"You must have. Everyone has someone," he insisted. "Uncles, parents, sisters, or close friends."

"First of all, I never really had any family ties," she said with a trace of bitterness. "I was forced early to stand on my own." She shook the mood. "Also, to be honest, I don't want to ever feel I'm a burden to someone. I handle my own problems. Being self-sufficient makes me feel less helpless."

"The only people who are really helpless are the ones who won't share their problems with anyone. That isolates them and they become weak instead of strong." He walked to the door. "I better return to the pueblo. I want to talk to Maria and see if she can tell me anything more about John's activities these past few days."

Sadly, Kelly watched him leave. Under different circumstances they might have been friends. Events beyond their control had conspired against them, and secrets she could not divulge had created a barrier of distrust.

KELLY'S NEXT TWO DAYS were spent finishing up the school year. Any spare time she could find, she utilized to call everyone who'd been acquainted with John. The story was always the same, no one knew anything. Justin, in the meantime, was interviewing people at the pueblo and urging the police to keep up their search for John's missing truck. His telephone calls had let her know that progress had been slow for him, also.

When the first day of summer vacation came, Kelly found herself already anticipating the work she'd be doing at the pueblo. Her plans for the summer reading program were now complete. This afternoon Elsie Whitecloud would be hosting a reception to welcome her officially onto tribal land.

John's family had been invited to the gathering. Although Maria would remain at home in case John tried to contact them, Clarita had agreed to come. Justin had also been asked.

A prickle of excitement washed over her as she heard a car pull up in the driveway. So many things were happening at once. At least no more attempts had been made on her life, and she was beginning to feel safe again. No one had come forward yet to accuse her of trespassing, and she had a new pickup. Actually it was a used one the insurance company and she had settled on. Perhaps the threat to her was over. If only they could find John! Then maybe everything would go back to normal.

Kelly hurried to the dresser and put on her earrings. Her white two-piece outfit flowed in smooth lines around her. The blouse was adorned with embroidery that matched the hemline of her skirt. The silver concha belt at her waist, intricately inlaid with Acoma geometric designs in coral and turquoise, gave it an elegant air.

Hearing the doorbell ring, Kelly went to answer it. Justin looked impressive in his dark blue Western-cut suit and bolo tie. "Come in," she invited.

She picked up her purse from the chair. "I'd offer you a drink, but I don't think we have enough time."

He smiled a purely masculine grin. "I thought by now you'd know about Indian time. It's a better system, you know. Give it a try sometime."

"Translated, that means going slow and easy, right?"

His eyes strayed over her. "On certain occasions it can have its advantages," he said quietly.

His words made her pulse leap to life. They also took her completely by surprise. She stared at him, unable to think of anything to say.

He chuckled. "You look sensational, and—" he stopped for a moment then added "—soft."

"I beg your pardon?" she said, smiling.

"Soft in a feminine way, a nice way."

Kelly felt her body respond as his voice caressed her. Then as quickly as it had begun, the spell was broken. He moved to the door and held it open. "Ready whenever you are."

Why had he moved away? Her hormones were in a turmoil. She considered grabbing him by the lapels and kissing him thoroughly. She smiled.

"What's that little grin all about?" he asked, letting her into his vehicle.

"I'll tell you someday...maybe."

"You're a woman of secrets, Kelly," he commented thoughtfully as they got underway.

"No, Justin, I'm not," she replied candidly. "I'm a woman who finds herself in awkward circumstances. You have no reason to believe anything I say, but I've never intentionally wronged anyone." Silence fell over them as they continued their drive.

"You're still keeping something back," he maintained as they reached the pueblo. "As an investigator it's my job to observe people. Their actions always say more than their words. In your case, all the indications are there." He pulled into an area beside Elsie's home where several other vehicles were parked.

They made their way to the door slowly, thoughts heavy on their minds. The minute Elsie spotted them, she approached. "Come in!

There's someone eager to meet you, Kelly." She smiled at Justin. "I'm going to steal her from you for a few minutes, but I'll bring her right back."

"He'll never miss me," Kelly replied wryly.

"Don't be so sure," Justin answered and winked.

Surprised, she stared wide-eyed at him. Before she could stop to think about it, however, Elsie urged her out the patio door. Murray Sullivan was the first to come toward them.

"Ms. Ferguson, you look exquisite." He took her hand and held it a bit too long.

She extricated her hand politely. "Thank you."

Elsie maneuvered her past him. "Come on," she said in a conspiratorial whisper. "I want you to meet our governor. He's really enthusiastic about the summer reading program and very supportive of education in general."

Elsie led her across the garden to a cottonwood arbor. Large wooden posts supported a single overhead frame containing a network of leafy cottonwood branches. The structure resembled a summer porch. Beneath the cool shelter was Clarita Romero and approximately two dozen men and women from the Pueblo community. All were engaged in animated conversation. "This is Governor Gus Pasqual," Elsie introduced.

Kelly shook his hand. The man's palm was hard and weathered, that of a person used to working outdoors. White shoulder-length hair framed his broad, well-chiseled facial features.

"I have heard a great deal about you." Pasqual trained his dark, indomitable eyes on her. "I'm glad that you'll be working with our children this summer. You have very special gifts as a teacher."

"I always do my best, sir, and I care about my students," she replied honestly.

"That's probably why you've earned their respect," he answered simply. He took Kelly's arm and accompanied her to the buffet table. "We will toast to the teachers and to the success of our children." He handed her a glass filled with fruit punch.

His voice carried, and a hush fell over the gathering. As Elsie quickly handed glasses to those guests who did not have a drink yet, the governor exchanged a few words with his aide.

Weaving past the small group between them, Justin and Clarita worked their way over to Kelly. Clarita gave her a smile, then spoke. "To earn this man's respect is not easy. He expects the best from others, and praise from him is rare."

Justin agreed. "You should be very proud of your accomplishments."

"Oh, I am! It's wonderful to work..."

Suddenly the glass she'd been holding shattered! A heartbeat later a deafening blast sliced through the air, echoing off the houses around her. A gunshot? Justin swept both Clarita and Kelly aside and pushed them to the ground as another crack reverberated through the pueblo. From beneath the buffet table, Kelly heard another two shots thunder out in angry succession. Both bullets impacted against the sides of the cottonwood arbor with a thwack, inches from where they'd been standing. Wood splinters flew everywhere.

Kelly shifted in Justin's arms, but his grip remained firm as he continued to hold them down. Her right arm and side felt wet and cold, and her palm throbbed sharply. Glancing down, she saw blood trickling through her fingertips.

Chapter Seven

The shots stopped as suddenly as they'd started. A deathly silence encompassed the scattered group huddled on the ground in twos and threes. Then someone stirred. Whispered voices urgently called to one another, slowly growing in intensity. Murray Sullivan appeared and helped Clarita to her feet while Justin gently lifted Kelly up.

"You're bleeding," he observed in a taut voice, seeing a tendril of blood flowing down her forearm. "Where are you hit?"

"I don't think I am," she glanced down at herself. The only pain registering was the dull throb in her hand. "I must have cut my hand on the glass when it shattered," she replied in a shaky voice. "One of those bullets came close, Justin. I'm almost sure I heard one whiz by me," she said, shivering involuntarily.

He glanced over at the cottonwood post she'd been standing next to. Three splintered gouges indicated where bullets had struck and passed through. "You're right."

She followed his gaze and her head began to spin. She swallowed convulsively, her eyes remained glued on the bullet holes in the post. Sheer determination kept her from passing out cold. Clarita put her hand on Kelly's arm to steady her. "Thanks, Clarita. Are you okay?" Kelly inquired.

Before Clarita could reply, Elsie came rushing up to them. "Are you three all right?" Seeing them nod, she continued quickly. "The governor is out in the front of the house waiting for Sergeant Suazo. He and the other officers should be here in another minute or two." Elsie, glancing downward, suddenly saw the blood on Kelly's hand. "Oh, good heavens! You *have* been hurt!"

"It's only splinters and a few cuts from the glass I was holding. It's almost stopped bleeding now."

"Come into the house with me. That needs to be cleaned and bandaged." As Clarita began to lead Kelly away, Elsie paused and glanced back at Justin. "Could you make sure everyone else is okay? If anyone needs help, have them go to the house."

Justin nodded, his thoughts already racing in a different direction. The glass in Kelly's hand had shattered before they heard the sound of the gun, so the sniper must have been some distance away. Lining up the glass and the bullet holes gave him a clear indication of direction. He needed to find the exact location and study the site. There was evidence to be gathered and clues to be studied, even though the sniper was undoubtedly long gone by now.

After verifying that none of the other guests had been wounded, he walked quickly to the parking area at the front. Stopping at his car, he opened the door and retrieved his pistol and holster from beneath the seat. A moment later, he spotted the sergeant coming toward him quickly.

"Why is it that I'm not surprised to see you?" Suazo growled. "Fill me in on what you know. Now that I'm here, the tribal police will handle the matter," he said curtly.

Justin shook his head. "A sniper incident qualifies as an attempted murder, Sergeant."

Suazo's eyes narrowed slightly. "So, you're taking over?"

"It's my duty. The FBI is responsible for investigating major felonies on Indian land."

Suazo did not comment further. His glare, however, reflected his feelings.

"Right now we have to get up on the mesa rim at a point southeast of here. That's where the sniper fired from. He's probably in the next county now, but I want to gather evidence while everything is still fresh. Why don't you follow me in your car?"

"We can go up in mine," Suazo countered. "I know this area better than you do, and I might be able to help you pinpoint the spot."

"All right, let's get going."

Suazo exchanged a few words with his deputies, then hurried with Justin to the police vehicle. Ten minutes later they turned off a dirt road and followed tire tracks leading toward a high ridge that overlooked the pueblo.

"If he had a high-powered rifle and a scope," Suazo commented, "he could have picked off his targets from up on that vantage point. The governor's aide said that the shots were all directed toward the arbor where the governor and a few others were standing. I keep thinking, though, that this is the second time the Ferguson woman has been directly involved in a violent incident. Do you think the sniper was aiming at her?''

Justin said nothing for several moments. "There's a good chance she was the target, but it's too early to make that determination. Clarita Romero and I were both close to the impact zone too.''

"Think what you want," Suazo muttered under his breath, then lapsed into silence. His eyes narrowed as he focused on the road ahead. "Tire tracks run up that narrow ravine, then cut across to the east and back to the main road. See them?''

Justin nodded. "Let's park here and take a look around.''

Suazo left the vehicle and walked ahead. Abruptly, he came to a stop and crouched down. "The vehicle was parked here, out of sight from anyone at the pueblo. Notice these boot prints?'' he asked. "About a size ten, wouldn't you say?''

Justin nodded. He recognized the distinctive imprint, having seen hundreds of them during his training days as an FBI agent. Back in Quantico, the marine base where the FBI academy was, paratrooper-style boots like those had been a dime a dozen. Here near the pueblo, though, they could become an important clue. Staying clear of the tracks, he followed the trail to the rim overlooking Elsie's home. "He must have knelt here and taken aim, using that boulder as a rest. The impressions are still in the sand.''

"Here's some empty shells, too." Suazo gestured with the tip of his boot toward a scattered group of center-fire rifle brass.

Justin stood pensively behind the spot the sniper had occupied. Had Kelly been the target, or was this incident unrelated? The governor and other notables had also been under the arbor, but some distance away. Clarita Romero, of course, was another possibility. Only he couldn't fathom any reason for trying to kill Clarita. Either way, he'd have to find a way to get Kelly to trust him. Things were getting out of hand, and this was no time to withhold information.

He walked slowly around the immediate area, circling like a bird of prey. His eyes, hunter sharp, searched the ground for evidence. The sagebrush directly ahead of him seemed to have a hollow spot in the middle. He went to it, then separated the branches, mindless of the way the stalky growth pricked into his skin. There in the middle, hidden in the bramble, was a bolt-action hunting rifle with a telescopic sight. "I've got something here," Justin said, pulling the 30-06 by the sling from its hiding place.

Suazo started toward him, then stopped as he heard a vehicle approach. "That'll be my deputies. I'll have Billy Clah photograph the area in case the wind damages the evidence before the FBI lab boys can get here.''

"Good idea. Make sure Clah gets good close-ups of the footprints. Also have him measure them so we can verify the shoe size. I'm not sure how soon the Bureau team can get here, so this might be the only chance we get. This time of year, the weather's always unpredictable.''

Justin watched Suazo as he approached the two deputies and gave them instructions. Suazo was a bit hostile, yet he was still conceding the case to him too easily. He'd expected much more resistance.

Suazo returned as Justin inspected the rifle, careful not to place his own fingerprints on it. "The bolt is half-open. A round is jammed between the clip and the chamber. Little wonder since there's sand in there everywhere. Our sniper is careless, it appears," Justin commented, more to himself than to anyone else.

He looked at the scarred forestock of the finely crafted rifle. Resting it on the sandstone boulder had taken its toll on the weapon, leaving telltale marks. He aimed the rifle toward Elsie's home, keeping his hands on the leather sling and well away from the trigger. He could make out individuals easily in the cross hairs of the 8X scope.

"Take a look," Justin said, handing the rifle carefully to Suazo, who'd been watching him intently.

Suazo took the rifle gingerly in order to keep from smearing any possible prints.

"What do you think? Would you have missed every one of those shots?''

The police sergeant sighed carefully and stared a moment at one of his deputies, centering the cross hairs on the man's head. "No way. But maybe our sniper was a lousy shot.''

"He hit that right front arbor pole with three rounds, all of them less than four inches apart. And he shot a glass right out of Kelly Ferguson's hand without touching anyone. I think he may have hit exactly where he wanted to.''

"Food for thought." Suazo shrugged. "Now let me get the serial number and I'll call it in." Suazo examined the receiver and scribbled the numbers on a pad. "Do you want me to pick up the Anglo teacher for questioning?''

"No, I think the situation with her calls for an informal interview, like with the rest of the guests," he answered, giving Suazo a challenging look.

"This case is under your jurisdiction by law, Nakai," Suazo admitted abrasively, "but you'd do well to use our help.''

"I realize that I need your department, Suazo. I have no intention of doing this alone, or upsetting those in the pueblo." It was clear to him now. Suazo saw him as the lesser evil. But now he'd undoubtedly realized that John's disappearance would play a part in his investigation. The last thing the tribal officer wanted was Anglo or Hispanic FBI agents investigating matters that could entail questions about the Pueblos' religious rituals.

"We're through here, Sergeant," Billy Clah informed him.

"Do you want the film sent to the FBI office? If Billy does it here, you could have the results this afternoon. He's really good with a camera."

"All right, have him take care of it," Justin agreed. "When it's ready, you can leave a message for me at the Romero house. I'll check in with them. Right now I'm going to go back to the pueblo and question everyone at the gathering. Someone might have seen or heard something that will give us a clue."

"If you ask me, this is all tied in to the woman. She's trouble," Suazo muttered. "My bet is she'd got a really good idea of what's going on. You should let us work on her a bit."

"No," Justin replied. "I'll handle her my way."

Suazo gave Justin a contemptuous look, but remained silent.

"Are you ready to go back now, or shall I ride to the pueblo with one of your deputies?" Justin met his eyes with a level gaze. It had been a mistake not to bring his own car. He didn't like being in a position of having to personally depend on someone like Suazo.

"I'll take you back, Nakai."

Justin noted that Suazo never missed the opportunity to call him by name. The habit annoyed him, and he had a feeling it's just what Suazo intended.

"What's your plan with the woman? Do you want me to keep her under surveillance, or do you intend to do that yourself?"

The faintly mocking tone in Suazo's voice angered Justin, yet he forced himself to remain calm. "I'll let you know."

As they approached the parking area near Elsie's home, a third deputy came up. "We're still questioning people, Sergeant, but so far we haven't turned up anything."

Suazo turned to look at Justin. "Nakai, it's your ball game."

Justin gritted his teeth. "Before you release anyone, I want to question the governor and a few of the others who were underneath the arbor."

Justin walked inside Elsie's house and called the FBI office in Santa Fe. After a brief rundown to the special agent in charge, he proceeded to the back where the reception guests were. People were understandably subdued. As Justin moved from one group to the other, he fared no better than the deputy. Even the governor, who'd been facing in the direction of the sniper, was not able to provide anything.

Justin was finishing with the governor's aide when one of the deputies approached. "Sergeant Suazo would like a word with you, sir."

Justin scowled at the deputy. "He knows where I am," he retorted.

"The sergeant said it would be better if you met with him at the front of the house, sir."

Justin pursed his lips. He didn't have time to play games with Suazo. He hoped for Suazo's sake that he had a good reason for doing this. Justin strode outside. As he reached the front of the house, he saw Suazo standing by his patrol car. "Sergeant," he said, in a crisp voice. "I'm here. Now what's so important?" He stood at the door and forced the man to approach him.

"I have some very interesting news. Your agency's computer network paid off. It managed to get me the registered owner of the rifle we found."

Justin waited, allowing Suazo to set his own pace.

"It belongs to John Romero," he said at last.

Before he could recover from the surprise, Kelly came toward them. "Hi," she greeted in a quiet voice. "Do you want me to catch a ride home? If you've got work to do here, I'll understand."

Suazo chortled derisively, then walked away.

Kelly gave him a sharp look, then focused her attention back on Justin.

Justin met her eyes, trying to guess what lay behind them. She looked so tired and frightened. He wanted to hold her and let her see inside his heart until she trusted him. Nonetheless, he forced himself to remain coolly professional. "I've still got some things to do before I can leave. Can you wait here for me? I'm sure Elsie won't mind."

"I'll wait," she answered. "Take as long as you need. If you hadn't pushed Clarita and me to the ground when you did this afternoon, I'm not sure what would have happened. Did you find whoever it was, or figure out why they were shooting?"

"Not yet, but we have some leads. Is there anything you care to tell me?"

"Now wait a minute," she said, instantly defensive. "This doesn't necessarily have to be connected to me, does it? I mean, there were several members of the tribal council under that arbor. Maybe it was just someone trying to scare the new governor, or something like that."

"It's possible," he admitted in a low voice, "but I think you and I need to have a long talk." He rubbed the back of his neck with one hand.

"I'll be here when you get through." Without further word, she walked back inside the house.

Justin watched her for a moment, then turned and walked to his car. As he pulled out into the street, Suazo drove up next to him. "Nakai, do we head for the Romeros' now? Mrs. Romero went back there about a half hour ago."

"I won't need you," Justin answered. "I can handle this."

"Well, it just so happens that I'm on the way there myself," Suazo replied with a grin. "So, if that's where you're going, we're bound to meet." Suazo pulled away and headed down the road leading to the Romeros'.

Justin cursed, his hand tightening around the wheel. He was more concerned than ever. He knew John too well to believe he was capable of hurting a friend. Yet the evidence was disturbing. He'd promised to help John, not make things worse for him. His muscles tensed. His face became a rigid mask. The last thing he needed now was Suazo antagonizing Clarita Romero. By the time he reached the Romeros', Suazo was parking his car. Justin pulled up next to him.

"Clarita Romero is not a guilty party here," Justin said, meeting him near the door. "Remember that. I don't want her upset."

"Just who the hell do you think you are, Nakai? I know these people. They're of my tribe, not yours. Don't tell me how to deal with them."

Justin was about to reply when Clarita Romero came to greet them. "I thought I heard someone out here. Has there been any news about the shooting or my son?" She looked hopefully at one man, then the other.

"No, not yet," Justin replied gently. He shot Suazo a warning look as they stepped inside the house.

Murray Sullivan emerged from the kitchen as they seated themselves in the living room. "Hello."

Clarita folded her hands in her lap and regarded both Justin and Suazo somberly. "You have more questions. Am I right?"

"Just a few," Justin answered as Maria appeared. He nodded to her and continued. "Where does John keep his hunting rifle?"

The question made Clarita pause. "It's locked in the back of his truck." She looked up at Murray. "You'd know more than I would. You went hunting with him several times."

"John kept a 30-06 locked in the steel box behind the seat in his truck."

"If you need a hunting rifle," Clarita offered, "I'm sure we can find one you can use."

His heart went out to the woman. She looked as if she'd aged ten years in the past few days. "Thanks for the offer, but that won't be necessary. I'll manage." He couldn't bring himself to tell her the reason why he was asking.

"What else is on your mind?" Clarita urged.

Her intuition, even under such trying circumstances, surprised him. "I need you to verify something for me. What size shoe does John wear, and does he own a pair of paratrooper boots?"

"John wears a size ten and a half, and he owns boots, many pairs, in fact. Only I'm not really sure what type they are."

Maria smiled. "He has one pair of paratrooper boots. I'll never understand why he loves them so much. They're really worn and he's had them repaired more than once. But away from the office, they're the only shoes he wears."

"Are they in his closet now by any chance?" Suazo asked pointedly.

Justin glared at him wordlessly.

"I'll check," Maria answered.

"Let me go with you," Suazo said. "I'll help you look."

Justin took a deep breath then let it out again. Control. Without that, there was no harmony.

"Murray," Clarita asked, "could you go pour some coffee for us? This shooting has gotten me quite tired. I think you can find the cups."

"Certainly, Clarita." Sullivan stood and left the room.

"Tell me what is happening," Clarita demanded in a quiet tone. "You have found out something, or you wouldn't be asking these questions."

Justin considered the best way to answer her. "We found a trail that might lead us to your son, but it's too early to tell yet. I wouldn't want to get your hopes up. As soon as we learn anything substantial, I will let you know."

"I want my son returned to me," she said softly. "He belongs here at the pueblo with his family and friends."

The words cut through him like a cold blade. For the first time in his life he felt like a betrayer. Yet, this was the only trail he'd found, even though its implications were grave.

"I will do my best to find John. You have my word on that. He is my friend and that's not something I take lightly."

Clarita stood slowly. "Do you have any more questions?"

"One more thing, but it's very important." He lowered his voice, not wanting Suazo or Sullivan to overhear. "The sniper that fired at us—we're still not certain of his targets or intention."

"Do you believe he could have been shooting at Kelly?" Clarita's voice quivered.

Justin looked at the floor. "Or you. But it's also possible he was trying to intimidate instead of kill. I think he missed deliberately."

Clarita sat back down wearily. "Then what do we do?"

"To begin with, stay here at the pueblo. Also, it would be a good idea to find someone to watch over you and Maria all the time, a person you can trust."

"Raymond, Maria's husband, is a security guard at the state capitol in Santa Fe. He will take his vacation now if I ask. He has already offered because of my son. I will talk to him. Maria and he can come to stay at the house with me. But what about Kelly?" Clarita added. "She lives alone, who will watch after her?"

"Does she have relatives nearby?"

"Only friends, like the Romeros." Clarita's eyes twinkled briefly. "There is room for one more."

"Well, it might be a good idea if she'll go along with it. She'll be working here at the pueblo already, where everyone knows one another." Justin answered, pleased with the idea.

Murray came into the room with a tray filled with four cups of coffee and a glass of water.

"If there's nothing else, I'm going to bed. Only remember, if you learn anything new, wake me, no matter what time it is."

"I'll make sure you're told immediately."

"Good night then, and Murray, thanks for the coffee. I'll save mine for later."

Maria was just coming out of John's room when she saw her mother walking down the hall. "Excuse me, Sergeant. I'll rejoin you in a few minutes." Placing her arm around Clarita's shoulders, she walked with the older woman toward one of the bedrooms at the back of the house.

Suazo went toward Justin and gathered up a cup of coffee from the tray. "The boots were not there, and Maria said the room looked like someone had gone through everything."

Justin nodded. "We'll speak later."

Murray took his water from the tray and cleared his throat. "I'm assuming this has something to do with the sniper incident at Elsie's earlier. Did you find John's rifle out there somewhere?" Neither Justin nor Suazo commented.

Maria returned and joined them. "I'm not sure how long my mother will be able to take this. My brother must be found."

"He will be, don't worry," Suazo answered. "This pueblo has always known how to help its own." Giving Justin an expressionless glance, he walked out the door.

JUSTIN ARRIVED at Elsie's home one hour later. He looked exhausted as he walked Kelly to his car. "I'm sorry I've kept you waiting for so long."

"Don't give it a thought. It's been a very hard day for all of us."

"How are you holding up?"

His concern was genuine. A warm sensation spread over her. "I'm tired, scared and a little sad. Today was supposed to be such a special day. It marked the start of my program here at the pueblo. Having the occasion marred by something like this—" She shook her head. "I have to admit, I'm surprised at how cool everyone was about this, especially Clarita. With John missing, it must have been doubly hard for her. And Elsie was a bit upset that the party came to such an abrupt end, but she wasn't rattled in the least. The rest of the guests seemed more annoyed than anything else."

"Why does that surprise you?" he asked. "There's really no other way they could have reacted. The incident happened. It's natural for the tribe to see it as another unpleasant crisis they've encountered and endured. The important thing is that they came through it."

"I wish I could look at it that way," she said in a shaky voice.

Her fear touched him. "It's not the same for you," he cautioned. Somehow, he had to find a way to break past the barriers of secrets she'd erected between them. Instead of starting the engine, he sat back in the car and decided to take advantage of their quiet moment. "The danger you're in has not diminished. I suspect that the sniper was trying to scare you, but he came awfully close. Clarita was next to you, so we can't minimize the danger to her also. Yet, the bullets were all clustered around the area you were standing in."

"I don't understand any of this," she said in a thin voice.

"I have to know what you're keeping back. Have you stopped to consider the possibility that John's disappearance is tied into it somehow?"

"I'd help you if I could, but I don't know anything about that. If I did I'd tell you in an instant. You have to believe that."

He exhaled softly. "Tell me something. How do you account for what's been happening to you?"

"I can't." And that was true in more ways than one. She could sense all the questions forming in his mind. He didn't trust her, and she really couldn't blame him.

"We come back to the same situation, then," Justin replied. "We know someone's trying to scare you and is willing to risk your life in the process. There is a step we can take to make things more difficult for your enemy, though. We can put you under protection." He started the car, but began to circle around the pueblo, rather than head out to the main road.

"You mean have a guard at my house?"

"No. Clarita has offered to have you stay at her place. Raymond will be there full-time, and he's a trained security guard. And I'll be there, too—when I'm not looking for John—and the sniper." Justin waited for her reaction.

"So that's why we're going the wrong way. You'd already decided for me, haven't you?" Kelly didn't know whether to be angry for his assumption or flattered because he was so determined to look after her.

"I knew you would make the right choice," Justin answered smoothly, a trace of a smile on his lips. "You're an intelligent woman."

"Well I'm certainly smart enough to know I'll need clothes and some other personal items from my house, and my school materials. We'll have to go pick them up."

"You're right." He stopped the car, then turned around in the graveled road. Soon they were heading for the main highway leading south to Santa Fe.

It was almost ten o'clock by the time Justin drove up the long narrow driveway and pulled alongside her new pickup truck. Keeping her close to him, he helped Kelly out of the car quickly and slipped into the shadows of an arborvitae next to her porch. He opened the door with her key and whisked her inside.

He motioned for her to wait as he examined the front rooms. Seconds later he joined her in the kitchen. Kelly sat down in a chair, trying to force herself to relax, and glanced at the familiar surroundings. A cabinet drawer stood ajar. That particular one had been her nemesis from the first day she'd moved in. Learning to shut it had become a habit after she'd collided against its corner repeatedly on her way to the refrigerator. Crossly, she slammed it shut.

"Wait here while I check out the back rooms," Justin said quietly.

Kelly stood at the doorway to the kitchen and watched him walk through the living room. He stopped by the hall door and wrapped his hand around the knob. All of a sudden she realized something was wrong. She *always* left that door open. The air-conditioning worked more evenly that way. "Stop!" she warned Justin.

Chapter Eight

"Someone's broken into the house," she whispered.

After a hurried exchange, Justin pointed to an overstuffed chair in a corner of the room. "Get behind that," he growled.

She moved quickly, realizing that he was placing her in a position where she'd be out of sight and also out of the way of an intruder trying to escape.

He turned out the lights and crouched with his back to the wall, with the door to the hall to his right. They waited for what seemed hours. At first she couldn't see, but soon her eyes adjusted and the familiar features of her living room became clear. Justin was in the shadows, barely visible in the subtle grays of the moonlight illuminating the room.

The tension grew, and her heart was beating so hard Kelly thought anyone would be able to find her by the sound alone.

A muted click told her the door had been opened. The next moment, Justin had disappeared, as silent as the night. For what seemed an eternity nothing happened, then a light in the bedroom down the hall came on. "Okay, you can come out now. Whoever was here is gone."

Relieved, she tried to stand up, but she'd been crouched behind the chair so long the action hurt. "Oh, pain," she muttered as her bones creaked. She stepped into the hall and walked toward the bedroom.

"Body stiffen up on you? Next time, do a little muscle flexing to keep the blood circulating. Works every time," Justin suggested, turning to smile at her as she entered.

"Who are you, my P.E. teacher? How long would it take your muscles to heal after rolling downhill in a truck?"

He gave her a sheepish look. "Sorry, I forgot about that."

"I'll forgive you this time. But, tell me, do you encounter this sort of thing often?"

"Not as much as I used to when I was working undercover. One good thing to remember whether you're stalking a criminal or watching a herd of antelope, is to avoid any quick movements. They'll take off every time."

"I'll file that away, just in case." Her gaze fell upon the dresser. Two of the drawers had been left slightly open. She glanced at the rest of the room. The bedspread was rumpled, showing the ghostly impressions of a small, heavy object that had rested there. Whoever had broken in had searched her place. They'd probably set the drawers on the bed while they checked out the contents. "Someone's gone through my things," she observed.

"I suspected as much. Why don't you have a look and see if anything's missing?" Justin suggested. "Pull the drawers out by the corners, in case we want to check for fingerprints later on."

She followed his instructions and examined the contents of each drawer. Her clothing had been disturbed. She'd never been meticulous about order, but she had her own method of putting things away. Nothing, however, appeared to be missing.

The thought of someone handling her undergarments made her feel sick. She fought the impulse to throw the entire contents of the drawer into the trash.

"I thought intruders tossed everything out onto the floor so they could do a search," she said. "Our uninvited guest is very neat."

"And very smart. You know someone was here, but without any overt evidence, you'd probably have a difficult time convincing the police," Justin replied. "They're using fear as a weapon against you."

"Well, it won't work," she replied, for her own benefit as much as for his.

Justin walked around her room, his eyes darting to and fro. "Do you have any idea what they might have been looking for? First someone searches the Romero home, at least John's room, and then here." He stepped closer so he could read her eyes.

"I wish I knew," she answered truthfully. She felt the warmth of his breath brush against her face and suppressed a shiver. "Maybe if we could find that out, we'd know what's going on." Kelly forced her mind on the task at hand. "Time to gather some things, I guess. We don't want to keep the Romeros up all night."

In less than an hour, they were underway to the pueblo.

"What's happened back there at your place is just a warning sign. I'm not sure what it is you're not saying, but I strongly suggest you confide in me. It's a crime to withhold information pertaining to a murder investigation."

"No one's been murdered."

"Yet."

"Don't worry about me," she answered. "Concentrate on John."

"In my opinion what's happening to you is connected to John." He considered telling her about the rifle, but then decided against it. This new incident had created too many questions in his mind.

As they stopped at a light, Justin looked across at her. "At least tell me why you don't think John's disappearance has any connection to all the trouble you've experienced."

"How could it?" She rolled her eyes. "For Pete's sake, you're his friend. Does any of this sound like John's doing? John wouldn't run anyone off the road, let alone take shots at another person. Most of all, John would never have harmed me, or allowed anyone else to do so."

"How close are you and John?"

"As friends we couldn't be closer. We can talk about things that matter to us because in many ways they're the same. For instance, he wants to make a contribution that counts to his tribe. That's exactly the way I feel about teaching."

Justin switched his gaze back to the highway as they left the city. "I like you, schoolteacher, and I want to keep you alive. But by holding on to secrets this way, you're sure not making it easy."

"You've got to believe me," her voice trembled, "I don't know anything that could help you."

"Why don't you trust me to make that judgment?" His voice gentled and his eyes turned to meet hers.

"I'm sorry," her voice cracked, but she cleared her throat and continued. "I'm doing what's best for everyone involved."

He looked away from her and said nothing. At that moment, she'd have given anything to be able to explain and make him understand. But because she cared for him, that was precisely what she could not do. She would have to accept the danger to herself for now, without involving him. He needed to be free to help John. They both did. For wherever John might be, he was probably in even greater peril than she was.

KELLY WALKED INTO the Romero kitchen shortly after eight, having slept in at Clarita and Maria's insistence. Her first class of the summer session wouldn't begin until nine-thirty.

Pouring herself a cup of coffee, she joined Clarita at the kitchen table. The elderly woman showed the strain of recent sleepless nights. "Tell me what I can do to help you," Kelly asked softly.

"Join in the search for my son. Do whatever you can to help," she answered simply.

Kelly nodded slowly.

As Justin entered the kitchen, Clarita looked up. "Did you rest well?"

Justin nodded. "Are you sure you want me to stay here at your home? Under the circumstances, I would understand if you'd want me to make other arrangements."

Clarita Romero gave him a weary smile. "Under the circumstances, I can't think of any place I'd rather have you be. From you, I know I'll hear any news almost as soon as it happens."

Justin chuckled softly. "You're a wise woman." Declining the offer of breakfast, he walked to the door. "Forgive me for rushing off but I'm eager to get started."

Clarita gave him an approving nod.

Giving Clarita a quick hug, Kelly followed Justin. "Where are you off to this morning?"

"I'm going to check with Suazo and his deputies first and see if any more evidence has been uncovered about the sniper. Then I'll have to run down any leads the police can give me on John's truck." He brushed her cheek with his hand, the caring in his eyes evident in the bright light of day. "See you this afternoon."

His touch left her skin tingling. A yearning she didn't quite understand surged through her as she watched him drive away. The emotion made her uneasy. Hunting criminals was at the center of his life, just as teaching was at the center of hers. She wasn't at all sure there'd be room enough in either for the kind of relationship her heart longed for.

The first day of the summer school program went by quickly. After the briefest of orientations, the teachers and students got right to work. Elsie concentrated on skill-building activities while Kelly tested and tutored individuals.

When the students finally left at three, Elsie and Kelly remained behind to prepare for the next session. It was almost five o'clock by the time Kelly arrived at the Romeros'.

Offering to help Maria and Clarita with dinner, Kelly learned that Murray Sullivan had promised to bring some chicken for everyone.

Murray was there promptly at five-thirty. As Raymond and Kelly were helping carry in the food, Justin joined them. "Ah, my favorite

chef, the colonel. His place is the most popular establishment in Shiprock. Who do we have to thank for the catering? Murray?'' Justin
grabbed one of the sacks and headed for the door.

"What did you find out today?" Kelly asked, rushing up to meet
him.

"I'll let everyone know at dinner, if it's all right with Clarita."

"We're all anxious to hear," Clarita answered as she moved to
open the door for them. "The table is all set and the iced tea is
poured."

Within minutes of the beginning of their meal, Justin had filled
them in on what he'd learned. Most of the news was disappointing.
Nothing further had turned up on John's missing truck, or on the
vehicle that had run Kelly off the road.

Although the Santa Fe police and Suazo had already been there,
Justin had also gone to John's legal office to speak with his secretary.
She had been able to offer no suggestions as to where John might be.

"Have you learned anything more about the person who broke into
my house?" Kelly asked.

"No, but it must have something to do with the break-in and search
here."

"Well, there might have been a break-in at Kelly's but whoever
searched this home didn't have to do anything except walk in." Murray shook his head slowly. "The only locks in the pueblo are at the
bank."

"It's our custom," Clarita explained patiently.

"What do you think they're looking for?" Maria asked looking at
Justin, then at Kelly.

When no one answered, Clarita spoke. "The connection to both
seems to be John. I wonder if this has something to do with the land
deals he was working on? He'd been preoccupied with business
lately." She paused, then shook her head. "But all his papers are at
his office or at the bank."

"That's true," Murray conceded.

"There's another connection between the break-ins," Kelly said at
length. "The friendship I share with this family."

"What could you have that someone would want to search your
home and ours for?" Clarita asked.

"Nothing that I can think of," Kelly admitted candidly. "So much
for that theory."

"What kind of lock do you have on your house?" Raymond inquired. "Since you live alone, I hear, you should have something like
a dead bolt. Those are hard to go through."

"I have an entry lock that I thought was foolproof," Kelly said. "Let me show you the key, and maybe you can tell me something from that." She placed her purse on her lap and reached inside. Feeling something soft and moist beneath her fingertips, she jumped up and shoved the purse away from her. As it hit the floor, some of its contents spilled out and a small dead bird appeared by her feet.

"What the—" Raymond exclaimed, as Maria turned her head away. Clarita stepped back from the table completely.

"Good grief!" Murray added. "It's a sparrow someone's mutilated."

Justin had seen the Romeros' reactions, and knew instantly what they were thinking. They were standing back as if a live rattlesnake was before them.

"What's going on? Why would anyone put a dead bird into my purse?" Kelly asked, recovering quickly. As a science teacher she'd developed an immunity to dead animals a long time ago. What she regretted the most was it seemed to have frightened the others. Taking a tissue from her purse, she spotted a folded piece of paper still nestled inside. She resisted the temptation to pull it out and read it. It was better to take care of the bird first, everyone seemed so alarmed by it.

Looking at Justin, who hadn't said anything or moved, she asked, "Somebody played a joke on me, right? Maybe one of my students today?"

He spoke at last. "I doubt if they would ever do something like this. Do you see how the bird's eyes have been gouged out, and cotton has been stuffed into its mouth? That reminds me of something I've seen on the reservation a few times." He glanced away automatically. For the Dinéh to view an unclean death, like this one, was perilous and the action was instinctive for him. "Mutilated animals are part of witchcraft rituals."

"Yes, *chuge ing*," Maria muttered. "Here, too, the same association is made."

"You mean someone's trying to put a curse on me?" Kelly asked incredulously. She picked up the bird with the tissue and placed it into one of the empty food boxes, leaving the container on the floor.

"Or give you a message," Justin suggested. "Perhaps you're being warned to stop or start doing something."

"I'm not well versed on all the witchcraft things, but this can only mean one thing—silence," Raymond said. "Only the bird's eyes and mouth have been tampered with."

"You may have become the enemy of a witch. That's very dangerous," Clarita said slowly. "Witches live by killing others. It's their way of existence." Clarita met her eyes. "What knowledge do you possess that could threaten any of them?"

Kelly shook her head and shrugged helplessly. The look in Clarita's eyes held a trace of suspicion, and that realization hurt worst of all.

"Well, this is a rotten way to end a fine evening," Murray interjected, rising at last from his chair, "but I'll have to say good-night for now. I've got some reports to work on tonight. I hope you enjoyed your dinner in spite of all this."

Somberly, Clarita walked Murray to the door. As he was about to leave, Kelly approached with the box containing the dead bird. "Murray, would you please throw this bird into the river on the way home? Maria tells me it's the proper way to dispose of an object that could be cursed."

"I suppose so, but why can't Justin or Raymond just bury it outside?" Murray wondered.

"That's not how it's done," Kelly answered. "Besides, I think the Romeros would prefer to have this as far away from here as possible."

Clarita nodded, careful to avoid looking at the makeshift coffin.

"Okay, I'll do it," he agreed, taking the box. "Good night, and let me know if you hear any news about John." Sullivan walked down to his car and drove off.

Justin appeared behind Kelly and put his hand on her shoulder. "When was the last time you looked into your purse? And who had access to it today?"

"I'm not sure when I last checked it, but it was probably at school today. I keep it in an unlocked desk drawer most of the time. I know I left it in the room during lunch when everyone went to eat. Anyone on the pueblo could have walked in then."

"Please, no more talk of witchcraft in my home," Clarita asked.

"Justin and I will go for a walk, Clarita," Kelly answered gently, then turned to Justin. "Is that okay with you? There are still a few things I want to ask you." Seeing him nod, she looked back at Clarita and gave her a reassuring smile. "We won't be gone long."

"You understand why I'm asking this, don't you?" Clarita caught Justin's gaze. "It's a subject that can bring bad things to the household."

"Yes, the Dinéh feel the same way," Justin answered. "Come on—" he reached for Kelly's hand "—let's take that walk."

When they were out of earshot, Kelly glanced at Justin. "You don't believe in witchcraft, do you?"

"I don't know. Logic tells me one thing, and my culture tells me another. It really doesn't matter what I believe in, though. All I have to know is that where witchcraft is present there's always trouble.''

"Poor Clarita!" Kelly whispered. "I wish this hadn't happened at her house. From her reaction this is something she takes very seriously. I wonder what she's thinking right now."

He glanced at her. "That there's a link between John's disappearance, witchcraft and you."

Chapter Nine

"Oh, but that's not right! These are just scare tactics someone's deliberately using against me. It has nothing to do with John." They continued walking around the huge plaza, heading in the direction of the Pueblo Market Center. A few children were playing around the houses, but most of the adults were indoors.

"How can you be certain? Look at the facts. The Romeros know you were almost killed the same night John disappeared. You were also shot at, or at the very least threatened by a sniper, at a special Pueblo meeting. Then, someone goes and searches both your place and John's room. Finally there's the mutilated bird accusing you of seeing and talking too much."

She was certain all right. John couldn't be connected to the attacks on her. The person who'd planted the bird in her purse must have been one of those in the arroyo that night. Perhaps she'd seen Pueblo witches holding some sort of ceremony that could not take place in the kiva. "How much do you know about Pueblo witchcraft and cults?" she asked hastily.

He gazed across the plaza pensively. Long moments of silence stretched between them as they walked along. Finally he spoke. "Not much, I'm afraid. My knowledge is limited to the beliefs of my tribe, and it's not something we talk about unless we have to. To the Dinéh, witches exist and are evil men and women who use special powers to harm others. It's said they often wear animal skins, particularly coyote or wolf." He turned away, his voice dropping almost to a whisper. "We call them Navajo wolves, or skinwalkers."

She thought about what he'd said, noting his obvious reluctance to talk about that subject. "I'm afraid I'm going to have to find out all I can about Pueblo witchcraft practices. We're obviously dealing with someone who's either trying to influence me through ancient methods or intimidate me by pretending to. I've got to admit, however, I'd much rather deal with witches and dead birds than with bullets.''

"If it's to be a matter of choice. But what if the witches plan to continue to use both?" he asked quietly as they approached the market center.

"Then I'm in very big trouble," she muttered under her breath. Justin's self-possession and rocklike sureness worked its way under her skin. At least here and for now, she was safe.

Looking around, she noticed several men talking. She glanced at their faces absently, then suddenly stopped in her tracks. "Adrian, what are you doing here?" Standing in front of the workbench of one of the Pueblo silversmiths was Adrian Lowell.

He turned and noticed her, apparently for the first time. "Hello, Kelly, good to see you again. How are things going now that school is out?" He looked at Justin with a smile on his face, then back to her.

"I'm working on a science reading program for the Pueblo children this summer," she answered, surprised he was being so nice. "What brings you to the pueblo?"

"My summer job is in the jewelry business, so maybe I'll be seeing you around here once in a while. I think the San Esteban silversmiths are the best craftsmen in the area, and so do my customers. By the way, aren't you going to introduce me to your friend?"

"Oh, yes, I'm sorry. Adrian Lowell, I'd like you to meet Justin Nakai. He, like me, is a visitor on the pueblo."

Justin reached out his hand and shook Adrian's. He noticed right away that Lowell had learned something from his time on the pueblo. The people here shook hands gently, not in some macho bone-crushing contest like many of the Anglos he had met. The Pueblo people, as well as the Dinéh, considered touching strangers an event that should be as limited as possible. "It's a pleasure meeting an acquaintance of Kelly's," Justin said noncommittally.

"Well, it's been nice seeing you, but we have to be going now," Kelly said, pulling Justin along by the hand. The two men nodded, parting wordlessly.

Kelly waited until she was several steps away, then glanced back. What she saw made her blood run cold. In the pale light of the single bulb over the market center, she could see Adrian staring at her. His expression was ugly and distorted. Quickly she turned away.

"What's wrong?" Justin said immediately.

"What makes you think something is wrong?" she managed.

"You looked back, and then really tensed up. You don't like that man very much, do you?"

"Does it show? You know, it's nothing he's done. It's just a feeling I get. He seems a little strange, and there's something not quite right in his eyes." She wondered if she was imagining everything.

"Like he's being hunted," he observed in agreement. "He has the look about him that sends out warning signals to security guards in airports. Be careful around him," Justin added calmly.

They walked along a bit further, keeping to the shadows near the buildings rather than in the center of the plaza. All of a sudden she remembered the paper in her purse.

"Stop here a second, I want to look at something." She pulled the tiny sheet from her purse and unfolded it.

"What have you got there?" he asked, interested at once.

"I found this in my purse right after the bird fell out. I didn't say anything then because the Romeros were so upset. But I think it's a note someone slipped in there." She held it up to read in the moonlight.

Scanning it quickly, she cursed angrily and handed it to him.

"'Kelly—we could have been more than friends. Why did you ruin it for us?'" he read. "It's signed 'J.'" He stood there for a moment longer, examining the typewritten note carefully. "What do you think about this?" he asked.

She didn't know whether to be embarrassed or angry. "Somebody is trying to pass this entire thing off as a message from John. But it's nonsense. John would never have written that note or sent the mutilated bird to me. The person who did, however, is someone who believes there was more between John and me than just friendship and is trying to play up the jealousy angle." She shook her head. "This must be very convincing in your eyes. That's exactly what's been on your mind, too."

"I haven't formed any conclusions yet. But this note is evidence. I'm going to have it checked out."

"Don't be fooled into thinking John wrote that. He didn't," she affirmed.

"I'm not trying to pin anything on John. I'm aware of the possibility that all the evidence could have been planted as a frame-up," Justin said, then remembered she didn't know about the rifle and the paratrooper boots. The mounting evidence preyed constantly on his mind, waging a desperate war against his own need to clear his friend. Maybe tomorrow his luck would change. "Why don't we go check

out this note at John's office tomorrow? I haven't seen a typewriter
at the Romeros'.''

"Sounds like a good idea. That's the best way to disprove the
notion that John's harassing me. But we'll have to get up early, I have
classes at nine-thirty.''

They turned and walked back toward the Romero home.

Kelly knew that Clarita would demand answers when they returned.
Only she still couldn't say anything. Even though Clarita was a member of the Pueblo, to expose her to the knowledge of a witchcraft cult
would only subject her to danger. Those groups operated by rules
meant to terrorize and capitalize on fears held by the people for centuries.

"We need to have a talk," Clarita said to Kelly, then glanced at
Justin. "Alone, if you don't mind.''

Justin gave Kelly a quick glance, then nodded and walked inside
the home.

Kelly sat on the wooden bench beside Clarita and waited.

"I need you to be completely honest with me. I want to know
about the connection between you and my son that's causing all this
to happen.''

"Honestly, I just don't know. John and I have been friends for a
long time, but if he was in trouble of any kind, he didn't tell me.
Personally I think someone's trying to throw Justin and Suazo off the
track by clouding the issue.'' She placed her hand on Clarita's. "I
wouldn't deceive you. If I knew anything that I thought would help
you find John, I'd have told the authorities. I value my friends too
much to do anything else.'' To tell Justin or Clarita what she'd witnessed that night would only complicate matters. Clarita would be
placed in a terrible position, forced to choose between respect for her
people's customs and the search for her son. Justin would share the
danger Kelly was in, and the penalty. As outsiders, they could both
be banned from the pueblo, too. And what would happen to John
then?

Clarita stood. "Your word is enough, but I had to hear you say
it.''

Kelly watched her walk back inside. Once the seeds of distrust were
sown, it was difficult to turn back the time. Her own inability to
confide in those around her made her feel lonelier than she had since
childhood. With a heavy heart she followed Clarita into the house.

The next morning Kelly was up in time to catch Justin as he prepared to head back to Santa Fe. This time she wasn't going to let him
disappear on his own and fill her in later. "Maybe if we both look

around John's office, we'll find something that could explain his absence from the pueblo. Or at the very least find a clue to follow." She gathered her school things from the living room.

He gave her a curious look. "What are you doing, playing Sherlock Holmes? That's my job. You already have something to do for the summer, schoolteacher."

"You asked me to help you on this case, remember? Also I promised Clarita I'd do everything I could to help locate John." She tapped her watch. "Let's go," she said in her best schoolteacher's voice. "Time's a-wasting."

He put the car in gear. What an incredible amount of restless energy Kelly had. She was always moving, always searching for a way to get involved in whatever was going on. Logically his attraction to her didn't make sense. She was the opposite of him in some very important ways. She was impulsive; her emotions always seemed precariously close to the surface. Yet, there was a vibrancy about her, a zest for life, that was impossible to resist.

When they arrived at John's office a short time later, Justin followed her inside.

"It's been so hectic around here," Angela said, hanging up the telephone. "First John disappears, then the police and FBI come around—" she smiled at Justin to let him know she remembered him "—and now someone has broken into the office."

"When? Last night?" Justin asked, then realized it must have been. The local police had instructions to call him if anything related to John Romero was reported.

"Yes. The police were here already. Papers and files are everywhere, but I haven't been able to find anything missing. I can't figure it out." Angela looked apologetically at Justin, then Kelly. "I've been so busy, I haven't been able to pick up. Maybe I should just close the office today."

"Would you mind if we look around a bit? We could pick up as we go and maybe find some sort of clue," Kelly asked before Justin could speak.

She shook her head. "Go ahead. I need John back here, and I'll do whatever I can to help things along." The telephone began ringing. "It's probably another client. They've been calling for the past two days. People are really concerned about him."

As she picked up the receiver, Justin walked to John's large office.

"Okay, now what are we looking for?" Kelly asked, following him.

"We can't read his files without a court order, but there's nothing that says we can't look at his calendar and address books. With Angela's permission to browse around here, it seems only logical to do so."

Hearing Angela hang up the receiver, Kelly peered out of John's office. "Do you mind if I type up a short note to myself on his typewriter?"

"No, not at all. He keeps some note-sized paper in the top drawer, if you need it. Only I've got to warn you. That typewriter is very old and a bit erratic. John seldom uses it, so we haven't sent it in to the repair shop."

Justin turned to her with that comment and reached into his pocket for the note Kelly had found in her purse. Two letters in the note had been higher than the rest.

"It doesn't matter. I just had an idea of something I want my students to use in class." With Justin watching, she reached in the drawer, looking for the paper. Taking one of the note-sized square sheets, she held it between her fingertips and studied it for a moment. It was the same type of paper that had been used to write the note. She recognized the watermark. After showing it to Justin, she placed it in the typewriter. Kelly typed a simple assignment sheet to head a student notebook, then the single sentence of the note.

Out of the corner of her eye, she could see Justin watching. Pulling out the paper, she saw that the *a*s and *e*s showed up higher than the rest. The *b*s were missing part of the loop, too. It was definitely the same typewriter that had been used for the note. Disgusted, she handed the paper to Justin, who made his own comparison. Then he folded the papers up and placed both in his pocket. Only the faintest trace of a scowl showed on his impassive features.

She leaned back in John's chair and stared absently across the room. Her eyes came to rest on a photograph of John's cabin, hung on the far wall. "That's an idea," she said.

He looked up from the calendar he was thumbing through. "What is?"

"The cabin. Has anyone searched there yet? I can't imagine John going up without telling anyone, but surely it's worth checking out. Maybe we'll find a clue there that will shed some light on this."

"I had the county sheriff go by there. He didn't find any vehicles around or signs of inhabitants. Maybe it's time to go inside and take a closer look. We haven't found anything anywhere else."

"Did you learn anything from his calendar?"

"Not much. He'd blocked off the week of the rituals and made no appointments for the Monday following it, either."

"I've been to John's cabin before. Let's go up there together. I'll know if there's anything missing or different," she said. "Also, I can save you some time trying to find it. It's hard to locate, believe me."

"What about your classes?"

"Well, I need some cooperation from you. I have to teach today, so you'll have to wait until I finish my last class. We get out early today, at two."

"All right." He glanced at the clock on John's desk. "It's getting late. I'd better get you back to the pueblo."

"Stop at Clarita's. John keeps the cabin door locked. If she doesn't have the key, I'm going to have to search for the spare."

Justin, at her urging, drove back to the pueblo quickly. When they reached Clarita Romero's home, Kelly shot out of the car. "I've got to hurry with this, or I'll be late." Seeing him take his usual unhurried, measured strides, she grabbed him by the arm and urged him along. "Come on!"

Justin laughed. "So impatient," he whispered, as they reached the door. "Are you always this way?" His deep, velvety voice caressed her.

Flurries of wanting filled her senses and made a shiver course up her spine. His eyes burned into her soul. Hearing the door open, she reluctantly tore her gaze away.

"Hi," Maria greeted. "Has there been any news?"

"Not yet," Justin answered.

As they entered the living room, she saw Murray Sullivan sitting beside Clarita. He glanced up at her and smiled.

"Good morning, Murray," Kelly greeted, then took Clarita's hand and gave it a squeeze. "I need to ask you a favor, Clarita."

"Name it."

"When we went to check John's office, I remembered the cabin he has up in the Santa Fe Forest. No one's checked there yet except for the sheriff and he never went inside. It's a long shot..."

Clarita's eyes lit up. "Yes, John goes up there whenever he needs time to himself."

"I don't want to get your hopes up."

Clarita stood. "I'll get you the key. It's in the kitchen drawer."

As Kelly followed Clarita out of the room, Murray turned to Justin. "I've been up there several times. John and I used to go fishing every once in a while. It's really hard to find unless you know the way. Why don't you let me take you up there after I get off work?"

"I'd like to get an earlier start," Justin answered. "Kelly'll be off at two and she's offered to come with me. She's been up there, too, so we'll be fine."

"Yes, I suppose she has," he said slowly. Giving Justin a knowing smile, he shrugged.

Kelly walked into the room flourishing the key as Murray was completing the sentence. She'd heard enough to know what he'd intimated. The grin she saw on Murray's face made her seethe. "I've been to the bank, too, Murray, but you don't have a thing to worry about."

Justin chuckled softly as Murray turned beet red.

"I've got to run. See you later," she said.

Justin watched her race across the sandy ground. One thing was for certain. She sure could make things lively.

IT WAS SHORTLY AFTER TWO when Justin saw Kelly emerge from the community center. A small gathering of children surrounded her. As she crossed the porch, she saw him and waved.

Justin waited as she approached. It was a hot day, yet she looked as fresh as she had that morning. There was a youthfulness in the way she moved and smiled that rivaled that of her students.

"Ready?" he asked.

"Yes, I'm through here." With a wave at Elsie she walked to Justin's car. Before she could enter, two of the girl students rushed up to her.

"Ms. Ferguson? I'm Henrietta and I need to ask you a *big* favor. Could you move Sludge over so that Loretta and I could sit next to each other? I had to sit next to Sludge all year long and I'm getting tired of looking at him. And he's always teasing me about my hair."

"I like your hair. It's a cute style," Kelly replied, looking at the girl's perm.

"Well, he keeps calling me a buffalo and I'm sick of hearing it."

"Why don't we try this. I'll move you to the seat across from Loretta in the next row. That way he'll have to turn around to look at either of you."

"Thanks, Ms. Ferguson."

Justin waited until Kelly and he were alone in the car. *"Sludge?"*

"Henry," she corrected automatically, then started to laugh. "When he was a little boy, Henry apparently played along the irrigation ditches. He was always getting muddy, and he had a tendency to move really slowly whenever his mother would call him into the house. His older brother started calling him Sludge and the name stuck."

Justin started laughing. "Sounds reasonable." He looked eastward at the ponderosa pine-covered foothills as they reached the highway. The sight stirred something deep within him. "I wish they'd reassign me to the Southwest and let me go back to doing field work. You're lucky to be out here. I've traveled around quite a bit but I've never found another place I can call home."

"I like it here, too, but I probably won't be able to stay either. My career goals will end up forcing me to move away sooner or later."

"What kind of goals? I thought you loved teaching," he asked. Westward, the stunted junipers of the desert mesa were slowly replaced by upland forested areas thick with tall piñon trees.

"I'll always teach, but if I remain at this level, working with seventh- and eighth-grade students, the most I'll reach in one year are one hundred and sixty kids. If I can get my doctorate, however, I can train future teachers in college." She paused and stared out the window at the thickening clusters of piñon and pine. "The drawback, though, is that I'll miss working with the kids, particularly since I've learned how to apply for grants and get funding for special projects like this reading program."

"Perhaps the classroom is where you belong. You've found your place, why keep looking?"

"I don't think it's a good idea to stop reaching," she answered simply. "When you do that you stagnate, and that's a bit like dying inside. Moving forward, making new trysts with life, that's what keeps people young and interesting."

"But if it takes you out of something you love, is it still a good thing?" Justin prodded.

"The American dream is based on having the drive it takes to achieve success. My primary concern isn't money, but that is a factor, too. I want financial security, and a professor's chair at a university would give me that. I also want the satisfaction of knowing that I've taken my skill as a teacher and advanced as high as I can go."

Justin nodded, but said nothing. Hers was exactly the type of thinking he was trying to distance himself from in the FBI. He disapproved of the perpetual search for something better that seemed so ingrained in most Anglos. A long-term relationship would never work between them, despite the attraction, even if they were both to miraculously stay in the same area. And now even that seemed doubtful.

The series of twists and turns they took to find the cabin was complicated, resembling an elaborate maze. "Are you sure you know where you're going?" Justin asked at last.

"I'm fairly sure. It's been a while since I've been here."

Justin gave her an exasperated look. "I didn't bother to get specific directions from Clarita because you told me you knew how to get here. *Now you're not sure?*'' His voice rose slightly.

"I'm fairly sure."

Others had always marveled at his ability to avoid losing his temper. This woman, however, had the uncanny ability to drive him close to the edge in a multitude of ways. He took a deep breath, then let it out slowly. To walk in harmony a man had to remain at peace within himself.

"Turn left here. If there's a wooden sign reading No Trespassers then we're only about a hundred yards from the cabin."

Justin proceeded slowly down the bumpy road. Then he saw the sign sticking up from an outcropping of Gambel oak. "There, is that the one you meant?"

She nodded. "I can admit it now that I'm exonerated," she said with a smile. "For about twenty minutes there I could have sworn we were lost."

He laughed, then shook his head. "I suspected as much."

"It's both our faults, you know. We should have learned from Hollywood. It's the Indians that are supposed to be the guides, not vice versa. When you break the rule, you take your chances."

"Spoken like a true teacher," he replied with a small grin. Pulling the car to one side of the road, he parked.

"Why are you stopping here?"

"I think we should be careful when we approach the cabin. If someone who doesn't want to be found is there, we'll want the element of surprise to work in our favor."

Justin led her on a diagonal course, keeping the wind at their faces. "The sounds we make will be carried away from the cabin this way," he explained.

A twig snapped loudly, followed by a crunch of leaves as Kelly followed close behind.

He stopped in midstride and urged her alongside of him. "There's a trick to moving noiselessly across brush. Let me show you."

"I was trying to be quiet," she defended, then smiled sheepishly. She was fully aware that even gale-force winds wouldn't have been enough to mask all the noise she'd been making.

"It's all in where you place your feet," he explained in a whisper-soft voice, "and being aware of where your body is at all times. Try to step in places that aren't heavily covered with leaves and scrub. Ease your foot down and place it level on the ground so that your weight is evenly distributed."

Kelly thought she was doing fine until she caught the fork of a fallen pine branch with her foot and dragged it over some leaves. He turned around and motioned for her to stop. "Okay, I don't think the sound carried," he whispered. "Let's go."

"Sorry about that. This goes against the grain, you know. Teachers usually try to make as much noise as possible. It helps us strike fear in the hearts of the students," she teased in a barely audible whisper.

He smiled. "Okay, now that we're reaching the tree line, we're going to have to be real still. I can see the cabin from here, and there isn't enough wooded area to mask our approach."

She nodded. "I'll do my best."

He led the way forward, then stopped in midstride. "There's an open area ahead. We'll dash across it, then enter the cluster of trees again. Keep your head down."

She went first, cursing herself for not being able to move more quietly. Though she'd improved some, she still seemed as noisy as a herd of elephants in comparison to Justin. She watched him cross over to where she stood. His movements were supple and he seemed to flow noiselessly across the landscape.

As they neared the cabin, a door suddenly slammed and someone rushed out the back. A solitary figure ducked through the thick cluster of pines on the far side of the cabin.

"We must have been spotted," Justin muttered an oath. "Stay here. I'm going to see if I can catch whoever it is."

He sprinted forward with surprising speed. Kelly watched him for a moment. Why on earth was she just standing here? She certainly hadn't come all the way out here just for the scenery. She shot forward and had managed to almost catch up to Justin before he saw her.

He didn't break his stride. "I told you to wait! Go back."

His tone angered her. She was behind, not ahead of him. She wouldn't be in his way. Besides, this placed her in a position to help him if he needed it. "No, I'm coming with you."

He swore with surprising eloquence, then doubled his speed.

Kelly could see a blurry shape dodging through the aspens and patches of scrub oak ahead. They were getting close. Suddenly Justin froze in his tracks, then spun around and dove toward her. They tumbled to the ground as a knife hurtled over their heads.

Chapter Ten

Justin took the brunt of the fall with his shoulder. Then, holding her against him, he rolled and pulled her behind cover. His gaze flicked quickly over her, making sure she was okay. An instant later he jumped to his feet, crashing through the brush after the person who'd thrown the knife. But it was already too late. He reached the top of the steep slope that overlooked the road just in time to see a blue pickup take off in a shower of gravel and dirt.

Sitting up slowly, Kelly glanced up at the knife stuck in the ponderosa pine right behind her. "Who the heck was that?" she asked, as Justin came toward her.

"I didn't manage to get a clear look, but he was wearing some kind of cap and a brown shirt. Good thing I caught a glimpse of his arm through the trees before he threw the knife. Did you happen to get a better look at him?"

She shook her head. "All I saw was a blur."

"He took off in a blue pickup, but I was too far away to make out the license plate." Justin stood immobile, his posture rigid, the tension of the chase still evident in his features.

Kelly tried to will away the fear that was causing her stomach to tie into knots. John drove a blue pickup!

Justin placed his handkerchief around the middle of the blade, and extracted the knife from the tree. "This should give us a clue. It's a custom-made hunting knife, balanced for throwing. Look at the handle, it's made from aged mule deer antler and carved to fit the hand of its owner. But the tip of the blade's broken." He studied the area where the knife had been imbedded. "It's not here, it was already missing."

"Now what? Do we go back to the cabin?" The thought made her apprehensive. What had been a place of pleasant memories had suddenly become tainted with the fear that shrouded everything she did lately.

He nodded. "No one's likely to be there now. Whoever was there is long gone. To be on the safe side, though, let me go in first." He removed his pistol from the holster at his waist.

They walked in silence, each deep in thought. When they approached, Justin started forward, thumbing off his pistol's safety.

Justin stood to one side of the door and checked the lock. "There's no sign of forced entry." He pushed the partially open door ajar and stepped inside. The cabin smelled musty and stale. "Leave it open," he told her. "We'll need some fresh air."

He walked to the kitchen and saw a bag filled with groceries on the countertop. He walked around, silently noting the light layer of dust visible on the table and countertops.

"The bed's been slept in," Kelly called out.

Justin went to the bedroom and looked at the crumpled sheets. A blanket had been tossed on the floor as if by a restless sleeper. He looked for any signs of personal possessions, but besides a mirror, a used disposable razor and some shaving cream on the dresser, there was nothing around. The razor didn't give much information about the user, because like him, John didn't need to shave more than three times a week. Taking care not to disrupt any possible fingerprints, he searched the interior of drawers and closets.

"John kept some hunting supplies in the hall closet," Kelly informed him. "I remember he showed me a storage bin he'd built in there."

Justin followed her out of the bedroom. "Don't touch the handle directly. Try the base of the doorknob to open it."

"Not necessary." Hooking her foot around the bottom of the door, she pulled it toward her. "It looks like someone's been here before us."

Justin opened the lid of the oak storage box. It was nearly empty. The compartment contained a couple of custom-designed hunting arrows placed on a special rack. The vanes were turkey feather, with the cock feather dyed red on the tip. The shaft was glossy black, with a yellow strip on either side of a wider green one. The arrows were incomplete, however; one was missing a vane, and the other had no pile or point. From their days in college together, Justin recognized the colorful design as John's personal configuration. The powerful hunting bow was gone, though he could see a packet of extra bow string that had been left in the bottom.

"What's inside the cardboard box there in the corner?" Kelly asked.

"I'm just getting to that." Justin opened it carefully, then dumped the contents onto the bed. It had been crammed to the bursting point with twenty- and fifty-dollar bills. "There must be a couple thousand dollars in here, and take a look at this." He held up a passbook for an account at the United Tribal Bank. "It's John's passbook." He exhaled softly, opening the book and looking at the figures. "This indicates that John is depositing all kinds of money into the bank. And here is a withdrawal dated last June 1 for three thousand dollars. What on earth has John been up to?" He'd posed the question to himself, but the anger on Kelly's face took him completely by surprise.

"You've spent too many years with the FBI, that's your problem. You're taking this as proof that John's guilty of who knows what! Well, I refuse to think that it was John we surprised here today."

"Look at the facts," he said softly. "It's John's cabin, these are John's things. The arrows are his own and the bank book, too. Who else would have come all the way out here and made himself at home, using a key?" As he heard his own words, he felt the weight of each and the consequences of what he'd learned. He no longer felt worthy of the trust the Romeros had placed in him.

"And you're assuming John threw that knife, I suppose." She crossed her arms in front of her chest and glared at him. "You're letting these *facts* interfere with your common sense. You should know John would never harm anyone. If you start from that premise then it's easy to discredit the evidence we've uncovered so far."

"In law enforcement we have to go by the facts, not intuition," he answered gently, hating the role he had found himself in. More than anything he'd wanted to help his friend and not bring more trouble down on him. "We can't just tailor the evidence we find to fit the outcome we want. There's everything we found here and the boot prints—"

"What boot prints?"

"When I went to the spot where the sniper fired those shots, I noticed some distinctive boot prints. Whoever aimed those shots wore paratrooper boots, and as it turned out, John wears the same kind and size practically everywhere except the office. Suazo checked and John's weren't in his closet." He heard his own words, and the import left him feeling like the worst kind of traitor.

Kelly threw up her hands. "Now you're going to convince yourself that John was the sniper? I don't want to hear any more of this!'' She went to the door.

Justin stopped her in midstride. Grasping her by the shoulders, he gently forced her to face him. "I admire your loyalty to John, but sooner or later you're going to have to face the facts. Do you think I like this? It hurts me to know that I'm hunting my friend, a man I've known and loved for years. But refusing to face the evidence is no answer."

Kelly felt his pain as keenly as he did her own. It pierced her anger, shattering it under a rush of tenderness and remorse. "I didn't mean to judge you. I'm sorry," she whispered. Her eyes captured his, pleading a dozen silent messages.

He brushed her face with his open palm. It felt rough against her cheek. She scarcely breathed as his lips descended over hers. His kiss was exquisitely gentle and it was her undoing. She felt the strength in his body, and her heart began to drum at a furious tempo. She parted her lips, inviting him to take more.

With a throaty sound, he deepened the union. Heat surged upward from some deep place inside him, engulfing him in waves.

She felt his fingers rake through her hair and hold her still. His hungry tongue thrust forward, mating with hers. Kelly gripped his shoulders, afraid that if she let go her knees would buckle. A deep moan of pure need vibrated through him, touching her soul.

His grip tightened, and she could barely breathe. Lightning bolts of pure sensation shot through her.

The kiss broke by mutual consent. They stood and faced each other, chests heaving, breathing ragged.

Justin said nothing, but his body betrayed him. Kelly realized that the longings that had driven her also raged in him. She turned away from him. "I'll help you search the rest of the cabin," she said, her voice shaking.

"Try to remember the way it was when you came here last," he answered, his voice lower and huskier than usual. "I need to know if there's anything different."

She didn't trust herself to look at him until she'd conquered the feelings that had nearly overcome her. "I don't see anything missing. Everything I remember is here, including the color reproduction of Kowalski's *The Lone Wolf*."

Justin nodded. "Let's lock this place up. We'll have to leave the money—it's evidence, and go to the ranger station on the road toward Jemez Springs. I'll call the office in Santa Fe and have them bring a team over here to look for fingerprints."

Two hours later Justin sat in the ranger station with the special agent in charge from Santa Fe.

"Officially, this is your case," Dean Jenkins said. "The paperwork has been filed, and cleared. We have a shortage of cars at the Bureau office right now, but we'll get you a car from the interagency motor pool. In the meantime—" he slid a portable radio across the table at him "—this will keep you from being completely out of touch. It does have a limited range, particularly in the mountains, but it'll serve for the time being." He paced around the tiny office. His thinning hair was streaked with white and meticulously combed in place. He trained his sharp eyes on Justin. "Now fill me in on the details of your investigation."

Justin summarized the events of the past few days. "I believe the attempts on Kelly Ferguson's life are connected to John Romero's disappearance. Only I'm not yet certain how those two events fit together. We've found evidence that suggests John Romero is the one trying to kill her, but I haven't been able to discover a motive. My impression is that we've only scratched the surface, and it's going to take a lot more digging before I can get some solid facts that we can use in court."

"Has Ms. Ferguson been able to shed any light on the mystery?"

Justin shook his head. "Not so far. She's afraid of something, though. It's my impression that she wanted to handle whatever was going on by herself. Only the trouble has escalated, and she's beginning to see that it's beyond her capabilities. In time I believe she'll tell me what she knows."

"Keep me posted," the man said, then stood. "If you need backup or if there's anything our office can do for you, let me know."

Justin nodded and went to rejoin Kelly, who was waiting outside. "Will you be going back to the pueblo soon?" she asked.

"I'll take you back now. Afterward, though, I've got to return to work. Will you be all right?"

She nodded, still shaky. "Someone's going through a lot of trouble to try to make it look as if John's doing this. We have to find out who it is."

"You could be of more help, you know, if you wanted to," he said, leading her to his car.

"You're wrong about that," she answered simply. "I'm doing all I can."

As they drove to the pueblo, silence hung between them like an impenetrable curtain. Justin's mind drifted back to John's cabin. He could still feel her body trembling against him. He'd wanted her then.

He wanted her now. His knuckles tightened around the steering wheel, and he took a deep, long breath.

By the time he'd parked in front of the Romeros' home, he felt torn between the desire to take her someplace where they'd be alone and relief that at least for now she would not continue to pose such a distraction. "If you need me, call the tribal police," he said. "I'll be there with Suazo for a while." As he drove away, he could see her in his rearview mirror, standing, watching him. Her image was still in his mind when he arrived at the tribal police headquarters.

THE FOLLOWING MORNING Justin sat at the Romeros' kitchen table, finishing some eggs Clarita had insisted on cooking for him.

Kelly walked in from her own room to join them for breakfast. Helping Maria with the coffee, she poured herself and everyone else at the table a cup.

No one had much to say. Their unrelenting concern for John etched deep lines on their faces. Clarita and Maria, finished with breakfast, stood. "I'm taking Mother to the store. Raymond is already outside, and he's going to be with us. Make yourself at home, okay?" Maria said.

Justin waited until they were alone, then attempted once more to question her about the night they'd met.

"There's nothing I can say that would help you," she answered wearily. "Why won't you believe me?"

"I questioned the story when you told it to me at the accident, and I'm questioning it still," he answered in a quiet voice. "You're leaving out something that you know, and at this point, I'm certain it's very important. It also makes me wonder how deeply you're involved in what's going on," he admitted.

"I know that," she answered, "but I still can't help you." The distrust etched on his features made her heart constrict. He'd never know how hard it was for her to keep silent. Yet, by seeking his protection she'd be endangering both Justin and John. That wasn't a trade-off she could live with.

"I've got class soon. I've got to be going." She walked to the door. "By the way, I spent quite a bit of last night at the library in Santa Fe looking up information on Pueblo witchcraft, but I didn't get far. There's very little on that subject, and what I did find was very vague." She'd also checked on the ceremonial masks she'd seen, though she could hardly tell Justin that. Although that collection had been extensive, she hadn't found any she recognized. As she saw herself mirrored in Justin's ebony eyes, she struggled against the temptation to tell him everything. "I'll see you later."

He was still sitting in the kitchen lost in thought when he heard Maria's car return. He walked outside and helped her unload the sacks of groceries. "Where's Clarita?"

"She stayed behind to visit with her friend, Mrs. Brownhat. I'm glad, too. She's been needing to get out of the house, only she's insisted on staying by the telephone in case John tries to reach her. Raymond's with her and is going to walk her back." Maria folded the paper sack and put it away.

"Have you been waiting for me?"

"Yes," he admitted. "There are a few questions I'd like to ask you. Important questions."

She returned to the table and sat down. "Then I'll try my best to answer you."

"Are you and John very close?"

"When we were kids, John and I were opposites in many ways. He was the thinker, the planner. I was always going out and getting myself into trouble. And—" she smiled "—he was always there getting me out of it. I knew I could count on him. Now that we're both grown, our relationship has changed, but we still depend on each other."

"Can you think of any reason why he'd drop out of sight?"

She shook her head. "Even if he was in terrible trouble, John would have found a way to let us know he's okay. Perhaps he wouldn't trust the telephone, but he'd make sure the message got back to us." She stared at her lap in silence. "I'd never say this in front of Mother, but the fact that he hasn't contacted us convinces me John's either being held someplace against his will, or he's dead." Her lips trembled slightly but she composed herself quickly.

Justin nodded thoughtfully. Yet if John was doing something that could place his family in danger, he'd undoubtedly stay away from them. "Tell me about his relationship with Kelly. I heard they kept company quite frequently."

"That's true, but it wasn't serious. I can guarantee that John and Kelly weren't lovers or anything like that, if that's what you were thinking."

"What makes you so sure?"

"When John started seeing a great deal of Kelly, I began to get worried. My brother is very traditional, and an Anglo woman would have difficulty understanding some of our customs. I know marriage is good, but it's hard at best. I didn't want to see him go into a relationship that had so many negatives stacked against it."

"And you told him all this?"

"We spoke honestly with each other. My brother feels a bond of friendship toward Kelly. He can easily understand the dedication she shows to her job, and he admires her for that and trusts her."

"And that's all? She's quite beautiful," Justin added.

"My brother's not blind." Maria smiled. "He finds her attractive, but he also knows she isn't right for him. From what he told me, Kelly feels the same way."

"You've cleared up some of the questions I've had. Thanks." He walked toward the door. "I'll see you tonight." Justin stepped outside into the cool morning air. Despite the breeze, today was scheduled to be a scorcher. He entered his car and placed it in gear. It was time to get started.

The day went quickly. Although he managed to speak to quite a few of the people Suazo had suggested, he still had nothing when the day was over. He wouldn't even have been able to conduct those interviews if Suazo hadn't been there. The ones who had been involved with the ritual had been extremely reluctant to talk about anything that had transpired that evening.

Cursing Pueblo secrecy, Justin returned with Suazo to tribal police headquarters at around five-thirty. He was eager to see the photographs the lab boys had taken of the cabin. Shortly before their last interview, Suazo had received word that the photos had been sent over to his office.

Justin sat across Suazo's desk, and ripped open the large manila envelope. "There's an extra set of copies in here for you also, Sergeant," he said, handing him a stack.

Suazo glanced from one shot to the other, only mildly interested. Then suddenly, he stopped and stared at the one in his hand. "This is the knife that was thrown at you?" He showed Justin the photo he was holding.

"That's it," Justin confirmed. "Why? Do you recognize it?"

"I sure do. That knife belongs to John Romero. It was made for him by his father. I was there the day he shaped the handle to fit John's hand."

Chapter Eleven

By the time Justin left the police building, he could feel tension knotting his muscles. The possibility that his friend was responsible for the threats on Kelly's life as well as his own made him go cold inside. Now was no time to let his emotions surface; he had a job to do. But how did one stop feeling?

He wanted to talk to Kelly alone again. She was quickly becoming his best lead. Tonight it would have to be all business between them. Yet even as the thought formed, he wished that weren't true.

When he finally arrived at the Romeros', he allowed himself a few moments alone in the darkness of the car. To do his best work he needed to find harmony within himself, and that was swiftly becoming more difficult. Concern for his missing friend and this woman who was playing such a prominent part in the investigation made objectivity difficult.

After talking with Raymond and Maria for a few minutes in the kitchen, he went to Kelly's room. He knocked on the door and waited.

"Come in," she called out. She sat in the middle of the floor surrounded by stacks of papers. "Hello," she greeted as he stepped inside. "Do you mind if I keep grading these? I'll need to give them back to the kids tomorrow."

He shook his head and closed the door behind him so the others wouldn't overhear their conversation. Even behind the thick adobe walls, he lowered his voice. "I wanted to tell you that Suazo positively identified the knife that was thrown at us. It's one that belongs to John."

Kelly glanced up, her knuckles turning white as she gripped the red pencil in her hand. "Knives can be stolen."

"True, but the case against John is getting stronger."

Kelly shrugged and returned to her grading. "I've already told you how I feel about that."

He sat down on a chair by the dressing table and watched her in silence for a moment longer, trying to find the right words. "Tell me more about you and John," he asked in a gentle tone. "What kept your relationship from growing into something deeper?" His need to know transcended professional curiosity.

She took a deep breath, then exhaled softly. "John's whole world revolved around his culture and his way of life. My different outlook put us at odds at times. We could work with it, but only so long as we remained just friends."

At last she was admitting that there had been some problems between them. It was a beginning. "So at the root of the problem was the fact that he was Indian?"

She nodded.

A prejudice of sorts? "Do you object to a marriage between an Anglo woman and an Indian?" He had to delve deeper and find out how her mind worked, what secret she was hiding.

"No, that's not quite it." She met his gaze candidly. "John appealed to me both as a man and as an individual I could respect. But John belonged to the Pueblo in a way I could never have. Even if I had married John, the tribe would have still considered me an outsider. Whenever the Pueblo had closed religious ceremonies, I would have been forced to leave my home until the rituals were completed. The most important part of his life, a part he loved dearly, would have been closed to me. He wouldn't have been able to even talk to me about it."

Justin nodded slowly. "You're right. What you say about the Tewas is true. Their ties to the Pueblo and their devotion to secrecy are very much a part of who and what they are. That's why the Dinéh found them so hard to understand."

"So that's why John and I never really let love develop between us." She smiled shyly. "That explains why I'm single, but what about you? Do you feel your line of work is incompatible with a relationship?"

He lapsed into thoughtful silence. "Not incompatible, but it doesn't make things easy." Her answer had revealed even more problems for them should they allow their own relationship to develop. "I also have a portion of my life that I'd never be able to share with the woman I love. My work would entail separations from time to time, danger and secrecy most of all. And it's bound to get worse."

"What do you mean?"

"I want to go back to doing what I do best. Promotions have given me more status and more pay, but supervising is not where I belong. I fit out in the field, doing the actual work, rather than just telling others what to do. You want to progress and see how far you can take your skills as a teacher as you climb up. My philosophy is exactly the opposite. I have no need for promotions. I found my place and I want to keep it." He paused. "But my life-style is bound to be hard on a wife. She'd have to be a very strong person. One who can cope with the uncertainties of my work."

Kelly began picking up the stacks of papers around her, avoiding his eyes. "That's harder than you think. I know what it's like to be put on the sidelines of someone's life, and I'd never let that happen to me again." Gathering her courage, she challenged him with a look. "You have no idea how much heartbreak there is in that."

She stood and placed the papers on the bed. "My mother died when I was ten years old. My dad didn't know what to do with me, so he decided to send me off to boarding school while he accepted overseas jobs. I suppose he thought that if he went far enough, he could get away from the memories." She shrugged. "I learned back then that it's day-to-day sharing in each other's lives that bonds people."

Justin could see the hurt, still raw, behind her control. She would ask more of him than he could give, or not ask it as she did with John. A strange hollowness in the pit of his stomach echoed his sense of loss.

Suddenly a loud crack of thunder reverberated around the room. A steady rain began to pelt against the hard-packed earth. The oppressiveness of the weather accentuated his mood. "So, it looks like we're finally getting some rain. The land needs it."

"With summer the rains invariably come. It's New Mexico's version of the monsoon season."

"Be thankful. I remember years when little rain came. Cattle went hungry, and crops dried up."

A long silence hung between them. Finally Justin spoke. "All the evidence says that John is trying to kill you. You've given me no reasons that would suggest why."

"That's because he wouldn't. I've told you the truth. If your facts don't fit in with it, then perhaps you should reevaluate them."

"I know you've been open with me tonight. But whether you continue to disbelieve that it could be John or not, one fact is indisputable. Someone is trying to kill you."

The words chilled her more than the damp breeze blowing in through the open window.

JUSTIN WAS IN Suazo's office the next morning. Murray Sullivan sat before a large table studying the photographs of the cabin. "I don't see anything missing. I've been at the cabin several times with John, and everything looks normal to me."

"Thanks, Murray," Justin said. "Letting us take your prints helped. We need to identify all the fingerprints we were able to lift at the cabin and see whose don't belong there. Maybe that will give us a lead."

Suazo watched Sullivan leave, his face contorted into a tight grimace. "I hate to say this but, from the evidence, it's beginning to look like John was the one staying at that cabin."

"Not necessarily. There were quite a large number of smudged prints that were impossible to identify. Those could have been caused by someone wearing gloves as they moved around the cabin. As far as I'm concerned, it's status quo with everything remaining inconclusive." Yet with the smudged prints, there was finally something to support Kelly's claim that someone was framing John. Still, it was too early to make any determinations, no matter how tempting.

"We do have the evidence of the rifle and the knife. That's solid and irrefutable," Suazo countered. "You can't discount it."

Justin stared directly ahead, lost in thought. "There're discrepancies here that bother me," he said at last. "Did John ever strike you as a man who was careless with his things? The John I knew was always fixing or maintaining the possessions he really valued."

Suazo considered it for a long moment. "That tallies with my perception of John. But what are you getting at?"

"John was too experienced a hunter to get his rifle jammed with sand, or mar the finish of the stock on a rock. He would have cradled the weapon in his hand using the sling." Justin stared at his notebook, lost in thought. "There are other things that don't add up, too. For instance, the dust that covered everything up at the cabin, especially on the dining table, indicates that whoever threw the knife hadn't been there for very long." Justin flipped the little notebook shut, then placed it back into his breast pocket. "The sheriff had looked around there only a few days ago. Also, it doesn't seem likely that John would have thrown away a knife his father had made for him. And the biggest question of all is why John would leave things behind that he knew would identify him as the killer. He was far too intelligent for that."

Suazo considered the information. "Men who act out of jealousy find themselves reacting rather than acting. That emotion can destroy a man. The Ferguson woman is quite beautiful." He paused. "There's something about the way she moves and talks that makes a man respond. John was around her quite a bit. There's no telling how far that relationship went. I still believe that she's at the center of this.''

''She's sure been singled out by someone who wants to terrorize her. But I don't think she knows exactly why.'' He stretched out his legs. ''What we have to find is the pattern that weaves it all together.''

''The overall picture *is* emerging. Only it's not one that satisfies you.'' Suazo swore as he watched the red light on the coffee maker blink off. Only cold gray water filled the glass container. ''Damn thing's broken again. Let me get some fresh coffee from the other coffee maker, and I'll be right back. You want a cup?''

Justin nodded, his mind busy weighing possibilities. Unless he solved this mystery soon, a woman he was very fond of could die. A man he loved like a brother was missing and being framed for the attacks on her. Despite all the logical arguments, he was going to do everything in his power to protect them both.

KELLY GLARED at her students. ''This is a small classroom. No one's going to get away with anything here. We might as well get that cleared up right now.'' She gave them ''the look'' and continued to pace, forcing their attention to remain on her as she walked around the room. ''Someone took the handle off the pencil sharpener. Now, since we all need pencils, and sooner or later a point's bound to break, I'd appreciate it if the handle was returned.'' She stopped and faced them. ''I don't want to mislead any of you. This is not a request. If the handle is not there when we come back from lunch, we will stay in this classroom for as long as it takes to find it. Clear?''

''Yes, ma'am.''

She waited several seconds, then nodded. ''All right. You're dismissed.''

The clatter of sneaker-clad feet filled the room, punctuated by rowdy yells from the boys and girls. She dropped back in her seat and smiled. Phew! They were a handful. She laughed, looking at the pencil sharpener. She had a budding mechanical engineer in the group, it seemed.

She spent several minutes taking notes and clearing her desk, then walked out to meet Elsie. ''How's your group doing?''

''So far this morning one of the girls dropped an entire bag of sunflower seeds all over the floor, and we had several rubber band shootings—with no fatalities. All in a typical day.''

Kelly laughed. ''I don't know about you, but I'm ready for lunch.''

Elsie nodded. "I hate to admit it, but when Frances dropped her sunflower seeds, I almost made a dash for them myself."

"By the way, I'm going to have to compile some information about your current group for a report. How do you feel about a working lunch?"

"As long as I still get to eat, I'm game."

Collecting the brown bags with their names on them from the mothers who were doubling as kitchen staff, they walked outside. "It was really great of the pueblo to make arrangements to give everyone a brown bag lunch. Being able to choose what goes in them, too, makes it especially nice." Elsie smiled in agreement.

They walked out to the shaded, open veranda and found a spot for themselves. "As you can tell," Elsie said, "lots of people agree with you. That's why the program blossomed. It now includes those who are in the pueblo during the day, like the medicine man." She gestured toward the fit-looking elderly man sitting in the midst of a group of youngsters. "And some of the tribal council members are here, too," she added, looking in the opposite direction.

They'd just sat down when Murray Sullivan approached. "Hello," he said, glancing at Kelly, then Elsie. "How are things going?"

"Just fine," Kelly replied. "What brings you here?"

"The soda machine inside," Murray confessed. "The one at the bank is on the fritz. I better let you get back to your lunches, ladies. I'll have to pick up my soda and run. If I don't return to my office soon, my secretary's going to quit. We're in the midst of reports."

Kelly began to collect the information she needed from Elsie as she finished her turkey and Swiss cheese sandwich. It was spicy with one of those gourmet mustards, and almost too hot for her. She was in the midst of a question when loud voices interrupted her. "What's going on?" she asked.

Elsie glanced at the pair arguing in Tewa. The tall, young man had his hands in his pockets, staring down at the medicine man as if disinterested. The medicine man was much shorter, but broad-shouldered and strong looking. Except for the telling lines on his face, he could have passed for twenty years younger. "The medicine man tends a very complex herb garden used for curing and for some of the religious ceremonies. He's complaining that someone has been taking herbs from his garden." Elsie listened. "The other man is a member of the tribal council and he's saying that our medicine man always finds something to complain about. He accused the medicine man of hiding the herbs himself just so he'd have some reason to stir up the others."

"It certainly looks like those herbs work for the medicine man. He appears to be in great condition."

As the pair seemed to calm down, Elsie smiled. "Now they're friends again. Those two disagree on virtually everything, but believe it or not, they're the best of friends."

"That explains why none of the kids seemed overly upset," Kelly commented.

Elsie chuckled. "They know these guys. Whenever they get together an argument is sure to follow. No one pays attention anymore."

Kelly went back to her report. By the time she finished gathering the information she needed from Elsie, her breathing had become irregular, and she was feeling light-headed. She felt hot.

"Do you have asthma?" Elsie asked, concerned.

Kelly shook her head in confusion. "I just feel sick all of a sudden. My mouth is so dry and my stomach hurts." She gasped for air, and tried to struggle to her feet. "My heart's pounding so fast! Elsie, help me!"

Chapter Twelve

The kids began to gather around, looming over her, distorted in her blurred vision.

"Do you want a doctor?"

Kelly tried to nod and reached out clumsily with her hand. "I..." Elsie's voice seemed to have traveled through a long tunnel before ever reaching her. Then slowly everything began growing dark.

"She's convulsing," Elsie said, her voice rising slightly. "You," she spoke to the summer war chief who'd just come over, "get the children away from here. Send them home for today. And go phone the clinic. Tell them we're coming."

As the medicine man, Gus Sandoval, stepped forward, she shook her head. "Thank you, Gus, but we'll do this her way. I'm taking her to the public health clinic across from the pueblo."

"You'll need to have someone watch over her while you drive," Gus said quietly. "Go get your car. I'll stay here, then ride with you."

Elsie dashed off and returned only minutes later. To her surprise, the elderly medicine man lifted Kelly easily from the ground and carried her to the car.

"You better hurry," Gus said, laying Kelly gently on the back seat. "I've been watching her and I think I know what this is. Did she get sick right after she finished eating?"

Elsie nodded. She drove away quickly and turned the corner to circle around to the main entrance to the pueblo. "We'd just finished our sandwiches, and she seemed to go very pale all of a sudden and start perspiring."

"Did she have any pain?"

"Yes," Elsie explained the symptoms, never taking her eyes from the road.

"I'm almost certain that she's been poisoned by deadly nightshade. Some call it belladonna. Only a small pinch of dried leaf or berry is very poisonous. I use the herb for those who have bad stomachs, but only a very tiny amount. I was telling Pete Sorrelhorse a while ago that someone's been stealing herbs from my garden. Nightshade was one of those missing."

He shook his head. "Pete thinks my herbs are mostly weeds, but they're not. Every plant has its use, for the rituals or for medicine. When they're in the hands of someone ignorant or evil, they could be used to harm someone." He watched Kelly closely. "I'm afraid that's what's happened."

As Elsie pulled up in front of the public health clinic, people from the staff, already alerted by the summer war chief, came out to meet them. A tall nurse and a sturdy-looking orderly took Kelly inside on a gurney.

Elsie tried to go along, but the nurse stopped her. "No, we need some room to work. Can you tell me what led up to this?"

Elsie tried to give her all the details she could remember. Then Gus Sandoval interrupted, telling the nurse about the deadly nightshade that had been stolen and the danger from atropine and other alkaloids in the plant.

"Will the doctor arrive soon?"

The nurse shook her head. "The woman with her now is a nurse practitioner, and she's in contact with the doctors in Santa Fe. I'll tell her about the possibility of nightshade, then as soon as we can, we'll come out and give you a progress report."

After filling out the medical forms that seemed to be as common to Anglo medicine as the stethoscope, Elsie paced by the examining room door. The minutes continued to tick by. The medicine man sat quietly in a chair, either meditating or engaged in prayer. "I'm going to try to track down Justin Nakai," Elsie said. "He should know about this." She smiled at the elderly man, who looked up. "You've been a very big help, Gus. Thanks."

Just then, the young nurse came out. "Mr. Sandoval was right. It is indeed a case of nightshade poisoning, and we're treating her now."

"Will she be all right?"

"It's too soon for me to say, but the nurse practitioner will be out in a bit to talk to you. Does she have any relatives who should be notified?"

Elsie shook her head, then a tiny smile appeared at the corners of her mouth. "There's one friend, though, I think she'll want nearby."

"Then make sure that person knows she's going to have a very few rough hours ahead of her."

KELLY OPENED HER EYES slowly. The light hurt, and she quickly shut them again. "What happened?" Her throat was dry, and she was as tired as if she'd been running marathons across the hot desert.

"You've been very sick." Clarita Romero approached the bed and smiled at her. "But you'll be fine now."

She tried to clear her mind. "I was eating lunch with Elsie and..."

"Don't think about it now."

"What happened?" she insisted.

Clarita hesitated. Then Murray Sullivan knocked and entered the room. "They've found Justin Nakai. He's on his way over."

"Justin?" Kelly repeated. "What's going on?"

Clarita looked at Murray.

"It looks like someone slipped something toxic into your food, Kelly," Murray answered. "The medicine man said he was missing some dangerous herbs and it could be that one of them turned up in your lunch."

She stared at him numbly for several seconds. "Someone tried to poison me?"

"Yes, but I'm sure you're going to be all right now," Murray assured.

JUSTIN RETURNED to his car frustrated from a long morning's work that had turned up no new leads. Despite all the effort he'd put into the case, there was still no trace of John or his truck. Today he'd been fruitlessly searching the local auto repair shops to determine if any blue pickups had come in recently needing repairs or repainting.

Justin glanced at the list and started toward the next shop when his radio came alive. Kelly was at the public health clinic. The news that she'd been poisoned made his gut twist with anger and fear. If anything happened to her, he'd have only himself to blame. He should have forced her to tell him everything that she knew. Gunning the accelerator, he sped back to the pueblo, a prayer on his lips. *I've only just found you, schoolteacher. Don't leave me now.*

By the time he arrived, the remains of Kelly's sack lunch had already been taken to a prominent Santa Fe testing lab for analysis. Suazo stood at the door to the clinic.

"How's she doing?" Justin asked quickly.

"She's asleep now. Clarita Romero's sitting with her, but the nurse won't let anyone else in. She needs to rest for a few hours before they release her.''

"How long before the lab can give us some news on the poison?''

"At least an hour," Suazo answered. "I've asked the president of the Parents' Association to wait at the community center. I figured you might want to question her about the lunches.''

"Let's go," Justin said, with one last look toward the closed examining room door.

When they arrived at the community center minutes later, Justin could feel the tension in the air. Several worried faces stared up at him.

Suazo gestured for one young woman sitting near the kitchen doors to join them. "This is Mrs. Destea. She's head of the Parents' Association, and she planned the lunch program and distribution.''

Justin led her into an adjoining room. "Could you tell me how the lunches were prepared and by whom?''

She explained their lunch program, then added. "No parent would have put anything in those lunches. I guarantee it.''

"Were the bags labeled?''

"Yes, and right after we finished we placed them in the walk-in refrigerator. Anyone could have gone in there. People are always coming into this building to buy candy and sodas from the vending machines. And none of the doors are locked.''

Justin spoke to the two others, and after receiving substantially the same story from each, instructed Suazo to let everyone go home. As the room cleared, Suazo came and stood beside him.

"Now do you believe me?''

Justin glanced at him. "About what?''

Suazo gave him an incredulous look. "About the woman. She brings trouble, Nakai. Let me question her. If I talk to her before she's released from the public health center, she'll be easier to manage. It wouldn't be too hard to lean on her and get the full story. My bet's still that she really got poor John Romero all turned around.''

Justin said nothing. The thought occurred to him that Suazo seemed almost too eager to pin the recent trouble on John and blame John's actions on Kelly. The evidence was growing but Suazo's impatience with the case surprised him. It was out of character for anyone in law enforcement, and it was definitely out of character for a Tewa. Was Suazo trying to sweep everything under the table?

"So, shall I go talk to her at the clinic?''

"No." Justin stared across the desert mesa. "There's more here than appears at first glance. For instance, what happened today couldn't be connected to John. He would have been spotted, since everyone in the pueblo is on the lookout for him."

Suazo exhaled softly. "He could have sent someone."

"True, but we don't have any evidence to substantiate that."

"One thing, Nakai. The woman poses a danger here at the pueblo. Violence follows her. Legally we can't force her to stay away, but we have to do something."

"The woman is my concern," Justin answered flatly. "Yet you're right about the danger. For her own sake, I will recommend that she quit her work here for a while."

Suazo snorted. "That's one way of getting around the legalities."

"I'm going back to the clinic. By the way, Sergeant, could you make out a list of John Romero's enemies here at the pueblo?"

"Romero's?" Suazo shook his head. "He's well respected. I've never heard anyone speak badly about him."

"Everyone has enemies," Justin answered. "For instance, you aren't pleased with his plans for the future of the pueblo."

"Romero is opposed by quite a few of us who prefer the old ways."

"I want to know everything John is involved in, his business and his personal life."

"I can question others about his business," he answered, "but as far as the personal, you're on the way to speak to her now." He started to walk off then stopped and turned around. "By the way, Nakai. Consider this. If the woman finds you attractive, is she likely to tell you that your old friend was her lover and whether there was trouble between them?"

Justin's hands curled into fists, then he slowly forced his body to relax. Over the years he'd learned patience and endurance, and to deal with Suazo he'd need it all. He drove to the public health clinic and went inside.

Murray Sullivan looked surprised to see him, then quickly greeted him. "She's fine," he said without waiting for Justin to ask. "Clarita's helping her get dressed now. Will you be needing me for anything?"

"Not unless you saw something today that might help."

Murray considered it. "I went over to the community center at lunch to get a soft drink. Our machine at the bank was jammed. I spoke to Elsie and Kelly then, but nothing seemed unusual."

"When you went inside the building, did you see anyone hanging around?"

He mulled it over before answering. "One of the kids ran in to get a candy bar from the machine, and a couple of the parents came in, grabbed one of the trash bins and carried it outside. That's about it."

"Thanks, anyway. If you remember anything else, let me know."
Justin watched Murray hurry to his car, then drive away.

Clarita came out a minute later, leading a still-shaky Kelly. "Good, you're here. You can help me take her to our home."

Kelly smiled. "Thanks, but I think I should go back to my own house for a few days. I'll be fine. All I need is a few hours of sleep and I'll be as good as new."

"You shouldn't be alone," Clarita insisted. "You're weak and still in danger. Stay with us a bit longer."

"I need to be by myself now," she answered gently. "I don't understand what's been happening in my life lately, but I've got to be able to deal with it. I seem to be in danger wherever I am, so I might as well be at home."

Clarita nodded. "All right, I can understand how you feel." She turned Kelly over to Justin's care. "See her to her home then, and find a way to look after her."

"The Santa Fe police will be keeping an eye on her house, so don't worry. In a few days, when she's stronger, she can pick up her things at the pueblo." Justin placed his arm around Kelly's waist, then glanced at Clarita. "Come with us. I'll take you home, too."

Clarita shook her head. "I'm expected down the street at Maria's. Raymond's waiting. I'll see you later."

Justin led Kelly to his car without a word. His anger threatened to come spilling to the surface, so he opted for silence. He knew that his frustration was as much with himself as it was with her. They were halfway to her cottage when he finally spoke. "I want you to stop investigating and quit your teaching at the pueblo until this is over."

Kelly blinked and stared at him. "Are you crazy? I can't do that."

"The danger involves not only you, but those around you," he said bluntly.

She felt tears stinging her eyes, but refused to let her gaze drop. She cleared her throat, then once she felt sure her voice wouldn't betray her, continued. "I wouldn't do anything to endanger my students, and I think you know that. But those kids really need me. They get further and further behind in school because their reading skills aren't up to par, particularly in a difficult subject like science. If I were to quit, everyone would lose. And I'm not going to let anyone intimidate me into leaving." She brushed several stray locks of hair away from her face. "I will, though, take special precautions. You're right about that."

"This must be a first!" he said facetiously.

"Well, you do have good ideas from time to time," she smiled.

"From now on, I'll make sure I never leave the community center at the same time that the kids do. I'll also move back home permanently. Living at the Romero house exposes them to additional danger. I'll continue to visit them, of course. Clarita wants me there, and the family needs my support. Since we're all aware of the risks, though, we'd stay on our guard. There are a few other things I can do, too. I'll start bringing my own lunch and avoid outside gatherings."

"All good ideas, although lying low for a long time would still be the safest." Seeing her shake her head, he conceded. "Okay, then. But there are other things we'll have to do. I've arranged for off-duty police officers to watch your house for you round the clock."

"I'm living a nightmare," she said, her voice taut with emotion. "I wish I could go back to being what I am, a teacher."

"Someday, perhaps. But first you must stay alive."

Chapter Thirteen

"It's time to start doing everything I can to increase the odds in my favor." Kelly tried to keep her voice from shaking. "You've known all along that I've been keeping something back. The reason was that by telling you I believed I'd risk your life as well." She paused. "But I don't think I'm going to be able to shoulder this alone anymore. I'm afraid that next time they'll kill me."

"That's very possible," Justin answered. "I'm glad you've finally realized it."

"No more secrets then, but I warn you, you're going to be disappointed. My story doesn't have anything to do with John. It's also going to cost you. Once you know, you're at risk, too."

"I've suspected that you've been trying to protect me. But I'll be much better able to take care of myself, and you, if I know what I'm up against."

Kelly told him exactly what she'd seen that night in the arroyo. "The masks were the most frightening of all. Maybe it was the circumstances or the half-light, but the moment I saw them I felt terrified." She leaned back in her seat, weariness taking hold of her. "You know, there's one thing that's been driving me crazy. There was something very familiar about the voice of the person who shouted. But he spoke in Tewa and my knowledge of that language is very limited. I wish I'd been able to figure out what he said."

"Would you recognize the voice if you heard it again?" Justin parked in front of her home and walked inside with her.

The air was stale because the house had been kept closed. But the familiar atmosphere was welcoming nonetheless. "I'm almost certain I would." She gestured for him to sit with her on the couch. "So what's your opinion now that you've heard my story?"

"Are you sure you want to talk about this now?"

"Believe me, just sharing this with someone else has done more for me than you can ever know. I probably haven't done much for you, though. If they're after me because I intruded on a ritual, and they learn from your actions or questions that I've confided in you, you'll also be a target. They might even stop letting you search for John. That's what I've been most worried about. To make things worse, ever since we discovered that witchcraft was involved, I've wondered if what I saw that night was a conclave of witches."

He leaned back and stared pensively across the room. For several long moments, he said nothing. "I may be wrong about this, since the Navajo way is very different from that of the Pueblo. Still, I think your guess may be right. It doesn't seem likely that any legitimate religious society would try, without hesitation, to kill an intruder. At the very least, it seems to me, they'd have tried to establish your identity first."

"That makes sense to me. They couldn't have known that I wasn't someone from the tribe. Yet they didn't even stop to consider the possibility of forcing the intruder to join their society. I always understood that was the way it worked."

"Also, if it was a holy ritual, why wouldn't they have picked a spot like the kiva, where no outsiders were likely to intrude? Even if the central portion was being used there are *sipofenes*, the other rooms around the kiva, available for private rituals." He rubbed his chin pensively. "If they were witches, then that would also explain the mutilated bird you received." He looked at her. "Of course, this is all speculation based on our limited knowledge of the Pueblo. With so much secrecy surrounding their beliefs and ways, it's hard to really make any conclusions."

"How can we find out?" she said, leaning forward. "Is there someone on the pueblo we can trust to talk to?"

"I could try to ask Suazo, but I doubt he'll tell me much. Those aren't subjects the sergeant will want to discuss with anyone. I think we'll have to depend on finding our own answers."

"For now, can you keep what I told you about that night between us?" she asked hesitantly.

"Yes, but if this turns out to be directly related to what's happened, you'll have to bring it all out into the open."

"If it becomes necessary, I'll do that." She tucked her legs beneath her. "I guess now you see what I've been trying to tell you all along. My story has nothing to do with John and brings you no closer to finding him."

"Is it possible that he was one of the people you saw there that night?"

"Not a chance," she answered flatly. "If you think that, then you must have forgotten everything you ever knew about John. He would never have gone along with attempted murder—for any reason."

An unbearable heaviness settled over him as he found himself wishing the evidence were less convincing. Wishing he could remain as staunch an ally of his missing friend as she had. "What you've told me sheds an entirely new light on this case. Suazo is a police officer, but he's also a member of the Pueblo. We don't know yet if he's involved in what you saw that night or not, so his participation in this case will have to become more limited. And I can't bring any Anglo cops in on this to help me out without alienating our potential witnesses. So it's going to be you and me. The rules we agreed on before still apply. Before you do anything, you check with me. Just remember that your life's at stake."

"That's not something I'm bound to forget," she answered softly. "Particularly not after today."

KELLY, IMPATIENT with herself, returned to her classes the very next day. The episode with the nightshade had left her with a tendency to tire quickly but otherwise, by the afternoon, she felt almost back to normal.

Justin drove up to the community center and slowed by the entrance doors. Spotting him, Kelly strode out to meet him. Everyone else had long since gone. According to her plan, she'd leave an hour or more after the kids from now on. The extra time would give her a chance to grade papers. Consequently, she wouldn't have to do much work at home.

"Where are we going?" she asked. "I got the message that you wanted to pick me up after work."

"First, I wanted to tell you that I got the lab results on the belladonna in your food. It was a synthetic form used in medicine. The pharmacist says it's prescribed fairly frequently for a variety of ailments. Prescription records are confidential though, so until we get a suspect we can't check it out further."

"Terrific. You have any more great news?" she muttered.

"No more news, only a request. I need you to guide me to the arroyo where you saw the men that night. Do you think you could find it again?"

She considered it. "I think so, but I won't know until I try. I was lost and scared at the time. Those roads back there all seem to turn right back in on each other like a giant maze." She pursed her lips, then grew determined. "Let's give it a try. Maybe if I see it I'll be able to recall something else that could help."

They traveled to the Black Mesa, taking the photograph they had found as a guide. Twenty minutes later they were in the right area, based on the photographic evidence. "This is one of the sacred hills of the Pueblo. When did you discover that you'd taken the wrong turn?"

"I saw the shrine." Her hands began to tremble slightly, but she forced them to be still. As they approached the crossroads, she said, "Go to the left. I remember always turning toward the sunset at first."

Justin followed her instructions. If this worked, perhaps they'd find something at the site that would furnish a clue.

It wasn't long before they found the arroyo. "This is it," Kelly said, sounding both excited and tense. "I drove down here, then stopped. I saw them just ahead. There was a lantern in the middle, where the man was lying down." She described the scene again, trembling as she recounted the story.

"Let's go take a look around."

"Are you sure?" She gave him a worried look.

"It's okay. Pueblo land isn't closed now, and besides there's no one around here for miles." He drove a bit farther into the wash. "We'll leave the car here, and continue on foot." He gave her a thoughtful look. "If you want, you can wait for me here. I can certainly understand how you feel about this place."

She took a deep breath. "I'm going."

Justin smiled despite himself. "You don't have to prove anything to me," he said gently.

"I'm not," she replied. "I'm doing this for myself. I can't let fear dictate what I do. If I give in to that, I've lost no matter what happens."

He nodded. "I understand."

"The ground's still damp from that big rain we just had. If there ever were any distinctive tracks out there, they'll be gone now," she commented.

"Tell me again what you saw," he said, walking down the arroyo, "and where the people were standing."

Guided by her words, Justin searched the ground for any evidence that might have been left behind. After a while, he glanced up. "The sun's starting to set."

"I know," she answered, her voice taut. "Look, maybe this is going to sound dumb, but I don't want to be here after dark. If those people come back..."

"That's not likely. It would be too risky for them to return after what happened." He started toward the car with her. "Still, we've done what we came here to do. No sense in hanging around."

Justin led her to the car, then slipped behind the wheel. "How about having dinner with me?" He put the vehicle into gear and pressed down gently on the accelerator. The wheels spun, but the car remained exactly where it was. "Great. Mud. Just what we need," he muttered, easing off the gas.

He let off the brake slowly, hoping the car would inch forward and build momentum slowly on the power of the engine in gear. Nothing happened. The car was stuck.

"Maybe I can rock us back and forth out of these holes the tires have dug in the mud. Hang on!" Quickly changing back and forth between forward and reverse with the automatic transmission, Justin tried to extract the car from the bog. But without traction the effort was futile. "I'm going to grab a shovel from the back and try to dig us out. At this point, that's our best shot."

Kelly got out with him and watched as he pulled off his bolo tie and rolled up his sleeves. "I'm sorry, this is my fault," he said. "I didn't realize it was this muddy at the bottom. The wind has blown some dry sand over the top of the worst spots."

He tried to level out the ground in front of the tires, but every time he extracted a shovel full of mud, more would slide in to replace it. After several moments he placed the shovel down on the ground. "This isn't going to work."

"What about gathering scrub brush and placing it down in front of the tires?" she asked hurriedly, glancing at the setting sun.

"With the ground beneath the tires this wet, it'd just sink down and get us in deeper." Justin crouched by the back and silently considered his options. "The muddy spot isn't such a large area, it's just a low place where all the water seems to have collected. I think the easiest thing to do is wait until morning. Once the sun comes back out and the temperature soars, this will dry quickly. It's a matter of waiting it out."

"What about your radio?" She paced nervously, her eyes darting up and down the arroyo.

"It doesn't have the range to reach the relay point in Santa Fe from here, and I don't want to try to reach Suazo." He gathered her into his arms. "Nothing will happen to you. I give you my word." His voice was husky as he brushed her forehead with a kiss. "Besides, the desert is a wonderful place by moonlight. Have you ever gone camping?''

She chuckled. ''Actually, no. I'm more the type who enjoys modern conveniences like soft beds and bathtubs.''

''It can be very beautiful out here once the moon is up. There're no streetlights to get in the way of the stars. Even the sounds are different.'' He began to gather small, dry twigs and branches. ''I'll start a fire. One bad thing about desert nights. Although it may peak in the nineties during the day, it can drop to the forties at night.''

''I've got a few candy bars in my purse,'' she offered, sitting on the ground in a dry spot. ''There's not much in the way of dinner, but they'll taste good.'' She rummaged through her purse and brought out two peanut butter cups, a chocolate caramel bar and a small bag of peanuts. ''This is what I've got to share,'' she said teasingly, ''but what are you contributing?''

He started to smile, but then forced himself to grow serious. Wordlessly he walked to the car and returned holding a blanket. He sat near her, the blanket before him. ''My blanket and my warmth,'' he murmured. ''They might appeal to you tonight, after it gets cold.''

Even before I'm cold, she thought. Vivid images rushed into her head, and she felt herself blushing.

Justin smiled, and her heart practically stopped. She handed him the chocolate caramel bar. Breaking it in two, he offered one piece to her.

Her hand trembled slightly as she took it from him, and he smiled noticing it. ''I know what Pueblo life is like from my own experiences,'' she added quickly, ''but what's it like to grow up as a Navajo?''

''It's very different from the Pueblo, I can tell you that. I grew up back in Shiprock, on the reservation. You know where that is?''

She nodded. ''By the Four Corners, north of Gallup. I've been through there a few times.''

''Well, my dad ran a service station near the San Juan River bridge. He worked there until his death, just a few years ago. My mom spend her life working as a teacher at the BIA boarding school on the mesa at Shiprock. During the winters we lived in the valley in an old stucco house close to Shiprock High School. When summers came, my dad would take all of us into the Chuska Mountains to an old hogan near Washington Pass. The place has been in our family for generations. Dad felt it would help my brother, sister and me get in touch with our heritage. He was proud to be a Navajo, and he wanted us to feel that way, too.'' Justin finished his share of the candy bar in one bite.

"I guess I got my desire to see new places and people from him. We'd travel to see relatives almost everywhere we had some."

Kelly longed to respond to his confidences in kind. "I'm not a very good traveler. My home is very special to me. I've filled it with things that I value and that mean something special to me. It's my nest."

"It was different traveling with family and going to stay with relatives. I guess you could call it a 'floating nest.' Anyway, back then I learned to be comfortable with myself no matter where I was."

As darkness descended around them, the light from their fire danced and glittered against the shrubs in the wash. Justin draped his jacket around Kelly's shoulders, then placed his pistol and holster on a flat rock beside him.

A coyote's long piercing wail sent a chill to the base of her neck. Kelly glanced around and shivered. "It sounds so lonely and sad."

"According to Navajo legends, coyotes are a sign of witchcraft. A Navajo who's led an evil life is believed to become a coyote after death." His voice trailed off. "Personally I doubt that very many Navajos believe that story anymore, but even so, most would never talk about it."

"What do you believe?"

He shrugged, but didn't answer right away. "Even though I live and work primarily in the world of the whites, I still retain the essence of much of what I was taught. Our ways become a part of who we are. In the Navajo language there is no equivalent word for *religion*. The reason is that to us it isn't something that exists independently of a person. The foundation of our beliefs encompasses everything about us. It's living life, searching for the patterns that give it harmony. It's accepting evil because it's part of every man. Then, by understanding its place in the scheme of things, we learn to defeat it in others and overcome it in ourselves." He smiled. "It's hard to speak about these things."

Yet he had. By that one action he'd shown her how much he'd come to care about her, and to trust her. "Thank you," she answered softly.

He leaned back, stretching out on the ground and guiding her to lie against him. He brought her lips to his.

His kiss was soft at first, neither urging or coaxing. Her heart leaped to life and a slow tendril of heat began to wind its way through her. She parted her lips slightly and slid her tongue forward to tease his.

With a groan he pulled her even closer. His mouth smothered hers, a raw urgency tugging at his restraint. She moaned softly.

His tongue invaded her mouth with a fierce male aggressiveness.

As his hand reached to stroke her breast, she cried out and pressed herself into the kiss. His thumb traced circles of fire over her aching nipple. Hungrily he drank in the small cries that left her throat, as her body responded to his.

"Tell me you need me, schoolteacher, as much as I need you," he said in a husky voice. "Say it."

She had just started to answer when a loud thump shattered the moment.

"What the—" Justin moved to one side and saw a fireball arc across the sky toward them.

Chapter Fourteen

Grabbing Kelly's hand, Justin pulled her behind a large outcropping of rocks.

"What was that?"

"Someone's using burning arrows. He's already hit the car," Justin replied. Spotting the glow of a small fire, he managed to approximate the location of their enemy. He fired several shots in that direction, then muttered an oath. "The camp fire made us easy targets before, but now we're going to make the game tougher for him."

She peered around the side of the boulder. "The brush around the tires is starting to burn."

"Don't worry. I don't think it can spread. Everything is still too wet." He watched and prayed that none of the flames would get near the gas tank. "Stay here. I'm going to work my way around to the other side of the car and try to reach the radio. We can't call anyone from here, but it might come in handy later."

He crouched low, taking advantage of the shadows, and stayed as far away from their camp fire as possible. Several feet from the car, he suddenly bolted forward. Justin jerked the passenger's door open, dove inside the back seat and quickly switched off the dome light. Several more arrows thumped into the car body as he reached over to the front and tried to find the radio he'd left there.

He felt a thump beside his arm, then heat singed his skin. He yanked his arm back, realizing that one of the flaming arrows had lodged in the front seat of the car. As the smell of burning upholstery stung his nostrils he quickly edged back out of the car. He'd managed to go about fifty feet when the interior of the car exploded in flames behind him.

He barely had time to gather his thoughts when he saw Kelly come out of cover and start running for the car. "No! Stay down!"

His voice reached her, and she stopped. The camp fire illuminated her clearly. An instant later an arrow flashed by, missing her only by inches.

Justin dove toward Kelly, pushing her to the ground. "Why didn't you stay where I told you? You could have been killed!"

She saw another flaming arrow land only inches from where she'd been standing and imbed itself into the ground almost to the vanes. "Is it them?"

"I don't know," Justin replied, needing no explanation as to whom she meant. Glancing around to determine his next move, he realized that the tops of the scrub brush that lined the wash were beginning to burn. Although chances were they were still too moist to burn near the ground, the fire was spreading from bush to bush. Soon the heat would dry them all out and they would burn completely. "We have to get away from here. The spring winds blow tumbleweeds into the arroyo and there's a whole pile of them farther down. If those catch on fire, they'll cut off our escape route." His eyes darted around the arroyo. "Besides, once the fire is all around us, we're going to become easy targets."

"We have no other place to go except farther down the wash. He's waiting for us at this end," said Kelly, trying to keep her whispered voice steady.

"Then we'll have to go for it." Justin urged her on, then saw that the tumbleweeds ahead were turning into a roaring wall of fire.

"We're trapped in the middle." Kelly turned her face away from the searing heat. "I've got an idea. The ground's really wet on the left side of the arroyo. Remember how we got stuck? Let's work our way across. If we risk moving closer to the fire, we might throw them off guard. We could also try to find a place to dig in and hold out."

"He'll be looking for us to try to get away from the fire, not head right into the hottest part of it. It might work. I just hope we can get enough air."

Staying in the shadows, they crawled across the muddy arroyo carefully avoiding the fire that was quickly encircling them. Justin placed a hand on Kelly's shoulder. "Let me scout ahead," he whispered. "I think I see something that might help."

"Be careful."

"Always," he replied. He moved forward slowly, his pistol and holster clipped onto his belt near his hip pocket. A few feet before him he could see a small, shallow pool of water. No bushes had burned there. Reaching the side of the wash, he inspected a shadowed spot the rain water had undercut. It wasn't very big, but a cave had been formed right into the wall of the arroyo by waters that had rushed down the wash and eroded away the soft sandstone. He studied the place for a moment, then returned for Kelly. "Come on. I've found a safe spot."

They made their way through the cold, ten-inch-deep puddle of water and arrived at the undercut feature Justin had found.

Kelly looked at the low indentation cut into the side of the wash and then back at him. "This isn't a cave. This is a hole. We won't survive in there."

"There're still puddles of water around here, and the brush is too wet to burn. We'll crawl in there and hide behind as much of the wet brush as we can scavenge. We'll be fine."

Kelly saw the line of fire drawing near. "I hope you're right," she said softly.

A few minutes later they were huddled inside the opening. They had soaked Justin's jacket, and were ready to hold it over their faces if necessary to protect their lungs from the heat and smoke. Justin's arms were around her tightly. "We'll get out of this alive, I promise," he whispered in her ear.

She wanted to answer, but her voice failed her. Instead she shifted slightly and buried herself in his embrace. The cold steel of the gun he held in one hand grazed her skin, and she shivered.

"It's okay," he whispered. "I love you. I won't let anything take you from me."

The crackling of the exploding tumbleweeds nearby almost masked his words. Had she heard him right? She wasn't sure. As the sounds came closer, he tightened his hold and pressed a kiss against her forehead.

Kelly wasn't sure how long they'd stayed in there. Hours turned into eternities. She'd dozed off, the smoke stinging her nostrils and making her dizzy from lack of oxygen. Then she'd woken up in the throes of a nightmare only to hear Justin's voice soothing and reassuring her.

A lifetime later, she opened her eyes and saw light filtering through the singed brush covering the entrance to their sanctuary. The soft golden glow was not of fire, but sunlight.

"We made it, I think," she whispered cautiously. Justin didn't say anything for a moment, and she thought her heart would stop. "Justin?"

He shifted and took a deep breath. "I'm okay," he said. "I've been listening for two hours now. If there's anyone out there, I haven't heard them." Gingerly he moved toward the opening and peered out. The area surrounding them was a macabre blend of light and dark grays. The singed ground still smoldered in spots, yet for several feet to either side of them the plants and the ground remained untouched. "I'm going outside." He handed her his pistol and showed her how to switch off the safety. "Keep this with you."

"You'll need it more than I do."

"I have a backup." He reached into his boot. "Please, for once, stay here and do what I tell you."

She nodded. "Whatever you say."

Justin glanced around before emerging. The wash was devoid of cover now, save for a few large rocks. Carefully he ventured out. No one was around now. Their assailant had probably given them up for dead.

Returning to Kelly's side, he helped her out of the recess in the arroyo wall. "We'll be all right. We're alone."

"In the middle of nowhere. Without a car." She gave him a wide smile. "But you know what? I don't care. All that matters is that we're both alive! If we made it through last night, we can survive anything."

He smiled. "Don't get cocky, we're not out of this yet." He studied the desert around them. "The first thing I'd like to do is search the area for clues. Whoever it was left us for dead, so he might have grown careless. Afterward we'll start hiking back to the pueblo."

"How long a walk is that?" she asked warily, trying to remember how far they'd come.

"A *very* long one. The way I figure, we're a good ten miles from the nearest gas station."

She nodded, then shrugged. "So, I'll need new shoes by the time we get there. Maybe new feet. Or maybe just a foot massage," she added playfully, giving him a hopeful look.

"We'll discuss it after I see what you have to trade."

She laughed. "Oh-oh. That sounds ominous."

"Not to me. I'm a good negotiator."

He grew serious as he approached what was left of their car. "What a mess!" he muttered. The interior was charred beyond recognition. Traces of chrome and painted steel remained around a blackened metal shell. The foul smell of smoldering rubber and vinyl drove them back. He crouched by the rear and retrieved an arrow from the ground underneath. The projectile had missed and passed beneath the car. Justin rolled the black painted arrow between his thumb and forefinger, then stopped as he saw the smoke-smudged green and yellow stripes on the shaft. One of the three charred turkey-feather vanes was red.

Kelly looked over her shoulder, her throat so tight she could barely breathe. Could it be that she'd been wrong about John? As soon as she finished the thought, guilt overcame her. If she started to believe it, then she wasn't much of a friend.

Grateful, she noticed Justin didn't bring it up, either. "There are footprints over here," she said as she scrambled up the steep sides of the arroyo.

Justin followed. "There were two men," he said studying the tracks. "I recognize one of these sets of footprints. They're paratrooper boots."

She turned away, but said nothing, pretending to look around for more tracks. "Look, there are some tire marks here."

Justin studied them for a while longer, then stood. "Let's start back. We should get going before it becomes really hot."

She nodded. She wanted to get as far away from this place as possible.

As they headed away from the arroyo, Kelly spotted a cairn of rocks to one side. "It's a shrine," she said softly. Backing away from it, they continued walking toward the open desert.

Cutting cross-country through the empty stretches of land was hot, consuming work. "It's rough going now, but in the long run this will take us to the highway much more quickly," Justin explained, seeing her struggle just to keep going. Exhaustion and the relentless heat were beginning to take their toll.

"I'll be fine," she answered. "I just wish the day hadn't begun so warmly, though. Maybe the afternoon rains will help." They might also be able to get some drinking water then; her mouth was infernally dry.

As they made their way, her mind drifted to what he'd said the evening before. It had been such a desperate moment for both of them. Even if she'd heard him right, and she wasn't at all sure she had, his words of love might have been meant only to comfort. Still, despite logic, a spark of hope burned within her.

"You know what your problem is?" Justin said without looking over at her. "You expend too much energy when you walk. You travel across the land as if you're attacking every step. God help you if you ever needed to hunt for food. With all the noise you make, the game would run for cover miles before you could get near."

She recognized his tactic immediately. He was trying to distract her from the grueling trek. It seemed almost ironic that despite all his powers of observation, he hadn't realized that his presence was enough to do that. "What do you mean I expend too much energy? Walking's walking."

"Ah, a philosopher," he teased. He grasped her by the shoulders. "Try to coordinate your movements so that you flow more. Avoid those swaying motions with your hands. Conserve your energy."

"Okay, but even if I did that, how would it help me get near game?" she countered. "I'm pretty big in comparison to the landscape around here and they can spot me easily."

"Animals usually have a very keen sense of hearing and smell, but quite a few are nearsighted. They see movement, but not details. So if the animal turns in your direction, the best thing to do is freeze. Also, you try to approach with the wind in your face, like we did up at John's cabin. If you see an animal from upwind and it hasn't noticed you yet, then you try to make a circle around it. Use whatever cover the terrain provides, like rocks and shrubs as you make your approach. Stay aware, though, that your shadow can give you away, and stick close to your cover so that its shadow blends with yours."

He stopped and pointed ahead. "We're facing the wind now, what there is of it," he said. "There's a skunk over there in that brush, probably hunting for mice and insects. Want to give it a try?"

"Not on your life!" she answered laughing. "That's all I need now!"

"Coward." He laughed and added, "Now watch a master at work."

Kelly watched him merge with the landscape as he stalked the creature for the next few minutes. His movements were subtle and his approach silent. He got within ten feet then stopped. The animal moved away, continuing across the mesa, foraging for food.

When the animal was out of his sight, he signaled for her to join him. "Now that you've been suitably impressed," he joked, "we can go on."

"I bet you learned that as a Navajo boy."

He grinned. "Well, you're half right. I was a kid when I learned it in the Boy Scouts." He pointed ahead. "We'll be reaching the highway soon. Maybe we'll catch a ride."

"I didn't realize we'd covered so much ground," she answered, surprised.

"We've been moving in this direction all along," he said. They reached the main road leading to the highway ten minutes later. Suddenly Justin slowed his pace. "There's a vehicle coming."

128   *Black Mesa*

"Where?" As she finished the word, she saw the traces of dust flying, then a car appeared. "How did you hear that?" He was as suited for the wilds of the desert as any creature whose survival depended on instinct.

He glanced over at her, and smiled. "How did you manage not to?" He waited a moment then added, "It's Suazo." He tensed slightly. "Now what's he doing out here?"

Chapter Fifteen

Suazo's vehicle turned abruptly and headed straight for them, raising a cloud of dust.

They had no place to run. Kelly could see Justin place his hand on the grip of his pistol.

Just when it seemed Suazo was about to run them over, he swerved again and skidded to a stop a dozen feet away. Grinning widely, Suazo glanced from one of them to the other. "What on earth are you two doing out here?" he asked. "And where's your car?"

After hearing their story, Suazo drove them back to the site. It took less than ten minutes in his vehicle. "Before we get rain, or the wind comes up, I'm going to take some photographs of the area."

Kelly sighed. "Afterward could you please take me back to the community center? I left my car there, and I'd really appreciate the lift."

Suazo glanced at Justin. "That's not my job. I've got to head back to my office."

Justin, in the front seat with Suazo, glanced back at her. "Let me see what I can do once we get there."

Suazo parked near the rim of the arroyo, then gave a low whistle. "Damn! It looks like you were hit by an air strike. There's not much left, is there?" he asked rhetorically, indicating the burned-out car.

Justin walked with Suazo as he inspected the area and took photos of everything. Kelly followed. "These footprints," Suazo commented, "are the same ones the sniper left behind."

Justin nodded. "There're two sets of footprints this time, though."

Suazo studied the second set. "It's one big man, considering the shoe size." He walked back to where an arrow was imbedded in the sand and pulled it out to examine. "You know who this belongs to?"

Seeing Justin nod, he continued. "John Romero is being implicated in a lot of things."

"When we went up to his cabin, I noticed that the bow John used was gone and only unusable arrows had been left behind. I guess this is what happened to the rest," Justin observed.

"First we find his hunting rifle at the site where the sniper had been, then later his knife, and now these arrows." Suazo shook his head. "And there's the matter of a blue pickup being responsible for the accident you had," he said, turning to Kelly. "John's pickup is blue."

Kelly, hearing Suazo's comment about the rifle, stood dumbfounded, unable to take anything else in. Justin hadn't told her about that all the time he'd insisted on having *her* cooperation. Anger welled up inside her.

Then, as she stared at him, images of last night, when he'd saved her life, replayed in her mind. Slowly her resentment subsided.

Her gaze fell upon one of the shiny black arrows with its yellow and green stripes. Had John been one of the men in the arroyo that night? Had his allegiance to whatever rite she'd intruded upon been so great that it had offset their friendship? She just didn't know anymore. The thought that her own life could depend on finding enough evidence to convict a dear friend filled her with sorrow. Of course, there was another more alarming possibility. Had John stumbled upon the same group she had? If they had caught him and were trying to frame him, then he was in even worse trouble than she was. She and Justin would have to move fast. Time was slipping through their fingers.

Justin continued his conversation with Suazo, his face an impenetrable mask. Pursuing his friend had to be taking its toll on him, yet he still managed to cope. Maybe he could help her come to terms with the heartbreaking revelations they were finding at every turn.

Suazo strode past her. "Come on. I'll take you to your car. You've been staring at me for the past twenty minutes, and I'm tired of it."

Suazo's statement took her completely by surprise. She followed him to the car, Justin a few steps behind her. Had she actually made Suazo feel guilty, or was there really some compassion in the man after all? Too tired to speculate, she leaned back in the seat and looked forward to being home.

THE NEXT AFTERNOON Kelly stood in front of her students. With all the excitement and gossip surrounding John's disappearance, the kids had been barely manageable. She could sense their frustration and desire to get involved. Afraid trouble would follow their exuberance, she formulated a plan. After class was over she asked five of her best students to remain behind.

"I've heard everyone talking about getting involved in what's been happening here at the pueblo. You, Henrietta, said that if it threatened your family and friends, you had a right to do something about it."

Henrietta turned scarlet and stared at the floor. "I still believe that, Ms. Ferguson."

"We all do," Pete added. "We don't like the way everyone's going around being afraid. That's not the way things are supposed to be."

Eugene chuckled cynically. "Welcome to the real world, dweeb."

"Hey! Come over here and say that!"

"I don't need to. I can take you anytime."

"Both of you! That's enough!" Kelly glared at one, then the other. "I'm going to give all of you a chance to do something. Do you want to help or not?"

Five eager heads all nodded at once.

"You're going to have to work together as a team. That might be hard for some of you. If there's anyone here who can't handle that, leave now, and there'll be no hard feelings." No one moved and Kelly suppressed a smile.

"What I want you to do is very important, but requires only that you stay alert. Don't go looking for trouble. Never put yourself into any danger! All of you wander around the pueblo during the day, playing, visiting, working. I want to know if you see or hear of anything suspicious. The best way of doing that is to do ordinary things and to watch and listen."

"We've been doing that all along," Pete, nicknamed Big'uns for his wide girth, confessed. "Sludge and I have, that is. We thought we could help everyone that way, and maybe things would get back to normal."

Eugene, who'd lived in a rough section of Albuquerque for several years and acquired "street smarts," met her eyes. "To be honest, I have, too. Only I was doing it on my own. I thought maybe I could find out something the grown-ups couldn't. No one notices kids, unless we're doing something wrong or we want them to notice us."

"Well, Henrietta and I haven't done anything," Loretta said, "but we'll start."

"Just remember. The trick is to listen. Asking questions won't do any good. You won't get the kind of answers we're looking for. Besides, at this point it's not what a person says, but what he or she does that will make a difference.''

"Don't worry. We know what to do," Pete said.

Kelly watched her students get organized. The leaders, Pete Aguilar and Eugene Blackhorse, made sure that kids would be spread all over the pueblo.

"Remember, your jobs are to watch and listen. *That's all.*" She paused. "You're my most trustworthy students, and I've got to know I can count on you to do it my way."

Eugene Blackhorse nodded. "I'll make sure of it."

Kelly met his eyes and saw the determination reflected there. She'd chosen well.

JUSTIN SAT ACROSS Murray Sullivan's desk, notebook on his lap. "Right now I'm trying to piece together everything about John's life prior to his disappearance. You can help by telling me about the kind of business he transacted here."

"As I told you before, John's my friend and I'll do whatever I can. I see Clarita every day, and I can't stand to see what this is doing to her."

Justin didn't comment. "John is in charge of the pueblo accounts, is that correct?" he prodded.

"Yes, we invest the pueblo's money but John's the one who holds the purse strings, so to speak." He stood up. "Look, I'll be honest with you. I don't really know much about this aspect of it. Let me introduce you to Russell Bench. He's the vice president of the bank and he handles those transactions." Murray walked to the door, then stopped. "You might want to meet our tellers, too. John was always taking time to talk to them, and they're in a position to know just about everything that happens here."

"That sounds good."

The two tellers on duty, both Pueblo women, were friendly, but regarded him with caution. Learning that one of them was on her way to the community center for soft drinks, he gave her a note to deliver to Kelly. In it he asked that she meet him at the bank at the end of her classes. He was hoping their experience in the arroyo had triggered some more memories.

"Who's the gentleman in the office over there?" Justin asked, walking on with Murray. "Is this your assistant manager?" Justin indicated a tall, heavy-set man with thinning hair at one of the cubicle desks.

"Oh no, he's Hamilton Clymer, a prominent Santa Fe businessman. He owns The Sandstone, one of the finest art galleries on the plaza. He has an account here and conducts business with many of the Pueblo artisans."

Murray led him through a long corridor, then to an office at the other end of the bank. Knocking on the door, he walked in. "Russell, this is Justin Nakai."

Bench, a middle-aged Anglo about Justin's height, stood and extended his hand. "What can we do for you today, Mr. Nakai?" His eyebrows furrowed, then a flash of recognition crossed his features. "Nakai, you said? As in the FBI agent?"

Justin showed Bench his identification and badge. "I'd like to ask you a few questions about John Romero," he said formally.

"I'm not sure how I'll be able to help you," he answered guardedly.

"I've told Agent Nakai that this bank would cooperate fully," Murray said sharply.

Bench opened his hands and turned his palms up, in a gesture of confusion. "I'll do my best."

"I've got to go back to my desk." Murray gave Bench a long look, then glanced at Justin. "If you have any problems, you know where my office is."

Russell waited until Murray disappeared down the hall. "Well, that certainly leaves no doubt as to what he wants me to do. The only problem is that I have no idea where John is. Frankly I don't see how I could help you."

"Tell me about the investment projects John and you were working on."

He hesitated. "This is confidential?"

"Of course."

"We had a number of financial ventures pending. Foremost in John's mind though, was securing some government money he'd applied for. The bank could have then made special, low-interest loans to off-pueblo tribal members. That would have enabled them to build homes on property adjacent to tribal land. John wanted to see Indians populating the areas bordering San Esteban. In effect it would have made the pueblo boundaries larger, though legally, of course, they would remain the same."

"It sounds like a very good idea. He must have had a great deal of support here."

"Some, but he also made enemies. Sergeant Suazo of the tribal police led a faction which felt the land was best left undeveloped, even by tribal members. The pueblo leases that land from the state and since the terms aren't really specified, the tribe is free to do whatever it wants with it. Suazo's group felt that developing the land would also bring Anglos into the area and end up disturbing the privacy of the pueblo.''

"He had a point, I imagine."

"John didn't agree. He felt that the pueblo would benefit from becoming less isolated. The businesses here would grow, and the entire tribe would prosper. Their customs could still remain intact, as long as their children were raised to adhere to them." Bench shrugged. "John never considered the Anglo culture a threat. He saw it as an excellent way of showing Pueblo kids the richness of their own heritage. He figured that any comparison would weigh in their favor."

Justin smiled despite himself. That sounded precisely like the John he knew. Practical, and perhaps just a trace arrogant about his race. "What's the status of the project so far?"

Bench rubbed the back of his neck with one hand. "Without John, that deal is going to fall through. The bank needs him to complete the paperwork he started and to sign the necessary forms. Unless he returns in the next few days there won't be time to secure the money while the funds are still available."

So now there was a new angle. Suazo stood to benefit by keeping John out of the way. Of course this still didn't constitute proof, only more grounds for speculation. "What part did Murray play in these transactions?"

"Murray and John are friends, but all financial negotiations are my department."

So, if Bench was right, Sullivan was an administrator and a figurehead. The real power rested with the man before him. "How well do you know John, outside of business, that is."

"Not very well at all." He started to say something, then clamped his mouth shut.

"What were you about to say?" Justin prodded.

Bench shook his head. "Forget it. Sullivan's my boss. If I get him angry, I'm the only one who's going to lose."

"Sullivan's not in the room," Justin answered quietly. "If it's something pertaining to my investigation, it would be better to tell me now."

Bench held up one hand. "Okay, just don't let him know I told you this," he said, then continued. "For a while now, I've been worried that John may have been involved in other financial activities the bank knew nothing about. I haven't got any real evidence against him, and that's why I've kept my mouth shut. I didn't want to approach Murray with something like this unless I could back up my suspicions."

"What exactly do you mean?" Justin queried.

"John's personal account has quite a large balance. The pueblo account he was managing, on the other hand, seems to have experienced a series of setbacks. There have been several large withdrawals made from it recently. I strongly suspect John's been transferring tribal funds into his own account." He stood and began to pace. "A few days before he disappeared, John walked into my office and caught me going over the tribal records. I'm afraid my expression might have given me away, and somehow he guessed what I was doing." He shook his head slowly. "Now that he's disappeared, it just makes me wonder even more."

"Did he withdraw another large sum prior to that?"

"Not that I personally know of, but he may have had accounts elsewhere too, who knows?" Bench returned to his desk. "Look, I've said too much already."

"How about letting me look at the bank's records?"

Bench stared at him coldly. "I can't do that, not without a court order or permission from the pueblo governor. I'd lose my job for sure. And just between the two of us, if you want to really get the Pueblo set against you, asking to examine their books is one way to do it."

Justin stood up and shook Bench's hand. "That's something to consider. Thanks for your candor. I'll be in touch."

As he strode down the hallway, Sullivan came toward him. "I was just going to check on how you two were getting along. Bench can be a bit of a pain at times, but he's a good man."

Justin nodded. "I've asked Kelly Ferguson to meet me here at the bank. Has she arrived?"

"Right here," a familiar voice replied. She strode toward them. Her light cotton dress flowed smoothly over the graceful curve of her breasts. Her hips swayed ever so slightly, causing a stirring in his groin. The woman would embarrass him yet, unless he did something about the feelings building inside him.

"You know, I've passed by this bank often, but I never realized how nice it is in here." She glanced at the flowering potted plants near the doors and the fresh-cut flowers that were placed by each of the tellers' windows.

"We like to show our bank off, Kelly," Murray said. "Why don't you both come by tomorrow and I'll have Russ Bench give you a tour?'' he turned to Justin. "Seeing how everything runs in a financial institution might also give you a clearer view of the way John worked with us.''

"I'd love to come," Kelly answered.

Justin smiled. "So would I. So it looks like we'll be here." He wondered if Murray knew *anything* about the bank's operations.

Kelly and Justin walked out of the bank into the hot desert air. "What did you find out at the bank? Anything interesting?" she asked.

He recounted what he'd learned from Bench.

"John wouldn't steal money from the pueblo," she scoffed, then gave him an incredulous look. "You know the man. Money meant nothing to him. His whole life-style and beliefs were centered on the welfare of the tribe.''

"I don't know what's going on, but I do know this." He stopped by his car, then stood in front of her. "These attempts on your life have got to stop. The best way I know to do that is to find John, and that's exactly what I intend to do.''

"We're uncovering clues someone wants us to find," she commented thoughtfully. "But it's what we're not meant to see that's important.''

Justin gave her a sad smile. "Your loyalty speaks well for you. I'd value a friend like you who'd be on my side no matter what was going on.''

"You have one," she answered softly. "Me.''

Justin sat behind the driver's seat, his gaze locking with hers for one breathless moment. Then, out of the corner of his eye, he saw Suazo drive by slowly. Justin turned his head, and Suazo nodded in return.

For the moment the spell was broken. A twinge of sadness crept through her. She turned her thoughts back to the business at hand. "By the way, I haven't been able to remember anything more about that night in the arroyo. Maybe by now Clarita and Maria have recalled something that might be helpful, however. I'll speak to them and see.''

"That sounds good. In the meantime, I'll talk to John's secretary again. She handles his law practice accounts, and there might be something interesting there.''

Justin checked his watch. "I've got an hour or so free before my next appointment. Why don't we go for a walk around the Santa Fe Plaza? I need to unwind.''

"Sure. Afterward can you drop me off at home? Elsie's car broke down so I loaned her mine. She's going to drop it by early tomorrow morning before I leave for school." Seeing him nod, she continued, "You know, I think everyone at the pueblo has been affected by what's happening. My kids, who don't really know John all that well, feel the impact his disappearance has had on their parents and their home. They're all eager to help, so before they got themselves into trouble, I decided to guide their efforts a bit." She told him of her plan.

He laughed. "Like Sherlock Holmes and his Baker Street Irregulars?"

She smiled. "Something like that, but at least this way I know they'll stay out of trouble. Listening is not something kids do terribly well, but they'll compete with each other and play detective safely this way."

"I think you did the right thing."

A half hour later Justin parked near one of the hotels, then headed for the maze of tiny shops that circled the plaza. "There's a place a little farther up that has wonderful *empanadas*. They stuff them with piñon nuts. It's been a while since I've been there, but do you want to give it a try?"

"Sure, I think I know the place you mean. There're about twelve little stores all clustered around an enclosed patio, and the bakery is back in the far corner."

"That's the place," he said, smiling.

Kelly saw his shoulders lose some of the tension that had held them rigid at the pueblo. He seemed content to just walk beside her and enjoy the shaded portals that kept the sweltering heat at bay.

They stopped at the bakery, then sat outside beneath the shade of a tall sycamore tree, eating. "I've missed these," Justin said, finishing the last bite. "I'm glad I'm back home, even if it's only for a short while."

Just then, one of the employees from the bakery came up to her. "Excuse me, are you Kelly Ferguson? There's a phone call for you."

"What? Who could that be?" She walked into the bakery with the employee.

Justin could see her go to the phone through the large front window of the establishment. "And how did they know where you were?" Justin muttered aloud, turning around in a circle to see if he recognized anyone in the area. Was she a target again?

She came back quickly, her cheeks flushed with anger. "It was just some crank, and I have a good idea who. Let's go."

"Did somebody threaten you?" Justin asked, protectively stepping closer to her, his eyes on the shoppers and diners around them.

"In a way, I guess," she answered. They walked out onto the plaza sidewalk again, and she remained silent.

"Are you going to tell me what was said, and who you think it was?" he finally asked. "It may be important."

She smiled at the uncharacteristic prodding, then grew serious. "It's kind of embarrassing," she admitted hesitantly.

"Go on," he urged gently. "You don't have to be embarrassed around me."

His voice flowed over her, soothing yet exciting her all at the same time. She took a deep breath before continuing. "I think it was Adrian Lowell. He asked me when I was going to get tired of my Indian lovers and find myself a real man." She couldn't look Justin in the eye. Adrian believed she and Justin were lovers. It wasn't true, but the thought of it was something that had been on her mind for some time. Was it that obvious?

"Do you think this Lowell person could be responsible for some of the things that have happened to you?"

"Not really. He comes on real strong sometimes, but I think it's all show. He wouldn't actually do anything except talk."

"Or leave notes?" Justin questioned, immediately remembering the message found in her purse.

She shrugged, aware of his meaning.

As they walked back to his car, their hands brushed. The basic need to touch him made her body tingle with awareness. She chided herself sternly. Doing anything to further the feelings growing between them was sheer lunacy. It only ensured an even deeper hurt later on. Their careers were sure to take them far away from each other. Any relationship between them would be hard pressed to survive. Now all she had to do was get her mind to convince her heart that the risk was too great. Her heart didn't seem inclined to listen.

She gazed at Justin furtively as he drove her back to her cottage. The powerful hands that rested on the steering wheel had been so gentle when they'd touched her. She remembered his last kiss, and a fiery warmth washed over her.

"What are you thinking about?" he asked quietly.

"Nothing," she answered too quickly. Seeing the look on his face she realized she'd given herself away.

Justin parked by the door and walked her to the porch. "Officer Sanchez is across the street," he said, gesturing, "so you'll be fine.

I'll see you soon." He brushed her hair lightly, but made no move to kiss her.

"Stay for a bit?"

He shook his head. "I can't. I've got to check one of my sources. Besides, it's better if I don't stay."

So he, too, had been having second thoughts about their relationship. She couldn't blame him for that, not when she'd been doing the same. "All right, I understand." As he turned away, she closed the door and walked inside.

JUSTIN RETURNED to his car. She wasn't looking at him today, and the thought depressed him. By getting distracted, however, he'd failed her and himself twice now. He should have been able to spot their assailants in the arroyo, or at the very least responded more quickly. And what of the person who had followed them today? Was it only a jealous admirer of Kelly's making trouble, or was it someone else? Someone with a connection to John Romero? His mind raced with possibilities.

His thoughts drifted back to the woman and what might have been, had he remained with her tonight. Their relationship was wrong for both of them, yet his feelings for her were strong. The need to make her his became more imperative with each passing day. He took a deep breath, his knuckles turning pearly white as he gripped the steering wheel.

Restless, he pressed down on the accelerator and headed out of town. He'd walk in the desert in the quiet of the night and, hidden by the shadows, restore peace to his troubled soul. Nothing in excess, particularly now. The pleasures the schoolteacher had to offer were not his to take. It was time to shift the balance of his thinking.

Still, his body burned with the need to feel her reaching for him and softly calling out his name.

KELLY TOSSED the covers back and lay in bed staring at the ceiling. She was completely exhausted, yet sleep eluded her. Images of Justin flashed continually through her mind. Yet the breathless fantasies soon became too hot to indulge in. An aching emptiness spread through her as she acknowledged the yearning that would never be fulfilled.

She let out a frustrated sigh and rolled onto her side. The wind rushing through the trees outside echoed in the silence of her bedroom. Suddenly her normally gentle wind chimes sounded shrilly and then quieted down quickly. She sat up in bed. Something was wrong.

Kelly crept to her curtained bedroom window. Standing to one side, she peered out cautiously. Through the dim grays of night, she could see the figure of a man standing near her patio door.

Chapter Sixteen

Was the off-duty cop Justin had asked to guard her checking the back of the house? Scarcely breathing, she watched the man walk to her back door and grasp the handle. Her heart lodged in her throat.

Wrapping her housecoat around her, she crept quickly down the hall to the front of the house where she could see the street. There were two cars parked down the gravel lane. One was the police car, the other some neighbor's white station wagon. Both were empty.

She heaved a sigh of relief. The cop was out making his rounds. Well, now that she was up the least she could do is offer him a cup of coffee. She walked into the kitchen and turned on the back porch light. "Officer Sanchez?" She started to pull open the door, then realized the chain was still on it. "Oh blast! I forgot..." As she fumbled with the catch, the man on the porch jumped forward. Jamming his arm inside, he grabbed her hair painfully in a tight grip.

Adrian Lowell's grip twisted her head at an odd angle. "Let go, Adrian, please! You're hurting me!" She tried to pull away, but couldn't make him loosen his grasp.

"I've had enough of your games. You're a tease, Kelly, you know that? You make a man want you, then you draw back. Well, no more. Tonight I'm going to show you that I'm just the man to satisfy your needs." He yanked harder on her hair until she cried out. "Now, unfasten the chain, or I'll kick down the door."

She tried to scream, but a hard pull on her hair sent her to her knees. "Please, stop!" Where was Officer Sanchez? "There's a cop around here, Adrian. Go now, before he finds you."

"Too late," he laughed. "I found him first."

She was too scared to want to know what that meant. Her hair was being pulled so tightly that it felt as if her head was on fire from the pain. "Please," she sobbed. She'd have to push the door shut, it was her only chance.

Surging forward with her shoulder, she slammed heavily against the door. With a yelp, Adrian let go and withdrew his arm. An instant later, the door closed.

But her safety was short-lived. As she reached up to fasten the dead bolt, his fist came through the glass pane in the door with a sickening crash. Splinters of glass flew everywhere. She jumped back as his bloody hand reached around and fumbled at the chain. Then the door flew open and Adrian stood there, rage in his eyes.

Trying to back out of the room, she suddenly realized he was as close to the hall as she was.

He took two quick steps and blocked her exit. "Stop fighting me," he shouted, his chest heaving. "I don't want to get this rough with you, Kelly. Don't you know that? I've been watching over you for a long time now. I make sure you're home safe each night and keep an eye on your place. I deserve a little of your attention."

"You've been here before," she realized, horrified. She felt his hot breath on her skin as he closed in on her.

Strong hands forced her to look at him. "Never inside, until now. Tonight you're going to reward my patience."

Suddenly a loud ratcheting sound came from behind them. Adrian whirled around.

The second his grip slackened, she twisted free and scrambled away.

Officer Sanchez stood at her kitchen door, blood from a swollen cut trickling down past his temple. "Don't move. Don't even breathe," he growled.

Adrian stared at the shotgun pointed at his midsection. As he started to step back, the officer raised the weapon to his shoulder. Adrian froze in midstep.

"Face down on the floor. Move it!" Sanchez yelled, gesturing with the shotgun barrel.

Kelly leaned back against the wall, then slid down slowly as her knees gave way. Emotionally exhausted, she sat and stared at the men before her. The officer stood over Adrian, handcuffing him. "Ms. Ferguson, are you all right? I was making my rounds when he hit me from behind. I've called for a backup." He grinned at her sheepishly. "Good thing I've got a thick skull."

Kelly forced herself to stand up again. "You're hurt," she managed, then walked to a cabinet in search of some cotton and antiseptic.

"Not now, ma'am," he said. "I appreciate it, but I want to keep an eye on this—" he stopped short and grinned "—scumbag."

She smiled, relief flooding over her. The man Justin had picked to protect her had certainly come through. Justin had taken care to watch over her even in his absence.

Two more officers came rushing in through her back door a moment later, nightsticks ready. Sanchez turned the prisoner over to them giving them a brief description of what had happened.

The youngest officer pulled Adrian to his feet, and shoved him toward the door. "I'll get him in the car."

The lanky blond patrolman who remained behind studied Sanchez's injury. "He gave you a good knock on the head." He grinned slowly. "Lucky thing for you he didn't hit you anywhere important. Then Mrs. Sanchez might have really been annoyed."

Sanchez started to retort when Justin strode through the door. "Sanchez, I got your call. Is Kelly..." Glancing around, he saw her standing in the corner.

She started to rush to him, but then caught herself, remembering that he disliked her impulsiveness. "I'm fine," she answered, stepping over to him and touching his arm lightly.

His gaze roamed over her quickly but thoroughly. "You sure?"

She nodded. "I wouldn't have been if it wasn't for Officer Sanchez. He came just in the nick of time."

Justin questioned the police officers, accompanying them outside. Kelly smiled as she heard him tease the injured of-ficer in the same "good old boy" fashion the men had used before.

He returned moments later. "Starting tomorrow, you'll have another guard outside until Sanchez recovers. And just to ensure the same thing doesn't happen again, he'll have a partner."

"You didn't have to, but I'm so glad you came tonight," she said, leading him to the living-room couch.

"You really gave me a scare tonight." He held her tightly, wanting to absorb her into himself. He forced himself to pull away, then paced around the room. "Why didn't you tell me more about this guy? Until now, I had no idea Adrian Lowell posed such a threat to you."

"Neither did I," she replied somberly. "I never dreamed he'd do something like this. The worst part is that he threatened me here in my own home. This is the one place where I'm supposed to be safe, yet right now I'm afraid to be alone here."

Justin couldn't hold back any longer. With a few bold strides he returned to the sofa and pulled her against him. "You don't have to be afraid, schoolteacher," he murmured. "I won't let anything happen to you." He lowered his mouth to hers, kissing her tenderly and slowly, drinking in her soft sighs.

Guiding her gently, Justin eased her back against the soft cushions. Her face was flushed, her lips swollen and her eyes misty. She needed him. The knowledge made his body burn with desire. In his arms, surrounded by his love, she'd find safety. "I'll take care of you. No one will hurt you." He took her mouth again, then tore his lips away, his breathing ragged. "It's so hard to fight what I'm feeling.

His gaze burnt into her soul. If he didn't make love to her she'd lose her mind. Just the thought that he might not, made her cry out his name and press herself tightly against him. "Don't leave me now," she managed, her voice breaking. "I couldn't stand being without you tonight."

Her plea tore through him. "Sh-h-h," he murmured, burying his mouth in the hollow of her throat. "You don't have to worry. I'll stay and watch over you." But was it possible? he thought. He had his limits, and the temptation to take her was making it impossible for him to think clearly. "You're so incredibly beautiful right now." He took her mouth again. "I'll stay here tonight on your sofa."

"Fine," she answered breathlessly. "We'll share. Like the blanket. You can have the top and I'll take the bottom."

He laughed in response to her teasing words and sensual smile. Then he pushed apart the folds of her housecoat. He pressed a kiss against the soft bare flesh that rested just above her nightgown. "The problem, woman, is that you've made me a very hungry man. Tonight, I'm going to insist on the top, the bottom and the whole thing."

Justin slipped the straps of her nightgown away from her shoulders and worked the garment downward. As his hands grazed her skin, she undulated beneath him.

"Tonight is ours," he whispered huskily. His lips parted as he bent over her, pulling the taut rosy peak of her breast into his mouth. A shiver coursed through her, and she twisted beneath him, seeking his body out.

"Now you, please," she said, pushing him away slightly. "I want to see you and feel you against me." Her words were breathless.

He felt the heat stabbing through him. Through sheer force of will, he stood and extended his hand. "Come. Undress me."

The timbre of his voice sent its reverberations right to the core of her. His request, simple and straightforward, had touched her, and she realized that she longed to do exactly as he asked.

As she reached for the lamp beside the couch intending to turn it off, he grabbed her wrist. "No. Leave it on. You'll see me, I'll see you. No barriers, no secrets."

Holding on to his hand, she stood naked before him. She wasn't sure if her legs would hold her as she felt his gaze searing over her.

Kelly unbuckled his belt, then unbuttoned his shirt. Each article of clothing came off, exposing more of him to her. When at last only one barrier remained, her hands trembled wildly.

"You wanted me naked against you," he said in a raw voice. "Finish it, *ayó' ófhn íí nii*."

She looked up at him. "Aye osh naynay?" She imitated the sound. "It means 'one who is close to my heart.'"

He'd never used any endearment before, and that one expression spoken in his own language filled her heart with tenderness. Courage and desire welled up inside her, and she removed the last garment that stood between them.

His body was powerful and tense. His mahogany skin was taut with hard muscles, and a light sheen of perspiration covered him as he struggled for control. "Now come to me." He opened his arms to her, indicating that it was not an order, only an invitation.

Her body melted against his, driving him to the brink. He lifted her into his arms and carried her to the couch. He lay beside her, his lips working on her nipples and belly.

She responded instinctively, her fingertips trailing down his chest, getting ever closer to the area she sought. She hesitated for an instant.

"Please," he rasped.

Her hands enclosed his hardness and he groaned, the sound ripped from the depths of his soul. Her slow strokes drove him over the edge. Grinding his mouth against hers, he positioned her beneath him and surged into her. He felt her strain toward him as he sank deep into her warm body then pulled away, only to reclaim her again.

Burning with the same intoxicating needs, they clung to each other. She trembled then gasped, and the last vestige of control left them both.

He remained still in the quiet aftermath, then finally placed her over himself. "If I could, I'd keep you here forever," he whispered.

"If I could, this is where I'd stay," she answered. Time was rushing them forward to an inevitable parting. Yet they had the present, and the memories forged now would be ones she'd cherish for the rest of her life.

Kelly awoke in the middle of the night and saw Justin standing across the room. Clad only in jeans, he stared outside through a slit in the curtains.

She sat up quickly. "Did you hear something?"

He shook his head, then turned around and walked toward her. Picking her up, he carried her to her own bed. "I'm not much of a guard when I'm with you. It's better if we stay in separate rooms for the rest of the night." He gazed down at her nudity, then kissed her lightly. "I wish it could be different."

As he left, an unbearable sense of emptiness came over her. The differences that separated them had not been erased. Yet in the midst of life-threatening danger, their hearts argued for love.

She turned over, pulling her pillow close to her for comfort. Forcing her mind to rest, she drifted off to an uneasy sleep.

The following morning she awoke to the sound of Justin's voice down the hall. She lay still and heard the one-sided conversation that signaled he was on the telephone. Dressing quickly, she walked out of the bedroom to meet him.

As she put on a pot of coffee, he hung up the phone. "I started calling the repair shops in the area at seven-thirty this morning after Elsie and her nephew returned your car. I'm still looking for a damaged blue truck, assuming it won't turn out to be John's," he said, frustration evident in the tight lines of his face. "I have an APB out on John's truck as well, but so far it's going nowhere. We're working in tandem with all other police agencies, but even with their support we haven't found something solid."

"We'll find John and then everything will clear itself up, you'll see," she encouraged. She drained the last of her coffee. "I've got to go. I have a class at the pueblo this morning."

"It's time for me to get going, too." He placed his cup in the dishwasher next to hers and together they walked to the door. "After you're finished today, why don't you come to the Romeros'? I'll wait for you there."

She got inside her car and started the engine. "Sounds good. Oh, and by the way, remember today we're supposed to get a tour of the bank."

He smiled slowly. "I wouldn't forget."

He watched her as she drove off. He was starting to get used to having her in his life. He probably couldn't afford that distraction. Banishing the thought of her almost as quickly as it formed, Justin strode to his car. It was time to go to work.

He drove to John's office mechanically, his thoughts drifting to his friend. A sense of hopelessness crept through him. Would he ever see John alive again?

He swore with great feeling, then pressed a little harder on the accelerator. The longer it took to solve the case, the less chance they had of ever finding John. Yet once the matter was solved, Justin might find himself without a friend and without the schoolteacher.

He pulled into the parking lot outside John's office, then walked inside. As he entered John's suite, Angela glanced up and gave him a worried frown. "Have you had any news from John?"

He shook his head. "I was about to ask you the same thing."

Her shoulders slumped, and she leaned back in her chair. "I made arrangements for another attorney to take care of pending cases. From now on, I'll be keeping the office open only in the mornings. Without John here, there really isn't any reason for me to put in a regular workday."

"Financially how is John doing?"

She smiled. "He isn't so rich he can afford to lose the number of clients he has."

"Does he have any money problems that you know of?" he insisted.

"John?" she queried with a smile. "No. He's very good handling money. He's invested quite a bit of it, and though his returns aren't spectacular, he could live comfortably off those investments if he wanted to."

"Think hard, Angela. Was John preoccupied lately? It's very important."

"I've been thinking about that almost continuously." She walked to the window and stared at the narrow street outside. "But there's nothing." She turned and gave him a direct look. "Business was good, and his life was going well. During this past month I only saw him perturbed once. And that," she said, smiling, "was due to the fact that he was doing better than he had expected."

"What do you mean?" Justin leaned forward.

"He was going over the tribal accounts and was bothered by the large profits their investments had yielded this past quarter. He was pleased, but I don't think he trusted the figures. He was almost convinced that the bank had made a mistake. He even called Murray Sullivan and asked to see a copy of the next bank examiner's report whenever it became available."

The news surprised him. In one way it was just like John to double-check, but at the same time it wasn't likely anything pertaining to the tribe's financial interests would have taken John by surprise. He'd have been keeping track of them for a long time.

"I wish I knew something that could really help you," Angela said quietly. "I'd give anything to have things get back to normal around here."

"Wouldn't we all," he said and stood. "If he should contact you..."

"I'll let you know immediately," she finished for them.

Justin returned to his car. Nothing was adding up in this case. He wiped the perspiration from his brow and turned on the car's air conditioner. It was going to go past ninety degrees today. He aimed the vent directly at himself. The heat was not going to improve his mood.

What had his old friend been up to? Had his biggest worry been too much money in the tribal coffers? Something was missing from the puzzle.

Justin stopped by three more body shops in the area. No blue trucks had been brought in for repairs. What had happened to the truck that had forced Kelly off the road, and where was John's truck? Could they be one and the same?

By the time he arrived at Clarita Romero's the temperature had soared to ninety-five degrees. The heat was oppressive, and not a cloud was in sight. Pulling off his jacket, he tossed it over one shoulder and started walking toward the house. He found himself wishing for a return to the days when it was considered respectable for a man to wear nothing but a breechcloth.

"Hello."

He heard Kelly's voice behind him and turned to greet her. Her cheeks were flushed with the heat, but she looked more beautiful and vibrant than ever. Her white gauze dress flowed around her, accentuating her sun-bronzed skin and auburn hair. "I'm glad to see you," he said, then wished he hadn't. For someone who was trying to use logic to conquer feelings that were not meant to be, he was doing a lousy job.

Kelly walked past him through the front door. Justin followed her, then had to stop suddenly to avoid running into her. She'd frozen suddenly, just after entering the house, transfixed by the sound of a familiar voice.

Clarita smiled at them and reached for the tape recorder, turning it off. "Is something wrong?" she asked, seeing the expression on Kelly's face.

"Um, no," she managed. Surely she was mistaken. "What was that you were listening to?"

Clarita sighed. "When John was in college, he'd send me tapes in Tewa, instead of letters. I've kept all of them. Listening to his voice makes it easier to wait for his return."

Justin said nothing, but felt a wave of relief. At least they hadn't given up. As long as they continued to believe John would come back to them, they had a chance. Faith, it was said, could accomplish miracles.

"Have you learned anything new?" Clarita looked at Justin hopefully.

He wished he had something to tell her. "All I have is more questions, I'm afraid."

"Then ask. The most difficult part of this is not being able to do more to help my son."

"Tell me what you know about John's tribal business. Was there anything he was excited or concerned about?" He sat across her on the sofa. His heart went out to her. With each passing day she seemed more weary and frail.

Clarita said nothing at first, lost in thought. "John was planning to purchase additional land for the pueblo. He was very excited about that. Apparently because of some investments, the tribe was going to be able to do it much sooner than he'd thought possible. Does that help you?"

"A bit," he answered.

"We'll find him, Clarita, you'll see," Kelly said.

Justin placed his hand on Kelly's shoulder. "It's time for us to go."

Saying goodbye, Justin and Kelly started toward the door. They were halfway there when Clarita once again turned on the tape recorder. As Kelly heard the familiar voice, a chill ran up her spine. For a second or two she was unable to move.

Clarita smiled at her. "You've never heard John speaking Tewa, have you? Would you like to stay and listen?"

Kelly didn't trust her voice. Shaking her head, she managed a thin smile and walked outside.

As soon as they were away from the front door, Justin stopped. Grasping her by the shoulders, he forced her to look at him. "What happened back there? You looked as if you'd seen a ghost."

"Remember I told you that one of the people in the arroyo yelled out something in Tewa? I'm certain now that it was John. His voice, through the mask, sounded just like it did on that recording."

Chapter Seventeen

"If John alerted the others, then that means he was involved in whatever was going on," Justin said in a flat voice.

"Maybe," she admitted. "But John might have been yelling out a warning, realizing the others were prepared to kill an intruder. The ones there took it as a betrayal, and that could be why they want to kill me and frame him. It's a great way to take care of both problems at once."

He smiled. "Loyal to the end." He started to reach out to brush a strand of hair away from her face, then stopped himself. "We'd better get going. We're expected at the bank."

"How did your morning go?" She'd become so attached to his moods that it had seemed as if she'd felt his hand before he'd touched her.

He told her about his talk with Angela. "The way it looks now we have two avenues of investigation. It's either a witchcraft cult that's established itself here in the pueblo, or it has something to do with John's financial dealings."

"Perhaps both?"

He considered it. "I suppose so. They don't have to be mutually exclusive. Practicing witchcraft together could bind a group very effectively." He glanced at her. "But I still think we're dealing with two separate issues. John, however, may be the link between them."

As they approached the bank's doors, Justin pulled her aside. "When we're in there, I want you to help me out a bit."

"Sure," she answered eagerly.

"If I reach up and touch my ear like this," he said, demonstrating, "try to divert Bench for as long as possible. I'm going to be searching for evidence that will allow me to get a court order for the bank's books, and I may need him looking your way for a while.''

''You've got it,'' she answered. ''We'll double team Bench, and he'll never know what hit him.'' It was at times like this that she could see how personal this investigation was to him. Justin was not the type to cut corners, yet for John he'd risk an ''unofficial'' search. The realization that he trusted her enough to enlist her help, also revealed how much faith he was placing in her. She felt closer to him than ever.

Justin gave her a long look. ''Remember we're on the same side. Don't change the game plan or the rules midstream, or you're likely to break up the whole play.''

''Don't worry about me,'' she said and went ahead toward the doors.

''Lately it seems to be one of the things I do best,'' he muttered under his breath as he followed her inside.

As they entered the lobby, Bench came toward them. ''I've been waiting for you,'' he said, shaking their hands. ''Are you ready for the grand tour?''

''Whenever you are,'' Kelly answered.

Bench walked them past the tellers' windows, then back to where the safety deposit boxes were kept. ''We're really a small branch here, so we don't have many compartments. We do provide a booth for the bank's customers, however, if they need to examine the contents of their safety deposit boxes.''

He led them down a carpeted corridor, then opened the door to his left. ''This is our data bank. All our lobby and office terminals are networked to this central unit. The daily transactions are backed up on multiple tape drives to prevent accidental losses. In addition, we print out two hard copies a week for our own use and then keep one in the vault for safekeeping.''

Kelly walked toward the computer. ''It's not much larger than my desk at school.''

''Believe me, if it had the ability to walk around, it could run the bank all by itself.''

''What would happen if a kid sneaked in here and did something to the system?''

''Spoken like a teacher,'' Bench said with a smile. ''That's one of the reasons this door is always locked. Only three people have access to this room. Murray Sullivan, myself, and the head teller.''

If the books had been altered, this is where it probably had been done. She searched her mind for some way to stay longer, but Bench was already at the door. "Now comes the grand finale," he said. "Our vault."

He entered three sets of numbers on a panel against the wall, then pressed his thumb against a clear portion of the screen. "It recognizes my codes, but unless I identify myself with my fingerprint, the vault will not open. It's also programmed to open only during certain hours. For instance, it would be impossible even for me to get in after six." He pulled the heavy door open and stepped aside, inviting them to enter. "This is the heart of the bank. In here we keep all the cash we need for transactions."

The bills were stacked a foot high on multiple-level shelves inside the nine-by-twelve room. "Good lord!" Kelly's eyes widened. "There's a fortune in here."

"Isn't this quite a large amount for such a small bank?" Justin asked.

Bench laughed. "I can imagine how it looks to you but believe me, there are no large denominations in here. I admit though, this many small bills together makes an impressive sight."

Kelly saw Justin touch his ear. Placing her hand on Bench's arm, she gave her most dazzling smile. "Russell, you've been so kind! I've really enjoyed this today." She stepped closer to him deliberately.

Bench's eyes strayed over her bosom, and he grinned. "Anytime, Kelly, anytime."

Just past Bench, she could see Justin bending over a stack of bills. As Bench started to turn around, she pretended to trip over her own feet.

Bench caught her in his arms. "You okay?"

She laughed. "I'm sorry, I've just never been in a vault with so many appealing temptations." She was flirting outrageously, but it seemed to be working to give Justin the time he'd asked for.

Bench laughed loudly. "You're a woman after my own heart, Kelly," he said. "And thanks for the compliment, even if I did have to share it."

She held his eyes and then sighed inwardly with relief as Justin came and stood beside her. "We'd better get you out of here, Ms. Ferguson," he teased. "Money always corrupts, and I'd hate to see you run afoul of the law."

Bench smiled at her and winked. "I've enjoyed having you here today." He glanced at Justin. "You, too."

Justin didn't comment, only nodded.

Kelly shook Bench's hand. "Thanks again."

As soon as they were outside, Justin glared at her. "Was that the only way you could think of to distract him?"

"It worked, didn't it?"

"The last thing in the world you want to do is get too much attention from a man like that. And you had him practically drooling."

She looked at him quickly, then laughed.

"What's so funny?" he demanded.

"You. Anyone would think you're jealous."

"It's just an observation."

"I see." Her lips quivered as she tried to suppress a smile. "By the way, I saw you searching through those stacks of bills. What on earth were you looking for?"

"Anything that would indicate Bench was lying. He told us everything was in small denominations so I wanted to check. When I did I learned that the first few bills of each stack were small. The rest, however, were comprised of one-hundred-dollar bills and over."

"Good grief! That would mean there's an incredible amount of money in that bank."

"I have enough now to get the court order I need. And this way, too, I'll be able to keep the gossip around the pueblo down to a minimum."

"What do you mean?"

"I could have gone to the tribal council and asked them to let me take a look at the pueblo accounts, then to John's family for permission to see his banking records. Yet it would have done a great deal of damage to the Romeros to cast doubts on John's business ethics. Gossip in a pueblo this small would have hurt them."

She felt a powerful rush of love as she looked at him. "So you decided to find another way."

"I can be patient."

"A minute ago, I'd have never noticed," she teased.

"That was different." He clamped his mouth shut in a thin hard line. "I've got to see about getting that court order. In the meantime, what are your plans?"

"I'm going to visit with Clarita. That way at least I feel I'm doing something for my friend." She paused. "I'm so worried about John! What if he's been hurt, what if—"

He pulled her into the shade of a young cottonwood. "Stop it," he said, grabbing her shoulders. "Playing that game is a sure way of driving yourself crazy."

"Don't you worry about things like that?"

"I don't allow myself to speculate as much as you do. Why don't you concentrate on the tasks that are yours to do, like teaching the children and helping me gather information?''

''I'll try.'' They started toward the Romero house again. ''Still, we should both work from the premise that John's in serious trouble and needs our help fast.''

''Agreed.'' Justin watched her go inside the Romero house. As she disappeared from his view, he felt the need to be with her again. She could certainly get under a man's skin. He returned to his car slowly. It worried him at times to think that she didn't understand how much he felt the absence of his friend. Could she see past his words and know what lay beyond them in his heart?

Spotting Murray Sullivan across the street, his thoughts returned to business. He had to get that court order and then return to the bank as soon as possible. By the end of today he expected to have some very solid answers. The time for patience had come and gone and the time for action was upon them.

It took some doing, but two and a half hours later, Justin placed the court order in his breast pocket. Now he was ready to face the others at the bank. Yet how prepared was he to find the answers? A sense of unease crept over him.

By the time he parked in front of the bank, he had brought his thinking back into sharp focus. The stakes were high. He'd covered himself by telling Dean Jenkins where he'd be. If the others didn't hear from him later, the FBI would know where to start looking.

Justin walked through the front doors and ran into Murray Sullivan. The tall blond Anglo who stood beside Sullivan gave him a curt nod and maneuvered past him.

''You'll have to excuse him. Clymer's having a bad day,'' Sullivan muttered.

''I've seen him before, but we haven't met.''

''He's the Santa Fe art dealer you saw here the other day.'' Sullivan walked back inside the lobby with Justin. ''What brings you back here?''

Justin reached inside his pocket and pulled out the court order. ''Shall we get started? I'd like to take a look at John's financial records and the pueblo accounts he was managing. I also want to see the bank's general accounting information for the last quarter, especially the printout that shows the beginning and ending balance for each account and the number of transactions.''

Murray stared at the papers in surprise. ''I don't get it. I mean I can understand you wanting to check into anything that pertains to John, but what's our bank got to do with any of this?'' He kept his voice deliberately low, his eyes drifting over the bank's customers nervously.

"I'm not sure, but I want to cover all the bases. Shall we get started?"

Sullivan walked to Bench's office, then explained what Justin wanted. "I'll go get some printouts for you. Why don't you use Russell's office? His desk is larger and you'll be out of the mainstream more, down at this end of the bank."

Justin nodded. "This will be fine."

Bench studied the legal papers Justin had given Murray. "This stipulates that you get the bank records for the last quarter only. The current books, which are still ongoing, are not included."

Justin met his eyes. "Those are the records I'm interested in for the moment. I'll probably be checking the rest sometime soon. Is that a problem for you?"

Russell shook his head. "I just don't understand what you hope to gain by studying our day-to-day operations. This bank is not to blame for anything John Romero may have done."

His tone and attitude angered Justin. He leaned back in the chair and regarded Bench stoically. "I'm not saying that it is. Nonetheless, I'd like to take a look at the records. Leads come up in the most interesting places."

Russell Bench stared back at him defiantly. "Maybe I shouldn't have told you about John Romero. I was trying to help you, now all you've done is created a lot more work for me."

"It's for a good cause," Justin replied. "Besides, how will I know if there's anything unusual in either John's or the tribe's accounts unless I have something to compare them to?"

Russell nodded slowly, somewhat mollified. Minutes later he relinquished his desk and began bringing in the paperwork Justin had requested.

Hours ticked by slowly. He'd minored in accounting and business, but going through these books took every bit of patience he possessed. From what he read the bank's records matched the information in John's savings passbook. According to the computer printouts, John had been withdrawing tribal funds for unspecific investments, at the same time his own accounts had been increasing substantially. Another court order, however, would be needed to check out everything. The judge had limited his access to all the records until he could present evidence of a crime.

Much still remained unanswered. A withdrawal coinciding with the amount of cash found in the cabin, for example, was not in the bank records he'd been checking. It had either been posted after the close of the quarter, or perhaps it never had been made by John at all.

Searching for substantial evidence, he studied the transaction rates and cash reserves the bank had reported on hand. The figures quoted, logic told him, were much too small to account for all the money he'd seen in the vault. He continued looking for other discrepancies, but finally admitted defeat. Most of the transactions taking place on Fridays showed deposits that would indicate payroll checks, as was to be expected. Only one seemed to show anything unusual. That particular account seemed to have numerous daily deposits made into it. Even if the account belonged to a business at the pueblo, he couldn't imagine anyone making that many small deposits. It would have made far more sense to wait and make several larger ones.

Russell Bench knocked lightly on the door, then came in. "It's past closing. How much more time do you need?"

Justin picked up the printouts and began stacking them in front of him. "I can leave right now."

"I hope your time was productive," he said, reaching out to take back the bank's records.

Justin placed his hand over the thick stack of computer paper. "I'll keep these for a while. The court order stipulates that I may examine them for seventy-two hours."

"I didn't realize that you meant to take them with you."

"I'll return them when I'm finished. You have duplicates of everything I have, so what's the problem?"

"None," Bench answered smoothly. "I'm just concerned about the bank's reputation, that's all." He lowered his voice. "Have you found the discrepancies in John Romero's account?"

Justin nodded, but said nothing.

"Do you think John might have run off because someone caught on? If a matter like this was ever brought up in front of the pueblo council, John would pay dearly. And it wouldn't end there. His family would be disgraced."

"We have no conclusive evidence yet of any wrongdoing. I'd appreciate it if you didn't discuss this with anyone." Justin's tone was clipped.

Murray Sullivan came into the office. "Kelly Ferguson is waiting for you out in the lobby."

Justin was torn between the desire to see her and annoyance that she refused to stay safely on the sidelines. "I'll be right out." Placing all the materials in a box Bench had provided, he strode outside with the records.

"I saw your car outside. Are you ready to call it a day yet?" she asked pleasantly.

He watched the intensity in her eyes and the nervousness that made her stand a bit rigidly. Something was up. "Yes, I am. I'm on my way to the Romeros'."

"Good. I'll ride with you. My car's still there."

Justin waited until they were in the car. "Okay, you didn't just drop by to see me. It's written all over your face. What have you found out?"

"I'll never make a poker player," she mused. "Or maybe you're just overly observant," she added hopefully. When he said nothing, she sighed. "Okay, never mind, here's what I got. Sludge's cousin lives diagonally across from the bank. She went out of town the day after the ceremonial and just came back recently. She was surprised to hear that John was missing, and she was eager to help. She told Sludge and Big'uns that John made a phone call from the booth in the bank's parking lot on the same afternoon he disappeared. After he finished, she saw him get into his pickup and drive down the road that leads out of the pueblo." She twisted in her seat to face him. "The bank seems to be in the middle of this somehow," she added quickly.

Justin glanced at her. "Don't jump to so many conclusions. Wait until the evidence comes together." Quickly he too recounted what he'd learned. "Now I'll check with my sources and see whose account that is. It may turn out to be nothing, but then again, you never know." He kept one hand on the wheel and another on the gear shift. "I'll send the records to an accountant in the Bureau who's a banking expert and see if he can find anything more."

"Will you ask for another court order to look at their most recent records?"

"I wouldn't get it, based on the information I have now. I'll have to bide my time and continue working." He parked by the Romero home.

"We can't just keep waiting! John's life might depend on what we do or don't do," she urged. She glanced at the house, worried that her voice might carry.

"I'm doing my best, damn it!" He drew in a long, deep breath, then forced his body to relax. He couldn't remember the last time anyone had managed to get him to lose his temper.

"I know," she replied into a contrite tone, getting out of his car. "I guess I'm just scared."

Maria met her by the door. "Mother's cleaning John's room. I tried to help, but I just can't do it!"

Kelly placed a hand on her arm. "Let me. You can keep Justin company."

Kelly walked to John's room and saw Clarita dusting his shelves. As she walked in, the woman glanced up. "I want John's room to be clean for when he returns."

Kelly felt her heart constrict. "I'll help."

A few hours later Kelly emerged from the house. They'd gone over everything in John's room until it practically sparkled. She gave Maria a shaky smile. "Everything's okay now."

Justin stood beside her as Maria returned inside. "This must have been hard on you."

"It was. His books, his favorite jacket, everything that defined him is in there. I feel his absence now more than ever."

Justin struggled not to reach for her. "I understand what you're going through better than you realize," he answered quietly.

With one last look toward the house she started to her car. "I'll see you tomorrow. I'm going home. I'm beat."

"No, wait. Let me drive you there. You shouldn't be alone on the highway after dark."

"I'll be fine. Besides, I'll want my car tomorrow morning."

"I can pick you up, or if you prefer, I'll follow you home and make sure you're okay."

She shook her head. "I appreciate what you're trying to do, but I really need some time to myself. I've got to find a way to unwind before I become a total shrew."

"All right." He walked with her to the car. "Make sure the patrol car is there and check with the officers before you go inside the cottage. One of them will go in with you to search the rooms as an added precaution. It never hurts to be on the safe side."

"Thanks for worrying," she said, slipping behind the driver's seat.

"You have that effect on me," he admitted, his eyes never leaving hers. "Take care."

Justin watched her leave. He hadn't told her yet, but he'd decided to ask for a permanent transfer back to the Santa Fe area. The Southwest was a part of him, and outside it, he felt like a stranger.

Maybe once Kelly learned that he'd be staying it would tip the scale in his favor and cause her to decide to remain in Santa Fe, too. He hoped so. He considered telling her of his plans and trying to convince her to stay. Yet, pressuring anyone he cared about was not his way. That was a decision she'd have to make on her own.

He heard the door behind her creak open. Clarita stepped out on the porch. "Kelly means a great deal to you," she said. "I've watched you when you look at her."

It hadn't been a question and it required no answer. Justin watched the faint rays of moonlight as they spilled from behind the cloud cover. "The woman is special...to me."

"You've made a good choice," she said simply, then returned inside.

Good choice? Hardly. Their future, as things seemed now, could hold nothing except disappointment and separation.

KELLY SWITCHED the headlights on to bright, trying to chase away the night's black veil. Justin might be willing to wait for those bank records, but playing by the book wasn't always best when time was slipping away. Whether he knew it or not, he was about to get her help.

The night seemed to close in around her. Glancing at the clock on her dash, she brought her speed up. She really hadn't remembered how isolated this stretch of road could be.

A brilliant flash of light reflecting off her rearview mirror caused Kelly to glance back. From out of nowhere, two headlights had suddenly appeared close behind her. Her heart lodged in her throat. How could she have missed someone following her, particularly out here?

Only one answer made sense, and she stiffened with fear. They'd been following her with their lights off and now they were ready to close in!

Chapter Eighteen

Kelly floored the accelerator pedal, trying to pull away from her pursuers. As the speedometer climbed past seventy, bright red flashing lights instantly erupted from the vehicle behind her. The sound of a loud siren pierced her ears.

A police car out here, tailing her? As she studied the vehicle, she realized that it was Suazo's four-wheel-drive Ford Bronco. Confused, she pulled off the road and parked.

Grinning, Suazo approached the car, flashlight in one hand, ticket book in the other. "Speeding on Pueblo land is illegal, Ms. Ferguson."

As she saw his expression it all made sense. He'd known she'd try to make a run for it once she saw someone tailing her. "You set me up, knowing how I'd react! And now you have the nerve to give me a ticket? That's entrapment!"

His eyes bored through hers. "I'm a police officer, Ms. Ferguson, and unless you show proper respect for the law, I'm going to have to take you in and impound your vehicle."

"You'd really do that, wouldn't you?" The question was rhetorical. Kelly shook her head. "I don't understand you. Why do you dislike me so much?"

"You're trouble, lady, and the pueblo would be better off without you. In fact, if Romero is implicated in what's been going on, it's my bet that somehow you're the reason. I strongly advise you to stay away from San Esteban. If you don't, you'll end up being killed in spite of police efforts to protect you. I can almost guarantee that."

She felt her body start to tremble and didn't know quite how to respond. Gathering her wits quickly, she forced herself to stare back at him. "I'm not intimidated by threats, Sergeant, if that's what this is."

"No, it isn't," he answered easily. "It's an observation, accurate too, I think. The signs are all there. You have a way about you, it seems—" he grinned "—of making persistent enemies."

She shook the ticket from his hand. "I'll keep that in mind, Sergeant, though I'm not sure why you're choosing to blame all this on me."

"I have all the reasons I need to want you away from the pueblo." He walked back to his patrol car.

All the way home her hands shook with anger as she gripped the steering wheel. She was tired of being the victim. From now on she'd pursue her adversaries as relentlessly as they had her, until they were brought to justice. The dark cloud of fear that threatened the lives of her Pueblo friends had to be driven away forever.

The following morning Kelly left home early. Parking down the street from the bank, she waited for Carol Black Feather to come by. Elsie, after learning about the Irregulars, had recruited herself and her niece, Carol. Carol was the bank's head teller, and in a perfect position to get a good look at the current records.

It was shortly after eight-thirty when Kelly spotted Carol coming down the street. "Hi!" Stepping out of her truck, she went toward the woman.

"Hi, Kelly!" she said with a smile. "My aunt said I should expect to see you, only I thought you'd come by the bank."

Kelly shook her head. "I wanted to speak with you *before* you went in to work. I need to ask you a favor, but it may be risky."

"If it concerns John Romero, I'm in," Carol said, then blushed. "I mean, I'd do anything to help find him."

Kelly looked at Carol and smiled. She'd kidded John dozens of times about things like this. John's good looks attracted quite a few women, though he hardly seemed aware of it. "Justin and I could both use your help. I'm afraid that we've hit a snag in the search for John, and we just can't afford to wait. He's probably in very serious trouble, or he'd have contacted us by now."

"Tell me what you need done." She leaned against the wooden post railing that bordered one of the shops.

Kelly explained why they couldn't get the current bank records. "I just want you to take a look at them for us. If there's something that doesn't look right, let me know."

Carol's shoulders slumped. "I wouldn't be able to see the computerized printouts unless one of the managers is with me. That's

Murray's policy. They watch those really carefully. Not too long ago Russ misplaced a set, and they had all of us looking. It was really crazy at the bank then. Russ found them later though, and everything went back to normal.'' She grew silent. "But maybe there's another way. The bookkeeper who normally mails the statements out has been sick, and we've been taking turns covering for her. If she's not back today, then I'll volunteer to stuff envelopes. While I'm doing that, it'll be easy for me to look for anything unusual.''

Kelly smiled widely. "That's great!"

"If she is there today, then I'll hurry through my own work and offer to help her. They don't like us to stand around anyway without having something to do.''

"Thanks, Carol. I really appreciate it.'' She started to walk away, then turned. "When we find John, I'll tell him how much you helped.'' Carol's face lit up, and she smiled broadly.

Kelly was on the way back to her car, when Justin's vehicle pulled up alongside her.

"Good morning,'' he greeted. "You're here early.''

"I had an early meeting with someone, and now I'm headed over to the community center. If you have a few minutes, why don't you meet me there?''

He nodded. "I've got to make a telephone call, then I'll be over.''

Fifteen minutes later, as Kelly was copying questions onto the blackboard, he walked into her empty classroom. "Don't let me interrupt,'' he said. His eyes strayed over the cotton T-shirt top she was wearing, and midcalf-length denim skirt. Her figure was soft and full, made for a man's touch.

She finished copying the assignment, then turned around. "I wanted to fill you in on something that happened last night.'' She eased herself onto a corner of the desk and sat facing him.

After telling him of her encounter with Suazo, she could feel the tension emanating from him. "You know, Suazo's never been fond of Anglos, but he really has a problem with me. I don't know whether to be afraid of him, or just angry.''

Justin walked to the window and stared outside into the courtyard. His hand was curled into a tight fist. "Leave Suazo to me.'' His words were measured and filled with purpose.

"If you say anything to him, it'll get worse. He strikes me as that type of person,'' she warned.

He nodded. "I'll handle it.'' He would have liked to take her someplace where he knew she'd be safe and leave her there until the danger was past. A man had a duty to protect what was his. The thought came to him suddenly, bringing a surprising revelation. Perhaps it was time to acknowledge what had been happening all along. This woman was *not* his, though lately he'd found himself wishing she were. "We'd both better get back to our jobs," he said, going to the door. "We have work that needs to be done."

He could feel her eyes on him as he walked away, but he forced his mind to focus on the investigation. It was time to check up on Suazo's whereabouts during the times that were critical to the case. The officer disliked John for many reasons, and his badge didn't mean he was innocent.

When Justin walked through the doors of the tribal police station moments later, Suazo was standing near a small portable fan, sipping a cola. He studied Justin's face. "So, Nakai, what brings you by?"

Justin could sense that the man knew Kelly had told him about their encounter the day before. Denying him the pleasure of second guessing one of the reasons for his visit, he shrugged. "I need to find out more about the pueblo, and how things work around here."

"Are you talking about our ceremonies?" he asked, instantly on guard.

"No, I don't think you'd talk about that."

"You'd think right, then."

The telephone rang, and a small Tewa woman came into the room. "Sergeant, it's that call you were waiting for."

Suazo nodded. "I'll take it in the next room."

As he disappeared, Justin walked up to the desk of the young woman. "How long have you worked here?"

"Almost five years now," she admitted with a polite smile.

"Well, with the deputies and the sergeant, you probably have plenty of company around," he commented, as if making casual conversation.

"Actually if it wasn't for the telephone and the police radio—I'm the dispatcher too—it could get really lonely here. I only see the sergeant first thing in the morning, and then right at the end of the shift. He's usually out patrolling. If it wasn't for all the extra reports he's having to fill out lately, you'd never have caught him in here at all."

"The day of that sniper incident he responded fast," Justin commented.

"He was out on patrol then," the woman confirmed. "And during our ceremonies, Sergeant Suazo puts in some very long hours. He and the other officers make sure the pueblo has the privacy it needs."

Suazo walked inside the room and gave Justin a cold stare. "Sharene, have you been giving away our secrets? All I need is the FBI watching to make sure I put in an honest day's work.''

Justin chuckled softly. "What are you so nervous about?" he said in a teasing tone. "Have you got something to hide?"

"If I did, you certainly wouldn't find out," he answered cynically. "You've lost your insight, FBI man, by spending so many years trying to think like an Anglo."

"It's useful to have the ability to think the same way another man does, no matter who he is," he answered ambiguously. "That's one way to always keep the advantage."

Suazo stared at him, eyebrows furrowed. Before Suazo could continue the conversation Justin turned and walked out of police headquarters. As he headed to his own car, he considered what he'd learned. In each of the instances, Suazo had managed to arrive at the scene of the crime almost immediately. Either the man had excellent police instincts, or he was more involved with the trouble than they'd thought.

It was after four when he saw Kelly coming toward the Romero home. Glad for a chance to get away from Murray, a near-permanent fixture lately at the Romero home, he walked outside.

She looked radiant with the sunlight playing over her copper hair. He'd come here, knowing she'd stop to see Clarita before going home. Tomorrow was Saturday, and he knew he'd have to keep a close watch over her. From the look in her eyes earlier, he could tell she was eager to start investigating on her own.

Seeing him, Kelly rushed up. "We've got to go someplace where we can talk," she said conspiratorially. "We got the break we needed, thanks to one of my undercover operatives."

"*What* undercover operatives? You mean your Irregulars?"

Clarita stepped outside, Murray Sullivan following a few feet behind. "Will you two be joining us for dinner?"

Kelly walked to Clarita's side. Being invited to eat at someone's house was considered an honor, and if you couldn't accept, explanations were called for. "I have an idea that might help with Justin's investigation, Clarita," she said in a low voice. "It's important that I speak to him as soon as possible."

Clarita nodded. "Then go."

Kelly weaved her arm through Justin's, urging him on. "It's a good thing I got tired of being patient. Wait until you hear what I've found out!"

Justin felt a terrible sinking feeling in the pit of his stomach.

"Come on," she said, urging him outside quietly. "Let's go for a drive. It'll give us a chance to talk." As Justin started walking to his own car, she stopped him. "Let's go in my truck. It's my show, this time."

She was enjoying being in charge, but her exuberance worried him. He gave her a guarded look.

"Remember when you told me there was no way you could get the bank's current records without more evidence?" She smiled and glanced over at him.

He held his breath and hoped she hadn't done anything illegal. "If you've done something I may have to arrest you for, then don't tell me."

She laughed. "Good grief! Relax, will you?" She grew serious. "You need me in this investigation because I'm able to get to sources you can't reach. That's exactly what I've done. One of my Irregulars is the head teller. She's Elsie's niece and also happens to like John quite a bit."

He sat up abruptly. "You didn't steal those records!"

"No, we couldn't," she admitted, "but Carol managed to get a look at the statements going out for this month. She came to talk to me during lunch today. Something struck her as very odd. She knows everyone at the pueblo, yet she kept coming across names she'd never even heard of. She wrote down several and then looked the people up in the phone book. They weren't there. She's convinced those people don't exist. And if they're off-pueblo families, then why on earth would they have their accounts at this branch?"

"Phony accounts. That's an interesting development."

"Now maybe you can get that court order."

"On the basis of what? This evidence isn't much more than hearsay. I'd need proof."

"She couldn't get any of the statements. She tried to make a copy of one and almost ended up getting caught," Kelly said in a dejected voice.

"I should be angry with you, but I can't fault you for caring," he said gently. "I know you're doing this because of John. Only you have to learn that sometimes these tactics can set us back. What if Carol had been caught? That might have precipitated a massive cover-up, and placed her in a great deal of danger."

"She knew the risk. Besides, that's what friends do for each other."

To her it was a matter of helping a friend, and no cost was too high. But he'd sworn to uphold the law and was bound by honor to that oath. Could he make her understand what the law meant to him, while helping her see it in a different light?

He watched her as she concentrated on the road. Tonight over dinner he'd talk to her. There was much he could share with the woman in his life, but a certain amount of separation was a good thing. The kind of togetherness she was searching for lacked balance. And without that, she'd undermine the very relationship she was trying to protect.

"Why don't you pick your favorite restaurant in Santa Fe and let me take you out to dinner?" he asked. As he leaned back in his seat, his pager poked him in the side. Muttering under his breath, he slipped it off his belt and set it on the seat.

"Okay. Is there something specific you wanted to talk to me about?"

So, she was starting to read him well, too. "Yes, but I'd rather wait until your attention isn't diverted by the road."

She drove through the plaza, then found a parking spot on a narrow side street. "The restaurant's right over there. It doesn't look like much, but the food's great."

He came around to her side of the car and opened her door. "I'm looking forward to relaxing over a good steak." Justin was halfway across the street when he reached around to the back of his belt. "I forgot I slipped off my pager when I was inside your car. I'd better go back and get it."

Justin returned to Kelly's car and reached for his pager on the front seat. Slipping the clip on over his belt, he started to cross the street again. Suddenly he heard the roar of a car engine accelerating. As he turned his head, he saw a tan sedan hurtling directly toward him.

He started to run, but instinctively knew he'd never get away in time. With a desperate burst of energy, he leaped forward. Ducking his head, he dove through the restaurant window as the fender brushed his pant leg. Glass shattered and flew around him. Justin bounced off a table and landed hard on the wooden floor. He heard screams, then a loud thud somewhere outside. Lifting his face off the cutlery-littered floor, he saw the shocked faces of the diners around him. He scrambled to his feet, surprised he wasn't badly cut, and dashed toward the exit.

Kelly rushed toward him as he emerged from the building. "Thank God you're okay." She glanced at the sedan. "Oh no! The guy's getting away," she yelled.

He looked in the direction she was pointing. The car that had tried to run him down had crashed into a lamppost just one store further down the street. A man in a plaid shirt and baseball cap staggered out of the disabled car and sprinted shakily down the street.

Without hesitation, Justin dashed after him.

Kelly, unwilling to be left behind, spurted after them instantly. Seeing Justin go through the church garden, she cut across in the opposite direction around the block. Maybe she'd be able to head the man off and block his escape.

As she shot around the corner, she collided against their fleeing adversary. The impact sent her sprawling to the ground before she could grab him. Undaunted, the man regained his balance and continued on. One work glove lay on the ground before her.

Justin hurried up to her, stopping for half a second. "Are you all right?"

"Yes, go!" She waved him hastily on as she reached out to pick up the glove.

Justin saw their quarry cut across the street. Horns blared, and brakes squealed, but Justin continued his pursuit, weaving through the cars.

Justin's breath began to come in ragged spurts, the thin air taking its toll after so many years at lower altitudes. Determined not to lose the man, Justin raced beneath the cottonwoods toward the Governor's Palace. Pueblo silversmiths and Navajo artisans sat underneath the shaded portal on the sidewalks, displaying the jewelry and rugs they'd brought there to sell.

Loud voices penetrated as the two men, like fox and hound, shot through the crowd, dodging street vendors by the narrowest of margins.

Seeing the man head for an alleyway, Justin increased his speed. He wouldn't lose him now. As Justin entered the mouth of the alley, he saw a truck pull up on the other side and his would-be killer jump in.

Muttering an oath, he drew his pistol and aimed at the tires. Suddenly two pedestrians stepped out on the sidewalk right in front of the truck. Instantly Justin bent his arm at the elbow, breaking his aim, and dashed forward again. By the time he reached the other end of the alley, however, the truck was several streets down and speeding away.

Kelly, gasping for air, caught up with him seconds later. "I'm sorry. I tried to help, but I couldn't hold him."

"Did you expect to?" He looked at her torn blouse, disheveled hair and the muddy patch of dirt on her cheek and started to laugh. It was an odd mixture of dismay at her foolhardiness and relief that she was all right. "You've got guts, I'll give you that, but what on earth made you think you'd be able to stop him?"

"I never intended to wrestle him to the ground. I just wanted to slow him down so you could catch up." Her eyes blazed with anger. "I was trying to help you, not be your comic relief."

"I'm sorry. I shouldn't have laughed. Did you happen to get a good look at him?" he asked, heading back to the accident site.

"No, I ran into him, then fell. All I remember was his shirt. His face is a blur."

He muttered an oath. "So he made a clean break after all."

"Well, he may have been able to get away, but he left his glove behind. Maybe we can get something from that." She handed it to Justin.

He shook his head. "An inexpensive cloth glove like that could come from almost anywhere. I doubt we'll get much. One thing, though—if he bothered to wear these, you can bet the car's stolen."

Walking slowly, they returned to the scene. "I can't figure out how they knew to find us here," she said at last.

"I recognize the sedan," he said, approaching the vehicle. "It appeared behind us on the road between the pueblo and here. It turned off when we got to town, so I didn't worry about it. He must have signaled his partner in the truck to follow us for a while. When they work in shifts and stay back, it's very hard to spot a tail. From now on we're going to have to be more careful. We know that there's more than one person involved in this."

A crowd had gathered around the restaurant. Working his way toward two police officers, he identified himself and made his report. "Your department can run down the sedan's plate and check the car for prints. I've got a partial license plate on the truck." He scribbled several numbers on a slip of paper. "I want your men to keep an eye out around here for a truck with these numbers and a missing taillight. I'll also request a statewide check." He handed the glove over. "The driver of the sedan dropped this. You'll probably want the lab to run a few tests, then have it sent to our office."

"What color was the truck you saw?" Kelly asked Justin in a small voice.

"Blue," Justin replied, knowing what she was thinking.

"What kind of description can you give us on your assailant?" one of the officers asked.

"I never saw his face," Justin answered, "but he was wearing a plaid shirt, jeans and work gloves. He was about five foot ten or eleven, and had light brown hair. He was wearing a plain red baseball cap." He glanced at Kelly. "Can you add anything to that?"

She shook her head. "I wish I could," she answered sadly.

"The description you've given us could fit just about anyone." The cop pursed his lips. "What about the driver of the truck?"

"I never saw him," Justin replied.

The second patrolman came up to them. "Agent Nakai, I was told to relay a message to you," he said. "The captain said you might be interested in this. Someone named Adrian Lowell was released this morning from the county jail."

Chapter Nineteen

The next morning Justin sat in the Santa Fe FBI office staring at a letter that had been forwarded to him from Kansas City. It had arrived there a couple of days after he'd left. An agent friend checking his mail had noted the San Esteban return address. Knowing Justin had been assigned to the Pueblo case, he'd sent it along.

Justin studied the note for the third time. This message from John seemed like one more piece to an endless puzzle. John had been asking for his help and advice on a financial matter concerning the pueblo. Unfortunately he'd included no details. He'd only asked that Justin extend his stay, if possible, until the matter was resolved.

Justin tapped his fingers against the desk, lost in thought. Once again things were pointing to the bank. Had John been alluding to the bank's operations, or maybe the pending land deals? It was time to take another look, though this time from a different angle. First he'd need photographs of all the bank's employees to send to FBI headquarters. They'd be able to make positive identifications and run background checks. The problem was how to get the photos without tipping his hand. He smiled, thinking of Kelly's Irregulars.

Special Agent in Charge, Dean Jenkins, came into the room. "I've just read over your report, Justin. Things are getting hot for you. Do you want one of our men as backup?"

"He'd stand out in the pueblo, Dean, and restrict my access to the people. It would only slow my investigation down."

Jenkins nodded. "We got a message for you from the state police a few minutes ago. A pickup matching the description of the one your hit-and-run driver escaped in was seen between here and Albuquerque. Apparently the driver stopped at a gas station outside Santa Fe and drove off without paying. No license number was available."

"I'm going to visit the Albuquerque Bureau office today. I want to coordinate our search efforts for the truck. In the meantime, I'd like to run a background check on Lowell."

"Our computers show he doesn't have a criminal record. He's never even had a traffic ticket."

"I'd still like to get a comprehensive file on him. He's definitely a suspect, and an unstable one at that." Justin paused. "I'd also like a complete background check on Russell Bench, Murray Sullivan and the rest of the bank employees who have access to the accounts." He handed Jenkins a list of the bank employees.

"By the way, the Santa Fe PD verified that the sedan that tried to run you down was stolen. Their lab, so far, hasn't turned up anything useful to us on the glove."

"I expected as much. Even hair or fibers won't give us a positive ID which is what we need. We already know his general description."

"I don't like the idea of your being on assignment without backup. Be very careful out there."

"Count on it." Justin stood, eager to get away from the office. Being enclosed in a sterile, temperature-controlled room day in and day out had practically driven him out of his mind. He'd never go back to supervising again. The field was the only place for him.

As he returned to his car, he thought of Kelly. He'd never had the chance to talk to her about his job. Then again, maybe the timing was all wrong. If she were to guess the direction his thoughts had been taking, that would only complicate matters between them. Right now she needed a clear mind to stay alive.

He pulled up in front of her cottage, nodding at Officer Sanchez, now back on duty. It was Saturday morning, and he had every intention of keeping her with him today. That was the only way to guarantee she'd stay out of trouble.

Kelly answered the door a moment later. "Hi! How do you feel? You must have bruises everywhere from that dive you took through the restaurant window."

"I'm a little sore, but okay."

A familiar and powerful emotion surged through him as he saw the concern in her eyes. "I'm here to find out if you want to do a little investigative work with me today."

"Of course, I'd love to."

"First of all I want to use your Irregulars."

"I knew you'd come around!" Kelly smiled broadly. "They're the perfect undercover operatives." She saw his expression change and stopped. She was rushing him again. "Oops, I'm sorry. Go on with what you were going to say."

"I need photos of Bench, Sullivan and all the other bank employees. I'm going to have the Bureau run extensive checks on all of them and confirm their identities."

"No problem. Let me make a few calls and I'll get the wheels rolling." She made a few quick phone calls. "Okay," she said moments later. "That's been taken care of. By the end of Monday, we should have all the shots you need."

He stood. "Now are you ready to go into Albuquerque with me? I want to visit the Bureau office there, then check in with the APD."

She grabbed a windbreaker from the hall closet. "Ready anytime you are. By the way, we never did have that talk *you* wanted last night over dinner."

"It wasn't important."

"That's not the way it seemed." She gave him a puzzled look.

He glanced at her as they got underway. "I worry about you, that's all. With this case, death seems an ever-present possibility, not only for John, but for you and me."

"I know. That's precisely why I feel we have to get more aggressive in seeking answers. We're at risk already, so we may as well push. Sometimes you just have to take chances if you want to progress."

The silence stretched as wide as the treeless horizons as they continued toward Albuquerque less than sixty-five miles away. "Tell me about your summer reading program. How's it going?" he asked, wanting to divert his thoughts. It was difficult having her so close to him in the confines of the car. Her perfume tugged at his senses, tempting and wrapping itself around him.

Desire and other gentler feelings mingled inside her, forming a special magic that was as pervasive as it was irresistible. Did he feel it, too? With effort she focused on his question. "The kids have been terrific. It's great to work with them and see them do well. That's when you know you've become a part of their future. I think if I gave up teaching at this level, I'd really end up missing it." Kelly didn't know if she should tell him she'd already requested a two-year extension of her summer grant. Maybe she'd wait to see if it was approved first.

"If you're continually looking for something better, you can lose sight of the good things right in front of you. True happiness lies in how you perceive what's already yours."

"That makes more sense to me now than it did a few weeks ago.

Still, to a large extent, the situation is out of my hands. If the attempts on my life are attributed to a member of the pueblo, everyone will start avoiding me. Unless the person is totally discredited, there are many who'll conclude that I bring evil with me. They'll stay as far away from me as possible. It's not fair, but it's true.''

Justin nodded slowly. "You're right, it could happen." So she was considering staying. That news pleased him. Yet the obstacle she'd mentioned was not one that could be easily ignored. For years he'd lived as a Navajo in the world of the *Bilagáana*, the Anglos. How ironic that his future would end up depending on the traditions of yet another culture older than either.

Justin pulled up to the entrance of the underground parking garage at the FBI office in Albuquerque. Showing his shield and identification to the security guard on duty at the barrier, he drove through.

"There's a man here who can access the computer at the state police department. I want to get a printout of all vehicles whose licenses match the letters and the number I managed to get off that truck's plate the other night. The good news is that they don't match John's."

"Finally something in his favor."

"It was definitely a New Mexico license plate though, so let's see what that turns up. I have a feeling it'll be a lengthy list, but we can cross-reference against the make and approximate year of the truck I saw. If you don't mind, you could help me sort through the list."

"That's why I'm here." She paused and smiled. "And also, no doubt, because you're afraid that if I weren't with you I'd start investigating a lead on my own and get myself in trouble."

He grinned back. "I didn't say that."

"You didn't have to."

As they stepped out of the elevator into the main lobby, Justin led the way to the back of the building. Entering a large computer room, he glanced around, then grinned. "Hey, Sky Hook," he greeted the tall, lanky Anglo in a sports shirt sitting before a computer monitor. "You still play a mean game of one on one?"

"You never could block my shot, shorty." He grasped Justin's shoulder in a friendly gesture, then returned to the computer. "Well, I've just finished running one of the programs, so you caught me at a good time. What do you need me to do?"

"I want you to access the state police computers."

"You have authorization for this?" Sky Hook looked around to assure himself they were alone.

"I could get it, but it would probably take all weekend, and right now that would work against me."

"Now I see why you wanted to meet me today," he muttered. "Well, what the hell. What are friends for?"

"Thanks," Justin said quietly and handed him a piece of paper. "These are the letters and the number I managed to get off the plate." He explained what he needed. "See what you can come up with."

Twenty minutes later they sat with a stack of computer printouts before them. Dividing it into three piles, they pored over the materials.

"Does this have something to do with that guy who tried to run you down?"

Justin nodded. "You heard about that?"

"Everyone has. The guys here are keeping a lookout for that truck. We like to take care of our own, you know."

"I've checked my stack," she said leaning back in her chair. "None of the plates listed match the type of vehicle you saw."

"The same here," Sky Hook added.

Justin rubbed his chin in a pensive gesture. "There's the possibility, of course, that the license plate was stolen and placed on the truck."

"That's my guess, too," Sky Hook commented. "It makes sense under the circumstances. They'd cover their tracks the best way they could."

Thanking his friend and promising to come back at a later date to visit, Justin drove to the main office of the Albuquerque Police Department, less than a half mile west and north of the Bureau's offices. After being assured that the information on the trucks had been passed to all patrol officers, he returned to the car with Kelly.

"The truck that the man who tried to run me down escaped in was last seen heading toward Albuquerque. I don't want to go back to Santa Fe without making more of an effort to find it, but it's stupid to just drive around."

"We have to start thinking like the crooks. If you and I had a hot vehicle we wanted to hide or abandon, but we couldn't call attention to it, where would we take it?"

"It could be hidden in someone's garage, and if that's the case, we have virtually no chance of finding it."

"That's true, but if it were me I'd want to distance myself from the incriminating evidence. I think it's far more likely they'd park it among other cars and walk away," she said, then added, "How about taking a drive through the parking lots of the two largest shopping centers?"

"It could be there, but I doubt it. After the stores close and everyone leaves, the truck would have become obvious."

"True," she admitted, then brightened. "I've got it. How about the parking lots at the airport? Cars are left there for days sometimes. Some people pay weekly rates so their vehicles will be waiting for them when they return from a trip."

"That's a great idea," he agreed. "Let's give it a try."

Thirty minutes later, cutting across town on the freeway, they were busy circling the north lot nearest the airport terminal. Justin traveled up and down each of the rows with his characteristic patience.

Kelly helped him search the rows, then suddenly sat up. "Wait, don't turn yet. Keep going over to the next section. I just caught a glimpse of the front of a blue truck. I noticed it because it's been backed into the slot."

He studied the vehicles directly ahead. "Yes, I see the one you mean. Let's go check it out."

As they approached, she saw the top of the leather-covered steering wheel, and the bumper sticker advertising the intertribal ceremonials. Her heart plummeted. "That's John's truck."

"Let's take a closer look. It's hard to tell anything from here."

"I'm sure I'm right," she answered, but accompanied him anyway. Justin looked inside the driver's window and then walked to the back.

"This is his truck," she repeated.

Justin glanced at her, his lips pursed thoughtfully. Opening the tailgate, he jumped easily onto the bed of the truck. A tarp lay rolled up against the end. Squatting before it, he unrolled the canvas partially, then stopped. He hadn't expected this.

Kelly came around and watched him. "What did you find?"

He took a deep breath, and for a moment debated whether or not to tell her. "It's saturated with dried blood," he said finally.

"A body?" She barely managed the words.

"No, but whoever or whatever was wrapped in this was either dying or dead." He stepped away from it.

Chapter Twenty

Field investigators from the local FBI office as well as two Albuquerque Police Department detectives clustered around the truck.

Justin stood at the front of the vehicle, Kelly at his side. "I don't see any sign that this truck has been damaged by a collision."

"We'll take a paint chip and see if it matches the color rubbed onto Ms. Ferguson's vehicle. Then we'll let you know," one of the Bureau's men said.

"So we've finally found John's truck," Kelly observed, a trace of sadness in her voice, "but where's the truck that tried to run me down?" She swallowed back the bitter taste at the back of her throat. All this time she'd held on to the hope that John would be found alive, but seeing the tarp had jolted her confidence. Had someone abandoned John's truck here after killing its owner?

"The only thing we found inside that's of interest so far," one of the detectives said, "is a matchbook from a bar in Madrid, a town southeast of Santa Fe. I've contacted the state police already. They're going to have the officer working that area stop by the bar and ask around about the missing Pueblo man." He paused. "One last thing. The date on the parking stub matches the day Romero disappeared."

"Good work. Keep me posted." Justin led Kelly aside.

"At least we've finally found one piece of evidence in John's favor," she said, a trace of irony in her voice. "The date on the stub also matches the day someone tried to run me off the road. That means it couldn't have been John's pickup that was involved. It would have been impossible to have it repaired and brought here that fast."

"Come on. You can help me now. There's a few things that need to be done as a follow-up."

"I'm ready to do whatever I can," Kelly responded. What she

really felt like was having a good cry, but that would have helped no one. Instead, she forced herself to focus on the need to find the people that had brought so much misery into their lives.

"I've got a photo of John in my wallet. It's not a recent one, but he hasn't changed much over the years. Let's go inside to the airline ticket counters and talk to everyone there. Maybe someone will remember selling him a ticket."

It took a moment for the meaning of Justin's words to sink in. "You're assuming he killed someone, then took a flight out of here, aren't you?" Kelly demanded angrily. "Has it occurred to you that it could be the other way around?"

"I'm checking into all the possibilities, that's all." His face remained expressionless. "The lab boys will check the blood on that tarp against John's type. While they're doing that, I've got to cover all the angles. If you find this too difficult, wait for me."

She watched him walk off, then ran to catch up. "I'm going," she said stubbornly.

"Sometimes I just don't know how to get through to you," he said quietly. "You're determined to ignore the duty I have to my job and to myself. I'm trying to keep you alive, and the best way I have of doing that is to follow the trail that leads to John. I'm afraid of the answers I'll find, but I have to find them. We may have already lost John and I'm afraid of losing you, too." He met her eyes and held them. "That doesn't sound like the brave, stoical Indian that Hollywood makes us out to be, but there it is. We're human."

She felt her throat turn into a solid lump. "I'm sorry if I've said things that hurt you. I didn't mean to."

They stopped at the curb, waiting for traffic to clear. "I know," he answered, reaching out for her hand and giving it a squeeze.

Inside, they went from one airline counter to the next. Finally, with nothing to show for their efforts, they returned to the parking lot. John's truck was about to be towed away.

Justin exchanged a few words with the men, then walked her to his car. "We may not have turned up any clues questioning the airline ticket personnel, but finding John's truck is a big break in the case. There's bound to be fingerprints in the truck and on the parking stub. That'll clear up a lot of questions."

Kelly stared out the window. "What will we tell Clarita and Maria? Should we at least wait until the technicians verify the blood type?" Her voice sounded strangled even in her own ears.

Justin considered it. "No, I don't think so. I gave Clarita my word that I'd keep her up on developments in this case as they happened, and I'm going to honor that. When we reach the pueblo, I'll stop and brief Suazo on what's happened. Then I'll go to Clarita and tell her.''

"Would you mind dropping me off at Elsie's first? I don't want to be around Suazo unless it's absolutely necessary. Besides, I need a chance to check with my undercover operatives.''

"Think of them as Irregulars. It'll give you a better perspective on it.'' His mouth twitched, but he suppressed a smile.

As they drove back, Kelly couldn't seem to divert her thoughts from John and Clarita. She really couldn't decide whom she was worried about most. Though the elderly woman showed a great deal of inner strength, there was a limit to how much one person could take. And what about John? Would they ever find him again? "You know, I usually get angry when I start thinking of all that's happened to me. But then when I start thinking of John and what might be happening to him, I get scared.''

"We're doing our best and that's all we can do,'' he answered. He drove across the pueblo and stopped in front of Elsie's house. "I won't go in with you. I want to get over to tribal headquarters and call the lab in Albuquerque. It's much too soon for them to have turned up anything, but it'll help if they know I'm waiting.''

She nodded. "I'll see what I can turn up from my end.''

"I SAW JUSTIN drop you off,'' Elsie said, coming outside to meet her. "You look like you've been through hell. Come inside and we'll talk. I've got a new lead to tell you about.'' She led the way to her kitchen.

"What's happened?''

"I heard from Big'uns's mother. It seems she and her neighbor, Mrs. Garcia, have seen Hamilton Clymer meeting Russell Bench at the bank quite often after everyone's gone. The women have been using that route to go back home after church. Their circle has been saying a rosary each night for John.'' Elsie placed a glass of iced tea before Kelly on the kitchen table. "They also discovered that Clymer carries a large briefcase to and from those meetings.''

"I'm going over to Clarita's now. Justin will be heading over there as soon as he can. I'll let him know what you've managed to uncover. It could turn out to be important.''

"Oh, by the way,'' Elsie added, reaching inside one of the kitchen drawers. "I've got a roll of film for you here.'' She handed Kelly a small envelope. "Sludge and Big'uns got the photos of the bank employees you asked me for this morning. Most of the people the bank employs live right here, so it wasn't too hard for the boys to track them down. I managed to find a photo of Murray Sullivan and Russell Bench taken at the bank's grand opening last year. I went ahead and put it in there along with the film canister.''

Kelly glanced inside and brought out the photo Elsie had mentioned. Her vision misted over as she noticed John's image. He'd been standing just behind the bank employees. "Damn, I miss him," she said under her breath.

"What's going on in the investigation?" Elsie asked. "Have you learned something new?"

She told Elsie about finding the truck and the blood. "I'm so worried about him. Things are really looking bad." She walked slowly to the door.

"There's no reason to lose hope yet. Hold on to that," Elsie said softly.

Kelly's steps were leaden as she traversed the pueblo. The caring and love that bound the Romeros together had always touched her deeply. It was such a contrast to the lack of warmth within her own family. Her heart went out to Clarita. Would any words console a mother who faced the possibility her only son might never return?

Kelly's eyes filled with tears. As she went up the dirt path to the Romero home, an almost crushing heaviness settled over her.

She crossed the living room and had just seated herself beside Clarita on the sofa when the telephone rang. The elderly woman's eyes became like two fathomless pools of water.

Justin grabbed the phone on the first ring and identified himself. "Put out an APB," he said after listening for a moment, "and hold him for questioning when you find him. Anything else?"

A few minutes later, Justin hung up the phone. He looked at Maria, then Clarita. "They've lifted a partial thumbprint from the airport parking stub. The last person to drive John's truck was a man by the name of Vince Larranaga. He's a local. He doesn't have a police record but is known for always being one step ahead of the law. Right now he's got a civil suit pending against him for land fraud." He clenched his jaw. "We'll find him."

"It doesn't sound like anyone my son would have for a friend," Clarita said in a firm voice, "and John's law practice didn't deal with that sort of thing."

Kelly picked up the envelope from the side of the couch, and handed it to Justin. "Those are the photos you asked for this morning."

His eyebrows shot up. "That was fast. Good job."

Despite the tension filling the air, his words lifted her sagging spirits. He'd never actually commended her for anything before.

As Maria tried to console her mother, Justin and Kelly stepped out to the porch, to give them some privacy. "I've got this nagging feeling that I'm missing something important," he said. "Yet, the harder I try, the more elusive it becomes."

She stared across the sun-drenched streets of the pueblo. It was a different world here. Yet, evil had wound its way into this peaceful village and was striking at its people. "We've followed up all the leads we have. What more can we do? The only consolation we have is the knowledge that we must be getting close or they wouldn't be trying to kill us both. And they must want us very badly. Leaving us to die in the fire they set in the arroyo that night is a gruesome way to commit murder."

"That arroyo is also where you last saw John, right?"

"Yes," she replied. "I'm certain it was his voice I heard."

"Remember after the fire, when we were out there looking for evidence? We came upon a shrine. I didn't think much of it at the time since we were too busy trying to stay alive, but now I'm beginning to wonder. Maybe we should have checked that out."

"A shrine? Why? Disturbing something like that is a sure way of getting people around here very angry."

"It could be a grave disguised as a shrine," Justin countered. "I remember overhearing something about the Tewas and witchcraft at one of the intertribal ceremonials once. When certain kiva societies initiate members, local witches feel compelled to follow suit so their enemies won't gain an edge. If they can't find anyone willing to join them, they'll use the corpse of someone whose death they've caused."

"John?" she asked, her voice scarcely more than a whisper.

"Perhaps. Or maybe the man you saw lying down. We have to look into this." To go to a place contaminated by death went against his deepest beliefs. Even his years of experience in the FBI hadn't lessened his distaste for it. Nonetheless, he knew his duty. "I'll have the deputy get in touch with Suazo. He should come with us."

"You can't be serious! We don't even know if he's part of what's going on around here. We have to leave him out of this."

"We can't," he countered. "If we go snooping around Tewa shrines without him, any cooperation the pueblo's giving me will grind to a halt. And you're considered a friend of this pueblo. That would be taken as a violation of their trust. Face it, we don't have a choice. We have to take Suazo with us."

Kelly exhaled softly. "All right."

"This may be very unpleasant business," he warned. "You don't have to come."

She stood straight and faced him. "I'm going."

He hesitated, then nodded. "All right. Let me tell Clarita that we have to leave, then we'll go to the pueblo police station."

Kelly rode in stony silence beside Justin as they traveled to the other side of the pueblo. She wasn't really relishing meeting with Suazo, but she had to agree it couldn't be helped.

Kelly entered the tribal police station slightly ahead of Justin. Suddenly Suazo came rushing around a corner and practically collided with her. "What are you doing in here?" he demanded. Then he saw Justin. "I was on my way over to the Romeros'. Has there been any word on the blood type?"

"Not yet, but we have something else we need to talk to you about." Seeing that Suazo still stood in the hall, blocking their way, he added, "Shall we go into your office?"

He nodded reluctantly. "Yeah, let's go." He waved a hand at the chairs and made himself comfortable at his desk. "Okay, what now?"

Justin explained about the shrine. "I want to check it out. It might be a grave site."

"Or not. We don't look kindly on outsiders who want to go around disturbing our shrines, Nakai."

Justin met his gaze and said nothing.

The moments ticked by, yet no one said a word. Kelly shifted. Great. How long would this battle of wills continue?

Suazo toyed with a pencil lying on his desk. Standing it on end, he slipped his fingers down the length of it, then left that end up, beginning all over again.

Justin stared across the room at the daddy longlegs spider walking slowly down the side of the wall toward the bookcase.

Kelly glanced at her watch, then forced her body back to stillness. How did they do this? Finally Suazo spoke and she felt like cheering.

"And if I refuse your request?" he asked casually.

"I'll ask the pueblo governor," Justin answered in an equally relaxed tone.

Another lengthy silence followed. Kelly's nerves couldn't have been more frazzled had she been standing naked at gunpoint.

"Wait. I'm going to make a few calls and check some things out," Suazo said at last.

As he walked out of the office, Justin glanced at Kelly and grinned. "I thought you were going to pop out of that chair," he teased.

"Waiting is as hard for me as putting up with impatience is for you."

He smiled ruefully. "Your point is well taken," he answered.

Suazo returned a moment later. "I've spoken to both the winter and the summer chief, and to the winter and summer caciques." He turned to Kelly and added by way of explanation, "The latter two are our religious leaders. No one knows of any shrines in the area you've mentioned." He leaned back against his desk. "Which is not to say that there isn't one there."

Justin nodded. "It still bears checking out."

"Fine, Nakai. You want to go now?" He strode to the door and waited.

Justin stood and followed him out of the building. "We'll go in separate cars."

"Suits me just fine," Suazo said sharply. Without even a glance back at them, he slipped into his car and sped away.

"Charming as ever," she muttered.

"Time to go," Justin said as they got into his car.

"I know that in your profession you've dealt with this before. But I've read that Navajos traditionally are reluctant to intrude upon a place where a death has occurred," Kelly said.

"Given a choice, I'd rather not," he said grimly, driving toward the dust that hid Suazo's Bronco. "Unless a person has been properly buried, the Dinéh believe their *chindi*, the evil within them, remains and can harm the living. To the Dinéh, ghosts are the witches of the world of the dead." He shook his head slowly. "What we're about to do is not something I take lightly. My tribe sees death as the enemy, and existence in the hereafter to us seems shadowy and uninviting. Death and everything connected to it is something to be avoided. Suazo, I'll bet, would never believe that," he said, giving her a wry smile.

"Perhaps not. Yet, he has an advantage over you in this. From what I know, the Tewas believe in a happy afterlife, at least after the soul completes its four-day journey to all the sacred earthly locations. They go to 'the place of endless cicada singing.'"

"I've heard that." He stopped for a moment then, almost as if in defiance, added, "John told me that once."

It was his way of affirming that John was still alive. She tried to ignore the uneasiness that crept through her. Until recently her faith in his eventual return had remained firm, but suddenly she wasn't so sure. She swallowed the tears stinging the back of her throat. "When we find John, I bet he'll have quite a story to tell us."

Justin said nothing as he drove down into the arroyo.

Memories assailed her. Each time she'd come to this place, something horrible had happened. She tried to banish the awful feeling of dread that gripped her, but did not succeed.

A few minutes later she and Justin approached the small shrine, little more than a cairn of rocks on the desert floor. Suazo, who'd arrived first and located the spot, stood by watching both of them. She could sense Justin's reluctance to venture too close, but it was her own reluctance that troubled her the most. There was nothing to indicate conclusively that John was dead, yet somewhere along the way, she'd stopped believing him to be alive.

Suazo handed Justin a shovel. "Here you go, Nakai. You take it from here. I'm only an observer." His eyes bored through Justin's.

Justin's face remained expressionless. Taking the shovel from Suazo's hand, he began to dig.

Kelly's heart went out to Justin. Suazo was goading him into doing something that went against his beliefs. One look at Suazo's face told her that he was using this to see how determined Justin was to pursue this.

"A Pueblo man is missing, and this investigation concerns you directly. Shouldn't you be doing some of the digging, Sergeant?" Kelly demanded.

Suazo gave her a slow, smug smile. "These are federal lands. Pueblo land is behind us, on the south side of that fence we passed. Nakai is a federal agent and he's in charge of this investigation. Way I see it, it's his job. Besides, that prayer stick is phony. It isn't made right."

Justin gave her a sharp look, and she realized that inadvertently she'd made things worse. The real battle lay between the two men, and it was not something a third person could interfere in.

"I'm getting close to something," Justin warned after digging a while longer. "Why don't you wait for us back in the truck?" he suggested, glancing at Kelly.

"What have you found?" Suazo came closer and looked toward the end of the shovel. His jaw fell open, then he turned away.

Kelly stared at Justin, waiting and praying for confirmation that it wasn't John.

"Go now," he said, giving no indication of what he'd found. It was a body, all right. He felt the weight of John's lightning stones in his pocket. Was this the wisdom the stones had given them? Was his friend's spirit within the *xayeh* now?

Kelly didn't want to look, but she wouldn't run away, either. She walked a few feet away, but remained there.

"Have it your way," he muttered.

Scooping the sand away from the partially decomposed body uncovered by his shovel, he glanced up at Suazo. "Unless I miss my guess, that white powder all over him is quicklime."

"There's no telling how old the body is, not with that stuff spread over it. At least it keeps the smell down. You can't even tell if he was Indian or not, he's so dried up."

"It wasn't spread evenly, so not all of the body decomposed at the same rate."

Suazo stared at the corpse, then glanced away. "Sorry, Nakai, but there's not enough left of that face for me to be able to identify it."

Justin shook his head, then jumped out of the shallow grave. The odor of death clung to his body. Despite the heat of the desert, he felt cold. "There's something else beneath the body—pieces of wood and yucca fibers, I think, and some feathers."

Kelly's stomach hurt, and she felt sick, but she stood still, determined to hide it. Her eyes remained on Justin. There was a tightness in his mouth and lines of tension creased his brow. Going to his side, she took the shovel from his hand and tossed it to Suazo wordlessly.

Suazo met her gaze, then glanced at Justin. Without comment, he started back to his car. "How do you want to handle this, Nakai?" he asked, standing by his vehicle.

"Have the FBI team come out. Let them do whatever they can to identify both the man and the other contents of the grave."

"I'll radio it in," he answered. After he finished relaying instructions, he walked to Justin's vehicle. He crouched by the still open door on the driver's side, angling so that he could also look at Kelly. "So, it still bothers you," he commented, his gaze resting on Justin. "I wondered if you'd forgotten everything after living in the Anglo world all this time."

"Some things are a part of you," he answered flatly.

Suazo nodded. "I've got a message for you. The FBI lab says that the blood they found on that tarp is not John's. I told my deputy to tell the Romeros."

Kelly shook her head slowly. The news she'd been praying for was here. Only now it didn't seem to matter as much in view of the body they'd just found. It was as if fate had conspired to cheat them of even the slightest respite from their fears.

"I'm sure the Romeros will be glad to hear the news. They've been under a lot of strain. At least for a while, they'll breathe a little easier." Just then a glimmer of something uphill caught his eye.

Suazo followed his line of vision. A man was crouched on the bluff above, watching them. "You, up there!" Suazo yelled out, taking several long strides up the hillside.

Suddenly three shots ran out in rapid succession. As the blasts ripped through the stillness around them, Suazo dropped to the ground and then rolled.

"Get on the floor of the car, and crawl to this side," Justin ordered Kelly, pulling his gun from its holster.

Suazo scrambled behind a large boulder, drew his weapon and fired back.

Justin's shots reverberated almost in unison with Suazo's. Then as he peered around the front end of the car, Justin saw the man scrambling away from the bluff. A second later he heard the sound of a car being started.

"Like hell you're getting away," Suazo yelled, jumping into his own vehicle. He took off up the road, leaving a cloud of sand and dirt behind.

Justin and Kelly dove into the front seat of their car, and seconds later Justin joined Suazo in pursuit. "This is one I'm not losing. It's about time we caught some of the people who are intent on killing us." He pressed on, determination giving a rigid cast to his features.

Kelly knew she should have been afraid. They were darting through the sand and rugged terrain at breakneck speeds. Yet, nothing seemed to reach past the fog numbing her senses. She wanted to believe that the body they'd found could not have been John's. Yet, she wasn't sure. Her hope of seeing John alive again was slowly being destroyed. Yet without that hope, it would be all too easy to give up trying to find him. And that would be the worst betrayal of friendship she could imagine.

They spotted their assailant moments later by the trail of dust he was leaving. The blue truck contrasted sharply against the grays and muted greens of the rabbit brush and junipers. The man turned left at the bottom of a small hill, and began to circle around its base. Instead of pursuing, Suazo continued in a straight line going up the hillside. With Suazo out of the way, their assailant's car suddenly came in line with Justin's. The man opened fire.

Justin pulled the wheel hard to the left, away from the shots, then continued his pursuit.

Suazo hurtled down the other side of the hill and came out in front of the blue pickup, cutting across his path.

Firing, the man tried to drive past. One round pierced the window on the driver's side of Suazo's vehicle. Suazo ducked down as several more shots followed, then with one hand on the wheel, he aimed the barrel of his shotgun out the window and fired. A cannonlike blast ripped through the air.

As Justin and Kelly watched, the blue pickup went out of control. It smashed through the range fencing and continued on through the sagebrush and sand. Seconds later it bounced off a stock tank next to a windmill and came to an abrupt halt.

Suazo stopped several yards away, placing the Bronco between himself and the pickup.

Justin came up from behind and parked head on. "Stay on the floor," he warned. "If there's shooting, the engine will protect you."

As she heard Justin move away, Kelly reached for the passenger door and opened it slightly. Peering out from the crack near the hinges, she watched Suazo and Justin approach the vehicle, guns drawn.

Chapter Twenty-One

Suazo reached the vehicle first. The driver lay slumped over the steering wheel. With a quick jerk, the sergeant pulled him back and saw that his wounds had obviously been fatal.

Justin glared at Suazo. "Why didn't you take out his tires? We needed him alive!"

"He was shooting at us, Nakai, in case you missed that."

Kelly approached slowly. "Is it the same truck?" she asked softly.

"Stay back," Justin growled. "You've seen enough death already to last you a lifetime," he added under his breath.

She stopped, turning her head away. "Is it the same truck that ran me off the road?" she repeated.

Justin walked to the back and spotted the missing taillight. Studying the vehicle carefully, he moved toward the front and examined the fender. "It's got a new paint job." He ran his fingers over the thin metal skin. "It's my guess they had this reshaped too. I think it's the same truck that tried to run you off the road and the one we were looking for in Albuquerque. Only the plates have been changed."

Relief, bitterness and a sense of despair all joined into one soul-wrenching sentiment. In the past few weeks she'd come face-to-face with the worst elements of society. She'd tried to keep it from affecting her, focusing on the goal of finding John rather than the dirt they were uncovering. But now it seemed like too much to ask. Where was hope when despair took over? "Who's the man in the truck?"

Justin glanced back at Suazo and saw him removing a wallet from the dead man's pocket. "A New Mexico driver's license says he's Vincent Larranaga. It looks like him," Suazo added, noting the ID photograph.

"The man who left John's truck in Albuquerque," Justin said, leading Kelly back to his car. "I'm taking her to the Romeros'," he told Suazo. "Call the county sheriff and my Santa Fe office. I'll be back."

They drove in silence for a while, both lost in the turbulent seas of their own thoughts. "Will you be okay?"

Kelly straightened in her seat and nodded. "It started getting to me, that's all. I don't know how you do it, dealing with things like this on a daily basis."

"Restoring harmony is what my job is all about, not just enforcing the law. The universe sustains itself by maintaining a balance. I work to keep balance by reversing the chaos I see. In that way I find peace within myself. That's what's meant by 'walking in beauty.'"

"Your culture gives you strength to endure," she said. "I envy you that."

"Everyone needs something to believe in, a foundation of some kind."

"I believe in the kids and the future they represent. I believe that no matter how awful things seem to be, there's good that's patiently waiting to reassert itself." She smiled wearily. "I guess I lost sight of that for a while."

He dropped her off at the Romeros'. "I'll be back as soon as I can."

"Shall I tell them about the body?"

"No, not yet. With John's truck, it was different. But we have no proof that all this is linked to John."

Kelly walked inside the Romero home and found Elsie. "There's a rosary being said for John tonight," she explained, "and Clarita and Maria went over. They wouldn't leave the telephone unattended, so I told them I'd stay behind."

"I'm glad you're here," she admitted, sitting down on the sofa. "There's something I want to talk to you about." She met Elsie's eyes. "I need your help."

"You have it," she replied.

"Tell me everything you can about Pueblo witchcraft, particularly the masks or rituals they might use at this time of year."

Elsie's eyebrows shot up. "You ask for a lot, though you may not be aware of it." Elsie jammed her hands deep into her skirt pockets and walked to the window. She was obviously struggling with the decision of whether to discuss this. She glanced outside for a moment, then turned to face Kelly. "Academically most of us don't believe in that. Yet all of us believe in the influence such practices have upon us. You see, witchcraft is used for evil or amoral purposes and on that basis alone constitutes a threat."

Kelly paused, trying to figure out what she could say to convince Elsie to discuss this with her. It wasn't fair to ask Elsie this kind of question without some explanation. "I'm asking because this could tie in to the threats on my life and John's disappearance."

"The problem is that I have very little knowledge of the subject, and getting the information you want is going to be difficult, if not impossible. You see, people who do such things are associated with disease, death and misfortune. We take special care to avoid speaking about them because they're not something we want to call into our lives." Elsie gave her a tentative smile. "Can you understand any of this?"

"Elsie, I have to learn more about this, but I don't want to create any problems for you. Tell me this—if you were me how would you go about getting the information? I've checked the library but what's there is too general to be of much use."

Elsie fell silent, staring at an indeterminate spot across the room. Kelly was glad of the practice she'd had recently, waiting for Justin's decisions. It made the waiting this time easier.

Finally Elsie spoke. "There is one person who knows and who would talk to you if I ask. But you must promise never to tell anyone about your conversation with her. It could do her a great deal of harm."

"You have my word," Kelly said, swallowing. She wasn't quite sure what she was getting into, but there really was no other choice.

After the Romeros returned, Elsie led Kelly through the silent pueblo streets. Dusk fell softly over the adobe buildings, covering them in a soft watermelon-colored glow. Minutes later they arrived at a small adobe house under a tall cottonwood tree. Elsie stepped up to the front porch where several sweet-smelling herbs were growing in a window box. "My grandmother lives here, and she knows more about the pueblo and its culture than anyone I've known. I can ask her to talk to you, but the final decision is hers."

"I understand."

They stepped into a small whitewashed room, simply furnished with pine chairs and a long wooden bench with a blanket for a cushion. Elsie introduced Kelly to the elderly Tewa woman. Juanita's small body was weathered, yet her black piercing eyes shone with intelligence.

"What you ask is dangerous," Juanita said. "Anyone can be accused of witchcraft, and the consequences of such accusations are severe." She smiled sadly. "Old women are particularly subject to this. Our bodies are no longer pleasing to the eye, and our appearance can frighten. It was worse in the old days, but the problem is still there. Nowadays, instead of accusations that lead to a trial, there is gossip, and the damage is done in another way."

"I've promised Elsie never to say anything about this visit," Kelly assured. "But I desperately need your help." She explained her reasons, but as before, omitted details that would reveal facts pertinent only to the investigation.

"If there is witchcraft going on, and it has harmed one of the people then it's time to stop it." She sat very still, her hands folded in her lap. "Has the cacique been told?"

"No, but understand that I have no proof of anything. Right now all I'm doing is checking out possibilities."

Elsie stood. "If you'll both excuse me, I'd like to return to the Romeros. Clarita looked very upset when she came back." She gave her grandmother a hug and quickly left.

Elsie's uneasiness had been apparent, but Kelly was glad for time alone with Mrs. Whitecloud.

"My granddaughter trusts you. So I will trust you. But remember there is danger in what you have asked. The reasons witches threaten us so much is that we believe that their lives depend on the death of others," Mrs. Whitecloud explained in a clear but frail voice. "Without killing, they forfeit their claim to existence. They're our enemies because they must victimize us in order to continue being."

"Do they wear masks at their rituals?"

"Yes, they wear many guises. Sometimes they mimic ours but they're different in colors and patterns. Remember that our witches are not in league with the Anglo Devil. That's a European concept. We're taught that all the Tewas emerged from beneath the sacred lake. Some that came brought with them the knowledge of witchcraft from the underworld and that's why we've had to contend with them from the beginning." She stood up and extracted a book from a small shelf. "When I was a young girl, my brother went out one night and trespassed on a society of witches initiating a corpse. He was too frightened to move, so he stayed very still. When everyone left, he came running home. He drew these for us." She handed Kelly a yellowed sheet of paper. "To my knowledge these are what some of their ritual clothes and masks look like."

Kelly studied the drawings for a long time. Once again she found similarities, but not one of them matched very closely.

She returned the paper to Mrs. Whitecloud. "Thank you for your help," she said. "Perhaps someday I'll be able to repay you with some kindness."

"What you're already doing for the pueblo is more than enough. I've heard a great deal about you from my Elsie." Juanita walked Kelly to the door. "Has there been any more news about John Romero?"

"No, but perhaps soon," Kelly answered.

Walking quickly, Kelly headed back to the Romero home. Once again she'd failed to find any explanation for what she'd seen at the arroyo that night.

As she approached the Romero home she saw Justin standing out on the porch. "Have you learned anything new?" she asked, running up to him.

"Not yet. But I'll know something conclusive by tomorrow morning. The lab will be conducting their tests all night." He leaned against the railing. "I worried about you. Elsie just said that she'd gone for a walk with you, but then realized you needed time to yourself."

"I had an idea I wanted to work on, but it didn't pan out. How did you do?"

"The wood, yucca fibers and feathers we found in the grave look like they might have come from one or more ceremonial masks. From the colors and paints used, Suazo agreed it was likely. After the lab is finished with them, I'm going to try to get one of the pueblo artisans to reconstruct one for us based upon their knowledge and what you remember. From what I saw, though, I doubt all the pieces are there. They've probably scattered that evidence so we couldn't track it back to them."

"The only problem will be getting someone from the pueblo to do that job." She started walking away from the porch.

"Where are you going now?" he followed her.

"Home. I'll be here tomorrow first thing, but I need some rest." Her gaze traveled gently over him. "And so do you. You've had a horrible day." She hadn't forgotten the difficulty he'd had uncovering the grave. That task seemed to have taken its toll on him.

"I feel the need to cleanse myself," he admitted, "not only my body, but my mind as well. If I was at home I'd call in a singer. When the spirit is hurt, they come and the healing chants they know help restore the balance." He walked Kelly to her car. "But I'm not among the Dinéh and the *Hataalii* will not come here. I'll have to find my own way back to harmony."

"Maybe after it's all finished..."

He smiled wearily. "Yes, perhaps then."

The next day Kelly checked with the Romeros before going to class, but Justin had already left. Wondering what, if anything, he'd managed to learn, she was barely able to concentrate on her teaching. Just as school let out, Justin appeared at her classroom door.

Kelly sat immobile at her desk, unable to bring herself to ask the question foremost in her mind.

"It wasn't John," Justin said.

A wave of relief passed through her, easing the unbearable tightness in her chest. "Of course not," she said at last.

He smiled, but said nothing.

"Are you going to tell me the rest?" she asked impatiently.

He shrugged. "All right." He waited as she gathered her things. "The medical examiner managed to get some prints off one hand. The quicklime hadn't touched him there and the dry, hot sand mummified his skin."

She suppressed a shiver and steeled herself to hear the rest. "Go on."

"The man in the grave was named Nick Tyler. Bureau records show he'd served as an enforcer for one of the organized crime families. The M.E. says he died of a knife wound to the chest. Now comes the interesting part. The tip of the knife used to stab him was found imbedded in a rib. It's an exact match of the broken blade on John's handmade knife. Also, the time of death was most likely around the time John disappeared."

"If John killed someone, it must have been in self-defense. Only, what happened next, and where is John now?"

Justin accompanied her outside. "I don't know." He sat down on one of the benches.

"There are two possibilities—either John was killed soon after Tyler and is buried elsewhere, or he's alive and Tyler's friends have taken him prisoner."

"Agreed." He leaned back and stared pensively off into the distance. "If John's being held prisoner, then he must have some hold over his captors that is keeping him from being killed. That would tie in with the searches at John's house and his office. Also remember when they went through your school papers, then burned them? Maybe they thought you had whatever they're looking for. That would explain the search of your house, too. What we have to figure out is what could they be looking for."

"It's got to be connected to the bank somehow. That's the only irregularity we've found."

"We haven't ruled out the witchcraft angle, either," Justin reminded her.

"I wish I could make sense of the Tewa words John shouted. But to me they're just sounds, and impossible to identify. I have no frame of reference for them." She stood and paced. "You know, I failed John once in that arroyo. I've got to find him now."

Justin walked with her to his car. He could appreciate the way she felt. He, too, felt he had failed in his responsibility to John—failed his trust. He pulled the trunk open. "Inside this case are the pieces I suspect made up at least one of the masks. I tried to find someone who could put them together, but I can't. And Suazo refused to help. Can you get one of the artisans you know to do it?"

Kelly mulled it over. "I don't know, but I can try. First, take me to Elsie's."

It took three tries before they found a willing craftsman. Justin and Kelly stood inside the small shop. The scents of paints and fresh wood shavings tinged the air. "We need help," Kelly explained. "We have to find John, and the clues these provide could be valuable in our search."

The elderly Tewa man, Jesse Longacre, shook his head slowly. "If this was stolen from the pueblo, I don't want anything to do with it."

"No masks have been reported missing," Justin answered. "We believe it to be a fake, or one used for evil."

Jesse's eyebrows shot up. "That's a bad business." He studied the pieces Justin had set out before him. "I'll invoke the aid of my *Po wa ha*, my guardian spirit, then I'll see what can be done. Evil doesn't belong here."

Kelly gave him a description of the masks she'd seen in the arroyo, then waited with Justin outside the shop doors. "If this doesn't work, I have another idea we could try," she suggested. "Hamilton Clymer owns an art gallery. He sells mostly paintings, sculpture and very highly priced pottery, but he might also have some masks. Why don't we go over there and take a look?"

"It's definitely worth a try."

Twenty minutes later Jesse Longacre emerged. "This isn't a mask made for witchcraft purposes," he said, giving them a condescending smile. "This is a non-Pueblo-made fake, like the ones you can buy in Santa Fe. The colors are all bright, but it doesn't depict anything in particular. I almost expected to find a label saying Made in Taiwan."

Justin walked to the table where the partially reconstructed mask lay. "Is this what you saw?"

"Yes," she answered without hesitation. "Despite the parts that are missing, this sure looks like one of them."

"I haven't glued the pieces yet, but I've laid them out."

"You don't have to reconstruct it completely," Justin assured him. "Let me take some photographs, then we'll haul everything back to the evidence room."

Longacre handed them a sheet of paper. "I sketched it out as I went along. I think this is what it would look like when it's all put together."

"Thanks for all your help," Justin said. Placing the partially pieced mask and the loose pieces back into his case, he returned to the car. "Let's go check out Clymer. If these masks aren't real, it makes sense to try some of the tourist places around."

"I think this probably rules out actual witchcraft," she said as they drove toward Santa Fe. "The men wearing the masks must have wanted to create that impression in order to frighten away any intruders who stumbled on their activities. Of course, it also enabled them to blend with the ritual atmosphere at the pueblo."

"Now what we have to do is track down the source of the masks."

A half hour later, as they walked to Clymer's gallery, which was decorated to resemble an early trading post, Clymer spotted them. He approached and extended his hand, recognizing Justin from their meeting at the bank. "What an unexpected pleasure! What can I show you two today? My gallery has some very beautiful lithographs by Navajo artists."

"We're interested in ceremonial masks," Justin said.

Clymer's eyebrows shot up. "Well, I hope you realize that there are no genuine ones outside a pueblo. The best I have to offer are good replicas." He led them through a doorway to an adjoining room. "I don't have a big selection, though. I have two of the Oxua cloud beings, Dark Blossom, and Dance of Man. Some archeology students at the university make them for me. They're quite good."

Kelly showed him the artist's rendition of the mask they had found. "This is more what we had in mind."

Clymer stared at the sheet. "I've never seen any like this. If you'll pardon my saying so, it looks like the cheap tourist stuff some places around here sell. Mine, at least, are all authentic replicas." Clymer turned to help another customer. Realizing they'd get nothing further from him, Justin and Kelly left.

As they stepped out into the plaza, they heard loud voices from inside. Clymer stood behind a counter, arguing with a Pueblo woman. A moment later she came out. Glancing at Justin and Kelly, she approached.

"Mr. Clymer's not the honest businessman he appears to be. He's already lied to you once," she warned, "so be wary of what he says."

"What do you mean?" Justin asked. "When did he lie to us?"

"When he spoke to you about the masks. I heard what he said, and I *know* he's sold some that were completely fake. I remember seeing them here and asking him what he thought they were. He just laughed and said they represented dollars from his rich customers back east. My sister who makes pottery for him has a catalog like the one he mails out. It might have a picture of those masks in there."

"Would it be possible for us to see that catalog?"

"Come with me. She lives only a few blocks from here."

"Why are you helping us?" Justin asked softly.

"Clymer's cheated us for the last time. He takes my sister's pottery on consignment, but then doesn't pay us what he should. It's about time people were told about him."

On foot, less than ten minutes later, they reached a small apartment converted from a garage. A slightly older version of the woman who'd brought them appeared at the door. A moment later she produced the catalog.

Kelly found the masks toward the back. "Here, these are the ones."

Justin flashed his badge. "Would it be possible for us to keep this for a bit?"

"Go ahead, I have another inside. I kept them because it shows my pottery. Besides, I can't think of anything I'd like to do better than use it to turn Clymer's cheating against him."

Justin quickly walked with Kelly back to the car. "I sent John's bankbook by special pouch to our experts to see if it could be a forgery. If you have time, I'd like to stop by the office to check on their progress. I also want to talk to the accountant who's been going over the bank records."

"You're thinking that John's disappearance has something to do with Bench and Clymer, aren't you?"

"We have several suspects," Justin answered patiently. "It's too early to make a determination. For example, there's Suazo. He's harassed you repeatedly, and his whereabouts during the murder attempts still remain unverified. He's also been known to follow us. Most important of all, he's also managed to kill the only person we've had an opportunity to arrest, Vincent Larranaga. The possibility exists that it was done to silence the man. Larranaga was associated with real estate schemes, and could have been partners with Suazo and others in illegal activities meant to discredit John. Suazo and John were certainly enemies when it came to the land use issue, and John's absence will probably queer the deal that's in the works. Also, we have no way of knowing if Suazo was one of the men wearing masks that night in the arroyo."

"I've always said that Suazo couldn't be trusted," Kelly agreed.

"Of course there's Bench and Clymer and their tie-in with the bank." Justin drove across town to the office, less than five minutes northeast of the plaza.

"Don't forget Adrian Lowell," Kelly added. "I'm not ready to discount him. He really frightened me that night. Maybe he's the one who's been trying to kill me, and he's just making it look like John's behind it. He's jealous, and obsessed with me."

"And he's had dealings with Clymer, too. He could have gotten the mask from him," Justin finished.

"What about Murray Sullivan?" Kelly asked. "He works at the bank."

"I'm running a check on him too, of course, but I can't see Murray being involved in this. I don't think he knows what's really going on over there."

Justin parked near the side entrance to the Federal Building and walked inside with Kelly. Using an office that had been set aside for him, he gestured toward a chair. "Let me make a few calls first. Then I'm going to bring my boss in here to discuss a plan I've formulated."

He'd piqued her interest, but as usual, forced her to wait as he set his own schedule. "We can have the court orders we need in twenty-four hours," she heard him say. "I think we should move fast on this if we're going to do it."

Finally he hung up the phone. Lost in thought, he stared at the telephone absently.

She resolved to wait, at least another minute, before saying something. She shifted in her chair.

Hearing the movement, he smiled. "The accountant who went over the bank's records hasn't found anything illegal, but the number of accounts and transactions are unusually large for a bank serving that population. He suspects that there's something not quite right here."

"So what now?"

He walked to the doorway and waited for her. "I have one idea, but it'll involve you and it's risky."

"I trust you. John's depending on us. Whatever you've come up with is fine with me."

His eyes held hers, and for a moment she saw all the love she felt for him reflected back at her. It was all the reason they needed for being together. Could they really make it happen? "Let's go," he said at last, his voice gentle.

JUSTIN DROPPED KELLY off at her car. "It isn't too late to change your mind and let me use a policewoman as your double," he said. "We'll have plenty of backup, but the fact is you'll be setting yourself up as a target."

"So will you," she answered.

"It's my job."

"It's what I chose to do for myself and for my friend," she countered flatly. "They know my face too well to be fooled by someone impersonating me. I have to go myself to make it work. I only wish I didn't have to wear this bulletproof vest," she said, shifting her clothing. "It feels like I'm wearing a straitjacket for underwear."

"It's a very sound precaution, believe me," he answered somberly. "You'll go to the tribal police station now?"

She nodded. "I'll tell Suazo that I've remembered coming across some people on the mesa the night of my accident. One man shouted something and I feel that if I can recall what was said, I may be able to identify them. I'll say that I've decided to jog my memory by going out later this afternoon and retracing my steps that night. Then I'll ask him to relay that message to you if he happens to see you first."

"Be careful, and watch your back. I'll meet you behind the gasoline station near the pueblo. You can leave your car there, and we'll go the rest of the way together. Even if Suazo's mixed up in this, I doubt he'll follow you right from the start, since he won't know when exactly you're planning to get out there. Yet we're still making it easy for him to find you. You should be safe while you're at the police station. It's too public for him to try anything there. And remember, once you're outside the pueblo there'll be people guarding you, whether you see them or not."

"Don't worry about me. I'll handle Suazo, you handle the bank. And Elsie will make sure Bench is watched by the Irregulars. If he leaves the pueblo, your people will be notified immediately."

As Justin watched Kelly get into her car, he wondered if he'd made a mistake involving her. Her motives were good, but those were no substitute for professional training in a case like this.

As he drove across the pueblo, he forced his thoughts away from her. It was time to set the next phase of his plan in motion. Minutes later he walked into the bank and asked to see Murray Sullivan. Learning the man was not in, he went directly to Russell Bench's office. He's speak to Sullivan in confidence later.

"Come in," Bench greeted, leaving his desk. "Has anything new turned up about John?"

"Not yet, but I have some matters I want to discuss with you."

Justin sat in the thickly cushioned chair across from Bench's desk and leaned back. "We're going to audit the bank first thing tomorrow morning. At quitting time today, a guard will be posted at the front and no one will have access to the records until our auditors are through. We'll be looking at everything, but in particular I want John Romero's account gone over extensively for evidence of embezzlement. Also, we'll be checking into Hamilton Clymer's business here. He'll be notified officially at about the same time we come in tomorrow."

"You have the bank's full cooperation," Bench assured, "but why on earth is the entire bank being audited? It would have been much simpler if you'd allowed us to get the records for those two accounts. We could have conducted business as usual with the pueblo and not disrupted anyone."

"I'll explain why after the investigation is concluded," Justin replied cryptically. "I know you can understand the constraints I'm under. It's nothing personal, I assure you." He checked his watch. "It's time for me to be going. I'm meeting Kelly Ferguson just outside the pueblo. She claims to have remembered some details that could wrap up our investigation. She's out retracing the steps she made the night of her accident."

"Good luck," Bench said, walking with him to the door. As he reached the entrance, he saw a uniformed guard approaching. "Is this your man?"

"Yes, he'll make sure no one stays late tonight." He shook hands with Bench. "Until tomorrow, then."

Despite his outward calm, Justin's heart was thudding painfully. If Bench, Clymer and Suazo were guilty, they'd have to make their move tonight. He'd left them with no other alternative. They could choose to flee, or take the bait and come out tonight to try to kill Kelly and him.

If any of the three chose to make a run for it, they wouldn't get far. The Irregulars would monitor their activities inside the pueblo, and agents would follow them off tribal land.

Picking up his radio, Justin switched it to the special frequency the Bureau had arranged. No other police departments would be able to monitor their transmissions. "The trap is set," he said quietly. "It's a go."

Chapter Twenty-Two

Justin stopped by the Romeros' home. He was still debating whether or not to tell Clarita that the search for her son was reaching a crucial point. If things went according to plan, she'd probably have some answers soon.

As he walked inside the house, Murray Sullivan greeted him. Clarita and Maria were busy making tortillas in the kitchen and hadn't noticed his arrival. Deciding that the news he was bringing might only serve to unsettle them, he gestured for Sullivan to come outside with him.

"What's going on?" Murray asked, joining him on the porch.

"I'm going to have the bank audited," Justin began, not certain how much to tell Sullivan. "I have reason to believe that there's a big problem with the accounts John Romero was handling for the pueblo."

"You're not serious!" Murray blurted. "How can that be?"

"I've only told you so it won't be a surprise to you tomorrow. I don't want you to get dragged into this mess."

"I appreciate the warning, and I'll certainly be careful."

Justin started back toward his car. "I'll be back later. Please don't tell anyone about this yet, not even the Romeros."

Justin made his way quickly to the meeting place he'd arranged with Kelly. As he drove around to the rear of the building, he saw her waiting.

Kelly left her car and dashed to his. "I don't think anyone followed me out here. In fact, I didn't even see the men you said were supposed to guard me."

"You're not supposed to. If you had, then I'd worry," he answered, giving her hand a gentle squeeze.

Justin drove north along the highway toward Black Mesa. "The state police have loaned us their helicopter. It's on stand-by status back in Santa Fe, waiting for our call to get airborne. If any of our suspects take the bait and move in on us, we'll spring the trap from both sides at the arroyo. There's an entire team behind us that's ready to close in, and the helicopter will be available if they try to cut across the desert."

"I'm not worried," she said, then smiled shakily. "Well, not much, anyway."

He was about to reassure her when his radio came alive. Justin picked up the mike and depressed the side button. "Did you get that?" he asked Kelly when he finished.

"Some of it. The static made it hard to understand what the man was saying. I know it's about the photos you sent in, though."

"Russell Bench's real name is Randall Benchly," Justin explained. "He was an unindicted co-conspirator in a criminal case almost fifteen years ago. He was suspected to be the mastermind behind a money laundering scheme that involved prominent organized crime figures in Phoenix. No charges were brought against him because of lack of evidence, though others he'd associated with were prosecuted."

"Do you think that's what he tried to do here, launder money for his pals in Phoenix?" Kelly looked at the clouds gathering over the Black Mesa area. A thunderstorm of major proportions seemed to be brewing. Well, rain or not, they were committed to the operation now.

"It's a logical deduction. They set up a string of phony accounts and then disperse large deposits among them. The money is drawn out frequently and distributed over a wide variety of investments. That way the mob hides the vast profits made from illegal sources, uses the money to increase their wealth and leaves no easily followed trails that can be used against them."

"That would certainly explain a lot of the details we've uncovered about the bank so far," she said. Vast stretches of stunted junipers and piñons opened up before them as they left the highway. The sky was getting gray now, and the wind was beginning to kick up some dust devils.

Just then, Justin received another call on the radio. Kelly listened carefully this time, trying to pick up the message. "You've got company," she heard. "At least two men in a van."

Justin reached for the radio's Transmit button. "Start closing up the distance between us a bit, but don't move in until I give you the word."

She started to turn around and look, but caught herself and used the side mirror instead. The swirling dust made it hard to see, but something *was* back there. They crossed several of the smaller washes intersecting the main road, yet their tail remained far behind.

They were approaching the arroyo when the rain began to come down. "Great, just what we needed. Something to decrease visibility," he muttered.

As Justin drove down into the wash, he slowed, waiting for their pursuers to catch up. But suddenly a second car appeared at the top of the road on the far side.

Realizing that they were about to be trapped between two enemies, Justin spun the car sideways into the sandy bottom. He had just slammed down hard on the accelerator, trying to escape down the streambed, when a hail of bullets showered the car.

The windshield exploded into a thousand flying cubes, and Kelly instinctively ducked down to protect her eyes. Justin swerved and skidded to a stop, pushing her farther down into the seat as several more rounds thumped into the door panels just behind them.

"Get out," Justin yelled, pushing her toward her door. "He must be using an automatic weapon."

Scrambling in a half crawl, she yanked the door handle and pushed herself out onto the sandy bottom of the wash. The rain came pouring down unmercifully over her.

Justin tumbled out behind her, landing on top of her heavily. Another long burst of gunfire erupted. The car was being riddled with dozens of bullets impacting into the seats and engine compartment.

Rolling over quickly, Justin placed a hand against her back. "Are you okay?"

"I think so," Kelly managed, spitting out a mouthful of sand as she pulled herself out of the mud.

"Then take this and shoot back. Squeeze off the shots and keep the barrel out of the sand. Just point in the direction of that car, but don't expose yourself long enough to aim."

He placed his pistol in her hand.

"What about you?" she asked shakily, afraid to raise her head too far.

"I'm going to reach up and try to get the shotgun and the radio out of the car. Now start shooting back, but don't stick your head out where they can see you."

Kelly scooted up next to the front tire and aimed over the hood at the car that was still up on the edge of the arroyo. Too scared to think, she pulled on the trigger, hardly noticing how the weapon jerked in her hand.

Suddenly she heard a loud boom behind her and felt the impact of a lead fist hitting the fender just beside her head.

"There's the van behind us! Get by the front bumper," Justin shouted, grabbing her by the back of her shirt and hauling her to her feet. By the time she knew what was happening, they were on their knees by the headlights. Justin had aimed his shotgun over the hood, trained on the person who had nearly killed her an instant before.

"Take the car on your side, I'll aim at the one that came in from behind us."

The web of her hand hurt as the hammer jerked back into the soft skin every time she fired a round. She wasn't hitting anything, and worst of all she was expending ammunition they'd need to stay alive.

Peering around the bumper, she tried to place her shots better. Suddenly smoke appeared from underneath the hood of her target. The front end had caught on fire. "Will it explode?" she asked, surprised and pleased by her unexpected success.

"That only happens in the movies," Justin answered. "You probably just put a hole in their carburetor. Keep firing."

Smoke billowed out thickly for a few minutes, then died down in the ever increasing downpour.

"The rain's starting to get heavy. That'll make it harder for them to see us at this distance. I wasn't able to get to the radio, so let's use the reduced visibility to get away from here. We'll head down there while they're still shooting at the car." He pointed to a little embankment that flood currents had created along the bottom of the wash.

"We'll crawl along it until we get around a bend in the wash." Justin fired a few more shots, his gaze straying over their enemies' position. "The car will hide us initially, if we're careful. Once we get far enough away, we'll climb out of the arroyo and get on top of one of the mesas. Then we'll at least have the advantage of seeing them first."

"The people of San Esteban made their stand on Black Mesa more than once, and they're still around," she muttered, remembering what she'd read in the history books.

"Stay flat and use your forearms to pull your body forward."

"Just like John Wayne would do," she mumbled.

"Or Jay Silverheels. Now let's get going." He left the empty shotgun behind a tire, pointing toward their foes.

Water and fast-moving silt formed streams around them as they slithered through the wash. They were at the lowest part of the arroyo floor where an embankment had been created. The runoff was musty smelling and icy cold.

As the water grew deeper, Kelly wondered if this particular spot was prone to flash floods.

"What if a wall of water comes rushing down on us?" Kelly whispered after they had proceeded seemingly unnoticed for about fifty yards. The only sounds she could hear were the gurgles of running water and the steady drone of the pounding rain.

"Do you swim better than you repel bullets?" Justin answered back.

"I suppose so," Kelly muttered, suddenly aware of the numbness in her hands and knees from the rainwater.

"Then stay down here," Justin responded.

The sound of sporadic gunfire still echoed along the walls of the arroyo, but was now muffled slightly as they reached a bend in the wash bottom. Slipping quickly into a thicket of salt cedar, they found a narrow ravine that led them up to the top of the channel. Now that they were out of the arroyo, the thought of drowning was replaced by other more violent possibilities.

Justin led them from boulder to boulder up the steep slope until they were at the summit of the flat-topped mesa. Here the rain fell unobstructed over them. The drops struck the ground, exploding upward and splattering mud all over their legs. The distances seemed to merge into a silver-gray sheet as the menacing gloom all but engulfed them.

Just then, a new outbreak of automatic weapons fire caused them to pause and look down. They could make out small figures rushing their car in the arroyo. Their enemies would now learn that they had slipped away. Soon they would be on their trail again.

"Don't worry. From here, I'll be able to hold them off for a while even if they do try to climb up after us. I'm hoping, though, that they won't be able to find us. This rain will have washed away our trail, so that's on our side. Our biggest problem right now is that this thunderstorm is about to end. Soon the increased visibility will work against us."

"Were you able to see who they were?" she asked, her breathing slowing down slightly.

"No, how about you?"

"I was too busy ducking and running," she admitted sheepishly. "What I want to know is where's our backup?"

"We haven't kept in touch so that should put them on the alert. The team behind us should be closing in soon. They knew our planned route." He glanced at the clouds overhead. "The weather's probably kept the helicopter out of the area, however, or grounded completely."

She fell silent, watching through the gathering dusk for their pursuers and praying help would arrive in time. "I wish I'd been a better friend to John. He was in a great deal of trouble, and from what we've learned, he must have known it. I wish he'd come to me for help."

Justin crouched behind the large boulder. His eyes remained on the area around the arroyo below, like the eyes of some giant bird who felt challenged by a hunt in the storm. He glanced at Kelly, then brushed her hand lightly. "Perhaps John didn't feel he had the right to burden you with what was going on. There are times when people can't share certain parts of their lives, simply because those areas don't belong solely to them. When a man finds himself in that position, the only thing he can do is open his heart fully to those he loves and hold them in the deepest part of himself. It's a sharing of the soul, and the bonding is complete, even though the events can't be shared. Do you understand?"

His voice was a barely audible whisper that coursed over her like the caress of velvet against her skin. He'd left her with no doubt that he was referring to the two of them as well as to John.

"Stay here, and let me take a look around. I've lost track of them, and we can't afford to do that right now."

As he moved off, she felt a rock-hard lump at her throat. Here, on this desolate mound of earth, she'd finally found what she'd been searching for: the personal surrender Justin had offered her transcended her most cherished hopes. In the face of death, life had presented her with the best it had to give. She knew they had to find a way to stay together.

"It'll be dark soon," Justin whispered, coming up silently from behind her.

Startled, she jumped and spun around. "Damn! I didn't even hear you!"

He smiled. "I hope you remember all the lessons on stalking I gave you. Tonight we're going to have to use them to turn the tables on our enemies."

"I remember," she said resolutely. She'd made it this far and had no intention of giving up the fight now. If they lost this one, they'd lose their lives. If they won, they'd have the hope of a future filled with dreams to share.

"It's beginning to get dark, so we have to get started. Until it's completely dark, however, we're going to have to be careful not to show ourselves against the skyline. We're on higher ground than they are and that can make it easier for them to spot us. Also, since the wind's dying down, we'll have to keep our voices soft.''

"Justin, shouldn't the backup team have been there by now?" she asked in a hushed voice. "I would have thought..."

He nodded. "You're right, and I have no way of explaining it."

"Could the backup team have been killed?" She hated asking the question, but not voicing it seemed worse somehow.

"I doubt it," he answered, then shrugged. "Look, we can speculate, or we can start working on ways to stay alive." He crouched before her and put his hand lightly against her cheek. "We're in a lot of trouble, but I'll do everything in my power to protect you."

She nodded. "And I'll do the same for you. Where do we start?"

"We have to start setting traps. We'll create a diversion to separate the men so we can deal with them one at a time." Justin took a small coil of wire he'd removed from a broken-down fence nearby. "I got this when I scouted out the place. It took plenty of bending back and forth to break it loose, but it's going to suit our purposes just fine." He quickly fastened the thin wire about four inches off the ground between two sturdy bushes on either side of the trail. Then he placed a few small tumbleweeds about a foot in front of the wire. When someone stepped over the weeds, their feet would be in just the right position to catch the wire.

Justin led her through an area thick with junipers and sagebrush. Bending back a branch, he placed his handkerchief over the top of its tip and covered the cloth with rocks and dirt. "The weight will keep the branch bowed, but the pile of dirt will flow slowly off the cloth, like sands of an hourglass. When the branch straightens back up, it'll dump the rocks on the ground. We'll use that sound to make them believe we've split up." Justin reached for his pistol. "Are you ready? I'm about to issue them an invitation."

He worked his way to the edge of the bluff. "They're starting to come up. I figured that sooner or later they'd realize this was the most logical escape route for us. Everything else was too much in the open." He glanced back at her. "I'm going to shoot in their direction. It'll slow them down, but in about five minutes when it's completely dark, they'll move again. Only, by then we'll be ready. Stay behind cover, you don't want to get hit by a lucky shot."

Justin fired three times, and immediately a shower of bullets ricocheted off the rocks just above them. "I'd say I got their attention."

"Could you see any of them?"

"There were three men, but I couldn't tell who they are."

Darkness descended, shrouding them in a protective veil. Justin crawled to the rim and tried to focus on the moving shapes below. "Let's go." He checked the cloth one last time. "It's almost ready to give." Detecting movement near the edge of the bluff, Justin tossed a large rock to his right.

"They're over there," a man's voice whispered.

As they began to move in the direction of Justin's rock throw, another sound disturbed the bushes to their left. Their rock trick had done its thing. "They've split up," another voice said.

"I'll take the left, you take the right. Bench, you stay in the middle in case they try to join up again."

Justin and Kelly exchanged glances, but they remained silent as the men moved off. Crouching low to the ground, they waited just down the trail from the low-strung wire booby trap.

As Bench stepped cautiously over the tumbleweeds, his foot was snagged in the wire. His body was thrown forward, his shotgun sailing out in front of him. He landed with a hard thump.

Justin slipped out from behind the juniper brush in the blink of an eye. Before either Bench or Kelly realized it, Justin had his pistol at the back of Bench's head. "Don't make a sound," he ordered in a guttural voice.

Using Bench's own belt and handkerchief, Justin bound and gagged him. Once assured he no longer posed any threat to them, Justin grabbed the shotgun Bench had dropped.

"If he's here, then the other two must be Suazo and Clymer. They've gone off in separate directions, so we'll have to move quickly. I need to ambush those men."

"How did Bench get past my Irregulars?" she muttered, then added, "Let me lead one to you. I can make him think I'm lost and groping around in the dark. He'll come after me, and then you can get the jump on him."

"No way."

"Why not? It'll work, and it won't alarm him. He already thinks we're separated. We can use that to our advantage."

"If he doesn't kill you first."

"Hey, I'm fast on my feet," she teased. "Besides, do you have a better plan?" When he didn't answer right away, she added, "I thought not. Now let's get going."

He muttered an oath. "Your plan lacks preparation, but it might just work. If there ever is a right time for your impulsiveness, this is it." He glanced around. "Lure him back in this direction, and lead him past that rock." He pointed to a boulder almost seven feet in diameter. "I'll grab him as he comes by." Justin listened for a moment. "He's not too far from here. Come on." He led her quietly to a new position, much closer to their prey. "Be careful." Justin handed her his pistol, just in case.

She smiled and gave him a thumbs up, not trusting her voice. As soon as Justin disappeared from her view, she thought she'd be sick. She'd never been so scared in her entire life.

Making sure she scraped against the side of every shrub she could find, and then emitting a few yelps for good measure, she waited and listened. The man was coming back. Hearing him draw closer, Kelly started running toward the boulder Justin had pointed out.

She dashed past it quickly. Then, as her pursuer closed in, Justin came around from behind the rock. Swinging the shotgun like a baseball bat, he caught the man full in the chest. The crushing impact threw both men to the ground. Maintaining his advantage, Justin twisted his adversary's free arm behind his back and forced his face down onto the sand.

Groaning, the man turned his head to the side, spitting out the dirt. "Hamilton Clymer!" she identified in a whisper.

"Quick, help me tie him up," Justin urged. He took the clip from the AK-47 assault rifle Clymer had been carrying and tossed it away in the dark. They were counting on stealth not firepower, but they didn't want to leave a weapon around that could be used against them. Employing the same method he'd used on Bench, he quickly neutralized their second assailant.

Justin emptied Clymer's jacket pocket of ammunition and a penknife, then took the hand-held radio that had been looped around Clymer's belt. As he stuck it into his hip pocket, the radio speaker crackled alive. "Clymer, where the hell are you?"

Justin and Kelly exchanged glances. "That's Murray Sullivan." Her voice was scarcely more than a whisper lost in the wind.

Justin depressed the side button. "You're alone now, Sullivan," he said in a low, menacing voice. "Quit now and make it easier on yourself."

The only response was the static.

Kelly handed Justin back his pistol. "Now we know how they managed to stay one step ahead of us. With Sullivan so close to the Romeros, it was easy for them to lead us in circles," Justin whispered. "It also explains how Bench managed to elude your Irregulars. Sullivan must have helped him leave the pueblo."

"The bank's only a block away from the community center. He must have found it ridiculously simple to get into the kitchen and doctor my sandwich. And come to think of it, doesn't he take medication for his stomach? I'll bet that's what he used to poison me. He must have done it when he pretended to come over to get a soft drink. With his stomach problems he doesn't touch anything but water. It should have occurred to me before. No matter how you figure it, he was in a perfect position to cause the most damage."

A loud click came over the radio as Murray thumbed his Transmit button. Justin held his fingers to his lips, signaling to her to be silent. Another click came over the hand-held radio. Justin set it down next to a thick stand of brush and pulled her away silently.

She realized what their attacker was trying to do. By clicking the Transmit button and listening for the unit's speaker, Murray was homing in on them. He would follow the clicking noise their radio made and come right up on them. Justin was planning to use Murray's own strategy against him.

Seconds later, from behind the cover of an embankment, they waited and watched the spot where Justin had placed the radio. Minutes slipped by, and several times she thought she heard a footstep or the rustle of leaves. Justin never moved, his eyes like dark caverns in his face as he watched intently.

Suddenly a ripple of gunfire burst around the bush where they'd abandoned the radio. With a murderous yell, Murray sprang into sight, blanketing the area with bullets.

The sound of his weapon suddenly merged with a thunderous vibration as a huge apparition rose up from the canyon below, scattering dust and tumbleweed everywhere.

It was their helicopter backup, Kelly realized, her heart thumping. She almost stood up and cheered, but Justin held her down. It stopped abruptly to hover fifty feet overhead. The bright beam of a searchlight stabbed down, transfixing Murray Sullivan in its glare.

Sullivan covered his eyes against the blast of dust from the chopper's rotor backwash. Pointing his semiautomatic rifle in the air, he tried to fire blindly, but no shots rang out.

Justin was instantly on his feet, hurtling toward Murray as the banker tried desperately to remove the spent clip from his weapon. By the time Murray noticed him it was too late. With a bone-shattering tackle that made her wince, Kelly saw Sullivan topple to the ground.

As Justin pinned him to the earth, Kelly rushed out into the circle of light and waved to the helicopter above.

Justin pulled Murray to his feet harshly, his pistol at the man's back. "You betrayed some people who'd never harmed you," he spat out. "Don't give me a reason to kill you."

Justin held Murray as the helicopter landed fifty yards away. The headlights of several vehicles began to appear on the desert floor below them, and men started running about, flashlights and weapons in their hands. Justin smiled at her. "This Navajo is sure happy to see the cavalry, even if they are a little late."

As the agents rounded up the two other prisoners, Justin glanced at one of the men from the helicopter. "Where were you guys? You were supposed to support the pursuit team."

"At first we couldn't lift off because of the winds. You had your pursuit team ready to give you backup, so we figured you'd still be okay. But the rain was a lot heavier a little east of here, and one of the small tributary washes between them and you suddenly became a raging torrent. They couldn't get across." The pilot shook his head slowly. "That's the problem living out in this area. The rain comes down so suddenly that the runoff has no time to soak into the ground. One moment it's dry, and the next a wall of water from a thunderstorm a few miles away comes roaring down the arroyo."

"So how did they end up getting here?"

"They headed toward the pueblo and got help there. Sergeant Suazo brought them here using an alternate route."

The sergeant, just reaching the rim of the mesa, overheard the last part and added, "It's my job. Only you should have told me what you were really up to, Na—" He stopped. "Well, you should have told me."

Justin nodded. "You're right."

Suazo grinned. "Now maybe we all can have some peace and quiet." His eyes grew hard as he stared at Sullivan. *"Ké Pí Cháe tsaa í,"* he spat out in Tewa.

Kelly glanced at him quickly. "Say that again," she asked, "please."

Suazo looked at her, puzzled, then repeated it.

"That's what John shouted that night in the arroyo. What's it mean?"

"Literally translated it means 'redneck banker.'" His eyes bored through Sullivan. "The term 'redneck' doesn't mean the same to us, though. It's an insulting way to refer to Anglos. It alludes to their delicate skins and constitutions," Suazo said grinning mischievously.

"It *was* a clue," she said softly. "John tried to identify the people who had captured him." She turned to Sullivan. "You tried to use John to further your money-laundering scheme, didn't you!" she accused. "What he thought were investment profits being placed into tribal accounts were really deposits from illegal mob operations. But he was too smart for you and caught on."

"So you killed Romero," Suazo muttered, coming dangerously close to Sullivan.

"No, but he might as well be dead," Murray said boldly, his eyes locking with Suazo's in a deadly challenge. "Unless you make a deal with me, John will die or thirst or starvation, whichever comes first. He can't escape from where he's being held."

Hearing footsteps behind her, Kelly turned around. Both Bench and Clymer were being led toward them. As one of the deputies unfastened the belt from Bench's hand and began to slip the cuffs on, Bench broke free. Spinning around, he made a desperate grab for the deputy's gun and pulled it from his holster.

Bench turned, pointed the pistol at Justin and began shooting. Murray, caught between the two, was struck as he tried to scramble to safety. Justin, reacting instantly, returned fire, but was thrown back as a bullet impacted against his chest.

Chapter Twenty-Three

Kelly saw Justin fall, and her whole future collapsed with him. An instant later, an ear-shattering burst of gunfire erupted around her. Bullets slammed into Russell Bench's body, hurling him violently to the earth.

As she fought the need to cry out, she saw Justin stir.

"I guess these vests really work," he said, sitting up. "But it still feels like I've been punched in the chest by a giant."

Kelly didn't now whether to laugh or cry. As the other agents clustered around Murray Sullivan and Bench, Justin stood shakily.

"Sullivan's dead," Suazo said from behind them. "So's Bench. We'll have to question Clymer to see where they're keeping John."

One of the agents from the Sante Fe office shoved a handcuffed Clymer forward. Justin stood before him. "You know what we want, now start talking."

"I can't help you."

"The charges against you are bad enough already. Do you really want to add murder to them?"

"Believe me, if I knew anything I'd tell you. My job, until you guys started getting close, was just to transfer funds. I refused to get involved with the rest. Murray initially asked me to go up to Romero's cabin and make it look like he'd been hiding out there, and I wouldn't do it. They had to send Larranaga instead. Romero was their problem and I wanted to keep it that way. My only suggestion is that you check up at Murray's place."

"Have the Sante Fe police send a car to Sullivan's home and search everywhere," Justin ordered one of the men.

As Clymer was led away, Suazo joined them. "That Anglo has played it smart all along," Suazo spat out. "I don't think he would have taken John to his home in the city. It's too risky. I think we better start to work on a contingency plan."

They walked back to Suazo's vehicle together. "I have an idea," Kelly said, interrupting the silence between them. "Let's head to Murray's home ourselves. Even if John's not there, we might find a clue that will lead us to where he's being held."

Suazo nodded slowly. "I hate to admit it, but the schoolteacher's idea sounds good to me." He grinned at her for the first time.

The friendly gesture took her so much by surprise she stared at him for several seconds. Finally she managed to return his smile.

As they traveled to Santa Fe, a message came in over Suazo's radio. The transmission made their hearts sink. "I didn't think he'd be there," Suazo said. "I wish I knew how much time we have to look."

"Do you think they've hurt John?" Kelly asked in a barely audible voice.

"They must have wanted something from him," Justin offered, "or they wouldn't have kept him alive. My opinion is that they've probably worked him over to try to get whatever information they wanted, but not enough to seriously injure him."

"That's the way I see it, too," Suazo agreed.

When they reached Murray's home, two police vehicles were parked outside. They walked inside the spacious four-bedroom home and began to look around. "Let's split up," Justin suggested, and they all headed in different directions.

Time seemed to drag for Kelly. They were looking for something, but none of them had any idea what. Leaving the master bedroom, she entered a study. Against the far wall was an antique desk with a roll top. When she tried to push the top back, she realized it was locked. "Justin?" she called out down the hall.

Seeing him come toward her, she added, "His desk is locked, and I can't find a key. Any suggestions?"

"We'll force it. Let me see if I can wedge my fingers beneath it, then give a good yank."

Suazo came in behind them. "Let me help."

A few seconds later the latch popped and the roll top slid back. "Let's go through all these bills and papers. Maybe there's something here." He grabbed a handful, as did Kelly and Suazo. Then they began to sort.

"There're several tax slips in here for properties around the state. It seems Murray owned quite a bit of real estate," Kelly said.

Justin looked at the top of the forms. "These are the legal specifications for each. What we need to do is find out where they're located." He walked to the telephone. "I'll call the office, someone will be able to help us out."

Twenty minutes later they stood before the desk, staring at five addresses. "They're all in this quadrant of the state, at least. The question is do we check these out or keep looking?" Suazo asked.

"We're out of leads," Justin said slowly. "Let's check the nearest one ourselves and have the state police or local sheriff departments take the other four, as well as Bench's and Clymer's property."

"Okay, that means we take this one," Suazo said, pointing to the third address.

"Where is that place, anyway?" Justin asked.

"It's right outside Madrid. It's not far," Suazo answered.

"Madrid? We found a matchbook from a bar near there inside John's truck. We sent a state policeman to check it out, but he didn't get anywhere. At the time, though, we had no suspect photos or descriptions to show anyone."

By the time they were finally underway, it was almost dawn. Justin had obtained topographical maps revealing the layout of the entire area. Suazo glanced from one to the other. "The matchbook offers hope, but let's not count on anything."

"But he's got to be at one of these places," Kelly argued. "Where else could Murray have held him prisoner?"

"That's the question we may be asking ourselves in another hour," Suazo cautioned.

"What do you suppose John has that they'd want so badly? Elsie's cousins told me that they'd temporarily lost copies of some records at the bank recently. Bench claimed to have found them again, but now I'm beginning to wonder if that was true. Maybe John stole some printouts that would have shown what Sullivan and the others were doing," Kelly ventured.

"If he did," Justin answered, "then they would have been his insurance."

"John Romero is smart. That sounds just like the type of thing he might do," Suazo said.

Throughout the twenty-minute drive Kelly could feel the tension mounting in the car. To have found those responsible for the attempts on her life and the trouble at the pueblo had been a victory. But their real goal, to rescue John from his captors, still eluded them. She clasped her hands in her lap to keep them from trembling.

As they reached Madrid, Suazo drove along the highway slowly. The sun was nearly up and the hills were casting long shadows. Many abandoned miners' shacks littered the hillsides, with an occasional house occupied by some adventuresome soul. Those with signs of life were few and far between, however.

"Sullivan's cabin is right outside town. We'll be there in another minute." Suazo turned off the highway and drove down the gravel path winding north. "According to the map coordinates you gave me, it should be up ahead."

The empty road stretched out before them. Then, just as Kelly was about to insist they'd taken the wrong turn, a solitary cabin appeared at the base of a small wooded hill.

Suazo parked off the road. "You and I can go on foot from here," he said to Justin. "But the woman should remain in the Bronco."

"No, you can't trust her that way," Justin answered. "Believe me, it's better to keep her with us."

"What am I, not here or something? Stop talking about me as if I don't have any say in this." Kelly glared at Suazo. "Like it or not, I'm going with you."

Suazo shook his head resignedly. "Whatever," he muttered, reaching behind his seat for the shotgun.

They crept noiselessly toward the cabin, but there were no sounds coming from inside. As they neared the rustic hut, Justin glanced at Kelly. "You stay behind this tree," he whispered. "If you see anyone coming up from the side, let us know."

Justin stepped onto the front porch first, weapon drawn. As he approached the door, he heard a noise. Instantly he flattened against the wall. "FBI. Come out with your hands up," he warned.

His only response was a shuffling noise from inside.

Justin waited another second, then tried the door handle. It was locked.

Suazo appeared from around the corner. "No back door," he said in a harsh whisper. "Except for the windows this is the only way out. How about if I glance through the front window?"

"Go ahead."

Before Justin could say anything, Suazo picked up an old wooden chair and tossed it through the front window.

They waited. Suazo crept up close, looked inside, then shook his head. Muffled sounds from the interior of the cabin drifted out to them.

"Shall we go in?" Suazo asked.

"You kick it open, and I'll go through first. Cover me."

Suazo landed the heel of his shoe against the door, splintering it and breaking the lock. As it swung open, Justin dove inside, rolling to the side as he did.

Scrambling to his feet, he saw Kelly crouching next to John on the floor. "How in the world...?"

"I figured that if anyone was inside the cabin, they'd be too busy concentrating on you. You were making enough noise. I went up to the side window—" she smiled and shrugged "—you did tell me to watch them, and I saw John inside on the floor."

"I tried to yell," John explained, his words thick, "but I couldn't. They kept me gagged. When Kelly came to the window, she could see that I was alone. Didn't mean to put you through any extra trouble," he teased. "I would have found a way to escape, too, if Sullivan hadn't kept me drugged. That man seems to have a pill for everything."

Justin looked at his friend. John's eyes had been blackened, and his face showed bruises and minor cuts from repeated beatings. His feet were bare, his boots obviously having been taken by one of his captors to use as part of their deception. His empty knife sheath, still hanging from his belt, explained where they'd gotten John's hand-made knife. "I knew you were a tough old bird. What in the heck did you have that they wanted so badly? Was it those books everyone was searching for?"

John tried to laugh, then stopped. "Remind me not to even try smiling for a while, okay?" As Justin removed the nylon cords that had held his wrists bound, he rubbed them painfully. "I had a copy of their real books as well as a copy of one of their doctored books. That was my leverage against them. Murray called me the night of the ceremony and told me that he'd learned who was masterminding the bank's illegal operations. When he said he was afraid for his life, I agreed to meet with him. I'd always felt sorry for the guy—he was trying so hard to belong. By the time I realized that he'd sold me out, it was too late. First, they sent a goon to kill me, but I figured that was because they'd discovered I'd taken the books. I never even considered the possibility that Murray had double-crossed me. I walked right into his trap." He stood up with help, favoring his left leg. "How did you put it all together? Did you find the books?"

"No, where did you put them?"

John tried not to smile, but couldn't quite manage it. "In the bank, where they'd be safe. They're taped inside one of the ventilation ducts in Bench's office, right next to the grill. I managed to grab them, with the help of Elsie's cousin, Carol, but I figured that my chances of getting them out of the bank were slim. They were starting to get suspicious of me. I'm surprised she didn't turn the books over to you."

"I think she's been trying to protect you. While she was willing to tell us what she could to make you safe, Carol really didn't trust us enough to tell us your secret. She couldn't risk being wrong about us. And all this time Sullivan and the others have been making it look like you were hiding out, trying to kill me," Kelly explained. "Carol's very fond of you, I think."

John smiled. "I know."

Leaning on Justin, John walked to the car. "How did you find out what I meant in my letter? I didn't mention the bank at all. Or are you here unofficially?"

"Officially, but not because of your letter. I didn't even see that until a few days ago. You see, when they went after Kelly, it became attempted murder. Your disappearance was also part of the investigation. When Kelly drove into whatever was going on that night in the arroyo it put her right in the middle of it."

John looked at her. "That was you? I should have yelled in English," he muttered. "What were you doing out there anyway? Did you get lost?"

JUSTIN SHOWED Clymer's statement to John and Kelly. "Tyler, the man who jumped you," he explained, looking at John, "was only supposed to follow you. Unfortunately he got ambitious. He must have figured that with you dead it wouldn't matter if they got the books back or not. Unlike Murray and the others, he didn't think you'd have that covered."

"I didn't, not completely anyway," he admitted, "but I did some fast thinking when I saw Murray was one of them. I told them I'd left the books with a friend, and if anything happened to me or my family, they'd be sent to the district attorney's office."

"So they decided Kelly was the friend and that they could frame you for Kelly's murder, sealing that loose end in case she ever managed to figure out what you had yelled. If she did have the books, then they wouldn't have to worry about them with her dead, and if she didn't have them they'd still be covered. Eventually they'd have killed you, but with a murder rap over your head, it would have been assumed that you were on the run."

"When I first started asking questions and taking a closer look at the accounts I was managing, Bench offered me a deal. He said he could make arrangements to have non-Indian landowners 'persuaded' to sell parcels adjacent to the pueblo cheaply, if I stopped making waves for the bank. I played along with him, since I was trying to gather more information. My only mistake was telling Murray what I was doing."

John walked around the office, staring at the diplomas and the commendations on Justin's wall. "You know, this place has a feel of permanence to it. Is my wandering Navajo friend putting down roots?" he baited.

"I've received my transfer to this region," Justin answered, then glanced at Kelly.

She smiled broadly. "Then we both have reason to celebrate. I've received a government grant to set up tutorial programs among the other pueblos in the area. It's going to be a permanent part of their curriculum, and will keep me busy around here for quite some time."

"That's great news!" Justin said, an enormous grin covering his features.

John chuckled softly. "Speaking of permanence, I better be going. I've got a date with Carol Black Feather."

"Treat her well. She's quite a lady," Kelly said.

"I realize that," he said, growing serious. "And you don't have to worry about her. I've got plans for Carol. These last two weeks have caused me to start thinking of the future." John gave them a sheepish smile. "You know you're in trouble when you start looking at other people's kids and wondering what it would be like to have your own. I'm sure you know what I mean, old buddy." Chuckling, he walked out.

Justin stared after him. It was such a simple matter. Only one more thing to do, but he was as nervous as a cat on a rainy night. He paced around the office, then stopped in midstride and turned to Kelly. "Let's go for a drive."

"Is something wrong? You're not acting like yourself," she observed, following him out.

He shook his head. All the stumbling blocks were removed, now it was time to act. He headed for the foothills northeast of Santa Fe. The sun would set soon. As dusk neared, the dazzling array of reds and blues that made up the desert sunset lit up the sky around them.

Taking her by the hand, he walked with her to a spot overlooking the valley below. "This is a very special place. From here you can see both the pueblo and Santa Fe clearly. They're close, yet they each exist separately, blending and sharing the best of themselves with the other. Can you accept my love, schoolteacher, knowing that even when we're apart, my heart will always be with you?"

As the aspens rustled in the breeze, making their own song, Kelly's yes was a soft caress that touched his lips and his heart.

American HEROES
AGAINST ALL ODDS

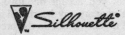

HARLEQUIN®   **Silhouette®**

Please address questions and book requests to: Harlequin Reader Service U.S.: 3010 Walden Ave.,
P.O. Box 1325, Buffalo, NY 14269 CAN.: P.O. Box 609, Fort Erie, Ont. L2A 5X3   PAHGEN

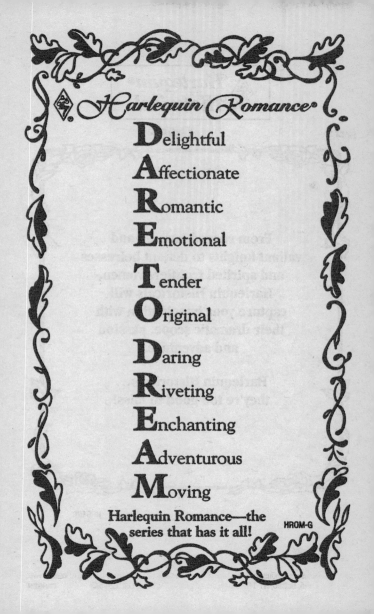

ℋarlequin Romance®

Delightful

Affectionate

Romantic

Emotional

Tender

Original

Daring

Riveting

Enchanting

Adventurous

Moving

Harlequin Romance—the
series that has it all!

HROM-G

Harlequin® Historical

From rugged lawmen and
valiant knights to defiant heiresses
and spirited frontierswomen,
Harlequin Historicals will
capture your imagination with
their dramatic scope, passion
and adventure.

Harlequin Historicals...
they're too good to miss!

HARLEQUIN®
Makes any time special.™

Upbeat, all-American romances about the pursuit of love, marriage and family.

Duets.
Two brand-new, full-length romantic comedy novels for one low price.

Harlequin® Historical
Rich and vivid historical romances that capture the imagination with their dramatic scope, passion and adventure.

Temptation.
Sexy, sassy and seductive—Temptation is hot sizzling romance.

SUPERROMANCE
A bigger romance read with more plot, more story-line variety, more pages and a romance that's evocatively explored.

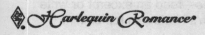
Harlequin Romance
Love stories that capture the essence of traditional romance.

INTRIGUE®
Dynamic mysteries with a thrilling combination of breathtaking romance and heart-stopping suspense.

HARLEQUIN PRESENTS®
Meet sophisticated men of the world and captivating women in glamorous, international settings.

Prescription: Romance™

"Any hereditary diseases run in the family?"

"None that I am aware of," Drew replied.

"Brothers? Sisters?"

"Three of the first, two of the second," he said wearily. "All right?"

Lizzy smiled. "Perfect."

"I'm not looking for a wife."

"I'm not looking for a husband," she said soothingly. "You seem like a reasonable man and I'd like to ask you a favor. Would you please have a baby with me?"

Prescription: Romance™

CONTRACT
DAD
HELEN SHELTON

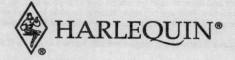

HARLEQUIN®

TORONTO • NEW YORK • LONDON
AMSTERDAM • PARIS • SYDNEY • HAMBURG
STOCKHOLM • ATHENS • TOKYO • MILAN • MADRID
PRAGUE • WARSAW • BUDAPEST • AUCKLAND

ISBN 0-373-83384-9

CONTRACT DAD

First North American Publication 1998.

This edition published by arrangement with Harlequin Books S.A.

® and TM are trademarks of the publisher. Trademarks indicated with ® are registered in the United States Patent and Trademark Office, the Canadian Trade Marks Office and in other countries.

Printed in U.S.A.

CHAPTER ONE

SUPPRESSING a smile, Drew gazed out of the window of his new fourth-floor office and studied the traffic and the ambulances that streamed below in the narrow streets around the Royal National's main entrance close to London's Regent's Park, letting his cousin's wife's chatter go over his head.

But when she repeated his name for the second time he turned back, his smile breaking through at her indignant expression. Strident and imposing even without the added bulk of her pregnancy, Jane rarely heeded her audience but, for once, it seemed she'd noticed his lack of attention.

'Repeat what I said,' she demanded, one hand on an ample hip, the other fishing in a huge jar of stuffed green olives which she seemed to have brought him as a gift.

'Bill's birthday party tonight?' Drew ventured, referring to the surprise party for Jane's husband. In the lead-up to the arrival of her baby Jane had stopped working at the hospital, and he'd assumed this call on him today was to remind him about the party she appeared determined he would attend. 'I mustn't be late.'

Sharply she said, 'That was five minutes ago.' She withdrew a handful of olives and clenched them in her fist. 'Drew Maitland, if you weren't Bill's cousin and oldest friend I would just…'

But she stopped and closed her mouth, rare for Jane in Drew's experience, and he tilted his head, immediately intrigued. 'What else?'

'Your actress,' she said baldly. 'Last week I saw a picture of her, draping herself over her new leading man.'

'We're no longer seeing each other.' Dryly and, he sus-

5

pected, with futility, he added, 'Not that that's any of your business.'

Jane smirked. She stuffed the olives in her mouth and swallowed heavily. 'Are you all right?'

'Fine.'

'What happened?'

'Nothing dramatic enough to interest you.' Seeing the sparkle in her eyes that suggested she doubted that, he leaned forward and tapped her snub nose with one sharp, rebuking finger. 'We realised we didn't have a lot in common.'

Outside of bed, that was, he added privately, acknowledging that the only reason his relationship with Suzie had lasted as long as it had been because her involvement in a successful West End production—one which had gone on tour during the year around Britain—had kept them apart for much of that time.

The sex had been good. Five—even two—years ago it might have been enough for him, but instead he'd grown dissatisfied. He'd become jaded, he realised, conscious of a cynicism that had begun creeping as much into his professional life as into his relationships. With Suzie he'd seen that he'd allowed convenience and physical pleasure to become priorities, without ever pausing to analyse whether they were attributes worth valuing.

With that understanding had come his startled recognition that as well as changes in his work he wanted a family. Not simply a wife, for Suzie had made it plain she'd have been happy to oblige him, but children, and there she'd drawn a line. Although she'd wanted him, pregnancy, with its potential to slacken her perfect body, had been out of the question.

Ending their relationship had been his first step towards redefining what he wanted from a life which, while superficially satisfying, now left him with a restlessness he found disturbing.

Career-wise he'd made changes quickly. His week-old

move to the National's specialist chest medicine team offered better patient facilities and resources and more secure funding for his research interests than his previous appointment, and already his enthusiasm for medicine had been revived.

Now Jane's news about Suzie finding another lover so quickly pleased him because she was a woman who needed male admiration to make her happy.

As far as his own personal life went, although Drew was open to the idea of meeting a woman who might one day become the mother of his children, now he valued his time alone. Time to find himself, he acknowledged, grimacing not for the first time at the hackneyed phrase and still uncomfortable about a leaning towards self-analysis which was very new for him.

The irony hadn't escaped him either that, despite his relative youth, he was now confronting issues that constituted the essence of the so-called male midlife crises. Crises, he'd always argued, were the creation of income-deprived psychotherapists, trying to argue up extra clients to justify their existences.

The delighted clapping of Jane's plump hands drew his attention back to her, and he smiled as she grabbed more olives. Her dancing eyes suggested she was pleased by his confirmation that his involvement with Suzie was over. 'So? What now?'

He sighed. 'What now what?'

'Are you seeing anyone at the moment?' she demanded sharply, popping the olives in her mouth one by one.

'As in a woman?'

'As in a monkey,' Jane said acidly, still chewing.

'No.' But her impatience amused him as much as it made him wary. He knew what was coming. 'No, Jane.'

'But I have the perfect person for you,' she protested, and he saw her swollen feet jiggle in her excitement. 'I've been meaning to introduce you for absolutely ages but this is the first time in years you haven't been dating. She's not on call tonight and she's coming to the party. It's fate!'

'Forget it.' Drew regarded her sternly, his alarm increasing in proportion to her enthusiasm. Despite his new-found paternal instincts, the thought of Jane trying to matchmake him with another one of her lunatic friends was enough to give him nightmares. 'I barely escaped alive last time.'

'Lynn's divorce had just come through.' Jane's frown suggested he'd still not been completely forgiven for failing to live up to the promises she'd made to her friend. 'She wanted to celebrate.'

'There's a time and place,' he said abruptly, lifting his eyes to the ceiling at Jane's sniff of disagreement. 'And what about the other one? Cleo?'

'*Caro* was upset about turning thirty,' Jane said defensively, her dancing feet stilling as she reached for more olives. 'She was looking for a little excitement.' She paused with the olives halfway to her mouth, narrowing her eyes at him. 'I thought men liked sexually aggressive women.'

'Again, there's a time and place,' he said dryly, watching her stuff the olives into her mouth, bemused by her apparent appetite for the things. 'No more friends, Jane. I'm not interested.'

'Lizzy's different to the others.'

'I doubt it.'

'You'll see.' Her smile was green with olives—and nasty. 'In fact, you've probably already met her since she's your chest team's X-ray doctor.'

He hadn't met her, but in his eight days at the National he had heard the consultant radiologist's name. 'Elizabeth Murdoch?' he said with a frown.

'Lizzy, not Elizabeth,' Jane said quickly. 'She spits when anyone calls her Elizabeth. Well? Have you met her yet?'

'No.' And he had reservations about meeting one that spat.

'But she takes your team's X-ray meetings.'

Drew hoped she wouldn't spit on the films. 'I didn't make the meeting this week.'

'Then tonight's the night,' Jane said happily, looking pleased with herself. 'It'll be so romantic.'

'Jane—'

'Just promise me you won't be put off too easily,' she added, taking another olive.

'I'm not interested…' But Drew frowned. Her words had been laced with just enough worry to rouse his curiosity, and reluctantly he found himself hesitating. Finally he sighed. 'Explain.'

'Just if she seems a little…eager,' Jane said delicately.

He closed his eyes briefly then sighed. 'What? More than the other two?'

'Oh, not for *sex*,' Jane said hastily, and Drew wondered if the sudden pinking of the tops of her already red and rounded cheeks could possibly be a blush. 'Not Lizzy,' she added. 'Never. Lizzy's not very *into* sex, if you know what I mean. She's not exactly like your… I mean, it takes her six months before she'd even consider sleeping…and even then there was only the one… Well, she's not like the women you normally date.'

'You mean, not like all your other friends?' More likely a hormonal flush, he told himself, reconciling the colour that hadn't faded with his knowledge of Jane. Unflappable in situations which would turn most people crimson, he found it difficult to conceive that the mere mention of sex would rouse the slightest embarrassment in her.

'Lizzy's…' But for once his cousin's wife really did seem nonplussed. 'She's old-fashioned. She's looking for a serious relationship—not some brief fling, that's not her style. She's very clucky,' she added, increasing his unease. 'Since I've been pregnant it's been hard to get her to talk about anything but the baby. She wants to feel it all the time and she's found one of those awful funnel things and keeps insisting on checking its heartbeat. She's read more pregnancy books than I have and I'm the one who's having the wretched thing.'

She darted an upward look between her lashes, clearly seeing his wariness. 'Don't look like that,' she urged. 'I just thought it was fair to warn you. If you understand her a little you won't be surprised by the way she might...act. Besides, you're thirty-eight. You're getting old. You need someone steady like Lizzy. It's time you settled down.'

'Not with a frigid, clucky radiologist who spits,' he said gravely, not correcting her assessment of his age.

Jane didn't look at him. She took two more olives and pushed the almost empty jar away. 'I've watched you with your nephews and nieces, and you're great with them. You obviously like children. You must want some of your own.'

'That's a different issue.'

'Lizzy's very lovely.'

'I believe you.'

'You don't want to meet her.'

'I'm happy to meet her.'

But, despite his assurance, Jane's face fell. 'She's kind and gentle and she'll make you a wonderful wife,' she said tightly. She folded her hands over the top of her baby with a careful wince that Drew realised he was supposed to notice. 'She keeps her flat very clean.' She darted him a sideways look, clasped her stomach and winced again. 'She's conscientious and her desk is always neat.'

Drew relaxed with a grin. He sat on the edge of his desk and folded his arms, regarding her. Manipulative as hell, he acknowledged, but for now—while he remained entertained—he decided it was easier to humour her. 'Does she cook?'

'She enjoys healthy food,' Jane said, her smugness suggesting she thought he wouldn't notice how deftly she'd sidestepped that. 'And she's good with animals.'

'Kind to old people?'

'Extremely.' Jane smiled, the pain in her stomach apparently forgotten. She reached for the olive jar again, pulled it to the front of the desk and fished in the bottom for the last few.

'Good at her job?'

'Consultant radiologist at twenty-nine,' she declared, munching. 'A year earlier than me, but to be horribly honest, she was always brighter. She's thirty-two now.' She swallowed the olives, then beamed. 'In line to be head of the department before she's forty, at this rate.'

'But ready for marriage?'

'And lots of children.' Jane nodded enthusiastically. 'Yes, Drew. You see, she's perfect for you.'

'You'll be maid of honour?'

'Bill can be best man,' she confirmed, clapping her hands. 'A small wedding, I thought, something tasteful. Your delicious brother can do the catering. We could have the reception at his restaurant.'

His mouth twitched. 'Honeymoon?'

'Provence. Or Tuscany. Somewhere dreamy and beautiful with cultural things as well. Lizzy hates beaches. She's pale and she always burns.'

Smiling slightly at the image of a ghost-like, sunburnt, spitting radiologist with a cleaning obsession and a neurotic fear of sex, Drew regarded Jane fondly. 'You know you're quite mad?'

'It'll be perfect,' Jane mused, apparently electing to ignore him. She peered into the bottom of the empty olive jar and frowned. 'Your children will be able to come and play in the pool.' She licked sticky-looking fingers. 'They'll be related, I suppose, yours and this bubble inside me. Is that second cousins?'

Drew frowned, realising that she was taking this far more seriously than he'd assumed. Alarm bells ringing, he lifted his hand. 'Stop,' he commanded. 'Janey, stop there. This is nonsense. I'm not interested.'

Her face fell again immediately. 'You mean you don't want to marry her?'

He laughed, unable to stop himself, his amusement increasing at Jane's apparent disbelief. 'Unbelievable as it may seem,' he conceded easily, wondering if she'd come to see him this afternoon with the sole intention of persuading him to marry her friend. 'No deal. No way. Pregnancy has addled your brain.'

'I'm in a very delicate state,' she cried. She braced her hands against the armrests of the swivelling chair she'd occupied for the last hour, levered herself out and waddled away from it. 'This is very important to me, Drew. I can't believe you could play with my feelings like that.'

'And I can't believe you thought you could manipulate me into anything so absurd,' he said firmly, one hand in the small of her back, urging her gently towards the door.

'You're totally suited.'

'I'm enjoying my solitude.'

'That's ridiculous.' Her mouth dropped open. 'You've never been without…anyone,' she said stiffly. 'You'll be climbing the walls in a week.'

He laughed. 'Not all of us are as sex-crazed as you.'

'But I've told her about you,' she said despairingly. 'I left a message on her machine about tonight. She'll be all excited.'

Despite his amusement, he winced at that. It occurred to him that, regardless of her good intentions, Jane had probably not done her friend any favours this afternoon. But, then, at least he was going to this meeting forewarned. When the poor woman made her advances he'd make it immediately clear he wasn't interested and so defuse the situation before she assumed anything else.

'Go,' he said affectionately, kissing one of Jane's round cheeks before shoving her out into the corridor outside his office. 'See you tonight.'

'You haven't got any more of those olives, have you?' Jane murmured, pausing with what looked like an afterthought and peering hopefully back towards his desk. 'Or black ones. They don't have to be stuffed—I don't mind.'

'Of course I haven't,' he said slowly, startled that she

could have forgotten she'd brought them herself. 'On second thoughts, no cab,' he said crisply. He had an hour before his ward round, and his bleeper would cover the short distance to Jane's home if anyone wanted to contact him. 'I'll drive you home,' he announced, shutting the door to his office, taking one warm arm and guiding her towards the lift. 'You're not safe alone.'

On the leisurely waddle demanded by Jane's condition towards his car he heard no more of the redoubtable Lizzy Murdoch, but Jane raised the subject again as he pulled up at the driveway of the house she shared with his cousin. 'Make sure you remember that it's Lizzy, not Elizabeth,' she said firmly.

'Rest assured.' He smiled when he came around to help haul her out of the car, amused both by her persistence and by the energetic wiggling she commenced to extract herself from the low seat. 'I don't want to be spat on.'

'Did I say that?' Jane managed a creditable imitation of astonishment, and he grinned admiringly. 'Goodness. I hope I haven't given the wrong impression,' she said carefully. 'I know you're going to adore her.'

'Hmm.' But he kept his doubts private now, watching doubtfully as she puffed her way to the front door. For all her high jinks and good spirits, she was very pregnant. 'Jane, sure you're up to this party? You could leave it until after the baby. Bill wouldn't mind.'

'Tonight's not just for Bill's birthday,' she announced, turning at the door to wave him away, the crafty twist to her mouth suggesting he hadn't hidden his exasperation well enough. 'It's going to be a special night for you too, Drew. For you and Lizzy. Seven. Sharp. Don't be late.'

'Seven sharp,' he echoed dryly.

'Drew...?' she called out when he was almost at the car. 'Promise me you won't...you won't *seduce* her.' Her expression had changed now, the calculation gone, and he could see she was suddenly genuinely worried by the possibility. 'I mean, I'm sure you'd be very good at that, only

Lizzy's had problems with men in the past and I doubt she'd cope.'

Unable to prevent a grin which, he saw, increased her alarm, he came back to her. 'I promise,' he vowed, not hesitating to make the commitment. 'No seduction.'

'Marriage or nothing,' Jane said earnestly, peering at him, her flushed brow creased.

'Nothing.' He tapped her nose affectionately. 'Bye, Janey.'

'You're going to fall in love with her,' she cried to his retreating back. 'That's *my* promise to you.'

He laughed at her from the car. 'Time you had that baby. You're going crazy.'

Returning to the hospital, he speculated about the chances of either not getting to the party or of being called away after a short time because of an emergency at the hospital. He grinned, imagining Jane's reaction to such an event. It would be safer to meet her Lizzy, he decided, rather than to engineer such an interruption. Besides, despite his confidence that they would be incompatible on a personal level, he'd be crossing paths with the radiologist professionally on frequent occasions in the future and for that reason it was important to establish a civil relationship.

He was on call all week for chest medicine, part of a one week in every four roster with his fellow consultants, but his colleagues had told him that—apart from the one day in that week when he was also first on call for general medicine—although he might be telephoned frequently for advice it would be rare for him to be called into the hospital after hours so the chance of the evening being interrupted was low. But after his late ward round of his patients that afternoon he made a point of telling his registrar that she wasn't to hesitate to call him if she needed help.

'Thanks, Dr Maitland.' Corinne's smile was friendly, her manner relaxed and as typically antipodean as her accent. 'But don't worry. Jane mentioned you were going to the birthday party and Dr Wright said he'd be happy to cover for the evening.'

Drew frowned. 'You're a friend of Jane and Bill?'

'Good friends,' she confirmed. 'I met them years ago through another good friend of mine—our radiologist, a very nice woman called Lizzy.' She gave him a look he decided could only be described as meaningful. 'Lizzy Murdoch.'

'Lizzy.' Drew nodded slowly, wondering. 'A very nice woman?'

'Lovely, even,' Corinne said quickly.

'Not Elizabeth?'

'Oh, no.' His probing was rewarded by seeing her shock. 'Never Elizabeth,' she said urgently. 'Not unless you want a swift kick in the ribs.'

Drew wondered idly whether he preferred to be spat at or kicked, deciding he'd prefer the latter. Lizzy Murdoch appeared to have several things in common with a camel that had once bitten him during a holiday in Morocco.

'Beautiful things come in small packages,' Corinne added cryptically.

He felt his eyes narrow. 'How small?'

'Five-two,' she said promptly. 'Higher in heels.'

'And this Lizzy is…?'

'Unattached and free as a bird,' Corinne chirped, her regard unflinching as it dropped to the bare fingers of his left hand. 'And you, Dr Maitland?'

'Single,' he admitted reluctantly.

'Perfect.' She beamed. 'My advice is to move fast because men are drawn to her like magnets and you might not get the chance to meet her tonight unless you do.'

Drew sighed. The meal trolley had arrived on the ward from the kitchens and he stepped back against the wall of the corridor so that it could be wheeled past, but when it cleared Corinne was still there, regarding him with the sort of speculation with which a fox might regard a basket of chickens. Odd, he registered, considering he was her boss.

'Like magnets?' he prompted, wondering how best to reconcile that with Jane's less flattering descriptions of the radiologist's eagerness.

'There's one in particular,' Corinne muttered, crossing to his side of the corridor. 'Dark hair, thin face. Rolex watch. Porsche. He's going to be there tonight. Look out for him. He hasn't met her but he's a predator. He's bound to go for her.'

'Really?' Drew decided things were looking up. 'I will look out for him. Thank you, Corinne.' He might even fetch the man a drink. Or two. More if it took more. He patted her thin shoulder. 'Thank you very much.'

'The man with the Porsche is totally sleazy,' Corinne hissed, to his surprise putting on a burst of speed so that she caught up with him when he walked away. 'I'm worried about him getting near Lizzy. She's not used to men like that. She won't know how to handle him.'

'I'll bear that in mind,' Drew remarked, wondering if it was Lizzy's smallness that inspired such protectiveness in her friends.

'You'll look out for her, won't you, Dr Maitland?' Corinne seemed urgent. 'Make sure she's all right?'

'I'll certainly look out for her,' he assured her, increasing his pace. 'Thanks, Corinne. See you at eight tomorrow morning.'

'Make it nine, if you'd rather,' she called after him, her voice fading as he turned the corner.

CHAPTER TWO

'LIZZY MURDOCH?'

A kind-looking woman, wearing a navy suit and a white doctor's coat, emerged from one of the consulting rooms and smiled vaguely around the crowded waiting room.

'That's me,' Lizzy called, jumping up so quickly that the tattered copy of *Time* she'd been pretending to read spun to the floor. Flushing, she stooped to retrieve it but she fumbled, then had to stoop again when it slipped out of her grasp. Finally managing to slap it back onto the neat pile beside her chair, she mumbled an apology for the delay and, aware that she had the attention of most of the other people in the waiting room, hurried after the doctor.

'Sorry,' she repeated huskily. 'I'm a bit nervous.'

'Please relax.' The older woman smiled warmly and gestured for her to take one of two comfortable-looking leather chairs placed across from a paper-strewn desk in the plush office, while she herself sat at a swivelling chair behind it. After introducing herself, she explained that the colleague Lizzy had seen on her last visit was away at a conference but that she'd read through the notes and understood Lizzy's case.

'And I do have the results from your swabs and blood tests, Dr Murdoch,' she added slowly, lifting layers of coloured paper which seemed to have been pasted into Lizzy's chart, while Lizzy herself sat stiff and tense. 'The final ones arrived yesterday.'

Dr Lennox looked up and Lizzy's breath caught when she saw she was smiling again. 'Smear and swabs normal,' the doctor announced. 'Pelvic ultrasound was normal, as I'm sure you must have seen for yourself during the examination. Oestrogen, progesterone, LH, FSH,' she recited, naming some of the main hormones involved in fertility, 'all normal responses. You're clearly still maturing eggs and ovulating normally. From a hormonal point of view, these results suggest there's absolutely no reason why you shouldn't be able to conceive perfectly naturally.'

Lizzy sagged back in her chair. 'I prepared myself for the worst,' she said faintly. 'When Catherine was told she'd left it too late to be able to have children...'

'Considering your sister's case and given your family history in general, you were understandably worried,' the doctor said soothingly. 'You're at high risk of premature menopause. If that happens, medically we can replace your hormones but we can't restore your fertility.'

'I've always wanted children,' Lizzy explained. 'Catherine's news panicked me. The thought that I might not have been able to have them...'

'The biological clock,' Dr Lennox said with a gentle, understanding smile. 'And I know how you feel because I was the same before my first baby. In your case, my professional advice is to start trying as soon as possible. Given your mother's and your sister's problems, I would suggest no delay. You're thirty-two now, which is older than I'd have advised you to leave a pregnancy if I'd seen you earlier.

Considering that your sister began trying to have a baby at your age, and the fact that she's only thirty-six now, I believe that you should aim to have your first baby within the next year. In your case, that might allow room for manoeuvring if things take longer than we expect. If you then decide you want more than one child there should still be an opportunity.'

'Within a year.' Lizzy nodded automatically. Which meant that she should be aiming to conceive within the next three months. Still euphoric from the results, she suppressed her anxiety, telling herself that the difficulties involved in achieving that were trivial compared with her fear these last few months while she'd been waiting to have her fertility examined. 'I'm still reeling. I really can't believe I'm OK.'

'I see from your notes that my colleague discussed the possibility of artificial insemination from one of our donors if your fertility results were positive,' the older woman added. 'Have you thought any more about that?'

'I'm still considering it,' Lizzy said quickly. 'Obviously, I have to think about it more urgently now. I would prefer to choose the father myself but there's no suitable man in my life at present.'

There had never been a suitable man in her life, she added inwardly. Only unsuitable ones. And not even many of those. She'd tried her best, of course, but it seemed that the sort of man she'd been looking for—heterosexual, kind and thoughtful, genuinely fond of children and not already married—wasn't especially common any more.

But she was optimistic by nature and, aside from the brief faltering of optimism that when she'd warned herself not to expect perfection from these test results, that hadn't changed. She had three months. 'Something will work out,' she said confidently.

'I'm happy you feel that way, but if you don't find your special partner in the next two months then you should make an appointment to come and see us in your third cycle,' Dr Lennox said gently. 'I don't mean to dispel your romanticism, merely urge a little caution. We may not have enough time to allow for a delay.'

'I know that's a sensible suggestion.' Lizzy tilted her head and a swathe of pale hair fell across one of her eyes, forcing her to tuck the strands firmly back behind her ear. 'And in my head I know you're right,' she conceded, 'even if it still sounds odd to me. Is this sort of thing—I mean, a single woman coming for artificial insemination—unusual?'

'These days, no.' The other woman's regard was warmly reassuring. 'Women now have careers which are important to them and often either through lack of opportunity or because of their high standards they choose to remain single. Our philosophy is that if they're financially and emotionally capable of giving a child a warm and loving upbringing, all of which our screening has told us you are, then the absence of a current partner shouldn't be a barrier to conception.'

'It might be years before I meet the man I want to spend the rest of my life with,' Lizzy confirmed. 'But, in my circumstances,' she added slowly, 'I can't delay having my first child while I'm waiting to find him.'

'Exactly.'

'Two months.'

'That's my advice.'

Lizzy felt strange. She wanted a child—several children—but she'd never envisaged not sharing the parenting. But time was running along—running out, in her case—and it was time to make decisions. She was perfectly capable of raising a child on her own, she told herself. In fact, she was more than prepared for that, financially and emotionally as well as career-wise, but the doctor's words forced her to acknowledge that it was likely that she'd also have to conceive that child alone.

Despite her joy at finding herself still fertile, that fact made her feel a little forlorn.

'All I have to do is find a healthy and willing donor,' Lizzy said firmly. 'In two months, if I can't, I can come back here. The most exciting thing is that physically I can have a baby.'

'I'm glad we could reassure you about that.' Dr Lennox came with her to the door. 'Remember to relax and stay happy. I wish you every success.'

'Thank you.' Lizzy suddenly found herself grinning wildly, the difficulties paling again as she realised the true meaning of her test results. 'Who needs the Underground?' she said happily. 'I could fly home.'

The other doctor laughed. 'Remember to keep up the vitamins and folic acid supplements. Lots of leafy green vegetables and wholegrains and make sure you get plenty of calcium.'

'Second nature,' Lizzy assured her, waving as she headed towards Reception.

'We'll forward a complete account to your home address,' an immaculately coiffed receptionist told her with a pleasant smile when Lizzy stopped to clarify how she should pay her bill for the consultations and the tests the private clinic had performed. 'Goodbye, Dr Murdoch. Good luck.'

Lizzy spent the brief Circle Line journey from the clinic, near London's Baker Street station, to her flat in a quiet corner of Bayswater three blocks from Hyde Park, squashed among a group of noisy Spanish schoolchildren.

Obviously excited about their journey, the children shouted and jostled and peered out at every stop, obstructing other passengers, but rather than being irritated, as everyone else on the train appeared to be, Lizzy regarded them benignly, enjoying their youthful good spirits despite their trampling of her feet.

There were several messages on her answerphone when she let herself into her flat. Two were from her friend and colleague, Jane, the first reminding her that she was expected for dinner that evening to celebrate Jane's husband Bill's birthday, and the second a cryptic comment that she had to be there early and that because there was a special man coming she should 'wear something low-cut'.

Lizzy winced, embarrassed anew at the thought of being thrust upon some poor male by a determined Jane. Still, she was hardly in a position to let that keep her away from now on, she acknowledged wryly, crossing her fingers with a silent wish.

She waited for the next message, her grimace relaxing into a smile when her friend Corinne's chirpy Australian accent roared into the room. 'Look out, Lizzy! Jane's told me she's going to try and fix you up with some drippy relation of hers tonight, her sister's husband's brother or something equally bizarre. An accountant.' Corinne's contemptuous tone told Lizzy what her friend—who thought that all the money in the world should be pooled, taxed heavily then shared evenly—thought of accountants in general. 'Cheap suit, bad haircut and beer belly. The works.

'I'm on call tonight,' the message continued, 'so I won't get there but, take it from me, the man's an octopus. I let him drive me home after Jane's last do and it took me twenty minutes to prise him loose before I could get out of the cab. My advice is to cover that gorgeous bod with a sack and stick a paper bag over your head. Wear loads of repellent. I know you're desperate, Lizzy, but life's just not that short.'

Then, as with Jane, Corinne had obviously called back immediately. 'Just in case you're even thinking about it,' she said cheerfully, 'the octopus hates kids. He says he'd rather breed rats.'

Lizzy crossed the accountant off the possibility list she'd just created in her head. Her baby needed a healthy, well-adjusted father with no major psychological hang-ups. As far as she was concerned, any man who disliked children had a serious problem.

'And my new boss might be there, too,' Corinne continued loudly. 'He's a dish. Dodge the accountant and check him out instead.'

Rather than battle evening traffic and the difficulties of finding parking, Lizzy took a cab to Jane's and Bill's Hampstead home, registering the cars double-parked outside with relief.

Hopefully, if the party was big, Jane would be distracted and it wouldn't be too difficult to avoid her lecherous relative, leaving her free to find Corinne's new consultant—not because he was 'dishy', but because in her role as the chest team's official radiologist they'd be in contact a lot professionally and it was important to cultivate a good working relationship.

Surprisingly, given the numbers of cars, the house was

quiet and dark. When she rang, the door opened immediately and a frazzled-looking and hugely pregnant Jane wrenched her inside. 'You're late,' she said, retrieving a large jar of stuffed green olives from the table by the door and tossing two of the little fruits into her mouth. 'Bill's due any minute.'

Without giving her time to say anything, Jane hustled her through deserted rooms and up a few stairs to a narrow cupboard on the landing. 'Thought I told you to wear something low-cut?' she muttered, casting Lizzy's neck-high and loose black dress a scathing look between mouthfuls of olives. 'You've got a great chest, Lizzy, best of all of us. I can't understand why you refuse to make the most of it.'

'Because I'm not an exhibitionist like you,' Lizzy said flatly, rolling her eyes. The size of her chest was a recurrent theme with Jane, who seemed convinced that if Lizzy just once agreed to appear topless, or at least exposed her cleavage—a cleavage which, while not large in general terms, Lizzy considered embarrassingly over-generous given her smallness everywhere else—then her single days would be over.

'Never mind,' Jane growled. 'Too late now. Get in there. Drew, Lizzy,' she muttered tersely to a large, shadowy male figure who, to Lizzy's astonishment, lurked inside the tall space. 'Remember, I told you about her?'

Jane snatched Bill's gift out of Lizzy's hands and pushed her into the cupboard, apparently unconcerned when Lizzy stumbled over heavy things which lay on the bottom. 'Lizzy, Drew. Keep quiet. Shouldn't be long now.' To Lizzy's alarm, Jane promptly slammed the door and turned a key, leaving her alone with the man she assumed was Corinne's octopus.

She blinked. Her eyes unused to the darkness, she was completely blind. 'It's a surprise party?' she whispered, pressing herself back into the depths of the corner to allow herself a couple of inches of space in case the octopus decided to advance.

'So we've all discovered.' He sounded amused. 'Jane forgot to tell any of us.'

'She's pregnant,' Lizzy said defensively, feeling the familiar surge of warmth that came whenever she contemplated her friend's condition. 'Very pregnant. Forgetfulness is hormonal. It's nature's way of concentrating a mother's attention on her baby.'

'Or, in Jane's case, concentrating her attention on food,' he remarked evenly, the narrowness of the space rendering him so close that his voice rumbled over the top of her head. 'That jar of olives she's working through is her second tonight, and I know she's eaten at least one during the day.'

'She probably needs the vitamins.' Lizzy heard him shift slightly and she recoiled when an arm brushed hers. 'Or the salt.' She stared fiercely into the darkness. 'I'm trained in self-defence,' she said baldly. 'Careful you don't startle me. With my lightning reflexes, I might accidentally break your neck.'

Her remark was followed by what she considered to be a suitably respectful silence but then he said quietly, 'It would be easier to avoid startling you if you got off my foot.' She flushed hot red.

'Oh, sorry.' She lifted one foot hastily, guessed from the soft sound he emitted that it was the wrong one and managed an inelegant shuffling step back to get off him, relieved that he could see as little of her as she could of him. 'You should have said something.'

'It wasn't uncomfortable,' he observed. 'You can't weigh much at five-two.'

'How do you know how tall I am?' she demanded. Surely Jane hadn't been so gauche as to give him her statistics?

'Is it supposed to be a secret?'

Lizzy frowned. 'Bill seems very late,' she ventured airily, changing the subject lest he strayed to more personal measurements, embarrassingly conscious that he'd probably overheard Jane's pointed comments about her chest.

'Bill's mobile's not working,' Corinne's octopus said pleasantly. 'He was on the ward at seven but nobody knows where he went. Jane's only guessing he's on his way home. She's panicking but she doesn't want us to know. She locked us up so we don't notice how many olives she's eating.'

'That's very cynical.' Lizzy eyed his shape. He was big, she could tell that much, and she liked big men. Odd, she conceded, considering she was the height he'd mentioned and finely built, but perhaps that was nature's way of giving her a normal-sized child. If her child was not to be overly short then a big man would make an ideal father.

His voice was much nicer than she'd expected from Corinne's description. Nice enough that she might even have found herself warming to him if she hadn't had prior warning. Nice and deep and richly threaded with an understated amusement which seemed powerfully appealing and very male.

Probably nasty, piggy little eyes, she told herself. A fleshy, greedy mouth and stained teeth. Definitely not the sort of man she wanted to father her child.

'Jane wouldn't have forgotten to tell Bill to come home,' she announced confidently. 'Not when she's invited so many people and hired caterers. She's pregnant, not stupid.'

'Perhaps it's her hormones?' She felt him laughing at her and that narrowed her eyes. 'Nature's way of concentrating her attention on her baby rather than on all the guests locked in cupboards around her house?'

'Bill *must* be coming,' she said sharply, ignoring him. 'Of course he'd come home on his birthday.'

'He's obviously not in any hurry. What time is it? Eight?'

'Eight-thirty by now,' she mused. 'I was late.'

'She locked us all away at seven-thirty.'

'What?' Lizzy's mouth dropped open. 'You've been in here an hour?'

'At least this cupboard's tall and there's enough room to breathe,' he said easily. 'She put Bill's immediate family in the main wardrobe in her bedroom and it's only half as high and there's eight of them. Must be getting uncomfortable.'

'His mother's claustrophobic!'

'She refused the wardrobe. Jane got cross and locked her in the downstairs bathroom.'

'How many others are there?'

'About fifteen hidden about the house,' the octopus told her. 'Another twenty-five or so in the pool-house.'

Lizzy pushed at the door, dismayed when it didn't budge. 'And everyone except me has been hidden for an hour?'

'No sense in looking forward to any olives,' he said dryly. 'She'll have finished them by the time we get out.'

'I don't believe this.' Lizzy pushed again but when the door still didn't shift she pressed her ear to the wood, straining her ears until she could hear faint noises from downstairs. 'She's watching television,' she said, aghast. 'She's left us here while she watches television.'

'Not even any alcohol to be going on with,' he noted. 'Next time I'll bring my own.'

'You seem remarkably calm about this,' she said, her teeth gritted as she fumbled in the darkness, searching for the doorcatch.

'Resigned more than calm.' She sensed him smile. 'There's no way out,' he told her. 'You heard her turn the key. It has to be opened from outside.'

'You don't think she's forgotten us?' Alarmed now, Lizzy knocked. 'Jane? Jane, can you hear me?' But Jane clearly couldn't because there was no reply. 'This is ridiculous,' Lizzy said briskly. 'She can't expect us to stay here for ever.' She hammered on the door. 'Jane? Jane, let us out.' When there was still no reply she glared at him. 'Do something,' she demanded.

'What would you suggest?' He sounded amused again.

'You're big.' And fairly powerful-looking, she remembered from the brief glimpse she'd had before Jane had shut the light out. 'Break us out.'

'The door's solid oak,' he said evenly. 'Sorry.'

She said something rude. 'Lift me up, then.'

'What?'

'Lift me up,' she ordered. 'There's a gap at the top of the door—up there, where the light's coming through. I'll call to her though it.'

The octopus sighed. 'Can't you karate chop yourself out?'

'I'm not that advanced.' She didn't explain that her self-defence skills came from a weekend workshop three years ago rather than long years of martial arts training, as he'd assumed. She braced her arms against the door. 'Come on, hurry. You said it yourself, I'm not very heavy.' She kicked her shoes off and lifted a stockinged foot for him to catch. 'I promise not to hurt you.'

'Here, then.' But, instead of grabbing her foot, he crouched and lifted her easily onto his shoulders, as he might have lifted a child, so that she sat with one hand on his head to balance herself, her legs on either side of him and her dress bunched at her hips.

Bending slightly and trying to ignore her embarrassment about being held so intimately close to him, her thighs practically around his neck, Lizzy peered through the crack. She had a view of the ceiling but nothing else. 'Jane,' she shouted. 'Jane! It's me, Lizzy. We're trapped. Let us out.'

But there was no reply. She repeated her cry, but still there was no sound from Jane. 'Perhaps she's gone out,' she said softly, mystified by the silence. Apart from the distant sound of television, there was nothing.

'More likely asleep,' he countered. 'She was asleep in the corner of the living-room when most of us arrived. We had to bang on the windows to wake her up enough to let us in.'

'Mothers need sleep,' Lizzy said abruptly. Then she leaned to one side, trying to improve her view. 'Jane!' But her shriek obviously startled the man beneath her because he shifted abruptly, and that, together with the fact that she was already lopsided, unbalanced her.

She swayed, cried out and clutched at the door for support, and the octopus's grip promptly tightened on her thighs.

Lizzy felt him go very still and flushed violently, realising that his hands had closed around her bare thighs above and including the tops of her stockings.

'That's enough,' he said, his voice curiously rough-edged as he released her, crouching so suddenly that she had to grab a handful of his thick, clean-smelling hair to stop herself falling. He yelped faintly, then bent his head and tipped her off so that she stumbled forward awkwardly, bumbling into a mass of hanging coats.

'If she didn't hear that,' he added abruptly, his voice still raspy, 'she won't hear anything.'

Hastily, Lizzy smoothed her dress down to cover her legs, relieved he couldn't see her expression. Despite Corinne's warning the warmth of his hands at her thighs had been disturbing and her legs were trembling. Stockings were much healthier than pantihose, considering she wanted herself in optimum condition to conceive a baby, but what she wore under her clothes was something she'd have preferred to keep private. Particularly from someone as lecherous as Corinne had implied he was.

'Perhaps you're right about Jane falling asleep,' she ventured jerkily, pressing herself back into the corner of the cupboard against the coats. 'She has been sleeping a lot lately. She gave up work four weeks earlier than she planned because she couldn't stay awake in the afternoons. It didn't matter, though, because we'd already appointed a locum to take over her work so we've coped without her. Jane's a very talented radiologist. Sorry I pulled your hair. Oh, in case you don't know, radiologists are doctors who've specialised in techniques to image the body—you know, X-rays and ultrasound scans, those sorts of things. She specialises in angiography, which means producing pictures of blood vessels. She's got a very good reputation. Thankfully her locum seems good. After the baby Jane's going to go back to work but only part time, I think, so the department's planning to appoint another consultant. Um…you're an accountant, aren't you, Drew?'

'No.' He sounded terse. 'Where the hell's Bill?' For the first time he hammered at the door himself but drew no response. 'And what are the others doing? They're not all locked in—in fact, everyone in the pool-house is free to wander about.'

'Bill's wine cellar's under the pool-house,' she ventured. 'He's hoarded hundreds of bottles down there.'

'Which explains why they're not all coming to find us,' the man called Drew said flatly. 'I'd forgotten about the cellar.'

Lizzy decided she couldn't call him the octopus any more. It wasn't fair. An octopus would have made at least a token attempt to grope her, but he'd released her legs as abruptly as if they'd stung him and now he seemed to be trying as hard to stay away from her as she was from him.

'Not much hope of rescue, then,' he added. 'An hour and a half of Bill's best vintages means they're probably senseless by now.'

'This is ridiculous,' Lizzy declared. 'I mean, really ridiculous. How could we have let her lock us away, like naughty schoolchildren?'

She wasn't sure how she knew but she seemed to feel him smile. 'Jane's rather intimidating.'

'She's bossy,' Lizzy conceded, 'but that's still no excuse. I can't believe I let her push me in here.' She looked at the slightly darker darkness that was him. Solid and calm, he didn't strike her as the type to let someone else, even someone like Jane, order him around. 'How did she get you in here?'

'It was the baby.' He sounded wry. 'It didn't feel right to argue with a woman carrying a child quite so prominently.'

Lizzy beamed. So, although he didn't want children himself, he held pregnant women in appropriate awe. 'You know, Drew, underneath, you're probably a very nice man.'

There was a brief and, Lizzy thought, startled silence. 'Underneath what?' he asked finally.

'Underneath all the greedy and grasping avariciousness,' she said happily. 'Underneath your arrogant assumption that you can reach out and grab a woman, regardless of the fact that she's desperate to get out of your cab. Underneath the materialistic, self-centred existence you so smugly call your life. Underneath—'

'That's enough!' The roar in the narrow space made her flinch. 'What the hell are you talking about? What arrogant assumption? What cab?'

'Don't be too hard on yourself,' she said quickly. 'You're an accountant. You deal with money all day and it's no wonder you've become blind to what's really important in life. Better people than you have been led astray—'

'I'm not an accountant.'

'Whatever.' Lizzy waved one hand vaguely. All money people were the same to her and, she suspected, to Corinne. 'What's really important, Drew, and I hope one day you look back on this little talk and see it as a turning point in your life, what's really important in life is—and this is something it took me quite a while to discover myself— what's really important, and I mean in all the world, what's most important is having babies. Babies and families. Nothing matters more.'

'Babies?' His voice was strangled but there was a long, almost, she thought, deliberate pause before he said, 'Look, Elizabeth—'

'Lizzy,' Lizzy said immediately. 'My name is Lizzy, not

Elizabeth or Liz or Beth or Eliza, but Lizzy. I don't mean to sound pedantic but it's on my birth certificate.'

'Lizzy.' It was a growl. 'What the hell are you talking about?'

'My name,' she said tightly, gritting her teeth. 'My name is Lizzy.'

'Not that.' He growled again. 'Before. Something about a cab?'

She frowned into the gloom. 'We were talking about your life,' she said finally. 'Haven't you been listening to me at all?'

'We met thirty minutes ago. What makes you think you know anything about my life?'

'Corinne told me,' she said slowly. 'Well, at least, she told me a bit about you. Enough to understand what makes you tick.'

'Corinne?' She could practically feel the cogs ticking over. Poor man, she thought sympathetically. Obviously not terribly bright. 'Corinne Jackson?' he added finally. 'Tall, dark hair, New Zealand accent, medical registrar at the National?'

'Australian accent.' But Lizzy nodded, pleased that he'd managed to work everything else out for himself. 'Corinne told me about you. Not a lot, of course, but enough to get the general picture.'

'The general picture doesn't sound particularly favourable,' he said tightly.

'It's never to late to change your ways,' she assured him. She reached out and briefly squeezed his arm, blinking her surprise at the power of the muscles beneath her fingers—unexpected, given Corinne's less than flattering description of the size of his stomach.

The arm withdrew rapidly and Lizzy shrugged. 'Really, I think you've burned your bridges with Corinne, though. It's not all your fault because she does prefer her men to be arty. She dates poets and artists and musicians, those sorts of people. She likes passionate, emotional men, not wimpy office types like you.'

'Wimpy?'

'Even if she hadn't found you repulsive I doubt you'd have stood a chance,' Lizzy said firmly.

'Repulsive?' But instead of aggrieved, she realised, as with his last comment he sounded rather thoughtful. Another point in his favour, Lizzy decided. If he could face the truth like this so maturely then he had potential. Shame he didn't like children.

'When you say repulsive—'

'Don't even think about it,' she ordered. 'Concentrate on changing yourself. It's not too late to improve. I'm sure that if you try hard enough some woman will one day find you attractive.'

'Some woman, one day?'

'You're not an ugly man,' she said kindly. 'Not that I can see you, of course, but, believe me, Corinne would have mentioned it if you were. But a new suit and a decent haircut will do wonders. Get yourself into shape, lose some weight, cut down on the beer and spend a bit of your precious money on a new outfit. And give babies a little more thought because women adore men who love children. It's a very basic thing, left over from the cavemen days. Believe me, genuinely paternal men are in huge demand.'

'Huge demand,' he echoed.

'Oh, just enormous,' she confirmed wistfully. A man like that would be in huge demand by her. For most of her adult life she'd been searching for one. 'You see, there aren't many around. At least not many unmarried ones.'

'You speak from experience?'

'Some bad ones.' Still unsettled by the memory of his hands on her thighs, she found herself chattering. She told him about Richard, a handsome surgical SHO whose passionate declaration of love for children had almost swept her off her feet. 'Until I discovered he already had three,' she said sadly, 'and a wife who thought her husband worked extremely long hours.'

She sighed. 'After him there was a medical registrar called Paul. We went out for ten months. He told me he wanted at least four children. I was planning the wedding when he started telling me about nannies and discipline and about how important it would be to get our babies' names down early for the boarding schools he'd chosen.'

'You called it off?'

'Children need to be loved and nurtured to develop their full potential,' she said stiffly. 'I realised I couldn't love someone who didn't agree with that. I couldn't ever send my children away to school and I certainly couldn't give them a father who wanted to stifle them.'

'And now?'

'And now nobody,' she said quietly. 'I never meet anybody.' But then she stiffened. Jane's brief introduction to him had included a comment about him knowing who she was. Perhaps she'd said something to him about trying to matchmake the two of them? Perhaps he was actually interested?

'I'm not desperate,' she lied sharply. 'The man for me has to love children—but it has to be genuine,' she added quickly. 'A woman can see through false sentiment about that. You, for instance, Drew. I can tell you aren't keen on them. Not keen at all. Now, while I encourage you to rethink that, right now I wouldn't be surprised if the idea of breeding children is less appealing to you than breeding rats. Hmm? Am I right?'

'You're certainly convincing enough.' He sounded amused again. 'Are you always this forthright?'

'Generally.' Something outside caught her attention. 'Listen,' she hissed. She banged against the door. 'Jane? Help! Someone, help. We're locked in.'

There were sounds of feet on the stairs.

'Let us out,' Lizzy shouted, hammering. 'Help.'

CHAPTER THREE

'LIZZY, is that you?' A woman's muffled voice came from the other side of the door.

'Of course it's me.' Drew heard relief in Lizzy's voice. 'It's Carol,' she told him, and he found himself nodding, although he had no idea who she meant. 'Carol, Jane's locked us in,' Lizzy cried. 'Let us out.'

'There's no key.' There was a high-pitched giggle and Drew rolled his eyes. Despite being muffled, it was obvious that Carol's voice was slurred.

'She's drunk,' Lizzy hissed, echoing his own conclusion. 'She must have been in the pool-house.'

'Jane's taken the key,' Carol continued unhelpfully.

'Can't you get it off her?' Drew demanded.

'We don't know where she is.' Another giggle. 'She's gone out. They both have. We came up to the house to ask for more ice but the cars are gone and there's no sign of either of them.'

'The cars are gone?' Lizzy groaned. 'Aagh!'

'Carol, listen carefully.' Drew spoke with deliberate firmness. 'Jane's locked Bill's mother in the downstairs bathroom. Let her out and then go and release his family. They're all upstairs in Jane's wardrobe and it's very small. Then ask around in case anyone knows how to pick this lock.'

'OK.' Carol sounded cheerful. 'You sound nice. Who is he, Lizzy?'

'It's Drew and he's an octopus,' she said loudly, and Drew stiffened, surprised that—despite the peculiarity of their encounter so far—she'd lost none of her power to

34

startle him. 'Please, Carol, go and do everything. I'll explain about him later.'

'You'd better.' Carol's voice was drifting away. 'Don't think I'm going to forget.'

Drew growled, not appreciating the thought of the planned discussion. 'Lizzy?'

'I just said that to distract her,' she said hastily, sounding suitably nervous. 'Otherwise she'll pester me like crazy. I promise, I really don't think you're an octopus. That was just what Corinne said and she always exaggerates.'

He vowed to have a few words with his new registrar. If her job kept her so under-occupied that she had time to create stories about him to entertain her friends then she clearly needed more work. 'Corinne has some explaining to do,' he muttered darkly.

'Oh, no, don't say anything.' A small hand clutched at his arm, and it worried him how much he liked that. It reminded him too much of the other part of her that he'd liked very much, the part his hands had encountered when they'd met warm skin above the stockings—the part he was trying very hard to forget. 'She'll kill me if you get in touch with her,' she added urgently, her soft, clear voice tinged with what sounded like genuine concern. 'I don't think she ever wants to see you again.'

He gritted his teeth. 'We'll see about that.'

'Her brother's got a black belt,' she said quickly, withdrawing her hand from his arm. 'He's very protective of her. My sincere advice is to stay away from Corinne.'

He realised he missed her touch and that made him irritable. 'Under the circumstances, that's not going to be easy,' he said, wondering if all of her was as silkily textured as her thighs. The women he was normally attracted to tended to be tall and willowy; he wasn't used to contemplating putting one in his pocket and carrying her away. Now, though, to his consternation, he found himself giving the idea serious thought.

'You'll just have to force yourself to keep away from

her.' She sounded very serious now. 'Corinne's a beautiful girl and I understand that you might have fallen a little in love with her but, frankly, she's not interested and you'll only make a fool of yourself if you persist. Facing that, Drew, will make you a better man.'

'Thank you, Lizzy.' Exasperation overcoming more... basic impulses, he glared down at the small shape that was this infuriating woman. Totally mad, he decided. Totally, totally mad. The body might be tempting but the head was full of popcorn. 'Thank you for all your advice this evening. It's been extremely...illuminating.'

'You're welc—'

'Now shut up,' he said tightly, 'because I've had enough.' His teeth were practically grinding. 'Just wait and listen. They're coming. With any luck, we're about to be rescued.'

There was lots of noise, loud chattering and laughing and bottles clinking and jovial comments, and eventually it sounded as if everyone at the party had assembled outside the cupboard.

'Have you out of there in a jiff,' a cheerfully slurred male voice assured them. 'Can't find a chain-saw but we've got Billy-boy's axe. Best get out of the way. Crouch low and I'll aim high.'

'What are you—?' But Drew cut off Lizzy's words, by dragging her to the floor at his corner.

'Get down, you fool,' he rasped, and crouched behind her, his hand twining in the silkiness of her hair and pushing her lower against the wall. 'Close your eyes. They're going to smash it.'

A heavy blow to the door and a splintering noise proved him right, but beneath him Lizzy moaned. 'Jane will be furious.'

'You'd rather stay here all night?' He eased himself away from her slightly, angered by his body's ignorant and instant response to the soft thrust of her hip against his leg. 'I'll commission a new door for them—every detail the same, if it makes you feel any better,' he muttered, trying to distract himself again from the memory of her stockings.

'I like your aftershave,' she whispered suddenly, shocking him into stillness despite another splintering blow to the door which still refused to shatter. 'It's very nice. Subtle.'

'I'm not wearing any,' he muttered tightly, holding himself away warily when she wiggled around to face him side-on, her movements, just when he needed it least, suddenly little short of provocative. 'And I'm surprised you're familiar with the word "subtle".'

Instead of withdrawing, Lizzy burrowed into him a little, the surprising voluptuousness of the breasts which now pressed warmly against his arm sending his blood pressure soaring. 'I'm sorry if I've offended you tonight, but—'

'It's for my own good,' Drew finished shortly, clenching his teeth and ducking over her again at the next blow to the door. The impact let in a narrow sliver of light and then the person with the axe simply inserted the blade and wrenched back, pulling a wedge of timber free and prompting a round of good-natured cheers from the audience.

'Out you come, Lizzy,' several people said brightly when the hole was big enough for her to get through and, with Drew carefully pushing and someone pulling, she climbed out.

Dazzled by the bright light spilling from the electric bulb above the cupboard, Drew could make out little more than a small, dark shape with a pale cap of hair before Carol's voice said, 'Poor Lizzy. How awful. Come and tell me all about it.' And Lizzie left, without sparing him a backward glance.

Poor Lizzy? he thought ruefully. Poor *Lizzy*? Less than an hour in a cupboard with Jane's poor Lizzy and he felt like he'd been ten rounds with George Foreman.

'Hard to understand why Jane and Bill decided to go out,' one of Jane's brothers said to him once Drew had downed a beer and started in on a cold cheese roll from the remains of the buffet which had been laid in the pool-house and had now been virtually demolished. 'Could it be a medical thing, her forgetting us?'

'Who knows?' Nobody seemed particularly worried, he realised. Everyone who'd been in the pool-house was tipsy, and the rest of the guests, including Bill's family, were already making up for lost time.

Bill's mother—his own Aunt Lily—thankfully looked none the worse for wear—relieved, though, that she'd been locked where she had. 'Bladder control isn't what it once was,' she confided, over what Drew noted was a mixture of one of her son's best clarets with a New World sparkling white. 'I've been doing my exercises but they haven't cured everything.'

He managed a noncommittal comment.

'What I absolutely can't understand is why she locked us in,' she continued. 'I mean, we couldn't have all jumped out when Bill got home and cried "Surprise!" because the doors were locked. Jane would have had to go around each group of us and unlock us all separately.'

'Jane's mad,' someone declared.

Drew nodded. That seemed to be the general consensus. Once again he looked around for Lizzy, or rather for someone who fitted his mental image of her because he still hadn't seen her, but she didn't seem to be about. Wary as he was, he still remembered his body's reaction to her and he was curious to see what she looked like, but no one seemed to know where she was.

He waylaid his cousin, Bill's older brother, who was weaving purposefully towards the cellar entrance, and asked him about Lizzy but he hadn't seen her either.

'Not for a while,' he said vaguely, clearly focused on his mission. 'Drew, where does Bill hide his Scotch? I know he's got a few single malts stashed somewhere but we can't find them.'

'Cupboard above the freezer,' Drew told him, glancing around the pool distractedly.

An attractive woman near the buffet eyed him speculatively but even if he'd been looking, which he wasn't, he told himself, she was tall and slender. He suddenly wanted small and curvaceous, and he found himself merely returning her smile with a polite one of his own and moving inside.

It was late, Drew decided, almost eleven-thirty, and, although the party was loud and lively even without the hosts, he wanted to be at work by seven the next morning. Besides, he reminded himself, he'd be meeting Dr Lizzy Murdoch in a more formal setting at nine in the morning at the X-ray meeting she chaired for the chest medicine team. Seeing how she performed in a professional environment was going to be interesting, he thought. Interesting but also, thinking of the popcorn he'd envisaged replacing her brain, potentially alarming for the health of his patients.

Lizzy's X-ray reporting session in her office early the next morning was interrupted by a visit from Corinne.

'Terrible night,' Corinne declared, helping herself to a cup of the radiology department's coffee. 'I've been up since two, pacing a very nice man who wandered into Casualty in heart block,' she added, referring to the process of installing a pacemaker to overcome the sort of arrhythmia where the electrical signals from the atrium failed to get through to the ventricles, thus disturbing the normal pattern of the heart rhythm.

'The general medical SHO hadn't even seen a pacing before so I got the job. He's all right now but I'm practically dead on my feet.' She sipped her drink. 'How was the party?'

'Great, if you discount the fact that Jane and Bill didn't bother coming,' Lizzy said crisply, frowning at a chest X-ray where the levels of the clavicle bones were uneven, suggesting that it had been taken with the patient slightly rotated rather than square-on to the X-ray machine. Without the film being taken properly, it was impossible to make assumptions about the size of the heart which, in this particular film, looked slightly enlarged.

Wondering how the film had slipped through the normally rigorous monitoring of the radiographers, she wrote a brief note to suggest that the patient should be brought up from the ward for another X-ray if his doctors were concerned about his heart size.

She told Corinne about being locked in the cupboard. She didn't mention with whom, but simply said, 'I met your octopus.'

Corinne looked up sharply. 'What?'

'He didn't seem that bad.'

'Oh.' Her friend's face stiffened. 'Really?'

'I thought he was quite pleasant.' Lizzy shuffled through more films, examining each one systematically and putting the normal films aside. 'He's prepared to listen to criticism at least.'

'I wouldn't know. I didn't manage to get him off me long enough to draw breath,' Corinne said acidly. She finished her coffee and levered herself off the desk she'd perched on. 'Did he say anything about me?'

'I got the impression he was very taken with you,' Lizzy told her, remembering his comments about him finding it difficult to avoid Corinne.

'Hardly surprising.' Corinne folded her arms. 'So what time did Bill and Jane turn up?'

Lizzy shrugged. 'Probably not early enough to stop all Bill's wine collection disappearing,' she ventured. 'Not before I left, at least.' Which hadn't been very late.

She'd been embarrassed about snuggling up to Drew the way she had in the cupboard when the axe had literally started falling. Despite Corinne's warnings about the sort of man he was, he'd been warm and strong and it had felt nice, being protected by him. Her behaviour hadn't been at all typical, quite the opposite, in fact, and, uneasily aware that she might have offered encouragement where she hadn't meant to, she'd left the party soon after being freed.

A pity he didn't like children, she thought, not for the first time wishing he'd been more suitable in that regard. All the other unpleasant aspects of his personality she could probably have discounted—she didn't have time to worry about anything other than finding good genes at this stage— but, regardless of how rampant his sex drive, she couldn't envisage a man who disliked children ever agreeing to her proposal. Morally, she knew, despite her desperation, that she couldn't deliberately conceive without the man's consent.

She measured the width of another heart in a chest X-ray she was inspecting, comparing it to the total width of the chest and finding that the left ventricle was mildly enlarged. Out of the corner of her eye she saw Corinne stir. 'Leaving already?'

'The new boss is a slave-driver,' Corinne grumbled, leaving her cup for Lizzy to clear. 'Ward round at eight every morning. Anyone would think the firm's turned surgical. I went into medicine because I thought starting the day at nine was civilised behaviour.'

Lizzy smiled. Corinne's consultant had recently retired and his replacement had only started the week before. Given her friend's difficulty in getting up in the morning, it wasn't surprising she was aggrieved at the changes. 'I didn't meet him last night,' she explained. 'I left too early.'

Corinne's new boss, Lizzy knew from the grapevine, was a chest and general physician with an excellent reputation who'd been poached from another prominent London hospital. His appointment was considered something of a coup for the National. 'Still, only another six weeks,' she counselled. Corinne's rotation changed in mid-August. 'Then back to shorter hours.'

'I'm thinking I might consider staying,' Corinne said quickly, surprising Lizzy because Corinne had been determined not to spend another six months in chest and general medicine. She wanted to specialise in cardiology and she'd been applying for heart jobs. She was talented and hard-working and very good at her job, and she'd had several offers. 'If they beg me, that is,' she added airily. 'See you at nine,' she said from the door, referring to the weekly session Lizzy held with her firm to examine the week's X-ray results.

Lizzy finished inspecting the films, typing her reports directly into the computer so they were immediately available for the ward doctors, then took some time for a brief chat with her registrar, Ray, about some of his own work before he went off to his Tuesday angiography session.

With a few minutes spare before her meeting, Lizzy tried to ring Jane but there was no reply from the house. There wasn't time to bleep Bill but she vowed to do it later.

The medical team arrived as Lizzy was sliding the films up onto a carriage of racks. She'd already darkened the room in preparation for studying the X-rays, and the four consultants and their eight junior doctors, plus a small group of medical students, filed into the seats in front of her, without her being able to see them very well. Lionel Wright, one of the hospital's senior physicians and a chest medicine specialist, introduced her to his new consultant colleague, and Lizzy smiled in acknowledgement, peering into the dimness but not getting much of a view.

'Corinne, perhaps you'll tell me some of the history for this patient,' she suggested, sliding the first set of X-rays across in front of the board and switching on the light behind it.

'Sixty-four-year-old man referred to us because of a three-month history of increasing breathlessness, cough with some blood-stained sputum, chest pain worse on the right, weight loss and general malaise,' Corinne said fluidly. 'Never smoked. He's lived and worked in Barking in East London all of his life until five years ago. On examination, his fingers are clubbed,' she continued, describing the blunting of the shape of the fingers sometimes seen in lung and other disease, 'and with the stethoscope there are loads of crackles at the base of the left lung and obvious fluid at the right base.'

Lizzy nodded. 'Multiple signs of asbestos exposure,' she said quietly, indicating with a pointer the linear white flecks of calcium at the base of the left lung and along the lining which appeared either thickened or containing fluid—on the upright chest X-ray it was impossible to be sure of the cause. She couldn't see the base of the right because it was even more obscured, again either by thickening of the lung lining or by fluid.

For the benefit of the juniors she explained. 'Remember that asbestos can lead to progressive lung damage thirty or more years after exposure.' She used the pointer again to trace the shape of the lungs. 'These shadows and the loss of a distinct heart border are classic signs.'

She moved to the opaque level on the right side of this chest. 'More disturbing is this area at the base of the right lung and the smaller one on the left. My suspicion is that this is both thickening of the lining and fluid in the lining and...' she shifted along to the next film, which had been taken with the patient reclining '...from this picture we see that the shape of the lung has shifted on the right, proving it is fluid which has moved, while on the left nothing has changed, suggesting the whitening is simply thickening of the lining—meaning both abnormalities are present.'

She turned back to her audience. 'There's a very high chance this is asbestos-related lung tumour. In this case, otherwise known as a mesothelioma,' she added, for the benefit of the students. 'The changes here are in both lungs, suggesting diffuse, or widespread, disease.'

She looked at Lionel Wright. 'CT scan to look more closely?'

'Please, Lizzy.' He nodded. 'A biopsy under CT control would help clarify the issue.'

Lizzy nodded, happy to oblige. It wasn't always possible to get a definite diagnosis by taking a biopsy but it was the most precise way of obtaining a sample of the damaged tissue.

One of the students raised his hand. 'I admitted Mr Webber. He's still relatively young and until last year he'd never been sick in his life. Is there a cure?'

Lizzy exchanged glances with Corinne, and Corinne said quietly, 'No cure.'

Films on the next few patients were more routine: a couple of chest views which showed a pneumonia that was now resolving; a few chest X-rays from patients who'd come in with chest pain which were normal, and one view of another patient with chest pain where the heart was enlarged.

'As a rough estimate, the heart shouldn't be larger than fifty per cent of the thoracic diameter,' she told the students, 'as long as the chest X-ray is taken symmetrically, like this, and by shooting the rays from back to front. When chest X-rays are taken with a patient staying in bed, the rays are shot from front to back with the film behind the patient, and that gives an exaggerated view of the heart's size on the X-ray.'

'He has a ten-year history of poorly controlled hypertension,' Corinne explained, 'which could explain the increased size.'

Lizzy nodded. High blood pressure caused the muscular wall of the heart's left ventricle to grow so it was better equipped to pump the blood against the higher pressures, but that meant the wall needed a stronger blood supply to bring it more oxygen and that increased the risk of a heart attack.

'Now presenting with myocardial infarction,' Corinne continued, confirming Lizzy's suspicions. 'The cardiac enzyme changes suggest only a small amount of damage and he's day six now post admission and doing well. No clinical signs of heart failure.'

'No radiological signs of failure either,' Lizzy said, noting nothing abnormal apart from the heart size. 'I suggest you repeat the film prior to discharge to watch that diameter.'

Next she looked at the films from the patient Corinne had had to pace overnight. 'Pacing wire in perfect position,' Lizzy confirmed. 'Early signs of heart failure with these tiny fluid lines…' she directed the students' attention to the thin traces at the sides of each lung field, '…and some engorgement of the upper blood vessels. Otherwise normal.'

The last films had been ordered by the house officer overnight for a patient who'd tripped on the ward on his way to the bathroom and hit his head and damaged his wrist. Because the films had gone straight from the department to the ward with the patient, Lizzy hadn't seen them, and the house officer came to the front and put them up himself.

'Right Colles' fracture,' Lizzy said, inspecting the wrist. 'Post-plaster films show an excellent reduction.'

The houseman nodded to his new consultant who, Lizzy saw, had sat forward. Confirming her opinion that the consultant was as yet unfamiliar with the night's accident and the patient, the houseman explained, 'The orthopods took him to Casualty and fixed him up. They're coming back today to have a look. There wasn't a skull fracture.'

'No fracture but it's not entirely normal,' Lizzy said slowly, frowning. She tugged the films off the rack and held them side on to the bright light to get a clear view. 'Expansion and double floor in the pituitary fossa,' she said sharply, referring to a double shadow in the bone at the bottom of the pituitary gland in the brain. 'Consistent with a pituitary tumour.' She directed the pointer at the curve of bone she meant. 'Subtle change, not easy to see, but, take my word for it, it's significant. Any signs of tumour?'

'He's a general medical patient admitted yesterday for investigation of indigestion,' the house officer explained. 'I didn't admit him and I'm not sure. There wasn't anything worrying in the notes but he did say that he's had a lot of headaches lately. I didn't notice anything on neurological examination after his fall but I examined him, thinking of trauma, not looking for other signs. I'll go back and check him thoroughly.'

'He needs an MRI,' Lizzy said crisply, referring to a magnetic resonance scan, a scan particularly good at clarifying pituitary tumours and especially the damage to the visual nerve pathways which a tumour could cause.

'He's got a pacemaker,' the house officer said quickly.

'Then a CT scan,' Lizzy said. The MRI scanner used a strong magnetic field which could damage pacemakers. 'I can make space on my list for this afternoon.' She wrote his patient number, along with the number of Mr Webber—the man with the suspected lung tumour—on a form in her pocket. 'But it'll have to be late because we're already stretched.'

'We'll liaise with the neurosurgeons about them taking over his care if it's appropriate.' Lionel Wright looked worried as he stood up, signalling the end of the meeting so that the other consultants and the juniors began to make their way to the door.

'Thanks, Lizzy,' he added. 'Spot on as usual. Sure we can't tempt you to St Margaret's?'

'Every minute of my week is filled,' Lizzy said. For more than a year now Lionel had been trying to get her to do a session at the private hospital where he held beds and private consulting rooms.

'The fees are set to go up next month.'

'The money would be very nice but I'm still too busy.' She helped the house officers put all the films back into their correct envelopes—beige for reported films, blue for unreported. As well as being busy, she was planning to have a baby, she told herself confidently. She had to look at slowly reducing her commitment. 'Same time next week.'

'A valuable session, thank you.' The new consultant stepped forward into the light from the X-ray board, and for the first time she could see him properly. Lizzy looked up at him and blinked. Tall and dark-haired with amused if guarded gold-flecked hazel eyes, he was extraordinarily attractive, and her eyes dropped immediately to his hands.

No ring, she noted—cautiously, that didn't necessarily mean anything. 'You're welcome, Dr...Maitland.' For a few seconds she'd struggled to remember his name and she felt herself flush slightly at his raised eyebrows. 'I'm afraid not all our sessions are that dramatic.'

'Oh, Lizzy's always got something up her sleeve.' With a pointed look at her friend, Corinne steered the consultant away. 'Dr Maitland, there's someone you should see in ICU. One of the other registrars rang me and asked if you'd give them your opinion.'

Lizzy didn't see Corinne again until she stormed into her office at one. 'Lizzy, you cow,' she raged. 'What did you tell him?'

Lizzy stared at her blankly. 'Who?'

'Dr Maitland.'

'What?'

'You know what.'

'But I don't.'

'He asked me if my brother was really a black belt. He wanted to know what I thought the problem was with his haircut. He implied you told him I called him an octopus.'

'What?' Lizzy stared at her, totally blank. 'But you were there. I barely spoke to him.'

'What else, Lizzy? What else?' Corinne wailed. 'If you've said anything else awful you have to tell me now.'

'But I didn't say anything.' Lizzy began to feel unwell. 'I told those things to Drew—you know, Drew the octopus.'

'The octopus is called Simon.' Corinne glared at Lizzy. 'Dr Maitland is Andrew Maitland. Drew to his friends. Remember, this morning, when you were introduced?'

But Lizzy didn't. Preoccupied with organising her films,

his first name hadn't registered. 'Oh, God,' she said faintly.
'Last night? That was him?'

'He's Bill's cousin,' Corinne cried. 'He *was* at the party
last night, wasn't he? I know because he told me he was
going. Tell me what you said to him.'

Lizzy felt sick. 'I don't believe it.'

'What happened?'

She told her everything. 'I swear I didn't mean any
harm,' she said, after she'd finished the story. 'I was only
trying to help him.'

'Does he look like he needs help?' Answering her own
question, Corinne shook her head as she lowered it onto
her hand. She blinked at Lizzy forlornly. 'You told him to
lose weight?' she said wearily. 'But he's perfect.'

'Isn't he?' Lizzy lowered her own head to her palms.
'He's gorgeous.'

'I saw him first.'

Lizzy lifted her head, her eyes widening at the watchful
gleam in Corinne's. 'You don't like doctors.'

'I can make an exception.'

'You're working for him.'

'So?'

'You like artistic men.'

'I like great bodies.' Corinne closed her eyes briefly.
'And nice eyes.'

Lizzy sighed. They were very nice eyes. 'Definitely not
married?'

'Definitely.'

'Gay?'

'Are you kidding?' Corinne's expression was scathing.
'Believe me, Snow White, I've had a lot more experience
than you. I can tell. He's not.'

'He's asked you out?'

'He's only been here five minutes,' Corinne said sharply.
'He's probably just getting around to it.'

'I know.' Lizzy smiled at her beautiful friend.
'Have fun.'

'Don't look at me like that, Lizzy.' Corinne looked unhappy suddenly. 'I'll do you a deal.' She pulled a stethoscope and a notebook and then a ragged rubber tourniquet out of the pocket of her white coat, before producing a fifty pence coin from the depths. 'If you weren't so desperate I wouldn't do this,' she told her. 'Toss you. Winner gets two weeks hands off and then it's a free for all. What do you say?'

'Tails.'

Corinne tossed. 'Heads,' she said quietly when the coin landed. But instead of the pleasure Lizzy had expected Corinne frowned at the coin, and then, astonishingly, she muttered, 'Oh, forget it, Lizzy. He's all yours. God knows, you need it more than I do.'

'Don't be silly.' Lizzy withdrew slightly. 'That isn't fair on you.'

'I've been out with a dozen men this year,' Corinne countered. 'You haven't dated once. Normally you're a terrible judge of men but this one's all right. Take advantage of my generosity,' she said airily. 'It won't happen again.'

'You're terrific.' Lizzy hugged her. She hadn't told Corinne or Jane any of the details of her clinic visits, but Corinne's gesture suggested she perhaps saw more than Lizzy gave her credit for.

'Two weeks,' Corinne said strictly. 'If he hasn't asked you for a second date by then the bet's off. You have to work fast. No wasting time or you'll miss your chance. OK?'

'Two weeks.' Lizzy nodded. 'What should I do?'

'Wear this loose,' Corinne told her, her mouth tightening as she tugged away the rubber band which had held Lizzy's short, blonde ponytail back. 'Put lipstick on and scent. Ask him out and wear the blue dress and no bra.'

'Ask him out,' Lizzy echoed, knowing she would definitely be wearing a bra. 'Where?'

'Dinner,' Corinne advised. 'Lizzy, you're quite beautiful, you know.'

'No, I'm not.' Lizzy had never been shy, but this was so important to her that she was suddenly nervous. She needed all the help Corinne could give her. 'Blue dress,' she repeated.

'And sort out the misunderstanding about what I said,' Corinne ordered. 'I don't need the boss thinking I've been gossiping about him.'

Lizzy went with her to the door. 'I promise.'

'I can't believe you called him an octopus.' Corinne groaned. 'Lizzy, how could you?'

'Was he very angry?'

'More bewildered, I think. He really wanted to know what was so bad about his hair.'

'I'll make it up to you, I swear,' Lizzy said hastily. His hair was lovely. Thick and dark and warm and nice-smelling and, despite her determination to approach him from a reasoned and clinically neutral position, her fingers tingled just thinking about letting them run through it. 'I'll make him think you're the greatest medical registrar in London.' She smiled. 'Which you are.'

'Oh, I forgot.' Several yards along the corridor, Corinne came back. 'Jane's had the baby. Gemma Rose. I went to see her. Seven and a bit pounds. She'd probably been in labour most of yesterday, although she didn't realise it because she thought the cramps were hunger pains. When she disappeared last night she drove to the hospital and she didn't mention you all so she must have forgotten about leaving you in the cupboards. Bill was still here, working, and he made it to Maternity in time for the delivery.'

'A girl.' Lizzy laughed, delighted, imagining her. 'I'll go and see her after work. What does she look like?'

'Tired. Still fat. Sweaty.'

'Not Jane, stupid. Gemma Rose. Big eyes? How much hair? Is she chubby?'

'Are you kidding?' Corinne looked blank. 'She's a baby. Babies all look the same, don't they? She's little and wrinkly and she's got a red face.'

'Like Bill's?'

'Like every baby you've ever seen.' Corinne's bleeper shrilled. 'I told her you'd probably come up later so she's expecting you. Bye!'

The CT list that Lizzy was scheduled to cover that afternoon was crowded, and it was almost five when the radiographer sent a porter to collect one of the two extra patients Lizzy had added to the list after her morning session with Corinne's team.

First was Ron Webber, the man with the probable asbestos-related tumour. A thin, pale man with solemn dark eyes, he smiled wanly at her as she helped him move from the wheelchair he'd been brought up in to a trolley and then across onto the CT bed. 'Dr Maitland's warned me that the news probably won't be good,' he said jerkily, puffing a little from the mild exertion. 'Will you know straight away from the pictures and the sample?'

'I'll have a good idea,' Lizzy said quietly. 'Did Dr Maitland explain that the sample will have to be checked in the laboratory to make the diagnosis definitely?'

'And that it still might not say for sure,' he confirmed. 'But he said the pictures will give him the information he needs. So will you tell me, please, Doctor?' His expression was serious and calmly determined. 'Tell me what you see, even if you can't be sure. I'd like to know as soon as possible. I need to make arrangements.'

'I'll speak to you afterwards,' Lizzy said gently. As a radiologist, her role was difficult. She was involved in his care only indirectly and, much as she approved of full and frank discussion with patients, ethically she couldn't offer such discussion without permission from the consultant looking after him.

Leaving two of the nurses to settle him, position him beneath the machine and explain what was going to happen, Lizzy returned to the shielded booth where Carol, their chief radiographer, was preparing for the scan.

'Did you know Jane's had her baby?' Lizzy asked, reaching for the telephone on the wall behind Carol's head. She called Blue Ward to see if either Corinne or Mr Webber's consultant was around, and the ward clerk went off to check.

'Little girl,' Lizzy added to Carol. 'I haven't seen her yet but I'll pop in tonight. That's why she left us all last night.'

'I still think she's mad.' Carol made a small adjustment to the machine. 'Can't complain about her parties, though. My head's still aching.'

'Slices from the top but I'm interested in the bases,' Lizzy instructed, once the staff had cleared the X-ray room and after Carol had spoken to Mr Webber through the microphone to explain that she was going to adjust the machine.

Lizzy directed Carol's attention to the X-rays on the board. 'We want to see what's behind that fluid.'

The ward clerk came back to the telephone and told her that Dr Wright was in the outpatient department with Corinne and that Drew Maitland had left the ward. 'Dr Maitland's looking after Mr Webber now,' she told her. 'You could try paging him.'

She gave the number but Lizzy was distracted by the first pictures coming through onto the screen and missed it, but before she could ask her to repeat it the ward clerk had hung up.

Lizzy grimaced. 'Carol, any idea what bleeper that new chest consultant's carrying?'

A tall figure appeared at the door. 'Eight-four-one-three.'

'I—I was just looking for you.' Lizzy looked up into glinting hazel eyes, immediately flustered. So much for Corinne's suggestion that she smarten herself up, she thought faintly. Tired, hot and wearing an unflattering lead apron to protect her organs from radiation when she performed Mr Webber's biopsy, she suspected she looked a horror.

CHAPTER FOUR

Lizzy was gorgeous, Drew acknowledged reluctantly, still shaken from the morning X-ray session where he'd discovered not only how exquisite and doll-like she was but also that she was superb at her job.

Although the night before had shown him that she was just as loopy as every other friend of Jane's he'd had the doubtful pleasure of meeting, he realised he'd have been happier if Lizzy Murdoch had turned out to be a little less impressive in the workplace and a lot less attractive. A *lot* less.

'Mr Webber asked me if I could talk to him about the results,' she was saying, that soft little voice almost apologetic as she stared up at him with luminescent green eyes. 'I wanted to ask if you minded.'

'I'm keen to talk to him myself,' he said evenly. 'It's difficult to wait for reports to come through and he made a point of wanting to be told everything immediately. I thought I'd watch the scan so I can speak to him directly.' His motives were pure, he told himself, even if his eyes dropped involuntarily to the ridge of what he knew must be her stocking fastening, visible through her skirt when she repositioned herself on a chair in front of the CT machine.

'Thanks, that's wonderful.' She smiled, a gentle, radiant smile that made him tense. 'Please sit down.' She jerked a stool out from under the desk for him, next to where she sat beside a red-haired women in a radiographer's uniform who beamed at him with apparent approval. 'These are the second set of slices, coming through now,' Lizzy explained, indicating the views on the screen in front of her.

The computer in the CT scanner converted X-ray pictures into cross-sectional images of the subject, rather as if the body had been cut into thin slices. 'Thickened pleura,' she reported, indicating the lining around the lung in the top four pictures, 'but otherwise still clear.'

The views became more abnormal, though, and the last sets of slices showed clear evidence of widespread tumour. 'Just one gentle attempt at getting a sample and inserting a drain,' he told her quietly, following her when she went to scrub for the procedure, while the radiographer remained in the office. 'He's very frail and the only reason we want to try and make a tissue diagnosis is to make his compensation claim more straightforward.'

'That's a very sensible approach.' She'd gowned now and he saw that she pinkened slightly when he stepped forward and tied her straps. Realising that he was flustering her, he wondered if she was nervous about performing a procedure like this with him watching her. Not that that was especially surprising, he told himself. As a chest physician, taking lung samples came into his special field of expertise, although, as a radiologist, she must be accustomed to using similar techniques.

As if to reinforce that point, she pulled on her gloves in neat, efficient movements then studied her trolley with a confidence which had to come from experience. 'What will you say?' she asked him.

'He asked for the full truth.' The green of the sterile gown was the same shade as her eyes, and his movements as he took the lead apron from the rack close to the door and slung it over his head were jerky.

'You can shelter from the rays in the booth,' she said quickly, but, even if she was nervous about him watching, Drew knew how anxious Mr Webber was and he wanted to stay with him.

'I'll stay.' A nurse had adjusted Mr Webber's position on the trolley so that he was on his side, and Drew relieved her at his bedside, steadying his patient's bony shoulder as

Lizzy approached. 'There'll be no pain,' he said quietly, explaining what the radiologist was about to do as she painted his back with a cleaning solution. 'Dr Murdoch will use local anaesthetic to numb your skin. After she's taken the sample she's going to put in a small drain to get rid of the rest of the fluid on that side, which will make your breathing easier. We'll leave the drain in for a day or two then take it out before you go home.'

After studying the stills, which the radiographer had projected onto a viewing screen in front of her, he noted with approval that Lizzy chose the finest needle on her trolley to inject local anaesthetic around the site where she'd take her sample. She waited for that to work then changed needles and infiltrated through the skin and carefully down. He saw the syringe jerk slightly in her fingers as it pierced the distinctive toughness of the lung lining.

While they waited for the anaesthetic to take effect, Drew talked with his patient. 'No pain?'

'I'm fine,' he puffed.

'Mr Webber, we're just going to turn on the machine for a few more seconds,' Lizzy said quietly, her eyes meeting Drew's briefly before she nodded towards the radiographer in the office where he knew her words would have been conveyed via a microphone. 'The pictures on the monitor will show me exactly where my needle is.'

'Screen,' she instructed, Drew noting that she studied the picture as she advanced her needle, pulling gently on the syringe as she went. 'Stop.' In the right place now, he saw she was applying more suction. 'Screen,' she ordered, while they both watched the picture. 'Stop.'

The sample, when she'd removed the syringe, was blood-tinged and Drew nodded acknowledgement. 'That's all we need,' he directed. 'Just finish with the drain and we'll send that fluid as well.'

He watched her smoothly insert a small drain, using a metal introducer, and while he connected it to an underwater seal to prevent air being sucked back up into the chest she sutured and taped the drain neatly into place at the side of Mr Webber's chest.

Impressed with her expertise, he unclamped it to make sure it was working, which it was, blood-stained golden fluid immediately flowing from the patient's chest into the bottle on the floor, then he clamped it closed for the journey to the ward.

'Finished now,' Lizzy said gently, pushing the trolley away. While Drew put a pillow under Mr Webber's side so he could turn a little more onto his back, without feeling any discomfort from the drain, he watched the radiologist shed her gloves.

'How are you feeling?' she asked their patient.

'A little easier.' His gaze bounced between Drew's and Lizzy's. 'What about the X-rays?'

'Not good,' Drew told him quietly. 'It looks like the sort of tumour we discussed earlier.'

'Not much else it could be,' Mr Webber replied stoically. 'I knew that when I wasn't getting any better. I saw two of my old work colleagues from Barking go the same way. Coming in a few months earlier, would that have made any difference?'

He'd agreed not to hide anything so now Drew answered frankly, 'None at all.'

'No treatment, then?'

'Dr Murdoch's drain will help the breathlessness. We can treat the pain that you're having with medication and radiotherapy, if needed, but, as we discussed earlier, there isn't any cure.'

'Will I be able to go home?'

'As soon as possible,' Drew confirmed. Once the drain was out and his breathlessness and discomfort as improved as they could be, there was no reason for him to remain in hospital. 'We'll aim for before the weekend.'

'That's something, then.' He nodded, firmly now, and Drew saw that he appreciated having a goal. 'Thank you, Doctor. At least I know what I'm dealing with.'

'Your wife's on the ward,' Drew reminded him. She'd been squeamish about coming to watch the scan, although he'd offered her the chance. 'Shall I speak with her now?'

'If you wouldn't mind. She's guessed, I think, but it might be easier, coming from you.'

A porter arrived with Mr Jackson, Drew's patient with the possible pituitary gland tumour and the next scheduled CT patient.

The porter seemed to be waiting to take Mr Webber back to the ward but he looked harried and was clearly relieved when Drew told him that he'd wheel Mr Webber back himself.

A nurse took care of the drain and bottle while Lizzy and Drew together lifted Mr Webber from the trolley to the wheelchair the porter had brought, exchanging telling looks behind his back. Although he appeared mentally strong, he was alarmingly thin and Drew made an inward note to organise an urgent referral for home nursing care. Both Mr Webber and his wife would need a lot of practical support when he went home if he was to avoid injuring himself accidentally.

'I'll come back and check Mr Jackson's scans later,' he told Lizzy, taking the samples of fluid and tissue which she'd just finished labelling so he could drop them into the lab on his way to the ward. His professional reasons for returning were sound but he found himself wanting her to wait for him, and that realisation made his voice gruffer than he'd intended. 'Will you be here much longer?'

'An hour or so after finishing here,' she told him.

'Thank you, Doctor.' Mr Webber's steady gaze swung from Drew to the radiologist beside him.

'Sorry I couldn't be the bearer of good news.' She spoke quietly but Drew registered the depth of concern in her regard.

'News, of any sort, was what I wanted,' Mr Webber told her. 'It's the waiting I can't stand.'

Lizzy found herself following the chest consultant as he

wheeled Mr Webber towards the door. 'If I'm not here I'll
be in my office at the back of the department,' she said
hurriedly, flushing when his gaze swung back to her almost
speculatively. 'If you wanted to talk about Mr Jackson's
results later,' she added even more rapidly, seeing that his
expression had turned guarded and wishing that she'd kept
her mouth shut.

After all, his remark before about finding her later had
been perfunctory, almost as if he'd hoped she'd leave early,
and he was probably only interested in seeing the scans
themselves, not in hearing her opinion.

'Otherwise you'll find my report on the computer,' she
finished lamely, turning back before she could see his no-
doubt-relieved reaction to that.

Mr Jackson seemed quite excited about his scan. An active, sprightly man, the plaster cast on his fractured wrist
did little to slow him climbing across onto the scanner bed.
'Now, don't tell me anything,' he said quickly, lifting his
hand when Lizzy returned from scrubbing her hands and
made a start on explaining what the scan would involve.
'All this medical mumbo-jumbo makes me dizzy. Do what
you have to and I'll just lie back and listen to the music.
You tell me when you're finished.'

When Lizzy and the nurse with him smiled he chuckled.
'You might have to wake me up, mind. I didn't sleep well
last night.'

'One thing before you sleep, Mr Jackson. Look straight
into my eyes.' Lizzy held one hand over his left eye and
wiggled the fingers of her other hand above them. 'Keep
watching me but tell me when you see my fingers moving,'
she instructed, repeating the procedure with his other eye
when she'd mapped out the vision in the right, comparing
his field of vision with her own.

As she'd suspected, his vision was disturbed. Despite the
crudeness of the test, which his own doctors would have
performed far more accurately, she could tell that he
couldn't see out of the outside upper corner of each eye, a

finding consistent with a swelling from the pituitary gland putting pressure on the nerves which came from the eyes and passed closed by.

'All right, Mr Jackson?' Carol's voice came over the microphone. 'We're putting you into the machine now and a light is going to move around your head. Just close your eyes and relax.'

Lizzy went back to the booth and waited for the pictures to come though.

'That was your Drew from the cupboard, I presume,' Carol said. 'Dishy. Is he really an octopus?'

'No.' Lizzy spared her a brief glance, annoyed that the drinks the radiographer had consumed hadn't blurred her memory. 'He's very nice.'

'I can see that.' Carol's attention seemed to be on the scanner but her brows lifted. 'I suppose you must know him pretty well after last night.' The radiographer smiled. 'Hours. Alone. In the dark.'

'Trying to get out,' Lizzy said crisply.

'Wondering if you were going to be trapped there all night.'

'Wondering if we were going to run out of air.' Lizzy adjusted the brightness slightly on the machine. All the slices so far, and they'd started from the top of the skull, looked normal. The pituitary gland, the part in which she was particularly interested, was lower. 'While you lot in the pool-house drank yourself silly.'

'I managed to get to work this morning,' Carol said defensively.

'Barely.' Lizzy smiled, pleased Carol had been so easily distracted. 'Looks like our patient's asleep,' she added, rising off her chair a little so that she could peer into the scanner.

Predictably, Drew Maitland hadn't appeared by the time the scan was finished. Telling herself that it was probably because she'd frightened him off, Lizzy wrote a brief summary in Mr Jackson's notes, which would go back to the ward with him, then took the films with her to her office for formal reporting onto the computer.

But she'd been wrong about scaring the consultant off—either that or his concern for his patient had overcome his obvious wariness of her—because he came to her office a short while later.

'Definitely a tumour,' she confirmed nervously, wishing she'd thought to tidy her hair and discard her unflattering white coat.

Under the pretence of adjusting the light intensity of her X-ray screen, she darkened the main office lights so he wouldn't be able to see her too clearly. She pushed up the films that held the relevant scans. 'Here's the mass,' she explained, outlining the darker coloured area with a pointer. 'It's not overly large as yet but it's expanded upwards at this point, explaining the visual defect.'

She felt his surprise. 'You examined him?'

'Only his visual fields,' she admitted. 'I hope you don't mind.'

'I don't mind, but I'm surprised,' he said. 'That's very thorough of you.'

Beyond her brief, she decided he probably meant, not taking offence because he was possibly right. 'There are no other lesions, and my impression is that this is a primary tumour,' she continued stiffly, 'unrelated to the previous bladder cancer I noted in his notes and, in all likelihood, amenable to surgery. How is he from the hormonal viewpoint?'

'Nothing abnormal yet,' he told her, 'but we're still waiting on most of the results.'

Lizzy nodded jerkily, self-conscious with him despite the professional tone of the conversation. The pituitary gland controlled the release of many hormones and, simplistically, the tumour could either produce the hormones, or the hormone-precursors itself, in an unregulated manner or it could squash or destroy the hormone-producing tissues, leading eventually to low levels.

'We won't have any more results through until late to-night, but there's a chance you've caught this early enough for him to get away with it,' he added.

'Lucky he fell over last night.' Lizzy looked again at the tumour outline on the scan. 'It's a good size for surgery. Probably a very high chance of a cure.'

'I've already mentioned him to one of the neurosurgeons,' Drew told her. 'He's expecting me to call.' His raised eyebrows asked permission to use her phone and she pushed it across to him.

Lizzy waited while he spoke to the surgeon, shifting her weight nervously from foot to foot to relieve some of the tension the consultant's nearness provoked, then she went with Drew up to Lilac Ward to show the surgeon the scans. He agreed with her assessment and told them that he'd see Mr Jackson the following day once more of the blood results were available. 'At this stage there's a very high chance of success,' he told them. 'Even an eighty per cent chance we'll be able to reverse the visual loss.'

Waiting with Drew for the lift to go back down, after talking with the surgeon, Lizzy gathered courage to ask him out. What about the things she'd told him in the wardrobe? He been pleasant this afternoon but not exactly friendly. Odds were he thought she was a complete idiot. Would he even begin to take her seriously?

Preoccupied, she didn't even notice the lift arrive, and it was only when he prompted her that she realised he was waiting for her to precede him into it.

'You look hungry,' she said baldly. 'Want to eat?'

'Someone recently advised me to lose weight,' he said evenly, his hazel eyes glinting brief, but, she thought, real amusement at her. 'I thought perhaps I should cut down.'

'I had the wrong person,' she mumbled. Even in a suit she could see his body was perfect. She doubted there was a shred of spare fat anywhere. 'I thought you were someone else.'

'That did occur to me later.' He smiled as he followed her into the lift.

Perfect white teeth, she noted approvingly, grimacing at the memory of the assumptions she'd made of his appearance the night before. Fleshy mouth, piggy eyes and yellow teeth, if she recalled correctly. Instead, he had to be the most physically attractive man she'd ever met.

'Let me guess,' he continued. 'You've confused me with an overweight accountant with a terrible haircut?'

'And horrible suits.' But Lizzy didn't want to go into it because it made her look too much like a fool. 'Basically, everything I said was because I assumed you were him,' she announced in a rush. 'I'm very sorry if I offended you.'

'I'm sure some of it was quite relevant,' he said calmly.

'No, it wasn't,' she said. 'None of it. And you have lovely hair.'

He gave her a vaguely startled look. 'Thank you.'

'So, will you come out to dinner with me?'

His eyes narrowed. 'Are you asking me out?'

'Well, it's late and we've been working and...yes,' she finished faintly. 'Is that all right?'

He hesitated and the silence strained her ears. 'It's all right,' he said finally. 'Just...unexpected.'

The doors opened and three nurses came in. Lizzy saw the interested looks Drew attracted, but it seemed he didn't notice because he was still looking at her.

Neither of them spoke until the lift doors opened again at the fourth-floor foyer—Radiology and Medicine—and both Drew and Lizzy got out. Lizzy blinked up at him. Now she'd actually made the invitation she had little more dignity to lose by pursuing it. 'Well?'

'Why not?' But he didn't look especially thrilled about it, she realised, trying not to let that bother her too much. 'Do you mean tonight?'

She held her breath. 'Yes.'

'I want to speak to Nathan Jackson on Blue Ward and I've some work to finish.'

'Which means I've got enough time to finish my work and visit Jane's baby,' she said quickly, her breath coming out in a rush. They arranged to meet in the hospital's main foyer, by McDonald's, at eight. 'We'll go somewhere special,' she told him, her confidence entirely assumed.

Gemma Rose was beautiful. 'Your nose,' Lizzy exclaimed to Jane. 'And look at all her tiny toes.'

'Ten,' Jane told her.

'And her gorgeous big eyes.'

'Two,' Jane announced.

'And sweet little ears.'

'Two of them as well.'

Lizzy looked worriedly at Gemma Rose's mother. 'You don't sound very excited,' she said disapprovingly.

'Nor would you be after a night without sleep and hours and hours without food.'

'Oh, I would be,' Lizzy cooed, making faces at Gemma Rose. 'Who cares about food when you've got this?'

'Me.' Jane glared at a nurse who wandered past at that point. 'They never feed you in this place. There're no olives anywhere.'

'Yes, well, from what I hear, I think you've had quite enough olives,' Lizzy countered. She touched Gemma Rose's thatch of spiky, black hair. 'It's so silky.'

'It falls out.'

But Lizzy heard the faint pride behind the grumble and she laughed at her friend. 'I see right through you, Jane Horricks. You're as pleased as punch.'

'I'd be more pleased if they brought me some food.' Jane's bulky body struggled up on the pillows. 'Be a darling, Lizzy, and stir them up. Play the heavy doctor, just for me. I was having a shower when the meals came and now they're ignoring me. I'm starving.'

'OK, but then I have to go.' Lizzy shook her head regretfully at the baby one last time. 'You are so gorgeous,' she told her.

'Time you got around to breeding,' Jane added with a touch of acid.

'I'm working on it,' Lizzy said absently, collecting her bag and deliberately ignoring Jane's sudden interest. 'What do you want? Since it's a private bed, I guess you can choose. Cheese and biscuits?'

'Olives and crisps to start. Smoked salmon and brown bread, rare fillet steak with steamed asparagus, fresh tropical fruits with cream—and don't forget a decent Burgundy,' Jane ordered.

Lizzy found an aide who promised to find Jane some leftover scrambled eggs and then had to hurry to get back to the foyer to meet Drew.

He looked doubtfully at her little Renault when she led him to it. 'We'll take mine,' he announced, his hand pleasantly warm at her elbow as he steered her away.

'It's not as small as it looks,' she protested, forced to skip to keep up with his long strides.

'Only from your perspective.' He looked down at her and promptly slowed his pace so dramatically that she realised he must have noted her puffing.

His amusement made her self-conscious. 'I'm quite fit,' she said defensively. 'I work out.'

'I remember.' The hand at her elbow tightened fractionally. 'Karate, isn't it?'

'Step aerobics,' she said. Less often, though, than she'd have liked. 'And I walk a lot.' Walking was an exercise she'd be able to continue when she was pregnant. 'Drew, do you like children?'

'I'd rather breed rats,' he said immediately, then his gaze narrowed on her expression. 'Why so horrified? Wasn't that what you expected me to say?'

'Is it the truth?' she asked rawly.

She saw him hesitate. 'No, it's not the truth,' he said finally, opening the door of the black Saab he'd led her to. 'I like children and one day I'd like to be a father.' He waited while she climbed into the car. 'Why?'

'Just interested.' Very, very interested, she realised. She waited for him to take his seat beside her. 'So you don't have any already?'

'What?'

'Children.'

'No.'

'Why aren't you married?'

'Why aren't I...?' His brows drew together. 'Why aren't you?'

'I haven't met the right person,' she explained. When he still didn't answer her question she tried another. 'Are you involved with anyone at the moment?'

'Not at the moment.'

'But you like women?'

She saw that her question must have astounded him because he'd gone absolutely still. 'Are you asking me if I'm gay?'

'Are you?' Lizzy met his stunned gaze unflinchingly. This was too important not to clarify the issue right at the beginning. Admittedly Corinne was experienced and a good judge of men but no one was infallible. Also, he was an unmarried, very good-looking, immaculately dressed man who had to be in his mid to late thirties. The possibility remained. 'Are you gay?'

But instead of answering, his hand lifted to her chin and tilted it rather determinedly towards him. Then he brought his head down and kissed her, a firm, almost frustrated, taunting kiss that nevertheless made her head spin.

When he took his mouth away he said grimly, 'Does that answer your question, Lizzy Murdoch?'

'Yes.' She could hardly breathe. 'I'm glad.' Her smile was tremulous but the sentiment was honest. 'Hepatitis B status?'

'Fully immunised,' he grated. 'Look—'

'HIV?' she said quickly.

'Never been tested.' His voice was very deep. 'I've never put myself or any partner at risk.' His firm, cool mouth was tight now. 'Is this what you call getting straight to the point?'

'Any hereditary diseases run in the family?'

'None that I'm aware of.'

'Brothers? Sisters?'

'Three of the first, two of the second,' he said wearily, his change of tone suggesting he'd decided it was easier to humour her for now at least. 'Mother and father in their early sixties and both well. Three grandparents in their eighties—one has just had cataract surgery. Four nephews and two nieces, all normal. I've had all my immunisations, have never been in hospital and still have my own teeth. All right?'

Lizzy smiled. 'Perfect.'

'I'm not looking for a wife.'

'I'm not looking for a husband,' she said soothingly, smiling reassurance, understanding why her questions had worried him. 'Relax.'

'Why wouldn't I be relaxed?' But his face was tight and his movements, as he pulled his seat belt across, were jerky. 'Am I allowed to start the car now?'

'Yes.' She fastened her own seat belt then frowned, realising she hadn't given their destination any thought. Deciding it was best to stick with the familiar, she directed him to a place she frequented near Oxford Street, about twenty minutes from the hospital, allowing ten minutes to find a parking space in the crowded little streets around the restaurant.

He sent her a brooding look when they stopped to read the blackboard menu outside, but he didn't say anything until after they'd lined up and collected their food and drinks when they had a brief argument about who should pay.

'But I invited you,' Lizzy protested, when he ignored the way she was fishing in her pockets for the exact change and simply handed a large note over her head to the cashier.

'You're not paying,' he said firmly when they reached a

pine table near the window and Lizzy tried to thrust pound coins at him.

'I feel terrible.'

'Don't.' He waited for her to sit, then sat himself opposite her, his back to the window so he was in shadow. It was still light and warm outside so the candles on the tables weren't yet lit. 'This looks interesting,' he said slowly, eyeing his food with what she interpreted to be vague unease. 'Do you think those red things are chillies?'

'Probably.' A forkful of chick peas halfway to her mouth, Lizzy blinked at him. 'Don't you like them? Want to swap?'

'I don't think so.' His first mouthful of his lentil bake was hesitant, his second marginally more so. She took some of her own food and chewed worriedly, watching him.

'We can go somewhere else if you don't like it,' she ventured after a few minutes when his enthusiasm didn't improve.

'It'll just take a little time to get used to.'

'Jane won't even come here,' she told him. 'If it hasn't got meat she's not interested.'

He rested his fork. 'How was Jane tonight?'

Lizzy grimaced. 'Her memory's completely gone,' she said. 'Tonight she didn't even mention locking us all up. I think she might even have forgotten any of us were there.'

'Did you say anything?'

'I didn't raise the subject,' she admitted. 'She was a bit touchy.'

'Bill's the one with the right to be touchy,' he said, 'once he discovers the state of his wine collection.'

'As long as we enjoyed it he won't mind.' Lizzy ate more of her chick peas. 'Aren't you hungry any more?'

'I'm fine.' But he'd only eaten one or two more mouthfuls and she saw he was studying his bake and the carob and tofu slice he'd selected for dessert with more thoughtfulness than hunger. 'Do you eat meat?'

'Occasionally. I prefer vegetarian or fish.'

'Fish.' He smiled. 'Good.'

Lizzy's breath caught. She lowered her fork. 'You hate it, don't you?'

'Hate's a strong word.'

'It's full of vitamins.'

'So is spinach. That doesn't make it edible.'

She stared at him in disbelief. 'You don't like spinach?'

'Is that a problem?'

'Not for me.' In fact, she realised she found it rather endearing. In fact, she was finding *him* rather endearing. 'But I love it,' she confessed. 'It's my favourite vegetable. Half the time I've eaten it raw before I even get home from the shop.'

She laughed at his grimace, and when he laughed back she realised she'd made up her mind. She pushed her plate away and looked at him, serious now. 'Drew, I don't want to beat around the bush any more. You seem like a reasonable and rational man and I'd like to ask you a favour.'

His face stilled and she saw that the wariness was back, but this was too important for her not to go on and she screwed up her napkin in her fists and held them tight under the table. 'I need your genes,' she said baldly. 'Would you please have a baby with me?'

CHAPTER FIVE

THE evening outside had darkened and a waiter came to light their candle. The couple behind them wanted to move and they both had to get up so that they could squeeze out. The girl trod on the coat Lizzy had left slung over the back of her seat, and in the brief flurry of activity and apologies Drew managed to get his head together. A little.

'Hence your questions in the car,' he said heavily, acknowledging her nod with a brief tightening of his mouth. There was no point in asking if she was serious—it was obvious in every taut, waiting line of her face. When another couple jostled her as they came to sit behind her he pushed his barely touched food away. 'We can't talk here. Let's go.'

'It's not what you think,' she said abruptly, sounding nervous now as they left the restaurant and started in the direction of Oxford Street.

Drew decided she couldn't possibly know what he was thinking because that was something about emigrating to Australia, but he let her talk, listening distantly to her words about her mother becoming menopausal prematurely, and about the lack of success her sister had had, trying to get pregnant, and the final, startling results that had revealed that Catherine had already left it too late to have children herself.

'Catherine and Duncan are trying to adopt now,' she explained, 'but it isn't easy. They want a baby but there aren't enough babies and they might end up fostering a teenager. I'm happy to do that myself if there's no alternative, but the gynaecologist I consulted told me that I was still fertile but that I shouldn't waste any time. She made it clear I should be trying to get pregnant immediately. But until last night I hadn't met a man I thought would make a suitable father.'

He sighed, wishing he'd taken his own best advice and stayed away from her. 'You don't even know me. This is ridiculous—'

'I've spoken with a solicitor,' she assured him hastily. 'Not about you, specifically, but in general terms. He can draw up a contract which would guarantee you no further responsibility and I swear that I will be the only person who ever knows your name.'

He stopped. 'No one will know my name?'

'I promise.' Her face creased and deeply earnest she swung around to him, holding up her hand in what looked like some sort of scout salute. 'Financially, I'm very secure and I've been thinking about children for years. I've set up a trust for them from an inheritance I received when I was twenty-five and part of my income goes into the same fund every fortnight. I have some solid investments, which my father tells me are very secure, and by the end of next year I'll have paid off the mortgage on my flat.'

He was shaking his head but, as if still determined to convince him, she rushed on, 'I specialised in radiology because I always planned to have a big family and it's a perfect field for a mother. There won't be any problem working part time and the hospital's crèche is excellent, and even if that changes Catherine, my sister, would be thrilled to help with child care.'

She blinked up at him, apparently assuming that he was taking her seriously. 'So, you see, I'm ready for this.'

He cleared his throat, wondering how best to break it to her that her readiness, or lack of it, was irrelevant to him, but instead found himself saying, 'You don't mind your baby not knowing his or her father?'

'My child will be deeply loved and secure. My brother-in-law and father are good male role models, and one day

I hope to fall in love and marry so he or she will have a proper father anyway.'

At some stage they must have started walking again because now they turned onto Oxford Street. With its brightly lit shops deserted at this time on a Tuesday night, apart from an intermittent swoosh from the buses and black cabs which swept along the road, it was very quiet.

'So you still believe in love and marriage?' he said dryly.

'Eventually I want all of that,' she said adamantly. 'One day. But my time's running out and I have to be practical. I can't sit around waiting for a husband who might never come. As I said, I want your genes—I need them desperately. But, don't worry, that's all I want.'

But Drew didn't find that remotely reassuring. Once he might have been tempted by sex, he acknowledged, the memory of how she'd felt when his hands had curled around her thighs enough to arouse him immediately, but that was no longer enough for him. He couldn't simply sleep with her to satisfy some adolescent craving then irresponsibly leave her with his child.

The whole point of the recent changes he'd made in his life was that he wanted a more fulfilling future, and that meant a committed and sincere relationship and children with a woman he could spend the rest of his life with. Lizzy Murdoch, dizzyingly unpredictable and possibly not quite sane, despite her undeniable physical charms, was not that woman.

His silence must have told her something because after a while she said quietly, 'I'll understand if you say no. The clinic can help me choose an anonymous donor.'

His hands curled into fists. 'You can never be sure what you're getting with those.'

'The samples are screened.'

'You can't screen for everything.' He didn't understand why he was arguing—an anonymous donor was obviously the best solution to her requirements—but still he found himself making sure she was aware of the dangers. 'There could be something hidden in the family history that the donor's either unaware of or chooses not to disclose.'

'I know.' Her little nod was forlorn and it tugged at his conscience. 'And it's so impersonal. Ideally, I wanted to know the father so I could choose someone of good character, obviously, or I wouldn't have asked you. But if I don't find anyone in two months then it'll have to be a donor.'

'Two months?'

'That's the time I've allowed myself,' she explained. She looked up. 'I suppose I sound very cold.'

'Not cold.' He managed a small smile. 'Desperate, I suppose.'

'I am *extremely* desperate.' She smiled back, apparently not at all abashed by the admission. 'If I wasn't so short of time it might be different, but I'm not even sure about having the two months spare.'

They were at Bond Street now and they crossed the road and began returning along the other side of Oxford Street, back in the direction of the restaurant, and then they continued to his car. 'I don't want to mislead you,' he said, realising finally that she might be taking his silence for assent. 'I'm not going to say yes.'

'Don't make a decision yet,' she said quickly, her expression immediately anxious. 'Think about it. Just a few days. Please.'

He nodded briskly, irritated with himself for doing so and thus taking the easy way out when he didn't have any intention of thinking about anything but avoiding her.

When he stopped beside her car at the hospital he stepped out and held her door open for her while she got in. 'I think you're very nice, Drew Maitland.' Her smile up at him was sweet and open, and if he'd needed further proof that she had no idea of how he was feeling her words gave it to him. 'Will I see you tomorrow?'

'Perhaps.' He shut her door, but leaned to look at her

when she wound down her window. 'You're an unusual woman, Lizzy Murdoch.'

He saw her frown at that but, not waiting for a response, he returned to his car and watched her leave the car park before he started his engine again.

Despite his determination not to think about her request, he slept poorly and had to work hard to maintain his concentration on the ward the next morning. From time to time during his round he was aware of Corinne frowning at him, as if she'd detected something of his distraction. He allowed himself a moment of grim amusement by contemplating her reaction if he revealed that her friend, Lizzy, the woman she'd been so keen to thrust in his direction, was responsible for this aggravating…knot in his brain.

There wasn't the remotest chance of him agreeing to her crazy plan, he repeatedly reassured himself, but still it bothered him that he couldn't shrug off persistent images of her with him again in that cupboard. This time, though, apart from her black stockings, she was naked. Not only clichéd but sick, he registered, disgusted with himself.

The neurosurgeon he'd consulted about his patient, Nathan Jackson, joined them on the ward towards the end of the round.

'I've talked with both him and his wife about scheduling surgery for next week,' he told them. 'They both seem fairly happy about that.'

Fairly happy was an understatement, Drew decided, when he visited the couple before his clinic. Both looked delighted. 'It's a major operation,' he cautioned, worried about their enthusiasm. 'With every chance of success, of course, but still not to be taken lightly.'

'Now don't you fret, Dr Maitland.' Mrs Jackson, despite a cloud of shock-white curls, was as sprightly-looking as her elderly husband, and she waggled her finger at him, nudging her spouse with obvious affection and prompting an echoing beam from him. 'We've been through worse.'

'Only five years since we sailed ourselves from New

Zealand to Southampton, me with a broken arm for the last fortnight,' Mr Jackson said proudly, holding up his plaster-encased wrist. 'The other arm that time.'

'And we cycled from Land's End to the Orkneys two years ago to celebrate our fortieth anniversary,' his wife added, 'him showing off his new pacemaker all the way.'

'It'll take more than a little operation to slow us down,' his patient declared. 'We're planning to take the grand-children trekking in Peru next summer, aren't we, Mim?'

'July,' she confirmed happily.

'I'm envious,' Drew told them easily, exchanging a grin with Corinne who looked hugely amused by the whole con-versation. 'And relieved I'm not your cardiologist.'

'He's a nervous man,' Mr Jackson admitted brightly. He tapped the skin over his pacemaker. 'Marvels, these things. Sometimes I think I've more faith in it than he has.'

'We'll let him know you're here so he can get it tested before your surgery,' Drew told him. 'The neuro people are keen to take you up to Lilac Ward later today but we'll come and see how you're going tomorrow.'

'Thank you, then, Dr Maitland.' Mr Jackson shook his hand. 'For everything. The surgeon told us this would have been much worse if it had been missed.'

'The credit's not mine,' Drew told him before he left. 'Our radiologist picked everything up on your head X-ray.'

'Lizzy's brilliant,' Corinne remarked—smugly, he de-cided—*en route* to Outpatients. 'Don't you agree, Dr Maitland?'

He gave her a hard look, holding the door to the clinic room open for her to precede him. 'Dr Murdoch seems very competent, yes, Corinne.'

But his registrar's answering grin was knowing as she skipped ahead, and inwardly he sighed.

'You know, if you ever want to have a…late night, Dr Maitland, you only have to tell me,' she murmured, eyeing him from under her lashes. 'If you've a date, for instance.

I'd be very happy to start work later, and I know the house officers wouldn't mind. Nine suits me.'

'We'll leave it at eight,' he said easily, amused despite her probing. Jane might have altruistic motives for wanting to match him up with her Lizzy, but it seemed that Corinne was merely concerned with sleeping in a little longer in the mornings.

Lizzy's afternoon ultrasound session started at two. The majority of scans requested were abdominal, and her first three patients were from the surgical wards, all having presented with abdominal pain and all turning out to have gallstones.

'Just one, but it's the size of a ping-pong ball,' she told one woman, who seemed fascinated by the moving images. She directed her attention to the rounded opacity, pressing the button that produced a still of the picture. 'This little ball here—that's the stone, and the dark streak behind it is its shadow.'

'Will the surgeon be able to get it out?'

'No problem,' Lizzy said reassuringly. She applied more jelly to the patient's skin and moved the probe around, checking the rest of her abdomen. 'Everything else—your kidneys, liver, pancreas and spleen—looks perfectly healthy.'

She finished her last case around five and then joined her registrar who was working in main X-ray that afternoon.

'I was coming to look for you,' he told her, indicating the stack of films from the session. 'I did an IVU for possible kidney stones on this man who's had some loin pain and is passing some blood in his urine. There is a little stone...' he indicated a small, white, rounded speck in the lower part of the tube that ran between the right kidney and the bladder '...but there's also this small defect in his right kidney. I don't know if it's significant or not.' He passed her the film. 'What do you think?'

'It's small,' she agreed slowly, studying the pictures. An

IVU, or IVP, comprised a series of X-rays of the urinary system, taken after giving an injection of dye. The progress of the dye with time showed how well the system was working, and was good at demonstrating stones, but didn't show details of the kidneys.

'Take a look at it under ultrasound,' she instructed, noting the patient's details imprinted at the top of the films. Forty-six and male, it was important to exclude malignancy. 'It's probably just a benign cyst but you have to be sure.'

'I'll call his doctors and let them know.' He gave her a quick smile when she stood to leave. 'Oh, that new physician on the chest team was here five minutes ago, looking for you. Did he find you?'

Lizzy's breath caught. 'Did he leave a message?'

'If he couldn't find you he was going to bleep you. I gave him your number.'

'I'll look around for him.' Her legs felt wobbly. 'Coming to the teaching?'

'Five minutes,' he confirmed. 'Just let me organise this ultrasound.'

Lizzy walked all around the department but didn't find Drew. She bleeped herself experimentally to check that her bleeper was working, which it was, but he still didn't call her. She toyed with the idea of calling him, but decided that would be too awkward. It was up to him to make the first move, she decided. Only, if he left it more than a day or two she'd have to hurry him along.

At six she took the radiology registrars for her regular weekly one-hour tutorial, tonight discussing some of the finer points of interpretation of lateral chest X-rays.

'A dry topic,' Lizzy acknowledged easily, smiling at their groans, 'and I don't even have any jokes to make it easier—sorry.'

But they were a pleasant, relaxed group of doctors, and as several had came into London from outlying hospitals for the lesson, and obviously appreciated the contact with their colleagues and main base, the session was enjoyable and lively.

Drew still hadn't contacted her by the end of the hour, nor by the time she'd caught up with the backlog of reporting she needed to do, before going home.

She was on call for the night so she let the telephonists know she was carrying a long-range bleeper, before leaving the department.

'The best thing about radiology,' she told Jane, stopping at the private wing to visit Gemma Rose again, 'is the on-call roster. I have to come in perhaps once a month at night. It's a dream.'

'I don't know how Corinne can bear to stay in medicine,' Jane added. 'She hardly ever gets any sleep.'

'And of all of us she needs it most,' Lizzy said. She jiggled Gemma Rose, smiling into her adorable little face. 'She's so grumpy when she's tired.'

'She's trying to impress Drew,' Jane declared. 'She's even stayed late this week to dictate all her discharge summaries.'

Lizzy kept her eyes on Gemma Rose. 'Does Drew sound impressed?'

'Drew's not an easy man to impress,' Jane told her, sounding annoyingly smug. 'Why, Lizzy? Want some tips?'

'No.' Lizzy glared at her. 'You're a pest.'

'I knew you'd fancy him.' Jane clapped her hands triumphantly. 'I would have introduced you years ago if I could have caught him unattached for a few days. Why do you think I told you to wear something low-cut on Monday?'

Lizzy's glare became accusing. 'I thought you didn't remember Monday?'

'I've just had more important things to think about,' Jane countered, one hand resting on her still-protruding stomach with such an air of injured martyrdom that Lizzy promptly felt guilty. 'And don't try and tell me you didn't enjoy his company.'

'Corinne warned me that you were trying to set me up with some ghastly relative of yours.' Lizzy changed the subject deliberately. 'But she mentioned an accountant.'

'Warning you off, was she?' Jane wiggled her fingers. 'I told her I might do something like that to make her wake her ideas up. I knew she liked Simon.'

'She didn't like him,' Lizzy protested. 'He groped her in the cab.'

'She really was worried.' Jane sighed elaborately. 'I should take this up professionally,' she mused. 'I am a born matchmaker.'

'You're a born raving lunatic.' Lizzy gurgled at Gemma Rose. 'Darling, your mother is silly. Yes, she is, she's silly.' She flicked her gaze to Jane. 'He's an accountant, you idiot. Corinne hates men in suits.'

'You are so innocent, Lizzy.' Jane held out her arms for Gemma, and Lizzy handed her across reluctantly.

'Now go home and leave me in peace.' Jane frowned at the little denim jumpsuit Lizzy had brought as a present for Gemma. 'And next time you come bring me some olives.'

'When are you going home?'

'When I decide.'

'I thought the maximum was three days?'

'They're too frightened to throw her out.' Bill walked in, kissed his wife and baby, deposited an enormous jar of stuffed green olives on the dresser, then beamed at Lizzy, before kissing her, too. 'Isn't she beautiful?'

'Adorable.' Lizzy kissed him back. 'Shame about her mother. Congratulations. How does it feel to be a father?'

'You know, Drew asked me exactly the same question about five minutes ago,' Bill said easily, making Lizzy stiffen. 'And the answer is—it feels great.'

'Strange question from a committed philanderer like Drew.' Jane looked sideways at Lizzy. 'Interesting.'

'Bye, Bill.' Lizzy smiled at her friend's husband, and her friend's baby, then scowled at Jane. 'See you tomorrow.'

Bill had implied that Drew was still in the hospital so,

instead of going directly to the car park from the private wing, Lizzy hurried back to the radiology department in case he was looking for her.

Ray was still around. 'One of the gynae registrars just called to say that she's bringing up someone from Casualty with a possible ectopic pregnancy for ultrasound,' he told her, explaining why he was staying late. 'But, no, no one's been looking for you.'

'We need a decent ultrasound in Casualty,' Lizzy declared, hiding her disappointment. She perched on the edge of the desk. 'Or at least a more portable one. The obstetric one is even further away than we are, and only the more senior staff are skilled enough to interpret the results properly anyway. There should be an emergency machine available in Casualty which we can run down and use when we're needed.'

Ray grimaced. 'But there isn't enough money.'

'There is never enough money.'

The clang of a bed being pushed though the double doors interrupted their discussion, and a porter and a nurse swung the bed into position.

Lizzy looked at the woman on the bed worriedly. Pale and tense, her eyes wide and fearful, fingers white where they clutched the side-bars on the bed, she looked devastated.

The gynae registrar hurried in a few moments later. 'Two days of lower right abdominal pain and some bleeding. Pain increasing tonight. Positive pregnancy test,' she told Lizzy briskly, while Ray gently introduced himself to their patient and the nurse lifted the white hospital gown to reveal a still-flat stomach.

'Last menstrual period two months ago.' The registrar had been carrying a litre bag of normal saline and now she exchanged that for the empty small one that had run through into the cannula in her patient's thin arm. 'Blood pressure slightly down. Pulse, a hundred. This is the second litre so hopefully the bladder should be full by now.'

Ray squeezed clear gel over the patient's abdomen and lifted the probe. 'We need your bladder to be full so it pushes the bowel away and gives us good pictures of the inside of your pelvis,' he said calmly. 'Try and relax, Mrs Sanderson. This machine bounces sound waves around inside you. I promise it won't hurt.'

Lizzy leaned forward to watch the screen. Mrs Sanderson's bladder was full and the pictures were good. She tensed when Ray located the mass in the right Fallopian tube, nodding confirmation when the registrar looked at her quickly.

Ray looked concerned. 'I'd estimate six to eight weeks.'

'My baby?' Their patient's wide-eyed gaze flew to his face. 'Is it my baby?'

'I'm sorry, Mrs Sanderson.' The gynae registrar took her hand while the nurse took the other and soothed back her hair.

The registrar explained about the embryo being in the wrong place. 'It's what I talked about downstairs. Instead of being in your womb, it's stuck in one of the thin tubes leading to it. We have to operate immediately to take it away before it bursts through.'

'And that could kill me,' her patient said huskily, weeping now. 'Oh, God. I can't believe it.'

'Uterus empty,' Ray said, finishing his examination. 'Both ovaries normal. Opposite tube normal. No other abnormalities.'

'I know you've been trying for a long time, but this doesn't mean you won't be able to have another baby,' continued the registrar, nodding acknowledgement of Ray's words and opening the drip so that the fluid began flowing more quickly. 'Your ovaries and your other tube look fine. But now we have to take you to the operating theatre. Shall I speak to your husband?'

'Please.' Mrs Sanderson lifted her legs and cried out. 'The pain again,' she sobbed. 'It's worse.'

'Let's go.' The registrar nodded thanks when Lizzy

rushed to open the doors and called urgently for a porter. 'We'll get you another injection as soon as we get to Theatre.'

Ray ran alongside, scrawling his report in the notes, while Lizzy helped the others push the bed to the lifts.

'Thanks, guys.' The registrar looked preoccupied as she accepted the notes from Ray. She cleared the first lift to arrive. 'Could one of you call Theatre One and let them know we're on our way?'

'I'll do it.' Ray rushed back to the department.

'What about Mr Sanderson?' Lizzy helped them push the bed into the lift. 'Want me to bring him up from Casualty?'

'That would save time.' The registrar nodded. 'Thanks. He knows what the probable diagnosis is so let him know the result if he asks. If you ring the bell at Theatre Reception on the sixth floor I'll come out directly.'

Lizzy found Mr Sanderson, waiting in one of the gynae cubicles in Casualty on the ground floor. Pale, obviously tense, he stood abruptly when she entered.

He brushed aside her attempt to introduce herself. 'Is it ectopic?'

'Yes,' she said gently. 'They've taken her to the operating theatre. Do you want to come up?'

'I do.' He looked numb. He followed her to the lift and when the doors shut he said abruptly, 'We've been trying for two years for the baby. We were over the moon. It seems so unfair.'

'I'm sorry.'

'I suppose it's hard for anyone else to understand how important this was for us both.'

'Believe me, I do understand,' Lizzy said quietly.

'But, of course, the most important thing is Sonya.' He rubbed his eyes with palms that Lizzy saw shook slightly. 'Will she be all right?'

'She's in very good hands.' The doors opened at the sixth floor and Lizzy guided him to the theatre reception.

She pressed the bell, as the gynae registrar had requested,

and the door swung open almost immediately. The registrar came out and thanked Lizzy, before walking across to Mr Sanderson.

Lizzy made for the stairs.

'We'll be operating in about ten minutes,' she heard the registrar say gently. 'The anaesthetist is with your wife now and as soon as he's finished I'll take you in to see her for a few minutes.'

She dropped into the department again to say goodbye to Ray and collect her bag. Because she'd arrived at work that morning before the night nursing shift had gone off duty but after the day shift had arrived for work, she'd had to park her car at the far side of the National's huge car-parking area, but when she finally reached the Renault there was a note from Drew underneath her wiper.

Timed an hour earlier, she read, "Didn't bleep you because assumed you'd already left. Dinner Friday night? Call me during the day to arrange time." He'd left his bleeper number.

She didn't sleep particularly well. Mrs Sanderson's problems had reminded her of everything that could go wrong with a pregnancy and had increased her sense of urgency about her own situation. She tossed restlessly for hours, and in the morning she peered at her strained face in the mirror with disgust.

'Relax,' she told herself, practising deep breathing. Stress could play havoc with hormones and for the next two months, when the balance of her hormones was so important, she couldn't afford to let herself succumb to it. 'Keep calm. Be serene.'

Outside Lizzy's flat Drew was aware of an uncharacteristic urge to cancel the evening altogether. It was years since he'd felt any similar nervousness about taking out a woman and he decided he didn't like the sensation. Telling himself impatiently that nervousness when it came to Lizzy Murdoch was entirely rational and reasonable, particularly when he was about to refuse her something she obviously wanted very much, he jabbed viciously at the bell.

But when she opened the door his breath caught and his mood changing immediately. Her hair gleaming and fragrant, her beautiful body *petite* perfection in a little blue dress that clung exactly where he'd have wanted it to cling if he'd designed the thing, she was enchanting. His hands clenched at his sides, he followed her inside.

'Like the dress.'

'Thank you.' Her flush suggested she might not be used to compliments. 'Jane and Corinne gave it to me for my birthday.' She added quickly, 'You look nice, too. I like your suit.' She was backing away now. 'Come upstairs. I want to show you something.'

'It's not huge,' she told him seconds later, leading him though the flat's open-plan living areas while he concentrated on keeping his gaze on his surroundings rather than on the feminine curves beneath her dress, 'but it's well designed and there's plenty of space.'

He looked vaguely into the rooms as she opened doors along the short corridor, lingering longer at her bedroom on one side—a pastel, very female room he'd have liked to explore further—only she was showing him the bathroom now and then a small guest room along the other side of the corridor.

'And this...' she opened the final door into a peaceful and light sunroom '...this will be perfect for the baby. What do you think?'

He frowned. 'Lizzy—'

'I'm not assuming anything,' she said quickly. 'I just want to show how well prepared I am.' She opened the room's side door and he saw that it connected with her bedroom. 'With this open I'll hear every noise, although for the first few months I'd keep the cot in my room.'

Idly Drew opened a cupboard, stiffening at the tiny outfits which hung inside along with a huge stuffed bear. 'I've bought a few things,' she said huskily, when he turned to look at her. 'For Gemma Rose if I don't get pregnant my-self,' she added, obviously self-conscious about her pur-chases. 'The clothes are good quality and they were all on sale. It seemed silly not to buy them.'

'Like it was silly not to buy this?' Sighing inwardly, Drew hauled out the massive bear, which had been bent into one corner. Golden and fluffy, it had kind brown eyes and was as big as Lizzy.

'Caught me in a moment of weakness,' she admitted.

'I know what that feels like.' He knew *exactly* what that felt like. He looked around, anything to keep his eyes off her. 'You're obviously very well equipped.'

'I've been thinking about this for a long time.'

'Doing it alone is not an easy option.'

'I'm ready.' She stepped though into her room and he saw her collect a sheaf of papers from the small table beside her bed. A small bed, he noted immediately, disliking him-self for being pleased about that. A single or only margin-ally larger.

'I had my solicitor fax me some notes today,' she told him, her voice delightfully husky now. 'An example of the sort of contract I mentioned the other night. I thought you might like to look through it.'

'Lizzy, there's no point—'

'Please, Drew.' She was so lovely and she used his name so appealingly that, to his disgust, he found himself swap-ping the bear for the notes, but when she turned around from stuffing the bear away he was looking at her, only the first few paragraphs of the stilted document read. 'This is very formal.'

'To protect us both.'

'It denies the father's right to have any contact with the child.'

'This is only a preliminary draft.'

'So you're prepared to change that?' He shouldn't even be asking, had no right to ask, but something about the defensive way she tilted her chin at him drove him on. That, and the tantalising glimpse of a creamy curve he'd had when her neckline had dipped as she'd bent forward to replace the bear.

'I'm prepared to negotiate.'

But the admission seemed to have been drawn painfully from her and he heard his voice demanding more. 'If I were the father, I'd definitely want contact.'

'I thought you might say something like that.' He saw her take a deep breath, and sensed that she was trying to stay calm. 'This isn't going to be as straightforward as I was hoping.'

'I'm sorry.' He didn't like himself for misleading her. It wasn't fair, not unless he was seriously thinking of going through with this—and he wasn't. The reason for this evening was to tell her that.

'No, you don't have to be sorry. I understand.' She'd leaned back against the cupboard that held the bear, and now she crossed her arms, the movement emphasising the shadow of her cleavage above the scooped neck of her dress and making him tense. 'In your position I don't think I could walk away from a child either.'

He kept his gaze fixed on hers. 'Am I making an anonymous donor sound more attractive?'

'Not yet.' He saw the small movement in her throat as she swallowed. 'Your sense of responsibility might be part of what makes me so sure you'd be an ideal father for my child. But I did say I was prepared to negotiate and I am.'

He was curious. 'What does that mean?'

'What do you want?'

He studied her for a few taut seconds, wondering what would happen if he told her honestly what he wanted at that moment. Would she still want to continue, or would she run a mile? 'What are you offering?'

'Whatever it takes,' she admitted huskily. 'I'm out of options. What can I possibly offer you to convince you to agree?'

CHAPTER SIX

'NOTHING,' Drew said abruptly, ashamed of himself. Aware that his determination not to take advantage of Lizzy wouldn't last much longer if she continued gazing up at him so invitingly, he swiftly folded the contract into his jacket pocket and swept her out of the room, his hand at the delicate small of her back. 'Dinner,' he declared tightly. The sooner he got this over with the better. 'Let's go.'

She snatched her keys from the coffee-table in the living room as he rushed her though the flat. 'Are we late?'

'It doesn't matter.' At least it wouldn't to their host. His car was parked close to her building and they joined the evening traffic on Bayswater Road. 'Does your liking of fish include prawns?'

'Everything except oysters.'

'Are you allergic?'

'They're like slime,' she told him, screwing her lovely mouth into a demonstration of disgust that made him laugh out loud, relieving some of the tension that had kept his hands clenched on the steering-wheel.

He took her to his brother's new restaurant, a modern and quiet fish eatery in a recent wharf development alongside the Thames. Michael, playing waiter, greeted them at the door, and Drew sighed at his delighted expression, sensing that he wasn't going to play this quite the way they'd agreed.

He hadn't wanted to bring Lizzy here, had merely wanted to utilise his brother's contacts to secure a last-minute quiet and private table somewhere else, but Michael had insisted. 'We're closed for refurbishment but the builders haven't arrived yet so you can have the place to your-selves,' he'd told him, and the idea had been tempting.

He wanted to have time with Lizzy to break his decision to her gently, time away from the distraction of interrup-tions and also—if he was to be brutally honest—away from the temptation of solitude, and Michael had promised to be discreet and unobtrusive. ''Fade into the background'' had been his exact words, if Drew remembered correctly.

Only it didn't look as if he was ready to do any fading because when he showed them to a table by a huge win-dow, overlooking the river, he lingered, surveying Lizzy approvingly. 'Hello, there.'

Drew rolled his eyes. 'Michael, Lizzy,' he said wearily. 'Lizzy, Michael.'

'Charmed.' He saw that she was surprised when Michael kissed her hand, but when he kept hold of it Drew growled his disapproval. He might not want her, but at least he had a conscience about it. His younger brother, he suspected, used to high-profile models and celebrities, would eat someone like Lizzy for breakfast.

'What have you got?' he asked. 'Prawns?'

'To start, and New Zealand orange roughy for main,' Michael said abstractedly, still smiling at Lizzy. 'Are you in medicine too, Lizzy?'

'Radiology,' she confirmed, and Drew was pleased to see she was trying to tug her hand free, less pleased at Michael's exaggerated reluctance to release it.

'At the National?'

'Cut it out, Michael.' Drew could feel himself growing irritated. 'Prawns and the roughy for us both and a bottle of that white I had last time. All right with you, Lizzy?'

'Fine.'

But Michael still lingered, and Drew sighed. 'Buzz,' he said tightly.

'Buzzing.' But his brother was grinning as he retreated and Drew realised that his entire family would have a totally inappropriate inch by delectable inch description of Lizzy before the night was out.

'This is very nice.' Lizzy swivelled in her chair and he saw her inspecting the chrome and black interior and the view of the river, reflections from the restaurant and wharf dancing on its surface. Twisting as she was, the fabric of her dress tautened across her chest, increasing his tension. 'And it's Friday night,' she continued. 'You'd think there'd be at least a few other people here.'

'Terrible reputation,' he said roughly. 'The food's sublime but Michael's atrocious. Try and ignore him.' He took one of her hands in his, marvelling at how small it was. 'Lizzy, we need to talk—'

But Michael, beaming, returned with a bottle of napkin-enclosed wine and he broke off, waiting impatiently while his brother opened the wine dramatically in front of them. He poured a little for Lizzy to try, forcing Drew to release her hand so that she could lift the glass, and once she'd tasted the liquid and nodded her appreciation he filled her glass and then splashed some into Drew's.

'Anything else?'

'Peace and quiet,' Drew said meaningfully, glaring when Michael winked at Lizzy as he retreated and made her smile. Once they were alone again he delayed what he'd wanted to say, suspecting that Michael would soon be back, asking instead what her family thought of her plans to have a child on her own.

'I haven't told them the details,' she said slowly, her eyes wide and achingly solemn. 'I didn't want them to worry before things were organised. But they're very supportive and they know how much I want children. My parents are both GPs, and practical and pragmatic people. They'll understand why I couldn't wait.'

Drew wondered. His own parents were also fairly liberal but he couldn't imagine them being pleased if one of his sisters had contemplated taking on a similar responsibility alone. 'And your friends?' he asked, thinking particularly of Jane who, he imagined, would be horrified. 'Have you discussed this with anyone?'

'Nobody knows. Nobody need ever know of your involvement,' she said quickly. 'I promise.'

But his involvement would be zero and that was the last thing that worried him. He shook his head dismissively. 'How do you picture the future?' he asked, suddenly curious about how she'd envisaged their relationship evolving. 'Purely theoretically, if I did agreed to go ahead with this, remember that my appointment to the National is a permanent one. We'll be meeting professionally very often.'

She hesitated then, he saw, and the fingers that lifted her drink to her mouth were not quite steady. '*If* I stay at the National,' she conceded.

'You're thinking of leaving?' His question was sharp.

'Not really.' She hesitated again. 'If my being there made things awkward for you...?'

'No.' Drew was appalled that she'd contemplated leaving a position she obviously enjoyed, but Michael was approaching with their prawns and he didn't continue.

Michael lowered their dishes with a flourish which, Drew was prepared to admit, the food deserved. Char-grilled prawns, elegantly garnished with lime and coriander and a tiny mound of roe, the dish looked and smelled delicious.

'House speciality,' Michael announced, arranging for each a lime-scented dipping bowl and fresh napkins. 'Enjoy.'

'Eat,' Drew told her, when they were alone again and she still sat, staring at him with worried eyes.

But she didn't pick up her fork. 'I can leave the National,' she said faintly. 'It won't be difficult to get another job. If that's what you want—'

'It isn't.' It was the truth—he hated the thought. 'Whatever happens, I'd prefer you to stay. Now eat.'

She did. Judging from her very pleasing enthusiasm, she enjoyed the food enormously. 'The best prawns I've ever tasted,' she declared, when Michael returned and collected the shell-laden plates.

'Thank you, Lizzy. An exquisite compliment from an exquisite lady.'

Drew rolled his eyes. 'Get lost, Michael.'

'Getting lost.' But Michael seemed to find that order as amusing as he had the rest, and he was chuckling as he meandered back to the kitchen.

'He's very good-natured,' Lizzy commented.

'He's a pest.' But Drew felt more resignation than annoyance. It was his own fault. He should never have told Michael he wanted somewhere quiet and private—it was always going to rouse his curiosity. He'd have to tell Lizzy his decision after the meal, once they were alone again. 'You mentioned your parents were general practitioners. Are the rest of your family medical?'

'My brother-in-law's a GP and my sister, Catherine, runs a preschool centre, as well as helping him part time with his books and reception work,' she explained. 'That's all there is. Is your family medical?'

'Unfortunately not.' He looked up when Michael approached with their main courses. 'If there were more doctors in the family there might be more sanity,' he added as the waiter lowered their plates.

'You mean more stuffiness,' Michael remarked.

'Stability,' Drew countered.

'Boredom.' Michael rolled his eyes expressively and made Lizzy laugh. 'Let me know when you're fed up with him,' he told her. 'I'm available.'

Lizzy laughed again, a warm, tinkling sound that drew a reluctant smile from Drew despite his irritation. 'Do you like children?' she asked Michael.

Michael was grinning, obviously delighting in the attention. 'Love them.'

'Ever had a hepatitis shot?'

Drew decided he'd had enough. 'He's twenty-nine and

he hasn't got a brain,' he growled. 'Get out of here, Michael, and don't come back until I shout.'

'He's very familiar,' Lizzy remarked. She picked up her knife and fork. 'Personally, I think he's wonderful but some people are fussy about things like that. Perhaps it's part of the reason why they've no customers.'

'They get by,' Drew told her, turning his attention, as she had, to the food although he'd have preferred to watch her instead. 'Like it?'

'Delicious.'

He agreed. Michael had prepared the fish simply, grilling it with butter, but the delicate flavour was superb. The asparagus and the rocket salad which accompanied it were equally good.

Lizzy refused coffee or dessert afterwards and Drew excused himself and went out into the kitchen to settle with a grinning, smug-looking Michael.

'She's delicious,' he hissed. 'Finally I understand why you dumped the beautiful Suzie.'

'I didn't *dump* Suzie,' Drew told him sharply. 'And, for God's sake, don't tell the world about this. We're not…together.'

Michael's brows lifted immediately. 'Interesting. Mind if I—'

'Yes.' Drew mock-swiped the top of his grinning face. 'Food was superb, as always, but your tableside manner needs work.'

'Bye, Lizzy.' Michael had followed him out and Drew saw that she was surprised when he bent and kissed her cheek at the door. 'Come back soon. Alone if you can't stand tonight's company.'

Lizzy was smiling. 'The food was wonderful,' she declared. 'I'm so sorry you don't have more customers. I promise to tell all my friends about you.'

Michael sent Drew a quizzical look, which he returned blandly. The little jolt to his brother's overly developed ego would do him no harm, he decided, electing not to explain the circumstances to Lizzy.

He parked close to her flat and walked her to the door, but stopped at the lower step, realising that, although they needed to talk and she'd invited him inside, going upstairs with her now was probably not a good idea. 'Lizzy, I should have told you straight out and earlier—' he began firmly, but her hand at his shoulder stopped him.

'Think about it some more, Drew.' She sounded nervous and her eyes were huge and shadowy in the faintly orange light that spilled from the lamps above. She was on the top step now while he stood near the bottom, and they were practically the same height. 'Please.'

'All right.' Cross about his cowardice but unable to stop himself, he leaned forward and kissed her mouth, keeping the gesture deliberately light regardless of the frustration he knew that would provoke. 'Goodnight.'

'Goodnight.' The words were soft and lilting, and he started to draw back. But before he could move anywhere she launched herself at him, wound her hands in his hair, as if to hold him there, and moved closer, her sweet mouth opening—forcing him to catch her when she stepped off her step.

He gasped involuntarily, surprise dulling his reaction, but she was tiny and very light and he recovered quickly and took her weight before she fell. His hands splayed under her buttocks and lifted her against him, accepting the promise of her open mouth with greedy urgency.

But even as he drank in the taste of her he knew he was making a mistake. Abruptly he pushed her away and replaced her on the step, holding her when her legs seemed to buckle beneath her.

'That's enough,' he rasped.

He was breathing fast and, despite her own dazed expression, he could tell she'd seen his weakness because she came towards him again. 'Drew...?'

'Lizzy, no,' he said tightly, his hands encircling her pale

arms and holding her away. It was a long time since he'd wanted a woman so much, but he couldn't—not now, not when he was in such a position to hurt her. Despite her enthusiasm, from what both she and Jane had told him of her past relationships, it was obvious she wasn't used to treating sex casually. If he stayed now and then refused to father her child, as he intended, not only might she never forgive him but he'd never forgive himself. 'This is sex. I can't base any decision on this.'

'But it's so good.' She snatched his hand and held it below her left breast, and he could feel her heart pounding though the silky fabric of her dress. 'Feel how excited I am.' She laughed like a child. 'After just one kiss! It's fate.'

He looked at his hand, felt her, stopped himself cupping her breast but couldn't pull away. 'It's not fate,' he said thickly, unbearably tempted. 'It's something much more basic than that.'

'That's what I mean.' She seemed overjoyed, her eyes and her face alive and eager and delicious. 'I've never felt like this before. It feels like proof that you're the right man for me to choose for my baby.' Her fingers encircled his wrist, felt his pulse. 'You feel the same,' she said urgently. 'Check your heart rate.'

'Believe me, I can guess what it is,' he said dryly, forcing his gaze from the breast just above his hand to her dancing eyes.

'Then...?'

'It's not enough.' Deliberately he drew his hand away and stepped abruptly away from her farther down the steps, holding his palm out to stop her when she seemed about to come after him again—telling himself that frustration had to be better than guilt. 'Not for what you want. And it's not what I want either.'

'But—?'

'Go inside.'

He kept his expression rigidly clear of compromise and, to his relief, she opened the door. 'Meet me tomorrow?'

'Next week,' he said rawly. Tomorrow he'd be frustrated and weak.

'We've only a week from tomorrow. I should ovulate Monday in eleven days so I thought five days around that, say from the Saturday before…?'

'I'll speak to you before then.' He waited while she slowly opened the door wider and finally walked inside.

Corinne came to Lizzy's office at seven-thirty on Monday morning, grumbling about the early start she'd had to make. 'Eight o'clock ward round still,' she repeated dismally, helping herself to coffee. 'I was sure I'd have talked him round by now.'

'At least it's warm.' Lizzy eyed her friend over the films she was examining. The July morning was balmy. 'Imagine in winter.'

'I'm not staying.' At Lizzy's surprised look, Corinne shrugged. 'Changed my mind. Cardiology calls. The only reason I briefly considered staying was the delectable Dr Maitland. But there's no point. He's not interested.' She sighed dramatically. 'I guess I'm finally getting old and ugly.'

'Funny, you still look young and gorgeous.' But Lizzy brightened. 'How do you know he's not interested?'

'Experience.' Corinne grimaced. 'Wore my shortest, sexiest leather skirt on Friday and didn't rate a glance. He's all yours, Lizzy Murdoch. I'm out of the competition. It's too depressing.'

'So you stayed home all weekend, feeling depressed?'

'Mmm.'

'Then why was your machine on the whole time?'

Corinne looked shifty. 'I might have popped out.'

'Both nights?'

'Popped out twice.'

Lizzy laughed, remembering Jane's comments of the week before. 'Getting your accounts done?'

'Don't be ridiculous.' Corinne gulped her coffee and

stalked out with an offended air. 'As if I'd even look at him.'

Ray brought her in some films he had questions about and then Lizzy had to hurry off to her ultrasound clinic. The departmental meeting took up much of her lunch break and then she went across to the obstetric block for the afternoon's combined clinic with two of the obstetric consultants.

The clinic was for mothers-to-be whose pregnancies were considered at relative high risk of complications. Her job was to provide expert interpretation of ultrasound scans and guidance during sampling of the fluid and tissues around babies, which the obstetricians occasionally requested, and in so doing either pick up problems early or reassure nervous mothers and doctors that things were progressing normally.

The obstetric registrar who had been looking after Mrs Sanderson, the woman admitted with an ectopic pregnancy last time Lizzy had been on call, updated her on her condition.

'Operation was straightforward,' she explained. 'We got there before the tube ruptured and so preserved most of it. Both ovaries and the other tube were unscarred and normal, as you noted from the scan. We didn't see any physical reason for her difficulty in getting pregnant, so fingers crossed, she'll find it easier next time. She's going home tomorrow.'

She leaned over with another set of notes for Lizzy to look at. 'This is a thirty-two-year-old woman in her thirty-first week, we think. History of early miscarriages and now some bright red painless bleeding the last few mornings. No previous scan because she's refused in the past, but this time she's agreed. I'm worried about the placenta and obviously I can't examine her, without checking its position first. Can you fit her in this afternoon?'

'Send her straight though.' Lizzy was ahead on her appointments and between patients. 'I'll look straight away.'

The mother-to-be was clearly anxious and, seeing how apprehensively she regarded the ultrasound machine, Lizzy tried to reassure her.

'The machine uses sound waves,' she explained. 'It creates a picture from the echoes that come back when they bounce against the baby.'

'Can you guarantee me one hundred per cent that it won't harm the baby?'

'No. Not a hundred per cent, no.' Lizzy shook her head. 'To the best of my knowledge, it doesn't do any harm, but no one knows enough to make an absolute guarantee to you about that and I can't do it either.'

'But if I don't have it...?'

'If there's a problem with the placenta then you may be putting yourself and your baby at risk,' Lizzy said frankly.

'The other doctor said the placenta might be growing over my cervix,' the woman said nervously.

'That can cause the sort of bleeding you've been having,' Lizzy confirmed.

'And if it is then I'll have to have a Caesarean.'

'There's no other way of delivering the baby. Labour, with the baby pressing down and the cervix widening, tears the placenta and that can cause massive haemorrhage.'

'So it's best to know in advance.'

'Vital for you and the baby.'

'Better get on with it, then.' She lay back and lifted her gown, nervously smiling her appreciation when Lizzy covered her legs with a cellular blanket. 'I'm sorry. I'm not deliberately trying to be difficult.'

'You want what's best for the baby.' Lizzy smeared her swollen abdomen with the gel that conducted the waves. 'I understand that.' She found the uterus easily, and moved the probe around to find the best picture, going from side to side looking for the cervix.

'Baby looks good. Sucking its little thumb, see?' She pointed to the screen. 'That's the head, there, this big pale shape, the mouth, and there's the thumb.'

'Oh, he's so big,' the mother whispered, her tone awed. 'Can you see if he's a boy or girl?'

Lizzy didn't look up from the screen but said carefully, 'Not yet. Are you sure you want to know that?'

The younger woman hesitated. 'I don't know.'

'Think about it,' Lizzy advised. Normally when mothers came to her they'd already made the decision about whether they wanted to know the sex or not, but this scan had been arranged at short notice and she'd been right to suspect that her patient hadn't been expecting the question. 'Some parents want to know but a lot want the surprise. Let me know in a while if you want me to look.'

She located the placenta and pressed the button on the machine that would produce a still, then took a second picture from another angle, looking up when the obstetric registrar came in and directing her attention to the screen. 'Central placenta,' she said quietly. 'Grade four in the old terminology.'

'That means your placenta is covering your cervix, as I suspected,' the registrar explained to her patient. 'The placenta is well supplied with blood and the bleeding that you're having is coming from tiny tears in the vessels there.'

'But I wanted a natural delivery.'

'I'm sorry.' The registrar touched her hand. 'It'll definitely be a Caesarean.'

'But the baby's all right?'

The registrar exchanged a quick look with Lizzy, and Lizzy nodded. 'Baby looks fine at the moment,' she confirmed. 'Very active.'

But the mother-to-be still looked alarmed and Lizzy understood. Although she still had every chance of delivering a healthy baby, the risks of complications to herself or the baby were significantly higher, given the position of the placenta. Briefly she imagined herself in the same situation and she felt sick.

'If you start bleeding more heavily then we might have

to deliver the baby early,' the registrar said gently. 'And, in the meantime, you're going to have to stay in bed and rest. Here. In hospital. So we can keep an eye on things.'

Lizzy saw the patient grow pale, saw the doubt and refusal that hovered on her lips, but when she spoke she said only, 'Can I go home and get my things?'

'If you must, then gently,' the registrar said. 'No lifting, absolutely no straining, and I'd prefer you didn't drive. It would be better to have your partner help you.'

'I'll call him.' She still looked numb. 'He'll probably tell me to stay. But the baby's going to be all right?'

'This is the best way we know to protect you both.'

'If something went wrong now, if you had to operate immediately, what would the baby's chances be?'

'It would depend on how badly you were bleeding,' the registrar said. 'If we can get another five weeks' growing time and perform the Caesarean electively, then baby's chances are practically normal.'

Lizzy touched her shoulder gently. 'Want to know about the sex, or are we finished?'

'Finished. I've decided I want it to be a surprise,' she said weakly, lifting her gown higher so Lizzy could wipe away the gel with a bundle of tissues.

'Thanks very much for fitting us in.' The registrar nodded as she took the notes and helped her patient from the trolley. 'Hope you don't run too late because of us.'

'I don't mind.' Lizzy went with them to the door and called in her next patient, who stood together with her partner. 'Goodness,' she exclaimed, returning the mother-to-be's happy smile with a surprised one of her own as she registered the size of the tummy beneath the maternity gown. 'Twins?'

'Triplets,' she was told happily, as the young woman preceded her into the room. 'One is really hard to see and the last two times they couldn't find him so the doctor told me I had to come and see the expert. Is that you?'

'That's me,' Lizzy confirmed with a smile, helping her up onto the step and then onto the trolley.

It wasn't long before she could announce to the pair that baby number three was fine. 'Just very slightly smaller than the other two,' she conceded, measuring the skull size, the length of his femur and then his abdominal circumference and comparing the results with his brothers' measurements and with his estimated age, 'but there's not much in it and nothing to worry about at present.'

She produced a still of each of the three babies for them to take away and gave them to the excited-looking father, smiling as they both exclaimed over the shots. She cleaned away the gel and helped the mother to sit up. 'Is it triplets because of fertility treatment?'

'Completely random,' the mother said wryly. 'And completely shocking. I had terrible morning sickness and heartburn and at first they told me it was twins but then my obstetrician found the other one.'

'You seem to be coping,' she observed, noting their fond smiles.

'Reality hasn't hit,' the father told her.

'Our parents are very good,' his wife told her. 'We'll have lots of help after they're born.'

'That'll help.' Lizzy knew that she was going to rely on her own family's help from time to time as well. She wrote a note on an appointment slip and gave it to them to take to the desk. 'I recommend repeating the scan in two weeks,' she explained, 'just to make sure the little one is keeping up. If he's fine then we'll be able to leave it longer next time.'

Her bleeper sounded as she was wandering back from Maternity to the radiology department and, because she didn't recognise the illuminated number she was being asked to call, she stopped at a phone in the corridor.

Drew's deep voice when he answered reminded her of the devastating embrace she'd forced on him on Friday night and her legs turned weak, but his words were imper-

sonal. 'I wanted to let you know that the results on the
sample you took from Mr Webber last Tuesday confirmed
our suspicions about mesothelioma. Thank you for your
help with that.'

'How is he?'

'We took the drain out on Thursday and he went to the
hospice on Friday afternoon for a few days to get to know
the place with a view to the future and also to fine-tune his
pain control,' he said. 'I called in to see him this morning
and his breathlessness hasn't returned and he says he's
quite comfortable. He'll be going home tomorrow.'

'That's a very good way of doing it,' she said, pleased
Mr. Webber hadn't had to stay in hospital. Drew hadn't
said anything remotely embarrassing but her face felt as if
it were burning. Determined not to pressure him any more
about the baby, but still reluctant to finish the conversation,
she asked him about Mr Jackson, even though she knew
she could have got the information from Corinne. 'What
did the neurosurgeons decide?'

'Surgery is scheduled for Thursday,' he told her.
'They've taken over his care and he was transferred to Lilac
Ward last week. They're confident the operation will be
successful.'

'I'm glad.' She flattened herself against the wall so that
two trolley-bearing porters could pass each other. 'Jane's
gone home finally,' she said, still not wanting to say goodbye. 'Bill said the nurses had to push her out in a wheelchair to make her leave.'

Chattering nervously, she told him about Gemma Rose
and about how cute she looked in the jumpsuit she'd given
her and about Bill's good-natured bemusement over the
ransacking of his wine and whisky stocks.

'She didn't even tell him we'd all been there for his
birthday,' she explained, smiling at Drew's laughter. 'He
noticed the chaos in the house but assumed that was Jane.
It was only yesterday when I was there for lunch that he
went out to the pool-house for the first time and discovered

the wine gone. Thank goodness the caterers knew to clean up the food or there would have been an awful mess.'

Drew told her about a Christmas party several years ago when Jane had destroyed her microwave by reheating a pudding she'd studded with five pence coins.

'I remember that,' Lizzy exclaimed, 'but I was on call that day and in the end I was too busy to get there. What about the time she poisoned us all with that vile ginger wine she made?'

'I was away that weekend,' he said, 'and on call the time Bill set fire to the lawn.'

'I was there then.' She laughed with him, recounting the story of extinguishing the blaze with wine-bottles of water from the pool.

'I can't believe we haven't met before,' she finished.

'Fate,' he said cryptically, his tone dry and his lack of any further comment making her frown.

'This afternoon I've been doing obstetric ultrasounds,' she said, talking quickly again. She touched her lower stomach with her free arm. 'I love watching the babies moving. My uterus has been contracting in sympathy. There was a set of triplets today, three beautiful little babies, all sucking their thumbs.' Then she straightened. 'Have you given things any more thought?'

She winced at his silence, cross with herself for bringing up the subject when she'd been so determined to give him space. But when he spoke there was none of the wariness she'd steeled herself for. 'Purely theoretically,' he said quietly. 'How were you proposing we do this?'

'How?' Her mouth opened. 'Um...how?'

'Technically.'

Lizzy flushed violently. 'My reading suggests it's better if I'm underneath,' she said jerkily, 'and you're on the top. But, really, I'm sure you have much more experience with this sort of thing than me, and...' she took a very big breath '...if you don't find that position particularly interesting—'

'No, Lizzy.' His graveness made her frown. 'I meant,

what technique for the insemination? In a clinic?' he suggested. 'Via a sample? Or did your reply suggest you wanted to approach this more naturally?'

'Oh.' Lizzy winced, understanding finally. Glad he wasn't there to see her expression, she said uncertainly, 'Actually, I thought the usual way.' In fact, she hadn't even considered the alternative, and now that she did she found it unappealing. She wanted to be able to look back on the time of her child's conception with the sort of emotional warmth that only closeness to another person could bring.

'I mean, I'd prefer the natural. But does your question mean you don't think you could? I mean, if you'd find it easier the other way—'

'There wouldn't be a problem,' he said deeply, and Lizzy cringed, wondering if there was and if he was just trying to be polite. Obviously, he had envisaged a more clinical approach, hence the question. 'I'd like to know more,' he said calmly. 'Are you free tomorrow night?'

'Yes.' She didn't care that he heard her eagerness.

But as she spoke a bleep sounded and he said, 'That's me. I have to go,' and hung up.

Lizzy lowered the receiver slowly, checked her watch, then confirmed the time with the clock in the corridor above the phone and blinked. It was six-thirty. She'd left Maternity at five-thirty, which meant she'd been speaking with Drew for almost an hour.

Disbelievingly, because the conversation had seemed disappointingly brief, she checked with the clock in the radiology department but, according to that both her watch and the clock in the corridor had been correct.

Ray was in the reporting room, going through his films for the day. 'That kidney defect I asked you about last week turned out to be a benign cyst,' he told her. 'I popped a needle into it under ultrasound guidance and the results came through today.'

'Good.' Lizzy frowned at the chest X-ray he was inspecting. 'What's this?'

'I was about to come and find you to ask you about it,' he said. 'According to the request form, she's a thirty-five-year-old woman with mild breathlessness, referred by her GP for an X-ray, but unfortunately she misunderstood when the radiographer asked her to wait and left the hospital before we realised.' He pointed to the round pale opacity in the middle of her right lung. 'What do you think?'

'Worrying.' The rest of the X-ray was normal and the opacity could be benign, but the differential diagnosis included several extremely serious illnesses.

She reached for the telephone and called the operator to check who was on call for chest medicine that evening. 'This needs urgent follow-up.'

Drew was on call, she discovered, covering for Lionel Wright who was away. She called him and briefly described the X-ray. 'I know the GP and I thought I'd ring him directly,' she said. 'Would you be prepared to see her if he can organise it?'

'Ask him to send her up tonight or first thing in the morning,' he confirmed. He took the details. 'Leave the film on your desk and I'll pick it up when I'm finished here. Thanks, Lizzy. I'll let you know what we find.'

Lizzy telephoned the GP, who agreed to contact his patient immediately. 'She's young but she's been a heavy smoker in the past,' he said worriedly. 'This could be very bad.'

'The chest team at the National's one of the best in the country,' she assured him. 'Whatever the problem is, Mrs Adams will have the best possible treatment.'

She looked at the films again, but when she called the GP back he'd already left so, instead, she rang Drew again. 'The breast shadows are very prominent,' she told him. 'She might be breast-feeding.'

'I'll check when she arrives.' He sounded pleased. 'Well done, Lizzy. You might have made the diagnosis.'

CHAPTER SEVEN

AT THE chest team's X-ray session the next morning Drew brought Rona Adams's films along to show the rest of the doctors and the students. She'd been admitted overnight and he'd had lateral films taken, but they added little to what Lizzy had already told him.

'The differential diagnosis of an abnormality like this is complicated,' he told the students. Focusing on keeping his mind on his job when examining the X-rays close up meant he had to come so close to Lizzy that he could smell the sweet, natural scent of her.

But it seemed his proximity unsettled her just as much because when he leaned forward his head brushed her shoulder and she stepped back hastily, stumbling on the edge of a chair in the process and forcing him to grasp her elbow to steady her. 'All right?' he asked softly, noting that the other doctors were too occupied, inspecting the films, to have noticed anything amiss.

'Fine.' She lifted her arm out of his grip, her face flushed, but the way she refused to meet his eyes gave him a fierce jab of pleasure that his awareness of her was not entirely one-sided.

'Mrs Adams has a two week history of breathlessness, and last night she began coughing up blood,' he said, addressing the entire group now. 'She's an ex-smoker so we have to consider a primary lung cancer, despite her youth.'

Beside him, Lizzy added, 'For the benefit of the students, many other things have to be considered as well. This could be benign, for instance some sort of infection—perhaps an abscess—or it could be a malignancy from another source. Lymphoma—or tumours of the lymph system—can cause

104

this, as can cancers from other places such as kidneys, breasts and bones.'

One of the students raised her hand. 'What happens if you don't find anything else wrong?'

'We'd have to biopsy the mass,' Drew told her. 'It's too far out in the periphery of the lung for me to reach through a 'scope so I'd ask Dr Murdoch here to take a needle sample from the outside under ultrasound or CT vision.'

'As a last resort,' Lizzy confirmed. 'If it is a tumour we risk spreading it by biopsying it that way so first we try and make the diagnosis in other ways.'

'But I'm being unfair,' Drew said, nodding towards the films. 'Dr Murdoch called me urgently about these scans yesterday and Mrs Adams was admitted as an emergency last night. She's the proud mother of a three-month-old boy.' He raised his brows at his house officers. 'Does that make it any clearer?'

He could see that Lizzy, who had mentioned the possibility of breast-feeding, and also Corinne and his consultant colleagues understood immediately, but the juniors were obviously puzzled.

'Pulmonary embolus?' one ventured, referring to clots in the lung.

'Possible, considering women around pregnancy are at increased risk of clots in the legs, but that wouldn't cause a round shadow like this.' He waited a few moments but there were no more suggestions. 'This is a secondary tumour from a choriocarcinoma,' he explained. 'She has a cancer that's grown from remnants of the tissue left from her pregnancy. It's rare but we do see it from time to time, even after miscarriages. The tumour has grown into her uterus and spread in the blood to her lung.'

The students looked upset. 'Is she going to live?'

'The best thing about this tumour is that the oncologists are confident it's still at an early stage, which means it's almost entirely curable,' he told them. 'They plan to start chemotherapy this afternoon, after finishing their investi-

gations, and within a couple of short cycles this lesion...'
he tapped the spot on the chest X-ray '...should disappear.'

'I'll keep you up to date with the films,' Lizzy said to
the group. 'With this diagnosis she'll need scans of her
pelvis and liver to help stage the disease so I'll bring them
along to show you next time and we'll follow her progress.
She should do well.'

They were the last films of the session and the group
started leaving. 'I'll take these back to Oncology.' Corinne
glanced quickly at him to ask Drew's permission before
she tugged the films free and put them into the X-ray envelope. 'Meet you on the ward?'

'Five minutes,' he told her, and cornered Lizzy, noting
the immediate and gratifying widening of her pupils.
Although they'd spoken on the telephone, this morning was
the first time he'd seen her since Friday night, but his memory of the feel of her against him had haunted him since,
slowly destroying every one of his good intentions.

Her confirmation the day before that she wanted love-
making rather than an impersonal laboratory procedure had
been his undoing.

The fact that he'd come up with thoughtful, logical, even
rational reasons for seriously considering her proposal—
after all, he did want a child and he, too, was growing older
and it might be years before he met a potential wife, plus
he believed she'd be an excellent mother, plus she seemed
amenable to the idea of him playing a significant role in
their child's life, a role he'd make sure was enshrined in
any legal agreement they made—hadn't overshadowed in
his mind the dull, cynical awareness that, underlying everything, he wanted her and he'd lost his determination to fight
that.

A few hours in bed together would appease his needs as
much as hers.

'About tonight,' he said softly. 'My place?'

'Fine,' she replied quickly and, apparently determined to
keep their exchange businesslike, mechanically recorded

the address he gave her in a notebook, without meeting his gaze again. 'I might be late, leaving here,' she murmured. 'Is seven-thirty all right?'

He noted the nervous glance she directed towards Corinne and the other doctors, filing out of the room, and realised that she wasn't happy about being seen talking to him. And why should she be? he asked himself, irritated with his annoyance at her gesture. She'd made it plain that all she wanted from him was procreational sex, and that suited him perfectly, didn't it?

Why, then, did he find himself contemplating backing her against the desk she clutched and making love to her until she screamed some gratifying acknowledgement of what he was confident he could do to her?

Self-disgust and an acknowledgement that, despite his intention to remain detached and civilised about their relationship, he was nevertheless reacting like a stereotypical territorial and egotistical male drew him sharply away. 'Seven-thirty's fine,' he said tightly.

Left behind once Drew had left the X-ray room, Lizzy gathered up the remainder of the films and reports, aware that her legs had turned shaky again. It was obvious he'd made a decision, she realised, but equally obvious from the way he'd stalked off that it was one he didn't want to share with her yet. But they were running out of time. Would he tell her tonight?

Every time she saw him, every word he spoke, added to her conviction that he was the right man for this, but had she managed to convince him?

She hurried back to the department, managing to fit in some reporting and persuade Carol to agree to a couple of urgent CT scans which one of the surgeons had asked to add to her list.

Rona Adams, the patient Drew had discussed at the meeting, did come to her clinic. She was obviously very anxious, but Lizzy found no evidence of tumour spread anywhere apart from her right lung.

'The doctors told me if everything else was clear on the scan then there's a very high chance I can be cured,' Mrs Adams said faintly, one slender hand coming out to touch Lizzy's arm. 'My baby's only three months old.'

'Everything else I've looked at is clear,' Lizzy told her, after exchanging an enquiring look with the physician who'd come with his patient to watch the scans.

'We'll begin the chemotherapy this afternoon,' he said. 'Let's get you back to the ward.'

Drew's home was in Notting Hill, a cosmopolitan and lively part of London a few minutes' drive west from Oxford Street. A narrow, three-storied terrace in a peaceful, leafy side street off Ladbroke Grove, it had been recently renovated, she guessed, gazing up at the tall ceilings and broad skylights over the stairwell when he opened the door.

Still in his suit, he'd obviously only just arrived home himself, and she wished she had been able to contain her impatience enough to arrive fashionably late but, although he contemplated her rather broodingly, once she was inside he brushed aside her murmured apology.

'This is lovely,' she declared, when he led her up wide stairs to a modern timber and ceramic-tiled kitchen and living area.

'Have a look around.' He opened broad glass French-style doors and Lizzy walked out onto wooden decking, which bore an outdoor table and chairs and barbecue, and gazed appreciatively over his garden. 'There's a residents' park through the back,' he explained, nodding to an iron gate at the far end of the small lawn. 'Wonderful for summer picnics.'

Romantic picnics, Lizzy speculated, not liking her dismay at the image of him sprawled on the grass with champagne and strawberries and another woman. 'How on earth did you find time to do all this?' she asked, following him back inside.

'I bought it as it is,' he said. He'd discarded his jacket

and her eyes rested on the breadth of his shoulders as he
bent to open the refrigerator. He extracted a bottle of white
wine and then a plastic box, which he put in the microwave
above the oven. 'The previous owners were architects,' he
continued, opening the wine. 'It took them five years to get
it the way they wanted and then they realised they were
bored with it and wanted a new project.'

He passed her a glass of the wine. 'To…decisions,' he
said cryptically. 'Thank you for coming tonight.'

'Thank you for asking me.' Her voice had turned husky
but she lifted her glass in another toast. 'To your beautiful
home, even if it makes my flat feel like a cubbyhole.'

'I found it charming.'

'Not compared with this.' She sipped the wine, finding
it cool and delicious, then gazed around. 'Buying something so big, you must have had a family in mind,' she said
curiously. 'How many bedrooms? Six?'

'Only four.' His regard was steady and no more readable.
'And I do want a family. One day.'

'That's nice.' Lizzy felt herself tense and she released
her breath with relief when the microwave pinged and he
turned away to check on it.

'Have a look upstairs, if you're interested,' he told her.
'Dinner will be a few minutes.'

Lizzy was *very* interested, and she took her glass and
followed his suggestion. She'd glimpsed formal rooms at
street level, and the kitchen level was open-plan—informal
living areas and a room which he clearly used as a study,
flowing into one space. Upstairs she found the bedrooms
and two hotel-like marble bathrooms, one that would be an
en suite to the main bedroom if the door to the common
area was shut.

She peeked into the main bedroom, but didn't walk inside. Large and airy, its window looked onto the park, and
from the door she could see the coloured shapes of the cars
along Ladbroke Grove, flickering through the trees.

The interior design was understated and pleasing—neutral colours and natural fabrics, polished pale wood floors, lofty spaces and plenty of glass, facing south. 'It's beautiful,' she said, when he came to find her. She was in one of the smaller bedrooms, watching two children playing with a ball on the path below. 'And so peaceful, even though we're still central. You must love living here.'

'Dinner's ready.'

They ate outside on the decking. Delicious filleted salmon with butter and lemon and tiny potatoes and peas. 'Not my doing,' he admitted dryly, when she complimented him on the food. 'Putting supermarket meals into the microwave is the limit of my talents.'

'But you can't have bought this from a supermarket,' she argued.

'From Michael.'

Lizzy laughed, remembering the waiter at the restaurant he'd taken her to on Friday. 'Cheat.' But she flushed with pleasure, flattered he'd gone to so much trouble for her. 'You come to my place next time. I'll make you my special spinach and lentil bake.'

His laugh was rewardingly warm. 'One way of guaranteeing you'll never see me again.'

'Yes, I have noticed that dinner guests never come back,' she mused. 'Jane and Bill always bring their own pizza.'

'Neither of them are health food types.'

'Meat or nothing,' she agreed.

Over coffee, the conversation turned more serious. Drew passed her a number of faxed sheets. 'I've spoken with my solicitor,' he explained. 'He's been through your contract and redrawn most of it. You should study it carefully.'

Lizzy caught her breath, her fingers tingling suddenly. 'Does this mean you're saying yes?'

'Not to your initial conditions,' he said heavily. 'If you want me to do this, Lizzy, it has to be done my way. Take it home and read everything. You might change your mind.'

'No. No, I won't.' She flicked though the pages, not reading just counting. There were six printed pages where her original contract had had five. All densely worded. 'Tell me what it says,' she said simply, trusting him utterly.

He took his coffee, left the table and stood at the edge of the decking and stared out into the garden, his back to her. 'Basically, it grants me most of the rights of a normal father,' he said finally, 'regardless of whether I choose to exercise those rights. The only exception is that custody remains yours, uncontested. However, I have full visitation rights up to what he's described as "reasonable".' He was quiet for a few moments.

'At a later date, if you and I can't agree on what "reasonable" entails we both agree to abide by the decision of an independent arbitrator.'

'But even if you have visitation rights I have full custody,' she said urgently.

'The contract enshrines your right to that,' he answered, not turning back to her. 'I agree never to try to take the child away from you.'

'And the birth certificate?' In the contract she'd given him her name was the only one that would be listed.

'Both of us,' he said firmly. 'There's not to be any doubt about his or her parentage.'

'What if something happens to me?'

'If you die, custody reverts immediately and fully to me, rather than to a member of your family.'

'But if I'm married—'

'The same applies.' Drew turned around then but he was in shadow and she couldn't see him. 'But you can trust me to be reasonable. My priority would be the happiness of our child. When I die if I have no other children my estate goes to him or her. If I have a wife and children our child receives an equal share of my estate.'

Lizzy's heart was beating fast and her palms felt damp. 'And if I agree to this then we can go ahead on Saturday?'

'Take some time. You might want to reconsider.'

'Nothing you've told me changes anything,' she said huskily.

'You seemed determined to do this on your own.'

'I think you'll be a fine father, Drew. I doubt I could make a better choice.'

He stayed very still. 'There's one more thing you should know, Lizzy. I want to be there.'

'Where?'

'For the birth. I want to see my child being born.'

'Oh.' Lizzy blinked several times. 'You'd actually be in the room?'

'In the room.'

'Not, Drew, *not* with a video camera?'

'What?' He laughed abruptly, a sharp, startled laugh. 'No! I don't even own one. Not a camera in sight, I promise.'

'I couldn't bear that,' she admitted weakly, wiping her palms on the side of her skirt. 'Bill wanted to film Jane and they had a huge row about it. He had some awful idea about us all going around there afterwards and having a party while we watched it. He couldn't understand why she didn't want the world to see her like that, but Corinne and I understood perfectly. Just there, watching, you mean?'

'Through everything,' he said quietly. 'It's my last condition.'

'It can get pretty messy,' she said uneasily.

'I'm aware of that.' He was amused now. Even though she couldn't see him, she sensed that. 'I might be a physician but I attended as many deliveries as you would have during my training.'

'I won't be lying on my back, being good,' she warned. 'I want to deliver squatting.'

'Deliver standing on your head if you want. If you and the baby are happy then I will be.'

'You're determined about this?'

'It's non-negotiable.'

'I'm embarrassed,' Lizzy said weakly. 'It seems very personal.'

'Hardly more than the moment of conception,' he said softly, coming towards her.

'You think I'm being silly.'

'I think you have some peculiar ideas.' A gentle hand at her chin tilted her face up to his. 'You're so brazen about some things and so shy about others. You want me to have sex with you but you don't want me to watch my baby being born?'

'I imagined that we'd have sex in the dark,' she said faintly.

'You must be joking.' It was twilight now but in the light from the house she could see his eyes suddenly dancing.

'That seems quite reasonable,' she protested, blushing fiercely.

'Not to me.'

'Not daylight?' she demanded, wrenching her chin away, aghast.

'Daylight, lamplight, moonlight.' He shrugged as if the choice wasn't especially important. 'But not darkness, Lizzy. Never darkness.'

'I've got an appendix scar,' she said abruptly.

'I don't mind.'

'Paul, my ex-boyfriend, said it was ugly.'

'He's an idiot.'

'He said it spoiled my whole body.'

'You have a beautiful body.'

'You don't know that.'

'Yes, I do.'

Her cheeks were hot and she wiped them with the back of her hands. 'You're very kind to say things like that but I still think I'd prefer the dark.'

One of his hands came out and stroked her hair lightly. 'Lizzy, I'm not remotely kind and I'm not going to give you a choice. I've told you that if you want this then it has to be my way. Everything has to be my way.'

'I do want it,' she said abruptly, pushing her chair back and slipping around the other side of the table towards the garden— hoping that the faint breeze would cool her face. 'I want a baby more than anything else in the world.'

'You still have a choice,' he said gently.

'And I want you to be the father,' she said quickly. 'I just didn't expect it to be so fraught.'

'Fraught?'

She sighed. 'Drew, to be honest with you, I have had the occasional boyfriend in the past, but I've only had sex with one of them.'

'Paul.'

'The one who wanted to send our children to boarding school,' she confirmed.

'And you didn't find it particularly enjoyable?'

'He was a little critical,' she explained. 'And, to be fair, I don't think he found any of it especially enjoyable either.' She flapped her hands in front of her face, trying to create more of a breeze. 'I assumed it would get better eventually but we weren't together long enough to find out. In every other way, and even talking about sex and things, I'm quite confident, but as far as the act itself....' She swallowed very hard.

'Well, while I would much rather do this the natural way, rather than with artificial insemination via a syringe in a clinic, just don't expect that this is going to be the sexual event of the year or anything.'

'You don't expect to enjoy it?'

'I don't mean me.' She swung around and smiled at him. 'On Friday when I made you kiss me...?' She flushed anew, just thinking about it. 'I've never felt like that before. It was amazing. My whole body was tingling and I'm sure that I...well, I'm just telling you this so you don't go into it with—' her voice fell away '—high expectations.'

'Don't worry about me,' he said softly.

'You're very attractive. I suppose you must be very experienced?'

'Take the contract home, Lizzy.' Still by the table, he retrieved the papers she'd left there. 'Read it carefully and make sure you understand. If you still want to go through with this there's another copy here which you can send to your solicitor for independent advice.'

Lizzy collected herself, understanding that he didn't want to talk any more now. 'Shall I call you tonight?'

'Tell me tomorrow.' He waited while she collected her bag then followed her when she set off down the stairs.

'Thanks for dinner.'

'I'll walk you to your car.' He opened the door for her, and took her hand again as they strolled along the curved street to where she'd parked.

'I scanned Mrs Adams today for the oncologists,' she said, drained by her confessions and needing to talk more neutrally. 'The lung seems to be the only secondary.'

'Good news, although not surprising considering her pregnancy was only thirteen weeks ago,' he said quietly. 'One of the team told me that the likelihood of a cure is better than ninety per cent.'

At the Renault he touched her hair. 'I've made you worry.'

'I really would prefer the dark.'

'You're not being offered the dark.' It seemed that her dismay made him laugh and she felt the light brush of his mouth at her forehead. 'I'm not going to pretend this is for the baby, Lizzy. I want children, of course, but this now is for me. You're very desirable. I want to make love to you.'

'I'm desirable?' she squeaked.

'Of course.' He squeezed her hand, his expression quite unabashed. 'Is that bad?'

'No.' She didn't know where to look and her gaze touched his eyes, his cheeks, his mouth, the darkened buildings behind him. 'No, that's nice.'

'Nice. Hmm.' His mouth quirked and she realised she'd amused him again.

He stood back and she unlocked her car and got in. 'I can tell you already about the contract,' she said weakly. 'I'll sign anything.'

'Tell me tomorrow.' He bent when she unwound the window. 'But take care, Lizzy. Make sure you know what you're doing.'

'I trust you.' She started her engine, not wanting to drive away from him but knowing he'd only find her more amusing for lingering.

She got to work early next morning and went searching straight away for Drew's office, finding it in the hospital's Department of Medicine on the fourth floor, the same floor as Radiology.

'What is this?' she demanded, slamming the third page onto his desk. 'I don't need your money.'

'Morning, Lizzy.' Irritatingly relaxed, he didn't seem remotely surprised by the way she'd burst in and looked up from the notes he was writing with a welcoming smile. 'The money's not for you but for the child.'

'It's a ridiculous amount.'

'Raising a child is expensive.'

'I explained that I had everything organised. Financially, I am very well off.'

'Then put it aside until the child's old enough to decide herself. I haven't told you how you have to spend it.'

'But I feel terrible.'

'I can afford it.'

'I won't take it.'

'Remove that clause and the deal's off.'

'Drew!' She waved her hands helplessly. 'I can't take this. You're already doing too much.'

'Not negotiable, Lizzy.'

'But this isn't how I pictured it at all.'

'You're not the only person involved.'

'But it's crazy.' She spun about, not knowing what to do, how to stand, anything. 'We met nine days ago. You don't know me. All I asked was one tiny and anonymous thing but instead you're taking on as much responsibility as me. More, even, because the baby won't cost anything near the amount you want me to take.'

'If you want just that one tiny and anonymous thing then you're asking the wrong man,' he said quietly. 'I could never justify that to myself.'

'You don't have to take on so much.'

'I can't not.' Apparently quite calm, he folded away the notes, placed them to one side and leaned back in his chair with his arms folded, regarding her enigmatically. 'I've told you, I also want children. I've thought hard lately. I'm almost thirty-seven. Perhaps this is *my* only chance.'

'Don't be ridiculous.' She glared at him. 'You're very nice. More pertinently you're a doctor, you're rich, you own a wonderful house and you are *extraordinarily* good-looking. If you wanted to get married and have a child tomorrow you could just click your fingers and have your choice.'

'Considering that when we met you told me I was fat, badly dressed and in need of a good haircut, I'm flattered,' he said dryly.

She stiffened. 'You know why I said that—'

'But you're ignoring the fact that at thirty-six, regardless of all my supposed attributes, I haven't yet met a woman I want to marry and have children with,' he continued firmly. 'My point remains valid.'

'When you do meet that woman,' Lizzy said grittily, 'what on earth is she going to say about you lavishing all this money on my child?'

'She'll understand.'

'You can't be sure of that.'

'I wouldn't become involved with her if she didn't,' he countered.

'I think you are mad.'

'You don't have to agree to anything.'

'I'm desperate,' she cried. 'My eggs are self-destructing as we speak.'

'Then sign.'

'I don't want your money.'

'You're going to have to learn to live with it.' He laughed at her expression. 'Cheer up, Lizzy. There are worse things than money.'

'I want this so much but I feel like I'm ruining your life.'

He laughed again. 'You're not ruining my life,' he said easily, swivelling his chair and tugging her down onto his lap. 'Silly woman. The money is such a small thing it never even occurred to me that you'd object.'

'I can afford everything myself,' she murmured, liking being held so close to him.

'Humour me.' To her delight he nuzzled her cheek close to her ear.

'You smell nice again,' she whispered. 'I love your after-shave.'

'I'm still not wearing any.' He kissed her throat. 'But you're wearing perfume.'

'Corinne told me I should,' she confided. 'She said men like it. Do you like it?'

'I liked you natural,' he said softly, and Lizzy vowed to throw the scent away. 'Do I take it you're going to accept the contract now?'

Her fingers dug into his shoulders. 'Yes.'

His mouth tracked back to her ear and Lizzy shivered. There was the sound of rapid heels in the corridor and then Corinne was there in the open doorway, staring at them with her mouth open.

Lizzy groaned. 'Hi, Corinne!' She jumped up. 'We were just talking,' she said brightly.

'Oh, yes?' Corinne looked smug. 'Then how did your blouse come undone?'

While Lizzy hastened to fasten it Corinne beamed at Drew, obviously enjoying herself. 'Your juniors are wait-ing, Dr Maitland. Queued up in Blue Ward and getting restless. I offered to come up and fetch you.'

'On my way, Corinne.' Drew's gaze, Lizzy noted, was dryly amused.

'Of course, if you'd prefer to begin your ward rounds at nine in future I'm sure we'd all be happy to oblige,' Corinne added, sending Lizzy a gloating look.

'I'll bear that in mind, Corinne. Thank you.' He lifted one shoulder ruefully, before following the grinning Corinne, and Lizzy smiled, relieved that he wasn't upset by them being discovered.

Corinne wouldn't gossip but she knew that Drew had no way of knowing that and so his good-natured resignation seemed admirable.

Lizzy tried to summon a little of that resignation when Corinne charged into her office at lunchtime.

'Tell me everything,' she insisted, perching on the edge of Lizzy's desk. 'Don't you dare skip one delicious detail.'

'He's very nice,' Lizzy said stiffly.

'Nice?' Corinne rolled her beautiful eyes. 'How many times have you been out?'

'Once or twice.' Lizzy pretended to study a skull X-ray.

'Where?'

'A fish restaurant on the river,' she said, describing it. 'I did mean to tell you about it. The food was divine but they didn't have many customers.' She shot her friend a sideways look. 'Your accountant can probably afford it—get him to take you there.'

'We'd never get a table,' Corinne said. 'That place is booked solid for months.'

'But we were the only customers there.'

'He must have booked the whole place.' Corinne clapped her hands, her eyes sparkling. 'How romantic. I bet he's amazing in bed.'

CHAPTER EIGHT

'CORINNE!' Lizzy waggled a finger, refusing to let herself be shocked. 'Stop it. You must be thinking about the wrong restaurant.' She described it in more detail.

'That's it,' Corinne insisted. 'I've wanted to go for months. Jane and Bill know the chef and they rave about his food. He's the hottest thing in London at the moment and he's just brought out a cookbook. Lizzy, it's definitely the same place.'

'But, I told you, there weren't any other customers.'

'And I told you he must have booked the whole place. This is incredible.'

'I don't even know if there was a chef,' Lizzy said urgently. 'I didn't hear any noise and the only person there seemed to be the waiter. I wouldn't be surprised if he did the cooking as well.'

'What did he look like?'

'Tall. Young. Dark. Called Michael.'

'Michael Maitland,' Corinne squealed. 'That's him. Lizzy, he did cook for you. I can't believe it. No one has ever done anything like that for me. Wait till I tell Jane.'

'Don't you dare!' Lizzy frowned. 'Michael *Maitland*? Do you think they're related?'

'Might be,' Corinne said slowly, and Lizzy realised she'd only just registered his name herself. 'Probably, given the circumstances.'

'Drew didn't say anything,' Lizzy added. 'But he was quite rude to him and he's not normally like that. If they were brothers it would make more sense.'

'Lizzy, the fact that he booked the whole restaurant just for you has to mean he's interested.' Corinne sounded

awed. 'Men don't do things like that without wanting something.'

'He's being nice to me,' Lizzy explained impatiently.
'It's nothing else. Firstly, believe me, I can tell and, sec-
ondly, he would have introduced his brother to me if he
was remotely serious. Besides our relationship isn't like
that. It's more businesslike.'

Corinne blinked. 'Didn't look very businesslike this
morning.'

'He feels sorry for me.' She met Corinne's doubtful gaze
unflinchingly, confident about the truth of that, even without counting the facts about her fertility—something she
wasn't yet ready to share with her friend. 'I told him about
what happened with Paul and about Richard turning out to
be married and about how I haven't been able to find a nice
boyfriend.'

'That night,' Corinne said sharply, 'did you wear the blue
dress?'

Lizzy frowned. 'Yes.'

'And?'

'And what?'

Corinne rolled her eyes. 'Ninny! Did he kiss you?'

'I kissed him,' Lizzy admitted dreamily. 'He sort of
pecked me politely but that was all so I kissed him again
but he backed off.'

'What?' Lizzy saw her friend was uncharacteristically
nonplussed. 'You spent the whole evening alone in a beautiful restaurant and you wore the blue dress and he took
you home and that was that?'

She sighed. 'Yes.'

'Did you wear a bra?'

'Of course.'

'You are so pathetic.' Corinne rolled her beautiful eyes
again. 'But still he didn't even want to come in for coffee?'

'I asked him and he said no,' Lizzy explained.

'No?' Corinne frowned. 'Oh. What have you been telling him?'

'I told you, he feels sorry for me.' Lizzy felt unaccountably forlorn for a few moments but then she reminded herself that, whatever his motivation, she was getting exactly what she wanted from Drew. 'But I still think he's very sweet,' she said faintly.

'You think Dr Maitland's sweet?' Corinne looked startled. *'Sweet?'*

'Kind,' Lizzy confirmed. 'Responsible. Thoughtful.'

'Thoughtful?' Corinne shuddered. 'Forget kind and thoughtful, Lizzy, because that isn't what you're supposed to notice with a man like that. Try powerful. Try exciting. Try just the sort of man you need to take you to bed immediately and keep you there for a week.'

'I'm not due any holidays.'

'The poor man obviously thinks you're a virgin,' Corinne said acidly, ignoring her. 'Hardly surprising, considering the way you carry on, and not that far wrong anyway. I'll have a word with him.'

'Don't you dare!' Lizzy surged from her seat, her panic only easing when Corinne grinned.

'Thought that might get a reaction,' she drawled. 'Not so sad and indifferent after all, hmm?'

'Like you and your accountant?' Lizzy snarled.

Corinne sobered with satisfying abruptness. 'That's a physical thing,' she said sharply. 'Nothing else.'

'Then why are you blushing?' Lizzy smiled, pleased with herself for getting the upper hand—rare, in her experience, with Corinne. 'Out. Let me work.'

'Forget Simon.' Corinne stood her ground. 'Lizzy, I'm serious about Dr Maitland.' She lowered her voice, her expression changing to one of earnestness. 'You know I'd never say a thing to him but you'd better. Men can be funny about things and if he thinks you're inexperienced... He's very attractive and he's single and, frankly, you're a fool if you don't at least make a play for him. You have to face the fact that you're not getting any younger.'

'Neither are you,' Lizzy said slowly.

'It's different for me. I don't even know yet if I ever want a baby. But you know you do, desperately, and when you think about the problems Catherine's been having...'

She left the rest unsaid but Lizzy realised what she meant and she was touched by Corinne's delicacy where normally she was so outspoken.

'Thank you for caring,' she said quietly, blinking fast to cover the tears that stung behind her eyes. She hugged her friend. 'I know what I'm doing and I'm fine. Everything's under control.'

'If you're sure.' Corinne patted her back but when she drew back her expression was still uncertain.

'Positive.' Lizzy sniffed. 'Now get out of here and leave me in peace.'

Late that afternoon when she returned to her office after her clinic the contracts she'd left in Drew's office that morning were in an envelope on her desk together with a note from him, suggesting she forwarded one to her solicitor for comment before making a final decision.

Lizzy called her solicitor then faxed him a copy of the contract, and he rang back an hour later, his calm manner despite his great age suggesting such agreements were not as novel as she'd assumed. 'Settlement terms are generous,' he told her gravely, 'but the matter of custody in the event of your demise is a concern. Otherwise a sound document, largely in your favour.'

'I'm happy with the custody clause,' she explained. 'He's very reasonable and I don't anticipate any problems.'

'Then I see no reason not to proceed,' he declared heavily.

Lizzy finished the conversation then lowered the receiver and did a quick jig around her office, before rushing off home.

She was still grinning the next morning and her expression drew raised eyebrows from Carol who came first thing to find her. 'Won the lottery?'

'Almost.' Lizzy beamed. 'More ultrasound requests for

this morning?' she asked, eyeing the forms Carol carried. The way she felt, she'd be happy to do a hundred if she were asked.

'Monthly sticky-bun bill from the bakery down the road,' Carol said tightly. 'No, make that the twenty-six sticky buns and one alfalfa sprout roll bill.'

Her disgusted expression told Lizzy what she thought of people who ordered alfalfa sprout rolls while the rest of the staff tucked into currant buns at the department's weekly morning tea, traditionally financed by Lizzy and her fellow consultants.

Carol showed Lizzy the figure she owed. 'You can pay it out of your winnings.'

Lizzy gave her the money. 'Alfalfa sprouts are full of vitamins.'

'Give me chocolate. Give me sugar. Give me alcohol.' Carol dropped the cash into the pocket of her uniform. 'The CT list this afternoon is full and the surgeons have four urgents they want added. I told the house officers to talk to you first.'

'They haven't yet,' she said. 'Can we possibly fit any in?'

'Might manage two or three if we both start early,' Carol said. 'The other one will have to be out of hours with on-call staff if it's really urgent.'

'I can stay late and do it myself if it is,' Lizzy said brightly.

'You really are in a good mood.' Carol's brows rose speculatively. 'I saw your dishy Drew in here yesterday afternoon, looking for you. Could that have anything to do with this good humour?'

'Really?' That must have been when he'd delivered the contract, Lizzy realised, feigning polite disinterest. 'Probably another urgent CT,' she commented, her weariness entirely faked.

But it must have been convincing enough because Carol,

with a casual shrug, continued on her way, almost bumping into the casualty officer who was coming to see her.

He had some X-rays for her to look at, two chests plus one abdominal film from a three-year-old girl. 'Mother is convinced she saw her choke on something she picked up from the floor fifty minutes earlier at kindergarten,' he explained. 'She banged her back and the choking stopped but nothing came out and she brought her up for a check. Clinically she's perfectly well. The films look normal to me, but with that history I wanted to be sure.'

Lizzy took the films to an X-ray box. 'And she's no idea what the object was?'

'None.' He peered at the film with her. 'Might not even be X-ray opaque.'

'There's no object visible here,' Lizzy told him, after inspecting the abdominal and chest films carefully. 'But, obviously, if it was something organic like a peanut it wouldn't be X-ray opaque and we wouldn't see it anyway.'

She saw that the radiographer who'd taken the chest films had correctly taken pictures with the child breathing in and then breathing out, essential if an inhaled foreign body was suspected.

'But there's a suspicion that the lung is slightly more inflated here when she breathes out,' she murmured, tracing the area she meant. 'It's still early and there are no signs of the lung collapsing behind the obstruction but that takes time to develop. My advice is to speak with the paediatric team. They might want to wait and watch but I think they'll find something down from the right main bronchus,' she said, indicating the main breathing tube on the right. 'I'd recommend they ask one of the chest physicians to have a look down there before any more problems develop.'

'Thanks, Dr Murdoch.' The casualty officer nodded his appreciation as he gathered the films together. 'I'll get onto it straight away.'

As soon as her ultrasound clinic finished, she rushed back to her office, fetched the contracts and went to find

Drew. Not in his office, or in Outpatients, or on Blue Ward, she found him finally in the bronchoscopy suite attached to main Theatres and the chest unit.

'Lizzy, come in.' Pleased to see her, although surprised when she appeared hesitantly at the door of the clinical room, Drew smiled a welcome and introduced her to his anaesthetist and to his small patient and her parents. 'This is Dr Murdoch,' he told them, 'the X-ray doctor who noticed the funny thing on your X-ray. All right if she watches us take a look?'

The child's parents nodded agreement and Lizzy took a gown from the rack by the door to cover her clothes. Drew paused momentarily to enjoy the way the fabric bunched about her tiny waist, outlining the soft, enchanting swell of her breasts as she tied the cotton garment securely closed.

Much more of this and he'd have to read up on reproductive physiology to see if he could persuade her to bring her fertility date forward, he decided grimly.

He worked at a bench to one side while beside him his anaesthetist talked softly to the drowsy toddler and her parents, all the while holding an oxygen mask above the child's face to help increase the amount of oxygen in her bloodstream prior to the procedure.

'What do you think of the films?' Lizzy asked him quietly.

'Subtle change, but I agree it's significant enough to investigate.' He didn't look at her again, concentrating instead on preparing the bronchoscope—a tube for examining the lower airways—for insertion into his little patient's lungs.

He nodded to his patient's parents as her eyes drifted slowly closed. 'I'll call you back in a few minutes,' he said, and a nurse escorted them quietly out of the room.

'Why aren't you using a flexible tube?' Lizzy asked.

'For children with suspected foreign bodies this is more suitable,' he explained. 'And a light, fast general anaesthetic is less stressful than a local for them.'

The anaesthetist signalled him as he put the child off to sleep and Drew moved quickly and smoothly to insert the tube, threading it lower into the smooth, pink airways. The dark and crinkly reason for the obstruction was clear almost immediately, and he raised his head and nodded for Lizzy to look. 'Quickly,' he instructed. 'Partially obstructing the airway, just where you predicted.'

She peered down then moved hurriedly back out of his way. 'What is it?'

'A piece of raisin or a sultana.' Sliding long forceps down the tube, he retrieved the fruit and removed the tube. The whole procedure had taken only seconds, and within five minutes the child was awake and talking sleepily with her parents, clearly not especially bothered by the drama.

'What would have happened if I hadn't seen it happen?' her mother asked Drew. 'Or if no one had noticed the change on the X-ray? We wouldn't have known anything was down there.'

'An infection would have built up behind the blockage,' he explained. 'The X-rays would have become obviously abnormal and we'd probably have done the same procedure as today.' He explained that the paediatric team would be keeping the little girl in hospital overnight but that, all being well, she'd be able to go home the following morning.

Leaving them in Recovery, Drew directed Lizzy out of the suite. 'Time for lunch?'

'Twenty minutes because we want to start the CT list early.' She drew the folded contracts he'd left her out of the pocket of her white coat. 'My solicitor has cleared these. I'm ready to sign.'

'Lionel Wright is a JP,' he said. 'I'll ask him to witness.'

The look she sent him as they hurried along the corridor towards the hospital canteen was startled. 'But then he'll know.'

'So?'

'So doesn't that bother you?' They were now in the queue for the sandwich bar and she'd lowered her voice.

'We have to be discreet,' she hissed. 'You know what hospitals are like.'

Inwardly he sighed, but then an awareness of the humour of the situation tugged at his mouth and lightened his expression. 'You really don't want anyone to know I'm the father?'

'Of course not.' He saw that her smile for the attendant waiting to serve her was shaky. 'Alfalfa and cheese salad, please, wholemeal bap, no mayonnaise.' She must have seen his wince because when he looked down she was glaring up at him. 'And I don't think we should see each other any more at work,' she muttered. 'Not socially like this.'

'Just for sex?' he whispered, her crisp little declaration goading him into teasing her.

'Exactly. And in secret.' She'd turned away from him to collect her bap, but the flush on her cheeks told him that she hadn't fielded his remark as calmly as she was pretending.

After collecting and paying for his own order, he caught up with her at a table by the window that overlooked the crèche's playground. He smiled at the way she wrinkled her little nose at his white schnitzel sandwich, refraining from telling her that in an effort to counter the canteen's invariably stale bread he'd ordered double mayonnaise.

'Stop laughing at me,' she said stiffly.

'I'm not,' he protested. Although in some ways she was right, the joke was on him and his own offended ego. 'I'm laughing at myself.'

'Why?'

'It's a long story.'

She waited until he'd finished a mouthful of his sandwich. 'And?'

'And perhaps I'll tell you one day,' he said softly, privately doubting it.

The cross way she attacked her lunch suggested he'd managed to irritate her. 'We should get a stranger to witness it,' she declared, her eyes on the envelope he'd placed on the table.

'Lionel Wright's discreet.'

Her look was scathing. 'This is as much for your protection as it is for mine.'

'I don't need protecting,' he countered easily. Despite her small size and angelic appearance, it seemed she wasn't accustomed to not getting her own way and he found himself enjoying their confrontation.

'People will gossip.'

'Let them.'

'I can't believe you're saying this.' She'd pushed her lunch away irritably and now regarded him with beautiful stormy eyes. 'Don't you care?'

'No.'

'What about if Corinne or Jane and Bill find out?' she demanded. 'Won't you be embarrassed?'

'Not remotely.' Giving up on his sandwich, as dry and unappetising as ever despite the extra mayonnaise, he lowered it, grinning at her disgusted expression.

'Look,' she said fiercely, 'they know me very well. I don't go out with many men. If you're seen with me, and then a few months later I start swelling up, they're going to know who to look at.'

He shrugged. 'They'd be right.'

'I was going to tell them it was a donor.'

'Isn't that what I am?'

'Yes, but not an anonymous one,' she hissed. 'You and I understand perfectly but others won't. Corinne and Jane might seem very modern but underneath they're quite old-fashioned. They try to hide it,' she insisted, 'and both of them will be supportive, but underneath they'll be shocked. They're both very protective of me and, frankly, I wouldn't want to be in your shoes if they even suspected you were involved. I'll try and shield you but I can't make any guarantees.

'Now, Corinne knows something, obviously.' Her lovely

face was quite flushed now. 'But if I tell her it's over, and we're careful not to be seen together again, we may just get away with it.'

Drew wiped his mouth with a paper napkin then pushed the wrappings to one side and eyed her mock-sternly. 'I probably do have this right but just confirm things for me, Lizzy. You want me to father your child, preferably avoid any involvement afterwards but obviously, by signing the contract, you're prepared to compromise on that, and now you've also decided you don't want to be seen in public with me, don't want any of your friends to know about me and, it would seem, certainly have no secret thoughts about any relationship outside of the purely temporary sexual liaison we've planned.'

'Exactly,' she confirmed, but at his grin her brows drew together when he grinned. 'What? What's so funny?'

'Life,' he said finally, remembering his smug wariness when Jane had first mentioned the name Lizzy to him. 'Just life.'

'So you see the other reason why I'm worried about you being there for the delivery,' she said urgently. 'I'd like to have my baby here at the National where I know some of the staff but if you're there people will guess—'

'I don't care.' He took her hand and grasped it tightly, despite the panicked way she looked around the cafeteria and tried to tug it away. 'Lizzy, I don't care.'

'This is for your sake,' she hissed, but her eyes widened at something behind him and he looked around and saw that some of the X-ray staff had come into the canteen. She was pulling at her hand, trying to force him to release her, but he held on. 'There'll be talk—'

Driven to exasperation, he used his grip to haul her around and into his arms. 'Then let's give them something to talk about,' he murmured, capturing her shocked and utterly tempting mouth.

But he'd underestimated his own susceptibility because, although he'd only meant to tease her, she was warm and unresisting and utterly desirable, and he couldn't stop himself from coaxing her mouth open and kissing her very thoroughly.

In the end it was enthusiastic applause that brought him back to the reality of where they were, and he released her, looking briefly into big green eyes as dazed as he imagined his own must be, before swivelling to wearily acknowledge the good-natured cheers and whistles of the grinning canteen staff and Lizzy's X-ray department colleagues.

'Finish your lunch.' His heart thudding alarmingly, he guided her back to her chair and collected the contracts she'd brought. 'If I get a chance I'll find Lionel Wright and check when he can witness these. If I have any luck I'll bleep you this afternoon.'

'I'm in CT,' she said faintly.

'I'll find you.'

'You shouldn't have done that,' she whispered, her eyes on a red-haired radiographer who was making her way purposefully towards them.

'Probably what made the idea irresistible,' he said softly, escaping.

On Friday Lizzy woke from a restless night to a fluttering nervousness in her stomach, and the feeling increased over the course of the day when she heard nothing from Drew about the contract or about whether he'd found someone other than Lionel Wright to sign it. When he still hadn't called her by late afternoon she bleeped him during a pause in her obstetric ultrasound clinic.

But Corinne answered the call. 'Dr Maitland is unavailable,' she explained, obviously not recognising either Lizzy's voice or the extension number in the ultrasound room. 'This is his registrar. Can I help?'

'Thank you, no,' Lizzy said thickly, slamming down the phone before Corinne guessed who it was and promptly regretting not finding out exactly what 'unavailable' meant.

A few minutes later her own bleeper shrilled but when she answered eagerly it was Corinne.

'Was that you with a fake voice?' she demanded.

Lizzy scowled. 'Where is he?'

'Why do you want to know?'

'Corinne…?'

But her friend just laughed at the growl. 'He's teaching,' she said easily. 'He's away, taking a training course for the college's membership exams, and he's given me his bleeper for the day. Of course, if this is a professional enquiry,' she added slyly, 'I can put you though to Dr Wright.'

Lizzy ignored that. 'Can I reach him?'

'No.'

'Is he due back this afternoon?'

'Monday,' Corinne said cheerfully. 'The teaching finishes around six so you could try calling him at home tonight.'

'I was going to call you anyway,' Lizzy added, not commenting on her suggestion. 'I wanted to check how Mrs Adams was.'

'I went to the ward this morning and she's fine on the chemo,' Corinne told her. 'The first cycle runs for eight days and the oncologists have told her that she shouldn't lose her hair so she's happy about that.'

Lizzy ended the conversation when a nurse brought in her next patient.

Still disturbed that Drew had made no attempt to contact her about how they were going to organise the weekend, she raced home after work but there were no messages on her machine.

Increasingly frantic that his lack of contact might mean that he was having second thoughts about them having sex the next day, she tried repeatedly to call him, but he didn't answer and it seemed he didn't have an answering machine of his own.

She called one of the hospital's telephonists, identified herself and managed to persuade her to part with Drew's mobile number, the phone he used when he was on call, but a recorded message told her that the device was switched off and wouldn't let her leave a message.

Finally, after ten, she drove to his home. It was darkened and there was no sign of his car so she pushed a note into the letter-slot in his door, asking him to contact her urgently when he arrived home, no matter what the time.

Back at the flat she made herself a very healthy sandwich and juiced several bunches of spinach, gulping two glasses of the green liquid to try and counteract the effect of the stress she was feeling on her system.

Later, she started fretting that something serious might have happened to him. If he didn't call by midnight, she vowed, making herself another sandwich and eating more spinach for good measure, if he didn't call she'd start telephoning hospitals.

He called at five to midnight. 'Are you all right?' she gasped, still very much awake.

'Of course.'

'Have you changed your mind?'

'No.' Even in that one little word she heard his amusement, and through the relief that made her sag back against her bed the unfairness of his tone riled her.

'I've been waiting to hear from you,' she cried. 'I was just about crazy with worry.'

'About me?' He sounded pleased. 'Lizzy, I'm touched.'

'Not you,' she shrieked. 'About your genes. What if something happened to you before I could use them?'

His laughter was warm against her ear. 'I've been working,' he said easily. 'Harder than I've ever worked in my life. I didn't know you were waiting for me to call. I thought everything was arranged for tomorrow. When are you coming over?'

'What about the contract?'

'I haven't had time to organise it yet,' he said calmly. 'There's no particular rush, is there?'

'Oh. I suppose not.' After all, they had a verbal agreement, and that was better than Lionel Wright knowing everything, she decided. She rolled onto her back, taking the telephone with her. 'Say tomorrow night around nine-thirty?'

'I'm doing a round at the hospital in the morning at eight but it won't take long so make it nine-thirty in the morning instead and we'll start early,' he told her cheerfully. 'Practice makes perfect.'

Lizzy's breath caught. 'How many times will we have to…do you think?'

'Oh, many times, Lizzy. Dozens, perhaps. This is too important to take any chances. Bring some chocolate to sustain you.'

'You're laughing at me again,' she said huskily.

'Only a little.' His voice was very warm, made her tingle in places she'd never tingled before. 'See you in the morning,' he said gently. 'Don't be late.'

Lizzy was at Drew's home two minutes before the appointed time but, despite her promptness, even if she hadn't held herself with unnatural stiffness on his doorstep, her expression would have revealed her tension. 'You're pale.' Drew brushed her soft, cool cheek with a single finger. 'Nervous?'

But it seemed she wasn't going to admit anything because she just muttered, 'Sleep-deprived.' She came inside when he stepped back. 'Why would I be nervous?' she said defensively. 'This is exactly what I want.'

She marched up the stairs ahead of him, her denim-clad rear rounded and tempting, but when she went to go up to the next level towards his bedroom he reined in his frustration, caught her hand and tugged her back down. 'Not yet, Lizzy.' She wasn't ready and there were things she needed to know. 'Breakfast. Have you eaten?'

'No.' Her relief was unflatteringly obvious in her quick smile and in the easy way she hauled herself up onto a stool at his breakfast bar. She took the cereal he passed her and poured some into a bowl. She added milk, shook her head at his offer of coffee and took juice instead.

'I saw Mrs Adams this morning,' he told her, deliberately steering the conversation to work. 'She's responding well to the chemo.'

'So Corinne told me yesterday.' Her happy smile now rewarded him for his efforts, and they talked companionably while they ate—about work and the teaching session he'd taken the day before.

Eventually he loaded the dishes into the dishwasher, but when he straightened he saw she was nervous again. 'Lizzy...?'

She stood up slowly and he could see how tightly she was holding herself. 'Yes?'

'I thought a walk,' he said softly. 'Around Portobello market and then up through Hyde Park, lunch and perhaps a movie in the West End in the afternoon.'

She blinked a few times and said enthusiastically, 'I'd love that. A walk's exactly what I feel like.' It came out all in a rush but then she hesitated, chewing at her lower lip with a delicate little movement that made him tense. 'But—'

'There's no hurry,' he told her, working hard to keep his voice calm, although what he really wanted was to take her to his bed immediately. 'My memory of gynaecology is that today's not really likely to achieve anything.'

'Tomorrow and Monday and Tuesday are definitely the best days for my cycle,' she confirmed faintly.

'So during the day today we keep things platonic,' he declared.

He saw her let out the breath she must have been holding. 'I'd like that,' she admitted.

He managed a smile. 'Good.'

As he'd suggested, they spent the rest of the morning exploring the antique and silver stalls strung along Portobello Road quite close to his home. They had lunch in a small pub he knew near by, and then they meandered, her hand firmly clasped in his, to Hyde Park, across it and up Piccadilly to a late afternoon romantic movie in Leicester Square.

Afterwards they strolled towards Charing Cross and down to the river. They stood at a lookout on the railway bridge, one of Drew's favourite spots in London, watching the barges and tourist boats passing beneath them, St Paul's Cathedral, lit by early evening sunlight, ahead of them. After a while he asked if she was hungry.

'Not really.' She lifted her head and he saw her appreciatively inhaling the gentle water-scented breeze coming off the river.

'A drink then. Have you had chickenpox?'

She blinked up at him. 'When I was a child,' she confirmed.

'Good.' He tugged her away from the bridge back towards the road and hailed a cab, directing the driver to Michael's restaurant. 'There's something I hadn't thought about until last night,' he said quietly, as they raced along past Westminster. 'Something important that might change your mind about wanting me to be your baby's father.'

Could barely hold. She stood with the creases of the skin bunching down at the cramped. 'He's a labourer to say the least unfit for much but for part of the family about still for free belongs.'

'You wanted—'

CHAPTER NINE

'MICHAEL'S your brother,' Lizzy said immediately. 'The waiter-cook. It's all right. I know already. Has he got chickenpox?'

Drew sent her a surprised look, remembering then that he'd never explained about Michael that night. 'No. Nor have I. We both had it when we were young. But that's not what I meant.'

'I don't mind that you didn't tell me,' she said quickly, making him frown. 'About him being your brother. It must be difficult when your family makes assumptions about women you introduce them to. I mean, it's not as if we're—'

'It's nothing to do with that,' he told her firmly, squeezing her hand. 'I didn't even realise I hadn't introduced you properly. This doesn't have anything to do with Michael, not directly at least.'

She looked bewildered. 'What, then?'

He sighed, wishing it had occurred to him right at the beginning. 'It'll be more real if you see it yourself.'

They were at the restaurant now. 'Everything but the kitchen's been closed for refurbishment for two weeks,' he explained, guiding her up the stairs. 'Michael cooked for us that Friday night as a favour. He opened again last night but his junior kitchen staff and a couple of waiters had to go off at the last minute because they discovered that they'd been exposed to chickenpox at a hygiene course he'd sent them on. None of them were sure if they'd had it before and he decided it was safer to put them on leave than risk exposing any customers.'

'You worked here?'

'Chief kitchen hand,' he said wryly, the corners of his mouth turning down at the reminder. 'He's managed to get agency staff for tonight but the rest of the family should still be here, helping.'

'You want me to meet them?'

'It's only fair,' he said deeply, pushing the door open so she could precede him. 'You might not thank me for not warning you.'

He saw that she realised the reason for his concern almost immediately. Annette, one of his sisters, met them as they entered, the twins wriggling under her arms. 'Pleased to meet you, Lizzy,' she said brightly, directing a vaguely scolding look in Drew's direction. 'When Drew was so mysterious about who he was bringing we hoped it might be you. Michael described you perfectly. I'm Annette.'

'Lizzy,' Lizzy said faintly. 'Twins.'

'Twins,' he confirmed, once she'd admired the laughing boys and greeted and been kissed and welcomed by a slightly harassed-looking Michael and the rest of the mob—Drew's other two brothers, his other sister and her husband and their three young children. He'd known they'd all be here at once—that was why he'd brought her now—but still the general noise and laughter and shouting and chaos of everybody helping to prepare the room for the evening made it hard to talk to her without being overheard.

'Annette's pair are the least of your worries,' he murmured, his hand holding her elbow tightly lest she run away. 'They're identical, a fluke. Worry about this.' He nodded towards where Michael and Nick, another brother, were arguing over a table setting. 'Twins,' he said quietly. 'Ten minutes apart.'

Then he waved his finger between Annette and James. 'Eleven minutes apart. James is the oldest but Annette's always refused to believe it.' And he indicated two of his other sister's children. 'Ben and Jason, fifteen minutes apart.'

'Four sets of twins in one family,' she whispered. 'It's impossible.'

'Unusual,' he conceded. 'But obviously not impossible.'

'Why didn't you warn me?'

'Until I saw them all together last night it simply hadn't occurred to me,' he said honestly. 'With the three lots not being identical we hardly even think about it.'

'My mother's sisters are twins,' she said faintly, 'so I've thought about it but never taken the possibility seriously. What do you think that makes our chances?'

'Still low,' he murmured.

'Higher than normal.'

'Worried enough to change your mind?'

Before she could answer him Annette brought drinks, a beer for him and freshly squeezed orange juice for Lizzy. 'Take them outside,' she advised, rolling her eyes as one of her nephews raced out of the kitchen, chased by a shouting chef waving a wooden spoon. 'There won't be any peace here until we open.'

They went out through the open doors onto the wharf beside the river. He saw that her movements were jerky and mechanical and he tensed, taking her elbow again and drawing her to the barrier so only he could see her expression. 'Well, Lizzy?' He still didn't know what he wanted her to say but he had to know. 'Up to you. Want to call the whole thing off?'

'They'd be company for each other,' Lizzy declared on the way to Drew's house an hour later, the time it had taken to tear themselves away from the chaos of Michael's restaurant. 'It would make work easier because I wouldn't have to stagger my maternity leave but I'd still have more children.'

She steadied herself with one hand on the seat beside her as the cab hurtled around Hyde Park Corner. 'There's room—I could put another cot in the nursery easily enough—but by the time they're a little older I'll have to think about looking...but, then, I don't have many people to stay so I could make the spare bedroom into a child's room.'

She chewed at her lower lip. 'It's not as if I can't afford it.' She looked at Drew quickly, seeing his frown. 'I could afford to move somewhere bigger—'

'The money I've offered you would, of course, be doubled if there're two babies,' he said abruptly.

'Mmm,' she said, looking away lest she provoked an argument. She didn't need any more money. She certainly didn't *want* any more money. 'I've lots of clothes,' she murmured. 'I wonder if they'd want their own or if they'd share?' She drummed her fingers against the leather of the seat. 'A boy and a girl would want different things, but then children's clothes are becoming more unisex—'

'Lizzy, stop worrying yourself. You know the chances are still very low.' His voice was lower now. 'You're talking as if there's no doubt there'll be a baby. Remember there's a chance this might not work at all.'

'Don't say that,' she said through clenched teeth. 'It's bad luck. Be positive.'

'You're depending on this too much. You're not doing yourself any favours by not being realistic.'

'I know my cycle,' she said firmly. 'I can feel it's the right time.' She gripped her fist, held it low to her stomach and pressed in at the aching she felt deep inside. 'I just know. Everything feels perfect.'

'What happens if it doesn't work?'

'I don't want to think about that.'

'Your hopes are too high. You'll be too upset if things go wrong.'

'I'll cope.' She looked away again, out of the window at the park, while they were stopped at lights. 'It won't affect you, you don't have to worry.'

'What if I'm not fertile?'

'What?' She looked back sharply, her eyes wide.

'I haven't been tested,' he said coolly. 'There's no way of knowing. What if I'm not?'

'We'll just—' But she broke off abruptly, startled. She'd spoken without thought, quickly and instinctively, but she'd been about to say that they'd adopt, and that was absurd. Regardless of how attractive she found him and how much she enjoyed his company and these days together, they weren't a couple. They didn't even have a relationship.

'If after two months you're not pregnant, we'll forget it and you'll find another donor,' he prompted.

'Yes.' She blinked. 'Of course.'

'Of course.'

But his regard was uncharacteristically narrowed, and it made her nervous. 'It will only be a waste of two months,' she said huskily. 'I won't mind. The gynaecologist told me that I had more time, just that I should move quickly. Besides,' she added, to try to reassure him, talking quickly to hide her unease, 'look at your family. Fertility runs rife.'

'Still sure you'll go directly to artificial insemination?'

'I suppose.' She shook her head at him. 'Stop it. I just want to concentrate on the plan as it is.'

'You could find another man.'

'No.' Restless now, she shifted in her seat, swivelled, changed to the flip-down seat opposite so that her back was to the driver's screen and then back again, all the while conscious that he was observing her every move, including the small, nervous flutterings of her hands which she couldn't control.

'Why not?'

'Not now,' she insisted. 'I told you I don't want to think—'

'You're not sounding very rational, Lizzy. What's happened to the carefully calculated neat little plans you described so proudly?'

'I'm perfectly rational,' she said sharply. She did have plans, careful, neat plans, as he'd suggested so scathingly, well thought-out and rational plans for the future and for her baby. If this didn't work then, of course, she knew exactly what she was going to do, but he was making her nervous and she couldn't think properly.

'In the cupboard that night you told me you never meet any men,' he said calmly. 'But that's not true, is it, Elizabeth?'

'Lizzy,' she hissed, resisting the urge to spit it. 'And of course it's true.'

'You meet men all the time,' he continued, his low voice drumming at her ears. 'I've watched. Men flirt with you constantly—at work, in the street, in restaurants. Lionel Wright can hardly keep his eyes off you, your registrar's the same—even Michael would have been interested if I hadn't been there.'

'Rubbish!'

'I'm being conservative, if anything.'

'In ten years I've had two boyfriends.'

'Still, it's odd,' he said softly. 'So desperate for the baby you crave, yet you've never taken a shred of notice of any of the men around you.'

'There haven't been any men, and this conversation is ridiculous,' she stormed, folding her arms.

'So why me?'

'You know why.'

'Do I?'

'The gynaecologist told me to hurry. I went to Jane's party. You were there.'

They were outside his home now and she jumped out, waiting for him to pay and for the cab to accelerate away before saying fiercely, 'The next day you looked good genetically and you seemed disease free. End of story.'

He got out his keys—his smile, she decided, particularly taunting. 'Pretty conveniently neat and tidy, isn't it, *Elizabeth*?'

'Lizzy,' she shouted, kicking the step which seemed safer than him in this mood. 'For the last time, it's Lizzy. And I am a neat and tidy person.' She stormed ahead to the stairs when he opened the door, not stopping at the kitchen level but going all the way up. 'Are we going to do this or were you planning to argue all night?'

His abruptly mocking regard put her teeth on edge. 'Still willing?'

'And able.' Furiously she threw her bag onto the floor beside his bed, then unbuttoned her blouse, cursing under her breath when the sleeves caught at her wrists and wrenching viciously at them until they pulled free. Her shoes, socks and jeans followed.

Her blue dress was neatly folded in a plastic bag in the back of her car but she was too cross to even consider going to fetch it. He'd agreed to this, she thought angrily, and he could just get on with it.

Bra and knickers the only things left, she hauled the bed covers back and jumped in, pulling the sheet back up to her neck. 'Well?'

But he didn't move. 'Well?'

'Aren't you going to take your clothes off?'

Instead, his eyes dropped thoughtfully to the floor and the scattered remains of her clothes. 'You just finished telling me you were neat and tidy,' he observed.

'Normally, yes, but these are trying circumstances,' she grated. 'You've got your dearest wish—it's still broad daylight—so can we just get this over with?'

'Is there a hurry?'

'My biological clock is speeding up.' She took a pillow from his side and wiggled it down under the covers, shoving it beneath her buttocks, then looked up in time to catch his sudden amusement. 'I read it in a magazine,' she said defensively. 'It changes the angle of the pelvis and increases the chance of conception.'

When he still didn't move she added acidly, 'As long as there's actually something in the vicinity capable of fertilising me, that is.'

'Didn't your magazine also tell you how delicate the male libido is?' he enquired interestedly, coming forward to gather her clothes, folding them carefully and placing them on the dresser at the end of the bed. 'The words "performance anxiety" ring any bells, Lizzy?'

Lizzy blinked. 'Performance anxiety,' she echoed, aghast. 'What do I do about that?'

He smiled. 'Say something exciting.'

Exciting? Lizzy felt herself pale. 'You've got nice hair,' she said abruptly. 'And I like your shoulders.' When he didn't react she bit her lip. 'And you smell nice and you've got good skin and I like your family.'

When he still didn't move she closed her eyes, pulled the sheet over her face and groaned, recognising that she was completely and utterly out of her depth. 'We can leave this until tomorrow,' she said finally, her forlorn words unnaturally loud to her under the tent of the sheet. 'Might you be better by then?'

'I'll work on it.' His tone was dry. 'Are you going to come out of there?'

'I don't know.' She was stiff with misery. Not only was this not turning out like any of her fantasies, but it seemed he'd lost even a trace of the desire he'd professed the night she'd come for dinner.

'Are you asking me to come in?'

'No.' She wished she could disappear. 'Watch television, if you want.'

'But I don't.'

He sounded amused, she realised faintly. He was laughing at her again. Before she could react there was rough, sudden movement at the bottom of the covers followed by the brush of air on her feet and warm hands at her ankle. She cried out when the hands tightened but he hauled her easily down the bed so her feet reached the end.

'What...?'

The touch of his mouth on the sole of one foot froze the protest in her throat.

'What, Lizzy?'

'Nothing.' It came out like a gasp and she wriggled her

toes, her breath coming faster as firm hands moved up her calves, hauling her even lower in the bed.

Her head still covered by the sheet, the pillow at her back now and her arms outstretched above her head, she couldn't see anything but pale, creamy cotton, but it didn't seem to matter.

Abruptly he swept the covers away and she lay exposed and stiff in the evening daylight, staring up wide-eyed into knowing, hazel eyes, which, to her relief, had turned warm.

'Now this,' he said softly, swiftly dealing with the front clasp of her cotton bra, lifting her arms and hauling the garment away briskly.

Involuntarily her hands rose to cover herself and his mouth tightened as if her sudden shyness amused him, but he didn't stop. One hand went beneath her, lifting her slightly, and he dealt with the fabric at her hips efficiently, sliding the cotton over her thighs to the bottom of the bed.

Firmly he pushed down the knees she'd instinctively lifted to hide herself and Lizzy could hear her heart hammering inside her chest as he sat beside her. She was finding it hard to keep breathing, had to keep reminding herself to breathe in and out, when her lungs just seemed to want to gasp.

Her gaze locked with his and she let him prise her hands away from her breasts but then she flinched when his palm grazed the tender, tightened nub at the centre.

'Cold?'

'No.' It was warm in the room and she shook her head, blinked, lifted her head, looked down at herself and saw the flush across the creamy flesh that he cupped. 'It just felt...funny.'

Still sitting beside her, he lowered his head and sucked the sensitive tissue into his mouth, teasing her with his tongue until her head began to muddle and she fell back against the bed and twisted, her hands fluttering at her sides, not knowing what to do with them until finally they rose to his head, twined in his hair and held him to her.

* * *

It was dark when she woke. She rolled onto her back, stretching with a yawn. Experimentally she glided one hand across to the other side of the bed but the sheet was cool and her smile stiffened, became awkward and tinged with self-consciousness, as she realised she was alone.

He was downstairs. Outside, on a chair on the decking.

With his legs outstretched and his feet bare, a half-empty bottle of amber alcohol beside him, his gaze was lowered broodingly to the near-empty glass in his hand. Lizzy hesitated, the skin on her arms goosebumping despite the soft warmth of the summer night's air.

'Drew…?' When his regard shifted to her she faltered, his shadowed expression unreadable in the dregs of light which filtered outside from the kitchen. 'Do you want me to go home?'

'No.'

Her fingers played at the lower button of her shirt. Not sure what constituted appropriate middle-of-the-night attire, she'd dressed completely, including footwear, but although he wore jeans his shirt was unbuttoned and hung loosely, doing little to conceal the muscled power of his chest.

Lizzy remembered the feel of his chest against her, the hard strength of his shoulders and back, and felt her mouth become dry. 'Can't you sleep?'

'Can't you?' Not answering her question, he swung the bottle so she could read the whisky's label. 'Drink?'

She said, 'Not that. Just water. I'll get it,' she added hurriedly, when he bent his knees, apparently preparing to fetch one for her.

Inside, she ran herself a glass of water, then splashed her face from the tap, wiping herself dry with a careless sleeve before going back out to him.

'I don't know what to say,' she admitted, taking the seat he'd swung around to the table for her so that she sat opposite him. 'I feel awkward. If you'd really prefer to be alone—'

'I'd tell you,' he said flatly, his voice low, rumbling. He took a mouthful of his drink, swallowed it then stared at the remains. 'Relax.'

'I wanted to say thank you.' She was glad of the darkness when his gaze lifted again because it had to be concealing the flush she felt covering her, despite her attempts to cool herself with the water. 'I've never...' She felt her flush deepen. 'Well, that was new to me,' she added jerkily. 'With Paul—' She broke off and took her turn to stare at her drink. 'I didn't know it could feel like that.'

When he didn't say anything she twisted her feet nervously beneath the table, not brave enough to look up again. 'Jane said she knew the instant she fell pregnant. I don't feel anything like that yet—at least I don't think I do—but still there's a chance I wouldn't realise even if I was, not for a few weeks and, anyway, if I'm not there's always tomorrow.'

She looked up, alarmed by his silence. 'We can still,' she said urgently, 'tomorrow and Monday and the other days, that's still all right, isn't it?'

'It's what we agreed.'

She frowned at him, trying to decipher his expression in the shadows, but with the light of the kitchen in front of her she could make out only his seriousness. 'But you don't sound very... Are you sure you haven't changed your mind?'

'Sure.'

Her breath caught, and she pushed her glass away and folded her arms on the table. 'Drew? Have I done something wrong?'

'No.' But as if her worry had finally communicated itself to him he made a small, harsh sound in his throat, pushed his chair back and came around to her. 'Nothing wrong,' he said roughly, lifting her out of her chair with an ease that demonstrated his strength to her anew. 'It's late. Back to bed, hmm?'

'Yes, please.' She almost whispered the words, concentrating hard to stop herself pressing her mouth to the hard curve of his shoulder beside her, bare now where her body had pushed his shirt back.

They made love again, and then once more in the morning when she woke.

'I have to stay like this for an hour,' she explained apologetically, blushing, when he returned from his shower, his brows rising when he saw her in the same position as when he'd left, except for the sheet he'd discarded in the night which she'd now retrieved and pulled up to her neck. 'I read it in a book. That means there's another forty-two minutes to go.'

He discarded his towel, and she saw his mouth quirk slightly at her hastily averted gaze. 'Are you cold?'

'Not at all.' She tilted her head, gazed up at the window and blue sky. 'I think it's going to be another hot day.'

'Then you don't need this.' Before she could grasp it, he'd torn the sheet away, balled it and thrown it towards the other side of the room where it fell in a soft cotton strip across the tiles.

Then he sat at her thighs and parted them, a firm hand going to her forehead and pushing her back when she sat up sharply. 'Flat, Lizzy,' he said softly. 'Stay flat. Forty-two minutes, remember?'

He'd obviously shaved when he'd showered and his cheek was smooth against her pale stomach when he kissed it.

'Drew...?' Lizzy lay back, her heart beating fast, her palms moist as they flattened against her breasts, her body arching as she felt the faint, teasing touch of his mouth drifting lower. 'I don't think I can let you do this.'

'The contractions will be good,' he murmured, holding her thighs apart when she strained to conceal herself. 'They'll help nature work. Relax. I won't hurt you. You can let me do anything.'

'I'll think of England,' she gasped, her breath catching

abruptly as he found his objective, sending a spasm of
alarm through her quivering body.

'If you can.'

She heard his amusement, but couldn't react, and let her
eyes close, suddenly nothing mattering as much as the
touch of his mouth against her.

They spent Sunday together, a lazy, gentle day passed
reading the papers and lingering over a makeshift picnic in
the park adjacent to the house. She drove to work directly
from his home on Monday morning, collected more clothes
and went back there in the evening.

On Tuesday night they ate at a restaurant he knew in
Notting Hill. It was a warm, balmy evening and Lizzy lifted
her head appreciatively to the gentle evening sun as they
walked home. Other strolling couples wore shorts and
T-shirts, and customers in the pub at the corner spilled mer-
rily onto the footpath and street. 'I love London when it's
like this,' she declared, finding herself supremely happy.
'It's so beautiful at this time of year.'

Drew smiled and, to her delight, his arm slid around her
back and he hugged her to his side, guiding her through
the crowds and not releasing her until they were at his
house. It had become their habit to have an evening drink
outside on the decking before bed, and she prepared herself
a spinach juice while he made coffee.

She joined him outside, eyeing him over the rim of her
glass. 'I'm on call tomorrow and I teach so I might be late
tomorrow night.'

He lifted one shoulder as if not especially concerned.
'When will you know?' But his brow creased slightly as if
her blank look had puzzled him. 'When will you know if
you're pregnant?'

'Oh.' Lizzy lowered her glass quickly, flushing. Of
course that was what he'd meant. That was the whole reason behind her being here, she told herself, cross that she'd
let herself forget again. Tomorrow would be her last night
with him. She didn't let herself dwell on why that thought

made her forlorn. 'About ten days,' she said huskily. 'The tests are very sensitive these days.'

She stood abruptly and collected her glass and his empty mug and carried them into the kitchen, where she stacked them into the dishwasher. 'Jane said she noticed things even before that. Her breasts were sore, she said, after only a day or two. I haven't noticed anything.'

'Early days.'

'I know.' She closed the dishwasher door slowly, the prickle of his gaze at her back making her self-conscious. Given the uninhibited intimacies of the past three nights with him, she recognised that she ought to be over that by now but, if anything, her nervousness with him when he looked at her like that seemed to have increased. The knowledge of what he could do to her, how he could make her feel, how he could make her respond, was overwhelming, and the undercurrent of that knowledge now threaded through her every contact with him.

With Paul she'd had no difficulty ignoring the sexual side of their relationship unless they'd actually been in bed together, and even then she'd not responded with any sort of enthusiasm. With Drew, though, things were profoundly different, and her response remained involuntary and total.

'I'm going to take a shower,' she announced, finally straightening from the dishwasher to face him again. She dried her hands on a towel, meeting his enigmatic regard with deliberate calm. 'Have you much work tonight?'

'An hour or two,' he said easily, but he didn't rise from the table and his gaze had turned almost thoughtful as he surveyed her. 'I'll wake you when I come up.'

'I won't be asleep.' Lizzy was confident of that. The thought of falling asleep, knowing what would happen when he woke her, seemed ludicrous.

On Wednesday night she took her usual teaching session with the registrars. It ran late and she didn't get to the house until nine. Telling herself that her forlornness was nothing to do with tonight possibly being her last night ever with

Drew but was, instead, a normal reaction to a long, tiring day, she rang his doorbell.

'I bought you a present,' she said glumly, thrusting it at him when he opened the door—drinking in the sight of him, strong and powerful in his tennis gear. She realised he must have been for a game while she was at work. 'I had lunch with Jane and Gemma Rose,' she added, when he lifted the bottle from its brown paper wrapping. 'It's one of Bill's favourites and she said it was very good.'

'Why do I get a present?' He closed the door once she was inside and looked at her, his regard enigmatic.

'It's a thank-you,' she muttered. 'For everything.'

'Everything?'

She tilted her head, determined this time not to let him embarrass her. 'It didn't have to be like this,' she said huskily. 'You could have been remote and clinical but you weren't. You made this time special for me and I want you to know how much I appreciate it.'

'This is uncharacteristically formal, Lizzy.'

'Yes.' She felt herself flush and wondered if he was mocking her. 'Well.'

'"Yes, well?" His mouth quirked. 'What does that mean?'

'Yes, well, formal is how it's going to be from now on, isn't it?' Lizzy stepped sideways and headed for the stairs. 'I'm sure we both understand that.'

'You're still worried about gossip?' He'd followed her to the kitchen and now grimaced his disgust as he watched her open the fridge and extract the remains of the spinach she'd bought the day before. 'I thought I'd stopped you fretting about that.'

'Your behaviour in the canteen that day was unaccceptable,' she said tightly, flushing at the memory of that kiss as she tore off some of the green leaves and stuffed them into her mouth. 'And foolish,' she added after she'd swallowed, meeting his amused regard bravely. 'But I think I've managed to cover it up.'

'Jane seemed delighted we spent the weekend together.'

Lizzy felt every ounce of heightened colour drain directly from her face to her chest. 'Jane was what?' she cried, aghast.

CHAPTER TEN

DREW allowed himself a few moments of enjoyment at Lizzy's panic. She'd been too smug lately, he decided. He'd indulged her, let her have her own way too much at the expense of his own well-being. It was time he shook her up. 'I said—'

'I know what you said,' she said hoarsely. 'What did you tell her?'

Her distress felt like fitting recompense for some of what she'd put him through that week, and he hesitated, deliberately taking his time. He leaned against the bench opposite her, crossed his feet and lazily folded his arms. 'This and that.'

But she didn't bite, her expression instead calming a little. 'She didn't say anything at lunch,' she said tentatively. 'Her memory hasn't been the best lately. Perhaps she forgot everything you said straight away? When did you see her?'

'Bill and I've been playing tennis. Jane came to umpire.'

'Jane came to umpire.' As she echoed his words he saw her face fall satisfyingly. 'So she hasn't forgotten anything—she just didn't know at lunchtime,' she said miserably. She tore off a little piece of spinach and ate it. 'And you told her—'

'As I said, she was delighted,' he said calmly, not taking his eyes off her pleasingly dazed expression until she turned away from him, crossed her arms on the bench and lowered her head.

'Do you have any idea what you've done?' she demanded, her fists clenching on the spinach they clutched. 'Jane can't keep her mouth shut about anything. If she knows, it's only a matter of time before Corinne—'

'Corinne seemed pleased, too,' he remarked. 'At least she seemed pleased for the millisecond she managed to prise herself away from Simon.'

Lizzy's head came up. Slowly she turned around. 'The accountant was there?'

'At Bill's,' he confirmed. 'I went there afterwards for a drink and they arrived to show off his new Porsche.'

'His new Porsche?' She shook her head vaguely, obviously beyond making any attempt to understand anything. 'So you're telling me that both Jane and Corinne know I spent the weekend here?'

'That we spend the weekend together,' he confirmed.

'But if I get pregnant?'

'Not much chance of keeping my identity a secret,' he said calmly.

'You're mad,' she whispered, wiping her green hands carelessly on her dress, before tearing more spinach from a paper bag into more little pieces and stuffing them into her mouth one by one.

'Says the woman with the green mouth.' Desire overcoming his revulsion at the vegetable she'd managed to coat herself in, he came to her, firmly disengaged the remains of the spinach stalks from her fists and dumped them into the bin. While she stood numbly silent he filled a glass with water. 'Get rid of the spinach before I kiss you.'

'It's very good for you,' she murmured, rinsing her mouth despite that. She showed him her teeth. 'Am I clean?'

'Enough.' His hands under her arms, he lifted her onto the bench. 'Does that mean you want kissing?'

'Yes, please.' Her arms crept up to circle his neck. 'Are we going upstairs?'

'No.' He loosened the buttons of her dress and bra and then bared her glorious breasts and tipped her back.

'Have I told you how much I love these?' he muttered against her throat, his hands sliding to her stockings, his thumbs stroking the soft, bare flesh above them.

'About a hundred times,' she whispered, closing her eyes.

In the morning while Drew showered Lizzy collected her things and packed them into the little case which she'd brought, finding herself struggling to hold back tears when she sat back on the bed and contemplated it. Telling herself that heightened emotions might be a sign of early pregnancy to try and lift her mood didn't work.

Drew came into the room, a towel draped carelessly around his hips, and she rose abruptly, trying to cover her confusion by tightening the belt of his gown that she wore and making for the bathroom with her head lowered.

But his arm at her wrist caught her and swung her around. 'Lizzy? Are you upset?'

'No.' She blinked furiously. 'Something in my eyes.'

But his concerned frown and the warm finger that brushed her cheek suggested she'd been less than convincing. 'Did I hurt you?'

'No.' Her face heated. Their love-making that morning, unexpected because it was Thursday now and out of her fertile time, had been passionate and urgent. Although he hadn't been as tender as usual, it hadn't been painful, but wrenchingly satisfying. 'I'm fine.'

She tugged her arm free and fled towards the bathroom. 'Don't bother making breakfast for me this morning. I'm not hungry. I'll just have juice.'

When she finally came downstairs he was reading the paper, the coffee beside him suggesting he'd either skipped or already finished his cereal.

He put the paper aside when she came in and Lizzy sent him a small, nervous smile, before depositing her bag in the doorway. Taking the glass of orange juice that was on the bench, she drained it quickly, worried that she was holding him up.

'I'll only be a second,' she said huskily, lowering the glass and wiping her mouth. 'Aren't you running late?'

'Why were you crying?'

'I don't know.' Grateful she had an excuse to turn away, she rinsed her glass and loaded it into the dishwasher. 'I never usually. It might be a good sign, I thought. Something to do with my hormones, perhaps.'

She smoothed her palms on the sides of her pants. 'I've thought about Jane and Corinne. The best course is for both of us to simply not say anything more. They'll be curious but they'll give up eventually.' She chewed her lower lip. 'I hope.'

'You're ashamed of what you've done?'

'Of course not.' Lizzy squirmed, the thoughtful coolness of his regard increasing her unease. 'Not ashamed, but it's a private thing. I thought it was just going to be between us.'

'There was nothing about secrecy in the contract.'

'I assumed we felt the same.'

'Jane and Corinne are your friends.'

'They're also extremely nosy.' Exasperation overtook her nervousness. 'We've been through this again and again and I can't believe you don't understand by now. They won't realise this was just an arrangement. They'll think you've taken advantage of me. They could make your life hell.'

'Perhaps I have taken advantage of you.'

'Hardly.' She snatched away the mug containing the remains of his coffee and rinsed it before she added it to the collection in the dishwasher, wondering if he was being sarcastic. 'How?'

'Sex without strings,' he said coolly, watching her as if her reaction interested him. 'Isn't that what men crave?'

'It could have been without strings,' she observed. 'Until you changed the contract and added them yourself.'

The casual way he received that suggested he wasn't especially concerned. 'What happens now?'

'I'll let you know as soon as I know anything.' She

checked her watch. 'Drew, you're really running very late—'

'Relax.' Instead of hurrying, he pushed his chair back almost lazily, and came to collect her bag. 'Corinne will be delighted. There's nothing she likes better than me arriving after eight. It's ammunition for her determined little campaign to delay my ward round by an hour.'

'She hates early starts,' Lizzy confirmed, darting ahead when he stood back to allow her to precede him downstairs.

Once he'd lifted her bag into the back of her car she hesitated and looked up at him, her hand on his arm stopping him when she thought he might walk away without saying anything more. 'This is goodbye, then.'

He frowned as if he didn't understand. 'I'll see you at work.'

'I mean goodbye to this,' she amended quickly, looking up at the house. 'I might not be back here again, not like this, not if things go well.'

'Is that why you were upset?'

'No.' Lizzy recoiled, horrified that he suspected that. 'No, of course not,' she said urgently, determined to dispel his doubts—doubts she refused to even allow herself to consider. 'Don't worry. This has been a…an agreement. We both understand that. I'm not in the least upset.'

'Is that supposed to reassure me?'

'It should.' She gazed up at him, blinking, not understanding the hard, almost frustrated darkening of his eyes. 'At least,' she said faintly, 'at least you must be relieved I haven't fallen in love with you.' She imagined that must happen to him quite often. Very often. She could imagine it happening very easily. 'That would have been a disaster.'

'Truly a disaster.' His tone was dry but his expression, to her relief, lightened now as if she'd managed to amuse him again. 'Goodbye, Lizzy.'

He bent his head and kissed her, a gentle, thoughtful, tender kiss that nevertheless quickened her breath. 'Call me when you know.'

She suspected a week later, but knew for sure on the Friday.

On call for the weekend, she waited until Monday to tell him, but when she went to his office after her last list his secretary told her that he was away for the rest of the day, covering a clinic at a neighbouring hospital.

'He'll be at Jane's tonight,' Corinne told her cheerfully, startling them both as she barged into the office, obviously having overheard Lizzy's enquiry.

She dumped a pile of notes on Drew's secretary's desk and waggled her hand in front of both their faces. 'Notice anything different?'

'A ring?' Lizzy shrieked, grabbing her finger. 'What? You didn't tell me anything.'

'I didn't know till last night,' Corinne said smugly, admiring the slim band with its solitary diamond. 'And I haven't decided. I'm just wearing it to see how it feels.'

'Not the accountant?'

'He's trading in the new Porsche for something small, and investing the balance in socially responsible projects,' Corinne announced.

Lizzy rolled her eyes. 'Not giving it to Greenpeace?'

'I'm working on it.' Her friend grinned. 'Early days, Lizzy Murdoch. Early days. He's crazy about me.'

'No more than you are about him,' Lizzy observed, noting the uncharacteristic flush highlighting Corinne's flawless complexion. 'Jane said that you even went to some posh business do in the City which was full of bankers and lawyers and money people and you behaved yourself because Simon asked you sweetly.'

'Not that I've changed any of my principles,' Corinne said quickly, smiling a goodbye to Drew's secretary as they left the office.

'No, you've just fallen in love,' Lizzy countered, her arm going around her friend as they walked. 'I'm really pleased for you, Corinne.' She hugged her. 'When do I get to meet him?'

'Tonight at Jane's, although why on earth it has to be a Monday night again, heaven knows.'

'Bill's been on call all weekend and is on again next, and she didn't want to wait any longer.' Jane was having a second attempt at a surprise—this time belated—birthday party for Bill, together with a head-wetting for Gemma Rose.

'At least I won't have any trouble recognising him,' Lizzy joked. 'Fat, bad suit, horrible haircut, hates children.'

'Actually, thin, great suits, terrific hair, as yet ambivalent about children,' Corinne amended sheepishly. 'Sorry. I exaggerated. I was determined you wouldn't get your hands on him until I'd had a chance to make up my mind, and Jane had told me she was going to try and get the two of you together.'

'Jane's a menace.' Lizzy laughed. 'She was teasing you. He wasn't even there that night.'

'But Dr Maitland was.' Corinne nudged her, and stopped in the corridor, eyeing her mischievously. 'So? You've been irritatingly reticent lately. What's going on?'

'Nothing.' She kept her tone carefully light, although inwardly she tensed. She'd barely seen Drew since that last day at his home—once at the team's X-ray meeting, and another time briefly in the corridor when he'd been with an interestedly observant Corinne. Although on each occasion she'd longed for some more personal acknowledgement from him, they'd merely exchanged cool greetings. 'I haven't seen him for ages.'

'So you keep saying.'

'It's true.'

'Then why were you looking for him?'

'I wanted to find out about Mr Jackson,' Lizzy said, inspiration striking. 'How he was getting on after the surgery on his pituitary tumour.'

'Awe-inspiringly well. Hoping to be discharged tomorrow,' Corinne said smoothly. 'Sailed through the operation and still trying to persuade his poor neurosurgeon to come along on his Peruvian trekking trip. Anything else I can help you with?'

'Mrs Adams?'

'Great. She finishes her second cycle of chemotherapy on Thursday and her tumour markers are falling already. Things are looking good.' She grinned. 'See, you could have asked me about them, Lizzy. You didn't have to bother Dr Maitland. Although I don't suspect he'd mind, not considering the way he was watching you during the X-ray meeting Tuesday.'

'Don't be ridiculous.' She knew Corinne was just teasing her but she didn't appreciate the reminder of how difficult she'd found that meeting herself. Trying to keep her mind on the films and her eyes off Drew that morning hadn't been easy, despite the fact that his almost brooding regard hadn't been remotely encouraging.

Corinne's bleeper sounded, dragging her away. 'See you tonight,' she called, making for the telephone which they'd just passed. 'Jane says don't be late and wear the blue dress and no bra.'

Lizzy rolled her eyes. 'Please don't tell me she's found another relative to introduce me to?' she called, but Corinne just waved her away, clearly already preoccupied with her telephone conversation.

Lizzy arrived late at Jane's. Nervous about Drew being there, she'd tried on several outfits and tried brushing her hair different ways, settling finally and almost in despair on the blue dress and her hair loose.

Like the last party, the street was choked with cars, and Lizzy was glad she'd decided to take the Tube. Also just like her memory of the last party, Jane was clutching a jar of green olives when she opened the door, and her mouth was full of them.

'Gem's asleep,' she told her through the olives, eyeing the stuffed rabbit in Lizzy's arms doubtfully as she let her in. 'No, you can't see her and, no, you definitely can't wake her up, and please stop bringing her toys.'

'They can't be good for you,' Lizzy remarked, putting her coat and the rabbit in Bill's study as Jane had indicated with a languid lift of a still-plump hand. 'Too much salt.'

'I don't eat the salt, I eat the olives,' Jane told her sharply. 'And Gem loves the taste of them in the breast milk.'

'She's too young to like olives. You're addicted.'

'Better than being a prude.' Jane looked pointedly at Lizzy's chest. 'What is it with you and bras?'

'Go away.' Lizzy crossed her arms.

'Lizzy,' Jane grumbled impatiently. 'We bought that dress for you so you could show yourself off. How can I find you a husband if you persist in concealing your best assets?'

'Don't find me a husband,' Lizzy snarled, conscious of the noise of the crowd milling mere feet away in the living room. 'I'm not interested.'

'Oh? Why's that?' Jane straightened, eyeing her interestedly now. 'Decided Drew's the one you want?'

'How that sweet little Gemma can have a monster of a mother like you is beyond me,' Lizzy said fiercely.

But Jane smiled. 'He's out by the pool.'

'Actually, I wanted to meet Simon.'

'Not here yet. But Drew's by the—'

'Pool, yes, I know, I heard you.' Lizzy glared at her before she stomped out of the study. She went directly to the living room to greet Bill and then joined a group of his medical colleagues, deliberately involving herself in a lively but worrying discussion about rumoured ward closures at the National.

When she could get away she crept upstairs and watched Gemma sleeping. Not until later when she was confident Jane was too occupied to notice did she make any attempt to find Drew. By then the house and garden were very crowded, but she spotted him by the pool, talking with two of the National's surgeons.

She began to walk across to them but someone tapped her shoulder and when she swung around Corinne, her arms wrapped around a very attractive, thin man with striking blue eyes and what looked like a custom-tailored black suit, was grinning at her.

'Lizzy, Simon,' she said gaily. 'Simon, Lizzy.'

They shook hands, his grip, Lizzy noted, firm and confident, although he looked a little taken aback.

'Lizzy…?' he said slowly, his friendly smile turning to a frown when he looked back at Corinne. 'You said Lizzy was short and fat with thinning hair.'

'She is short,' Corinne said abruptly, her expression turning vaguely sheepish before she beamed again. 'Lizzy's going to be my bridesmaid,' she announced, surprising Lizzy who hadn't known anything about it. 'Lizzy and Jane, the way it was Lizzy and me for Jane. September, I thought,' she added airily, 'before it gets too cold to have the wedding outside.'

Simon's delighted but startled expression suggested that the announcement was news to him, too, so, after murmuring her best wishes, Lizzy turned back towards Drew, leaving them to talk.

She hesitated by the buffet table laid out again in front of the pool-house and, as though sensing her regard, he looked up abruptly, caught her eyes and frowned. Making a signal with her hand, she retreated indoors and moments later he followed her. 'What is it?'

'Not here.' There were too many people around. Corinne and Simon were locked in a passionate embrace, obviously unaware of anything except each other, but that didn't mean everyone else was so unobservant. The thought of Jane gloating if she saw them together was unbearable.

She walked quickly upstairs and he followed her, but there were people up there, peeking at the baby, and Carol was at the back of the queue for the upstairs bathroom.

Drew took Lizzy's hand when she spun back down the stairs. 'Here, then,' he said quietly, to her alarm opening the door to the cupboard they'd been trapped inside that night.

She caught a brief glimpse of amused hazel eyes before he pushed her gently in. 'Stop panicking,' he chided. 'This is the door I had made to replace the last one.' There was a metallic, sliding sound and the door locked shut. 'The bolt fastens inside as well.'

But, aside from the light at the top of the door, it was still dark, and she clutched at him to steady herself. 'This is silly.'

'Not if you want privacy which, it seems, you do.' His voice was warm but she shivered when his hands lifted to stroke her bare arms. 'Well?'

'There's no baby,' she said faintly. 'I found out Friday night.'

'Oh.' His hands stopped their stroking and squeezed her shoulders gently. 'Are you all right?'

'I think so.' And she was. Much better than she'd expected. She'd known he'd been right to warn her not to get her hopes up too high but, to her relief, the arrival of her period had been far less traumatic than she'd anticipated. She was uncomfortably aware that she'd found a great deal of consolation in the thought of spending another five days with Drew. 'There's still this month,' she said huskily.

'And now.'

His hands slid to her breasts and her breath caught in her throat at the sudden rush of heat through her body.

When he shifted and lifted her against him so that her feet left the floor, all her breath rushed out of her throat again and she gasped.

'You feel good,' he murmured, his mouth at her throat making her arch back in remembered delight. 'This cupboard has certain possibilities we ignored last time, don't you think?'

Lizzy closed her eyes and tilted her head to allow his

mouth better access, letting him press her back against the cool bricks at the rear of the cupboard, her head spinning. 'Drew...?'

'Take this off.' He had her dress raised and he murmured his appreciation as she felt his hands slide over the tender skin above her stockings, then linger at the junction of her thighs just a little higher.

'I don't think we should be doing this—'

'And this.' Ignoring her weak protest, he took her dress away and dispensed with her bra, his mouth following the teasing brush of his fingers to her already aroused breasts.

'I can't,' she whispered, her voice sounding strangled as he mouthed the sensitive nubs, her fingers clutching at his hair—torn between pushing him away and the urgent need to pull him harder into her. 'No, Drew, please. Not now.'

As if her words had finally sunk in, he lifted his head, easily overcoming the shaking strength of her hands which had turned traitor to her will and tried to hold him against her again.

There was movement and he lowered her and then his hand was at her face, feeling its heat. 'You're embarrassed?'

'A little,' she conceded. Although that wasn't the reason she'd made him stop, it seemed good enough for now. 'The door's not that thick and there are a lot of people out there.'

She felt him smile and closed her eyes again at the soft, fleeting touch of his mouth.

'Get dressed,' he said softly. He crouched and retrieved her dress. 'Let's get out of here.'

He hadn't given her back her bra and she felt around for it with her foot, but when she couldn't feel it she let him fasten her dress regardless, vowing to creep back discreetly another time and retrieve it.

The stairs were empty and she was confident no one saw them emerge, but Jane's knowing smile as she trotted out of the kitchen, bearing trays of mini sausage rolls, made Lizzy wish she'd made the effort to find her bra after all.

'Lizzy,' she said brightly, her gaze dropping triumphantly to Lizzy's chest before she beamed broad approval at Drew. 'Well, you certainly look more...feminine.'

Lizzy promptly crossed her arms and scowled at her friend, but Jane wiggled her eyebrows at her unrepentantly.

'We're leaving,' Drew said calmly, taking one of the rolls Jane bore. 'Thanks.'

'My pleasure.' Jane nodded benignly at him, but her smile had faded. 'But, Drew, you'll remember what I said about—'

'I remember,' he said cryptically, leaving Lizzy mystified.

'And, Lizzy, you be careful,' Jane added, following them when Drew opened the door. 'Don't trust him too much.'

'She's all grown up now, Jane.'

Drew's firm hand at her back directed Lizzy away from Jane and down the steps as if he didn't want her subjected to any more of her friend's advice, inappropriate as it might be, but Lizzy dodged free.

'Jane, it's not what you think,' she said desperately. 'We're just going to talk.'

'Janey, stop interfering. Go back to the party.' Drew spoke before Jane could, his tone firm and brooking no argument, and with one last, now faintly worried look Jane turned obediently away, letting him pull the door finally shut.

'That was strange,' Lizzy mused, letting him take her to his car.

'She's worried I'm going to seduce you.'

'Oh.' She laughed, a short, startled laugh. 'After your tennis match that night I thought she knew you already had.'

'I was probably more discreet than you assumed.'

'Oh?' She looked at him quickly, puzzled by his set expression. 'You were teasing me?'

'A little.' He opened the door for her. 'You rise so beautifully.'

Lizzy vowed not to let him do that to her again. The idea that Jane had known about them together had genuinely worried her, not for her own sake but for Drew's.

'If she doesn't want me to be seduced she should stop telling me not to wear a bra,' she exclaimed when he took the seat beside her.

He sent her a sharp look but she waited until he'd started the car and pulled out onto the street before she explained, 'She's obsessed with this absurd idea that the only reason I'm still single is my underwear.'

'You do have enchanting breasts,' he said softly.

Lizzy stiffened. 'That's not true,' she said finally, staring fiercely at the windscreen. 'They're out of proportion.'

'They're perfect.'

'They're too big.'

'You only think that because your waist is so tiny. From a male point of view, you have an incredibly enticing body.'

'Can we change the subject, please?'

'Why are you so embarrassed?'

'I'm not embarrassed,' she lied tightly. 'I'm bored.'

They were nearing Paddington station now and he slowed for the red light ahead. 'Your place or mine?'

'Mine, please.' She folded her arms, her face still red-hot. 'Drew, what I said in the cupboard…I didn't mean just in the cupboard. I can't have sex with you tonight.'

He didn't say anything, but the atmosphere thickened abruptly and she knew he was annoyed. Outside her flat he pulled in to the kerb, parking between two delivery vans. He turned off the engine and they sat for a few seconds in silence before he said, 'Why not?'

'Because.' She studied her fidgeting hands, then jumped slightly, her gaze flying to his face when he captured her hands with his own firm one, his other arm sliding behind her and twisting her so she faced him.

In the orange light from the nearest streetlamp his face

looked tight and controlled, she registered. Tense. 'Why not?' he repeated.

'Because it's not the right time.'

'It's the wrong time in your cycle?'

'Yes.'

'But you're quite willing to share my bed again when it's the right time?'

'Yes.' It came out almost as a whisper. She wouldn't be able to resist him, she realised. She wanted him too much. In every way. She was as addicted to him as Jane was to her olives. 'Yes, I want to be with you then.'

But rather than welcoming her tentative approach, her faint hopes increased earlier by his comments about her body, his expression turned abruptly and chillingly cold. 'Out, Lizzy.' His tone and gaze glacially remote, he leaned across her and opened her door, letting it swing wide across the footpath. 'I don't want to hear any more.'

Lizzy shrank back against the seat, her fingers clutching the edge of the seat, not moving. 'I don't understand.' Was he saying that if she didn't offer sex on demand then he wasn't interested in it ever again? Did this mean he no longer wanted anything to do with her? 'What about our agreement?' she asked, clutching at the first thing that came into her head. 'We have a contract.'

'Remind me on the appropriate day.'

'The five days,' she said automatically.

'Make it three,' he countered harshly. 'The extra two were always overly cautious.'

'But what about...?' She gasped in a few deep, rasping breaths, stunned by how abruptly and how horribly things had changed between them. 'What about after that?'

'After that you'll have to go back to your clinic,' he declared. 'That's the plan, isn't it? Nothing's changed. Goodbye, Lizzy.'

Sick with misery, she didn't answer. Of course it had been sex for him. He'd never pretended anything else—it was only her own pathetic foolishness that had allowed herself to start hoping for more. Now she'd denied him he no longer wanted her—his haste now was probably because he was going to find someone more agreeable.

She clambered out, her legs shaking, and made for the entrance to her flat, hearing, as she opened it, the slam of her car door that suggested she'd forgotten to close it herself.

As soon as she was inside she heard him start the engine and accelerate swiftly away.

CHAPTER ELEVEN

DREW thought he'd done a rather good job of concealing his mood from his juniors and patients the following morning on his round, but the knowing way his registrar eyed him afterwards suggested he'd been less successful than he'd hoped.

'Headache, Dr Maitland? Hangover from the party, perhaps?' Corinne trailed him back along Blue Ward to the nursing station. 'You know, if you'd bleeped me and suggested starting later I'd have been more than happy—'

'Thank you, Corinne,' he grated. 'Your adaptability is noted.'

She beamed at him. 'Milk, ginseng and Worcester sauce,' she advised. 'Nothing like it.'

They were at the desk now and the ward's charge nurse, clearly catching Corinne's words, looked up interestedly.

'Paracetamol's better,' he declared. 'Two the morning after with a pint of warm water.'

'My husband swears by stout,' the ward clerk added. 'Half a pint as soon as he gets up cures whatever he's drunk the night before.'

One of his emergency admissions from the week before, a young girl with cystic fibrosis, wheeled her drip stand past. 'Fizzy vitamin B's good.'

'A child your age shouldn't know about hangover cures,' he growled.

She giggled. 'I'm eighteen.'

'Old enough to know better,' he said mock-sternly, and ruffled her hair, pleased to see her up and around. Five days ago he'd worried she might not survive her chest infection, but intensive physiotherapy and antibiotics had worked miracles. 'And, just for the record,' he told them all, 'I did not drink too much last night.'

Although, after leaving Lizzy he'd thought about it. For the first time since his student years the temptation to get blindingly drunk had been strong, and if he hadn't had to work today he might have given in.

Instead, he'd spent half the night pacing the floor reminding himself of how maddeningly, aggravatingly, irritatingly single-minded she was, and the other half pacing the floor convincing himself that temporary sexual frustration was infinitely preferable to involvement with a woman who would undoubtedly drive him mad within weeks.

He was relieved, he told himself, hugely relieved that things had turned out the way they had, and that she'd obviously escaped their involvement emotionally unscathed while he at least hadn't lost his head. In a few months he'd look back on this and realise he'd had a lucky escape. In the meantime, all he had to do was stay away from her.

For the second week in a row Lizzy started off the chest team's X-ray session trying to avoid looking anywhere near Drew.

The reasons now were different, she acknowledged. The week before she'd wanted to avoid him because she couldn't not think of making love with him, and that had flustered her and muddled her thoughts. Now, though, it was because she was frightened that she might make a fool of herself by getting publicly emotional and tearful—not something she'd ever worried about in her life about before, but she'd never before spent an entire night weeping either.

Although at the start Drew sat at the back, as he had the previous week, a few films into the meeting—once, she realised, he'd seen how hard she was trying to avoid him— he moved to the front beside Corinne, his regard narrowing with definite and worrying satisfaction when Lizzy automatically jerked to the other side of the X-ray board to put more space between them.

His questions, when the week before he'd been silent, his repeated moves to the board beside her to point out details on the films, his requests that she explain her findings, made it impossible for her to ignore either him or the thought of what it seemed she'd lost. Clearly, she realised faintly, he'd decided not to make this easy for her.

She put up a series of X-rays following the progress of one of his patients and he came up to inspect them, standing so close to her that she could almost taste him.

'Spontaneous pneumothorax in a nineteen-year-old man,' he said coolly, his gaze thoughtful as it grazed her features, the thoughtfulness laced with something deeper, she realised, when she backed hastily away.

He instructed the medical students to come up and they joined him, peering interestedly at the films as he guided them though them.

'Pneumothorax means free air within the chest, and you can see it here,' he explained, tracing the dense blackness of the air outlined by the chest wall and the compressed markings of the lung tissue which the air had squashed into the bottom and middle of the chest. 'In this case, occurring spontaneously in an otherwise fit, thin young man, probably because of the rupture of a bleb or bubble on the lung surface.'

Then his attention swung to Lizzy, making her flush. 'Would you agree with that, Dr Murdoch?'

She nodded jerkily. The students gathered around her had forced her closer to him again, and she could barely think.

One of the students asked what symptoms he had.

'Sudden onset of catching pain in his right side when he breathed in, and breathlessness,' Drew answered. 'He was exercising. He thought it was cramp and tried to work through it, but the breathlessness got worse.'

'And the treatment?'

He indicated the following film, moving closer to Lizzy in the process of examining it so that his arm brushed her side, but when she shrank away he followed her.

'A small amount of air will gradually be absorbed naturally so it can be left untreated,' he continued. 'A larger amount like this can be drained by simply putting a needle through into the space and syringing out the air, as you see here.' His arm lifted again and brushed Lizzy's arm, and he held that position while he indicated the small amount of residual air on the following film. When she braved a look up at him he smiled at her, a cool, knowing smile that made her stiffen.

He was doing this deliberately, she realised, appalled by his callousness. Nothing was accidental. He knew exactly how his closeness was affecting her but, instead of kindly keeping his distance and letting her overcome her misery in peace, he was enjoying himself by toying with her.

The next film was taken a day later and showed the air gone, the lung reinflated and essentially normal. 'That film was taken this morning,' Corinne added. 'We've discharged him on our round today.'

'The last X-rays for today belong to a young woman with severe asthma,' Lizzy said huskily, sliding the pneumothorax films back into the rack before pulling out the next set. Drew moved back to his seat and she began breathing marginally more easily. 'In this case complicated by a right, lower-lobe pneumonia.'

After she'd finished going through the films Lionel Wright thanked her and made his usual comment about her coming to work with him in private practice, a suggestion Lizzy countered with her usual comment about being too busy while she helped one of the house officers replace all the X-rays into their correct envelopes.

But when the students and doctors, including Corinne, filed out Drew stayed, catching her arm again when she made to move past him and blocking the doorway before she could get to it.

'I thought you weren't talking to me?' she snarled, tugging unsuccessfully this time to try and get away from him. 'I thought you didn't want to hear any more from me?'

'Usually I deal better with frustration,' he said easily.

'More likely you never experience it,' Lizzy countered sharply, the thought of him with other women turning her abruptly and searingly jealous.

'You might be right.' But she'd amused him again—she saw the glint of it in his eyes, and the gentling of his grip confirmed it.

When his thumb began to move against the sensitive skin of the inside of her forearm her breath caught, and she acknowledged that he was arousing feelings she didn't want aroused. 'I assumed you'd call up one of your old girl-friends,' she said viciously, unsuccessfully tugging again to get her arm away. 'I'm sure there must be dozens.'

'Interesting thought.'

'Isn't it?' She contemplated it, and scowled.

He laughed. 'Lizzy,' he chided, his voice deep and low and amused, his fingers sliding now to the soft underside of her wrist and making her squirm, 'you sound jealous. Now why would that be?'

'Wrong.' She wrenched her arm away. Succeeding this time in breaking the contact, she took several quick steps backwards towards the X-ray screens, desperate to put space between them. 'You were right last night. What you do in the twenty-five days of the month when I don't need you doesn't matter to me.'

'So you keep insisting.'

'You're a horrible person, Drew Maitland.'

He tilted his head. 'Why so agitated, then?' he asked, softly now. 'Hmm, Lizzy? What's bothering you? You're like a frightened rabbit this morning.'

'*You're* bothering me, and I'll see you on the tenth.' She gathered up her films and stormed towards the door, pride propelling legs which she'd feared might prove too shaky to support her. 'And, since you're so insistent on keeping it to three days, that's Sunday, Monday and Tuesday next month. Two weeks from now.'

He moved quickly, blocking the door before she reached it. 'All this anger is because I reduced the number of days?'

She clutched the film envelopes to her chest. 'Getting pregnant happens to be very important to me.'

'But we both know the window for fertility is only seventy-two hours.'

'I'm not a mathematical model,' she snapped. 'I'm a living woman. Natural cycles can fluctuate unpredictably.'

'And if I add another two days you'll be happy?'

'Happier.' And if he added another twenty days she'd be delirious, she added silently, knowing that it would never be in her best interests to let him discover that.

'I'll think about it.' The hardening of his expression and his abrupt withdrawal from the door suggested she'd finally said something to dent his taunting good humour, and he didn't object when she hauled open the door and stalked out.

Their meetings throughout the remainder of the week were all at work and, for Lizzy, all thankfully when others were around. The highly professional tone of their new relationship made it easier to fend off Jane's determined probing about what had happened after they'd left Bill's party.

'There's nothing between us,' Lizzy insisted, for what seemed like the umpteenth time, over a very late afternoon tea in the canteen on Friday after her clinic consisting of stale, curly sandwiches which they'd both decided to ignore after a single bite of each. She rocked a sleeping Gemma in her arms, wishing that the baby would wake. 'It's work, that's all. Just work.'

'Is this what you call work?' Jane hauled a lacy bra out of her bag and flourished it triumphantly in the air.

'Monster!' Flushing hotly, Lizzy snatched the garment and tucked it away in her pocket, looking urgently around the cafeteria—hoping no one had noticed. 'So I took it off. You don't know Drew had anything to do with that. I might have been hot.'

'So, don't talk about it if you don't trust me.' Jane sniffed then promptly held out her arms for Gemma. 'Give her back. You don't deserve her.'

'She's happy.' Lizzy held on to the baby. 'Corinne seems happy too.'

'Stop trying to change the subject.' Jane bent back to her bag and fished out a miniature jar of olives, opened it and took a handful. 'I won't give up,' she announced. 'If you won't tell me I'll try Drew.'

'There's nothing to tell.' Stiff now, Lizzy concentrated on Gemma, refusing Jane's offer of olives. 'I can't believe how fast she's growing.'

'You and Corinne could have a double wedding,' Jane added conversationally, her tone muffled as she munched.

'Her eyes are still so blue,' Lizzy cooed, silently urging Gemma to wake and open them. 'I wonder if they're going to stay that colour?'

'Don't you want to marry him?'

'Bill's got brown eyes, though,' Lizzy mused, determined to ignore her, 'but, then, his mother's are blue so he's got both bits of the genes so Gemma's might stay blue.'

'Lizzy!'

'Why are you doing this to me?' Lizzy hissed. 'Why can't you leave me alone?'

'Because I'm your friend and I love you and I'm worried about you,' Jane said sharply. She pushed the jar of olives to one side and folded her chubby arms, fixing Lizzy with a stare that could have melted bricks. 'You're sticking your head in the sand, Lizzy, as usual. I've let you get away with it for years, but enough's enough. You're so worried about being hurt like before that you won't stop and consider how suited the two of you are.'

Lizzy blinked. Either Jane knew something about the way she'd been feeling this last week or she was talking about something entirely different. 'When was I hurt?'

'When Richard turned out to be married, and with Paul.

I know you've never talked about it but that has to be the shortest engagement in history. Of course we realised you must have been hurt.'

'But it was me who called it off.'

Now it was Jane's turn to blink. 'He told Bill that he couldn't marry a woman who refused to bring up his children properly.'

'What he considered properly was appalling,' Lizzy explained. 'He thought they should be seen and not heard. He'd even chosen their boarding schools. *I* called off the engagement.'

'You never said.'

'I felt stupid because I hadn't realised earlier how mismatched we were.'

'We knew how much you wanted children. We assumed you'd been badly hurt.'

'But I wasn't.'

'Then why...?' Jane frowned at her. 'If you're not still pining from that, why can't you see how good Drew would be for you? He loves kids, he's a great doctor, he's caring and responsible, he's got a terrific sense of humour, he's wonderful-looking and very sexy and it's time for him to settle down. Deep down I get the definite impression he knows it. He's exactly what you need.'

'He's not interested in me,' she protested.

'He looked interested enough Monday night.'

'That's just sex.'

'Well!' Jane's obvious delight made her wish she'd kept her mouth shut. 'Well!' She was practically rubbing her hands together, Lizzy realised. 'That's a start.'

'I turned him down,' she snapped.

'Why?'

'Because.' Lizzy flushed, unable to bring herself to explain the irony. If he'd asked her a day later it would have turned out very differently. Telling herself that she was lucky to have discovered that his intentions outside of want-

ing a baby were non-existent before she'd made a total fool
of herself, she muttered, 'Just because.'

'You're not making sense. Do you want him or not?'

'No!' But Lizzy felt herself flush. 'Yes. Of course. I
don't know.'

'Well, make up your mind.' Jane shoved back her chair
irritably and collected her cup. 'More coffee?'

'Not for me,' Lizzy said huskily.

Gemma stirred when her mother walked away, one tiny
clenched fist coming up in a little stretch, and Lizzy smiled
down at her and rocked her gently again. Apart from the
times when she held Gemma, she'd thought less about
babies over these last few weeks than she ever had, she
realised. Strange, considering that over these weeks she'd
been actively trying to become pregnant.

But she'd been distracted. By Drew himself, she acknowledged, knowing that thinking about him had become
her major preoccupation. When exactly she'd fallen in love
with him she didn't know, but spending the better part of
the last few weeks trying to hide her feelings away certainly
hadn't made them any less overwhelming.

Of course it was little wonder things hadn't turned out
well. Their relationship had been doomed from the start.
Pressured by her gynaecologist's advice, she'd rushed him
and probably frightened him silly in the process. No wonder he was so guarded. If she'd taken things slowly perhaps
he wouldn't have been so wary of her and perhaps eventually something more might have developed.

Perhaps Jane was right. Perhaps it wasn't too late. Even
if it was, shouldn't she first do everything in her power to
make sure before she gave up?

She looked up blankly as Jane approached again. 'I have
to go,' she said urgently, trying to give her Gemma.

But Jane wouldn't take her. 'When I've finished my coffee,' she said airily. She took an irritatingly small sip. 'Two
minutes.'

Lizzy drummed her feet under the table, her nervousness increasing. 'He doesn't like spinach.'

'So purée it and tell him it's some foreign vegetable.' Jane looked smug. 'He won't know.'

'He hates lentils.'

'Dreadful things. You'll just have to give them up.'

'I don't think he's remotely interested!'

'If you don't ask you'll never find out,' Jane countered cheerfully. Then she swivelled. 'Oh, look. What a coincidence.'

Lizzy followed her gaze and saw Drew, coming through the plastic doors of the canteen. He looked immediately towards her, as if he'd known she was there, and she felt herself pale. 'Jane, you absolute monster,' she whispered. 'You called him when you went for coffee.'

'No time like the present,' Jane chimed. She took Gemma, tucked her back into her carry-cot and then deposited the olive jar beside her. 'I'll just move to the next table.'

'No, you won't,' Drew said smoothly, already by them. His hand at Jane's elbow and Gemma's carry-cot in his other, he steered her in the direction he'd just come. 'No eavesdropping. Bye, Janey. Go away.'

Lizzy saw Jane's pout of disappointment but, still bemused herself, she made no effort to intervene, and when Drew came back from pushing Jane out of the door she was still at the table.

'What?' he said quietly.

'What, what?' She blinked up at him and felt herself drowning in unexpected warm concern. 'What?'

'What did you want to talk to me about? Jane said it was urgent. Is something wrong? Were you wrong about not being pregnant?'

'No.' She blinked again, staring at him when he sat beside her. 'We're being manipulated,' she said faintly.

'Nothing new with Jane around.' His expression became resigned. 'You didn't want to see me.'

'No, I did,' Lizzy protested, still vague. 'I was going to come and find you but she stopped me.'

'Why?'

'Because she'd already called you, I suppose.'

'No, Lizzy.' To her further bemusement, he took her hand in his own cool and dry one. 'Not why did she stop you. Why were you coming to find me?'

'Will you come out with me tonight?' She faltered at his surprise but forced herself to continue. 'Dinner?'

His grip on her hand tightened. 'Why?'

'If you want we can have sex afterwards,' she whispered.

'What?'

'I'm not bleeding any more. I can have sex now.'

'What?' His brows lifted as if she'd said something astonishing then drew sharply together into a frown. 'Was that why you said no on Monday night?'

'Yes.'

'Why didn't you tell me?' he demanded.

'You must have known the timing.' She knew she was flushing. 'I thought you'd understand.'

'It never occurred to me.' He looked stunned. 'And even if it had, it wouldn't have made any difference. It's not as if we couldn't—' He stopped. 'Lizzy, why are you asking me to go out with you?'

'Because the first time I did it, all I was thinking about was a baby,' she murmured. 'I'd like it to be different this time.'

His eyes narrowed. 'How different?'

'I like you very much.' Her back felt very stiff where she held herself rigid. 'And I rushed you before. I'd like us to start again.'

She tugged her hand free and curled it on her lap with her other one—beneath the table so he couldn't see them twisting together. 'I'm not a bad person,' she said quietly. 'I'm quite polite and I'm very good at my job and I'm a good housekeeper. I can cook lovely vegetarian things. My desk is always neat and I'm a good driver. Well, my reverse parking needs work, but—'

'Lizzy—'

But she rushed on, focusing on her barely touched stale salad sandwich. 'I do get bad-tempered sometimes but not often and I'm quite stubborn and I know that I talk too much. I'm not as knowledgeable about cultural things as Jane is and I don't speak any foreign languages like her but I intend to learn Spanish one day.'

'Why are you telling me this?'

'Because I want you to like me,' she said quietly.

'I already like you.'

'And I'm trying to be honest so you know the bad things as well.'

'Then you've left a lot out.'

Her gaze flew up. 'Like what?'

'Like the fact that you're the most infuriating woman I've ever met,' he said softly.

'No!' She snapped back in her chair, appalled, her arms spreading in front of her on the table. 'No, Drew—'

'Like the fact that I never know what you're going to say or do next. Like the fact that in less than six weeks you've nearly driven me to beating my head against a wall.'

She lowered her head. 'I'm sorry.'

'Like the fact that you're so delicious I can't keep my hands off you.'

Lizzy's head snapped up again. 'What?'

'You don't have to convince me to like you, you idiotic woman. I'm in love with you.'

'I love you, too,' she gasped, the words bubbling up inside her like bursting champagne. She clutched at his hands. 'I do. Truly. I love you.'

'Thank God for that.' His hand went behind her head and he kissed her, a passionate, hard, exasperated kiss, which he ended when the cheers of the hospital staff seated around them forced them apart. 'Finally, she admits it,' he murmured.

Acknowledging the applause of the crowd with a brief lift of his hand and a rueful grin, Drew took her hand and led Lizzy, who was confident now that she was the colour of one of the hospital's bricks, from the canteen.

Pausing only to kiss her again in the corridor, a lingering kiss that made her head reel, he took her to his office, shut and firmly locked the door and kissed her soundly.

'What do you mean, *finally*?' she demanded when he raised his head.

'I've wondered,' he said softly, laughing at her. Sweeping piles of books aside, he sat on his desk and pulled her into his arms. 'Although you did your best to keep me guessing.'

'You're so smug,' she murmured, lifting her mouth for another kiss.

'Probably,' he conceded heavily. He pulled back, his eyes narrowed teasingly. 'But you did respond so appealingly. And, despite sending me away this week, you never found it any easier to keep your hands off me than I did off you. And I am smug because most of the time I couldn't conceive of possibly feeling as strongly as I did without it not being at least a little bit reciprocated.'

'I didn't know you felt anything,' she whispered. 'You never said...'

'The first time I met you you got under my skin,' he told her.

'What had Jane told you about me?'

'Nothing that matched the way I found you.' He kissed her nose. 'She'd led me to expect some neurotic, desperate spinster, likely to jump on the first man to cross her path, and what I got was a belligerent, karate-chopping woman with gorgeous legs who, when she wasn't insulting me, was making it very clear that she wasn't remotely interested.'

'Gorgeous legs?' she asked archly, pressing herself between his. 'You couldn't see me.'

'I could feel you.' He laughed. 'Remember when I lifted you in the cupboard? You were wearing stockings and your thighs were soft and warm and shockingly desirable.' His hands slid under her dress to the tops of the stockings she was wearing now. 'I knew I had to stay away.'

'But you didn't.'

'You didn't seem to give me much choice.' His voice lowered as his hands encircled her legs, 'though you certainly bruised my ego by not even recognising me in the meeting the next day. Later I guess Corinne told you, hmm?'

'Yes.' Lizzy stroked her hands through the delicious warmth of his hair. 'She said you asked her what was wrong with your haircut.'

Laughing, he withdrew his hands from her legs and smoothed down her dress, gathering her closer, his head against her breasts. 'I wanted reassurance that you'd mistaken my identity and, besides, I was curious,' he admitted. 'But just as determined to avoid you.'

'But you came out with me that night!'

'You bulldozed me into it,' he insisted.

Lizzy mock-thumped his shoulder. 'I asked you nicely!'

'You'd been flaunting yourself shamelessly all afternoon,' he chided, kissing her. 'You'd weakened my resistance. But when you mentioned having a baby...' He lifted his eyes to the ceiling. 'Jane had made it sound as if you were set on finding a husband so I was half prepared for that, but instead you made it plain you were only interested in one thing.'

'I shocked you.'

'Profoundly.' He grinned. 'All the time I'd been pretending to myself I wasn't interested I'd been plotting inside how best to seduce you, but instead you were ready to hand yourself to me on a plate.' His fingers worked at the button fastenings of her dress, and when he loosened it and lowered his mouth she shivered.

'You didn't take it that way.'

'I thought about it.' He kissed her midriff. 'But I already knew I was ready for children and the things I said about my age and not having met anyone special yet were true—at least, I kept telling myself the last bit was true. Your plan would give me an heir and your body. I told myself it made sense.'

'And the contract?'

'I keep meaning to get that signed.' His fingers went to the front fastening of her bra and bared her breasts. 'Subconsciously, I think I had other plans for you, Lizzy Murdoch.' He laughed at her expression. 'Don't be so indignant.' He kissed one tightened nipple. 'You're happy now, aren't you?'

'You're more manipulative than Jane,' she protested, guiding his head back to her breasts when he shifted away.

'You were just slow, recognising your feelings. You've been concentrating too much on a baby and not enough on yourself.' He nuzzled her again and then, to her dismay, tucked her away and fastened her dress. 'Soon,' he promised softly, holding her away. 'That night I took you to Michael's I really meant to tell you no. I told myself that the only reason I didn't was that he made such a nuisance of himself, but there was more to it than that.'

'Michael was nice.'

'And mad with curiosity,' he said dryly.

'I like your family.'

'Fortunate.'

'After that night you agreed to go through with the baby.'

'You must know why,' he said softly. He stroked her cheek. 'I could hardly keep my hands off you. Leaving that night was one of the hardest things I've ever done.'

'I remember.' Her whole body was blushing. 'That kiss was incredible. I didn't sleep a minute after that.'

'I don't think I've slept peacefully since.'

His rueful expression made her laugh. 'I thought then that the chemistry meant we'd be compatible parents.'

'Lovers,' he said softly. 'Which I knew already. But you were too focused on wanting to get pregnant to think about anything else. I tried to make you acknowledge something that day in the cab and at the house before our first night together, but you ignored me. That night, afterwards, I could barely think. The sex—' his eyes darkened '—was incredible. But it wasn't just that. I'd fallen in love with you and you still refused to admit to any emotions. You were driving me crazy with frustration.'

'I did know I had some feelings,' she whispered, returning his sudden kiss hungrily, 'but I tried to pretend I didn't because I never dreamed you felt the same.'

'You were crying that last morning.'

'I know.'

'After Bill's party on Monday when you wouldn't spend the night with me I thought that had to mean I'd been wrong about how you felt. Then at the meeting on Tuesday you were so nervous I thought there was hope again, but you told me you were just worried about the dates for the month.'

'I was trying to protect my pride,' she admitted. 'And I explained about why I said no that night—'

'I know now,' he said gently, kissing her again. 'Given your innocence, it does make bizarre sense, even though it wouldn't have made any difference to me.'

'I thought you were angry because I wouldn't give you sex when you wanted it,' she told him.

'I wanted you so much but it seemed as if I'd reached a brick wall with you. I was frustrated and angry and I was trying to salvage some pride myself, by pretending it didn't matter.'

Lizzy circled her hands around his neck. 'I'm prepared to promise never to resist you again.'

'A good start,' he growled, his mouth tracking along the side of her throat and sending little shivers of delight cascading across her skin. 'How about now?'

'No chance of resistance,' she whispered, letting him swivel and tip her back across his desk. Her hands went urgently to his shirt and then, once she had his glorious chest bared, the fastenings of his pants. 'I love you so much and it's been almost ten days. I can't think of anything else.'

'That's what I wanted to hear.' Drew discarded the rest of his clothes with a few brief, precise moments then returned to her. He tugged her dress free, followed by her underwear, leaving her stockings. 'You're ravishing,' he murmured, his mouth at her thighs.

'Then ravish me.' Lizzy pulled him up to her so she could kiss the mouth that was driving her wild with desire. 'Quickly. I love you.'

'Good.' His grin was lazy, but his mouth on hers became urgent. 'About time.'

They married in August, six weeks before Corinne so they'd be back from Provence for her wedding. Justin and Emma were born four weeks prematurely but in perfect health in April the following year.

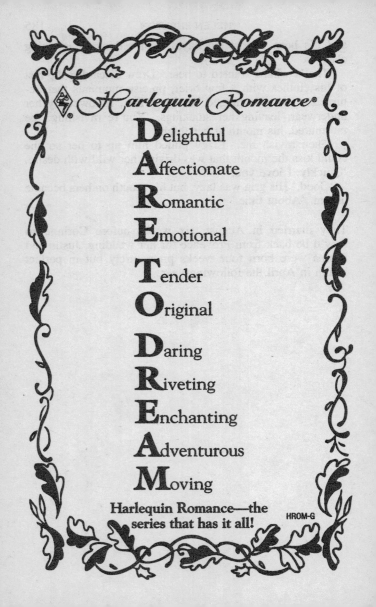

Harlequin Romance®

Delightful

Affectionate

Romantic

Emotional

Tender

Original

Daring

Riveting

Enchanting

Adventurous

Moving

Harlequin Romance—the
series that has it all!

HROM-G

HARLEQUIN ◆ PRESENTS®

HARLEQUIN PRESENTS
men you won't be able to resist
falling in love with...

HARLEQUIN PRESENTS
women who have feelings
just like your own...

HARLEQUIN PRESENTS
powerful passion in
exotic international settings...

HARLEQUIN PRESENTS
intense, dramatic stories that will keep you
turning to the very last page...

HARLEQUIN PRESENTS
The world's bestselling romance series!

Harlequin® Historical

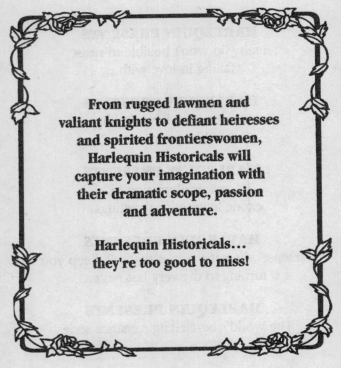

From rugged lawmen and
valiant knights to defiant heiresses
and spirited frontierswomen,
Harlequin Historicals will
capture your imagination with
their dramatic scope, passion
and adventure.

Harlequin Historicals...
they're too good to miss!

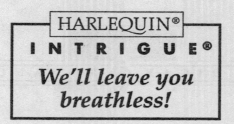

LOOK FOR OUR FOUR FABULOUS MEN!

Each month some of today's bestselling authors bring
four new fabulous men to Harlequin American Romance.
Whether they're rebel ranchers, millionaire power brokers
or sexy single dads, they're all gallant princes—and
they're all ready to sweep you into lighthearted fantasies
and contemporary fairy tales where anything is possible
and where all your dreams come true!

You don't even have to make a wish...
Harlequin American Romance will grant your every desire!

Look for Harlequin American Romance
wherever Harlequin books are sold!

HARLEQUIN SUPERROMANCE®

...there's more to the story!

Superromance. A *big* satisfying read about unforgettable characters. Each month we offer *four* very different stories that range from family drama to adventure and mystery, from highly emotional stories to romantic comedies—and much more! Stories about people you'll believe in and care about. Stories too compelling to put down....

Our authors are among today's *best* romance writers. You'll find familiar names and talented newcomers. Many of them are award winners—and you'll see why!

If you want the biggest and best in romance fiction, you'll get it from Superromance!

Available wherever Harlequin books are sold.

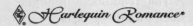

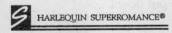

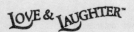